I0846963

CONTENTS

LUNA RUNESTORM

First edition

ISBN: 979-8-90046-100-7

DEDICATION

This is to all the people who always wanted to believe that love and magic were real.

They are. But I should warn you—both have a habit of stealing hearts... and not giving them back.

ACKNOWLEDGEMENTS

Thank you to all my Beta Readers, especially Ms Kathy and Annmarie. I wouldn't be doing this if you hadn't liked this book. Also to all my ARC readers and those who have left reviews! (those mean a TON to authors!)

Thank you to my teachers back in high school who encouraged me to tell stories, sorry I waited so long to actually do something with it.

And most of all, thank you to all the dogs in the world. Life is just better with a few of them around.

Oh, and one more thing.... thank you to Mr. Tom Hiddleston, for taking the MCU Loki and making him a complex and wonderful character. You reminded me of what I had seen in him when I read Norse mythology back in school. No, my Loki is not his, and he's not really the traditional Loki of Norse Mythology, but he's mine, and I hope you all love him as much as I do.

Chapter One

THE FIRST SIGNS

I set the dog's metal water bowl on the bottom step with a thump. Ash barrels toward it—a streak of blue-mottled fur, tags jingling, tongue hanging out. The air out here is heavy—sticky with early evening, a kind of slow syrup that glues your shirt to your back and makes even the wind lazy. You'd think, with the sun slipping behind the pines and the bugs hollering from the ditch, it would cool down. But Texas isn't that generous.

My phone buzzes—Sarah Mitchell's ringtone. She lives in Dallas and loves the big city. I've always preferred small-town life, or at least living near one. I like peace and quiet; I always have. Today, I don't feel like listening to her complain that I am hiding, that I never leave this place, so I hit ignore and continue with what I was doing. Guilt pricks at me for the thought. She is my oldest friend, but I am tired and busy, so I will call her later.

Mystic, the smart one, comes running up but doesn't touch the water. She noses the porch post and glances up with the eye that isn't smeared with black, like someone threw charcoal at her. She's looking for trouble, like always. I lower myself next to her and run my palm down her back. Her fur bristles against my hand, each wiry hair catching in my knuckles.

"You'll make yourself old before your time," I tell Mystic, scratching behind her ears. She leans into my touch, and for a second, I'm jealous of how simple her worries are. I know what it's like to burn out your nerves with worry.

The steps creak when I lean back. They're pressure-treated pine, stained and splintered, holding on for dear life against the slow rot. My ass hits the third step, and I settle there, knees up, head heavy. The dogs move in close. Ash leans into my hip, and Mystic perches at my feet, both waiting for what I'll do next.

I check my phone to see if FedEx is going to find my house today. It's miles from town and set back a hundred yards from the county road, surrounded by a scrubby yard that collapses into forest—tall, old pines, rough-barked and straight, with underbrush so thick you'd lose a car in there.

Mystic sniffs the air, then stares at me with that knowing eye. The look says, I've seen this routine. We're not alone.

"Relax," I tell her. My voice sounds older than I feel. "Nobody comes out here unless they're lost or they want something."

The sky shifts, changes gears, smears of orange and taffy pink bleeding into the treeline. The heat relents, just a fraction. I braid my fingers through my hair and feel the sweat at my scalp, the roots slick and tangled. Some girls would dye their hair purple as a dare or a statement. For me, it was armor—nobody expects much from a woman who wears her damage on the outside. It hangs wild, curling in the humidity, a shield even when it gets in my mouth. Especially when it gets in my mouth.

Ash finishes the water, then paces, not wanting to sit still. He glances at the woods, then back at me. His tongue hangs pink as raw meat. "You thirsty enough to drink a whole pond, buddy?" I ask. He chuffs. It sounds like laughter.

I don't look at my phone. I don't check the time. I don't want the world outside these woods, not while the light is like this. Maybe the sun does something weird to the air out here, bends it, slows it down. Or maybe it's just me, always hoping for some little magic that'll burn away the memory of...everything else.

That's when I see it.

At first, I think it's just a trick of the light. But I move, and they move with me, sliding along the ground, rearranging, forming new patterns. Some of them pulse, slow and lazy, like an animal breathing. "Y'all are about to trip me," I mutter to the dogs.

Mystic plants herself between me and the markings. Ash's hackles are up, but he's more confused than scared.

I step closer. The lines carved in the sandy dirt aren't lines at all. They're runes. I remember enough from school and old books to recognize them, sort of and years of reading various mythologies and maybe a few romance novels might have helped. They look like Norse tattoos or symbols from a History Channel show. They're darker than shadow should be, almost oily. And in the center of one, right in the heart, something glimmers—an amber glow, weak but real.

My chest tightens. Maybe it's the air or the not really knowing what they are. I crouch, careful, hands on my knees. The air around the markings feels colder, like stepping into the shade too quickly. I reach out, hand trembling just a little, and let my fingers hover above the lines but not touch them.

The shadows shift, slide, pulse. For half a second, I'm sure they're watching me back.

When my fingertips touch the edge of one of the runes, a chill races up my arm, sharp as ice water. Not painful, exactly, but wrong. My breath hitches, then I suck in a lungful of pine needles and old leaves.

"Fuck," I say, way too loud.

Ash presses against my thigh, tail stiff. Mystic lets out a low, uncertain whine, the sound like rusted metal.

I pull back, hands shaking now. The runes flicker, fade a little, then surge brighter, the amber in the center pulsing like a dying star. I want to touch it again, to see if it was real or if I was just imagining it. But my skin says no. My brain says run.

But I don't. Instead, I stare. The patterns are shifting—changing every time I blink. If I squint, I can almost read them, but they slip away, rearrange, spell something else.

"What the hell are you?" I ask, suddenly remembering the local 'rule' I was told when I first moved here six years ago: you don't talk to sounds in the woods.

Thankfully, there's no answer, just the slow, impossible glow. I feel a little silly for letting my mind even think that that rule is real.

My heart scrapes against my ribs, louder than it has any right to be. I stand and wipe my hands on my yoga pants. Both dogs stand with me, braced and waiting, as if some order or signal might come. I scan the woods, the sky, the dirt, looking for sense, for anything that'll fit the world I know.

I watch the porch light throw a sickly circle across the yard. The dogs cluster around me, more tense than before.

It starts with the bugs going silent. One second, the cricket orchestra is playing. The next, nothing. Even the mosquitoes hang back. The hair on my arms lifts in slow motion.

The dogs are both instantly alert. Mystic sprints ahead. Ash follows, then circles back to check that I'm with him.

The runes are everywhere now.

They climb up the cinder blocks, stretch across the water bowl, and even flicker at the edges of the porch light's little kingdom. On the ground, they crawl like snakes, slithering to find some pattern only they know. Some burn blue, some red, most just black—but it's the cold kind of black, the sort that sucks at your eyes until you want to look away but can't.

I swallow and taste panic. "Get back here," I hiss at Mystic, but she's not listening. She's found the largest rune—a circle of intersecting lines and hooks, as big as a washtub—right under the biggest pine. She steps around it, barking in short, controlled bursts. Each time she barks, the rune pulses brighter, as if challenging her back.

Ash whines and dances between my feet, almost tripping me as I walk closer.

Up close, the symbol glows so brightly it casts real light, a faint blue halo on the ground. The dirt at the center is perfectly smooth, like it's been licked by fire. If I breathe through my nose, I can smell ozone, sharp and almost sweet, the way the air smells right before lightning hits.

The air above the rune vibrates, like the world's smallest hummingbird is trapped there, wings beating a thousand times a second.

For one stupid heartbeat, I want to touch this one too, just to see if it's real or if my head has finally given up on facts.

I press down, barely brushing the surface.

The cold blasts up my arm, into my chest—a punch from inside. My heart flutters, skips, and catches up. I jerk my hand away and land on my ass, breath knocked out. My fingertips are numb, but the numbness is already gone, replaced by a burning that tingles straight through to my shoulder.

Mystic barks, but it's a different sound this time. Not a threat, but panic. She wheels and faces the woods, hackles raised, tail straight as a rod. I follow her gaze, expecting—what? A person, a bear, a goddamn ghost?

Nothing moves, but the trees themselves seem closer. The shadows at their bases are thick as tar, and the runes slither right up to their roots, disappearing into darkness. For one second, I swear the whole woods are watching me.

Ash presses himself against my leg, shivering. He's not cold. He's scared, and that scares me. This is the dog that chased a coyote out of the yard last spring, the dog that's never met a thunderstorm he couldn't out-bark.

I stagger to my feet, joints shaking, hands stinging. My left palm is pale, but the skin where I touched the rune is as red as a sunburn, the pattern of the symbol faintly traced there, a memory of something I didn't mean to keep.

I want to leave. I want to run for the trailer, lock the door, and never come out again. But I also want to stay because if I don't look, if I don't watch, who will?

The porch seems miles away. I call Mystic, my voice a cracked whisper. She backs up, not taking her eyes off the treeline, then finally bolts toward me, shouldering Ash aside and herding me like I'm her only job in the world. The three of us pile onto the steps, a tangle of limbs, fur, and pounding hearts.

I look back one last time. The runes are still there but are already fading, like they're embarrassed to be caught. The glow flickers, then dies, leaving the ground bare and ordinary. The woods sigh, and the bug sounds return—not all at once, but in little waves, as if unsure they're allowed.

I open the door, usher the dogs in first, then shut it behind us with my whole weight. I lock it. For the first time in years, I lock it.

Inside, I turn on every light, stand in the kitchen, and watch my hands shake. I wash the red mark with soap and water, but it stays. Maybe it's just my mind. Maybe it's nothing. I dry my hands, set the towel down, and stare at the wall.

Mystic paces, checking every window. Ash lies at my feet, a warm, heavy anchor.

I think about calling someone. But who do you call about a haunted yard? Nobody in town would believe it, not from me.

The trailer creaks, settling, reminding me I'm not alone. I walk the hallway, flipping lights on and off, looking out the windows. The woods are just woods now, deep and silent and old.

I slide down the hallway wall, curl up next to Ash, and close my eyes.

But all I see are those runes, waiting for me in the dark.

Pine needles slick with nightfall sting underfoot, but I don't bleed. The flesh I wear tonight doesn't break so easily. There's a secret in the trees, a hush that deepens when I slip between them. They recognize me, the old giants—know what I am, even if the mortals have forgotten.

I watch her from the shadows, where the world softens at the edges and anything is possible. She's smaller than she should be. Her hair is a strange, bruised color in the dusk, purple curls twitching like antennae, always testing for a signal from something unseen. Her soul runs hot; even from here, I can taste the little bursts of adrenaline, the slow decay of caution into curiosity. She lives her life like she's already a ghost—skimming the surface, never making a ripple unless something drags her under.

She thinks she's alone out here. I could laugh. She's more watched than the moon.

Her dogs know better. The blue one—the female, sharp and angry—has clocked me three times already, each glance a dare. The male is softer, but no fool. They remember older stories, the ones the first wolves told by starlight when the gods still bothered to walk.

But the dogs are nothing compared to the runes.

They writhe in the dirt, scrawled by shadows, hungry for meaning. Even now, as the mortal tries to scrub away their touch, they linger. They pulse with every shiver across her skin, every ragged breath she drags between her teeth. I stretch my own arm into the moonlight, watching the sigils inked along the muscle glow and stir, thirsty for the new pattern.

They're not mine, these fresh marks. Not entirely. But they know my blood.

I step out from the trees, just enough for the night to notice me. Not enough for her to see. I am nothing if not considerate.

The porch light behind her flickers, uncertain. She paces from window to window, a moth caught between glass and flame. She's scared, but she won't admit it—not even to herself. That's what makes her interesting. Fear in mortals is cheap. Defiance is rare.

I lean into the wind, drawing it through my mouth and filling my lungs with the taste of her: sweat, dog, and the faint trace of some chemical thing she uses to erase what the world left on her. Under it all, a wisp of blood.

Most mortals drown it in soap or sickly fruit, but hers is honest, sharp as a blade.

The runes in the yard answer mine, quicksilver along my forearms, my spine burning with messages I haven't read in centuries. They want something from her. Or maybe for her. I watch and wait.

She finally stops, hands splayed on the kitchen counter, head bowed like she's taken a punch. Her shoulders shake, barely. The blue dog stands guard at the door. The other glues himself to her ankles, tail sweeping the floor in slow, uncertain beats.

I watch her, letting my shape slip a little. Eyes first—they always betray me, gold in the dark, cat-slit and unashamed. If she looks out, she'll see them. I want her to.

She doesn't. Not yet.

She sits on the floor, back to the hallway, cradling the soft dog's head in her lap. She strokes him with a tenderness that aches, a little funeral for a day she can't explain. I can see the dream take her, the way her head dips, eyes fighting to stay open. I could slide in right now, whisper the right words, and she'd believe anything I said.

But the night is long. No need to rush.

A flicker at the window—her head jerks up, purple eyes wide, searching the darkness beyond the glass. She feels me. A delicious prickling runs up my neck, anticipation or hunger or both. I stand very still, letting the moment stretch. She looks straight at me, or where I was a second ago. I step back, just enough to become a rumor, a draft, the thing you doubt you ever saw.

The trees close behind me. The woods settle, pretending I was never there.

I hold the taste of her in my mouth, savoring it. The runes spiral up my arms, greedy and hopeful. I laugh softly, and the sound is too big for the space between the pines.

Tomorrow, or the night after, I have all the time in the world.

But the little ghost of a girl? She has just become the most interesting thing in it.

I vanish and leave the wind to wonder what comes next.

Chapter Two

A Chance Meeting

If you wake up every day expecting the world to punch you in the gut, most mornings just feel like a faint nudge. That's why I walk the dogs early, before small-town Texas drama kicks into gear and the park fills with people wanting to ask questions about my hair, my dogs, or why a grown woman with no wedding ring spends so much time alone.

But after last night, I was moving slower. I'd been thinking about it, and those glowing shapes had definitely looked familiar. In high school and college, I'd been obsessed with fantasy and paranormal stuff. Okay, I still was, but that's beside the point. It took a while to realize those marks really did look a lot like the runes I'd seen in various books, movies, and TV shows. I was so lost in trying to remember more about runes that I wasn't really paying attention when the familiar ringtone blared. I answered automatically, then realized—that was Sarah's ringtone, and I hadn't answered yesterday.

"Hey, good to hear from you. How's work?" I ask, hopeful the conversation won't go to hell. She hated when I didn't answer her calls.

Sarah sounds distracted. "I'm running errands. Long week. You didn't answer last night. I was worried."

"Nothing happened. I was busy. You should come visit sometime. It's actually really peaceful here," I offer, like I always do.

"Ame, you know I can't do small towns. Everyone knowing your business, nowhere decent to eat, no cell service..."

"We have cell service—"

"You know what I mean. Besides, I'm swamped with work. But YOU could come here! I found this amazing new restaurant—"

And there it is. The script we always follow: I invite her, she turns me down, then says I need to come see her. She then proceeds to tell me about a few jobs near her that would be great for me and how I need to return to the 'real world'. It never sinks in that I don't want to live in the big city. I like it here.

It's noon when I finally hang up, and I'm itching to get out of the trailer. I throw on gray yoga pants, a faded t-shirt three sizes too big, and sneakers that are more holes than fabric. Mystic and Ash dance circles around my feet, picking up on my nerves like they're radio waves.

The park's half-empty, just the way I like it. The whole place smells sharp and clean, like someone uncapped a bottle of Pine-Sol, minus the chemical smell. The playground's empty except for a couple of toddler moms chatting on the benches, their kids digging holes under the swing set like baby armadillos. The dog run sprawls at the far end, padded with soft grass and the occasional divot where someone's four-legged genius tried to tunnel to China.

I unclip their leashes. Mystic shoots off, laser-focused on a squirrel skittering along the top of the fence. Ash is more interested in the other dogs, tail wagging frantically, ready to make friends or get into trouble—whichever comes first.

I stand by the gate, arms crossed, pretending to scroll my phone but really just watching. That's me: always watching, rarely joining. I'm a world-class lurker. The dogs circle back every few minutes to check on me before launching back into chaos.

It's peaceful, but the peace is fragile. I can feel it—like a bubble just waiting for the slightest breeze.

That breeze arrives in the form of a man.

He doesn't just enter the park—he strides into it, every step deliberate, a slow-motion wave of confidence parting the air around him. He's tall. Like, offensive to short people, tall. His jeans fit perfectly, neither cowboy nor city slicker, and his shirt—button-up, black, sleeves rolled just so—has a weird shimmer when he moves, like it can't decide whether to swallow the sunlight or reflect it.

I watch him because everyone else is watching him. Not because I've never seen a man who looked and moved like him. I don't want to be obvious, so I glance at Ash, who's gnawing enthusiastically on a communal tennis ball. I quickly remove it from his mouth and hand him his own toy. Mystic picks up on my tension and immediately goes on alert, pacing between me and the new guy.

He's heading right for us. Not just in our general direction—he's making a beeline, no hesitation, eyes locked on mine and smiling like he's running for mayor and I'm the only voter in town. Why is he looking at me like that? I look like I just wrestled an alligator and lost.

I stiffen, trying to shrink into myself. Maybe if I act busy tying my shoe, he'll pass by.

I'm so busy focusing on my feet that when I straighten up, we nearly collide.

"Whoa—sorry." My voice cracks, instantly betraying me. I stumble backward, but he's faster. His hand catches my elbow, fingers cool and dry, grip gentle but certain.

The contact is electric. I know, I know—every bad romance novel ever—but it's not just the skin-on-skin, not just the jolt climbing my arm and lodging somewhere behind my ribs. It's the sense of recognition, a déjà vu so strong I almost drop my phone.

"Are you all right?" His accent hovers just shy of British, but with something else underneath, something I can't place. His voice is low, textured. Like dark chocolate, if chocolate could talk.

"I—yeah, fine, just—" I gesture vaguely at my shoes, as if improper footwear is an acceptable explanation for spatial incompetence.

He smiles, slow and dangerous, like he's testing how much I'll forgive. Not "good teeth" devastating. More like "I just sold my soul and somehow I'm okay with it" devastating.

"Didn't mean to startle you." He doesn't release my arm until he's sure I'm steady.

Mystic barrels in from the side, hackles up, placing herself firmly between me and the stranger. He crouches with surprising grace, extending his hand palm-down for her to sniff. She circles twice, then retreats behind my legs, still suspicious.

"She's protective," I say, the tang of old fear prickling the back of my neck, remembering the last time Mystic tried to protect me. "We've had a lot of practice being on guard."

"She's smart." He straightens to his full, ridiculous height. "Danger comes in many forms. Sometimes it even says please and thank you." His eyes flicker, green-gold with a ring of something almost luminous around the edges. They linger on mine a half-second longer than is polite, as if he's memorizing the details.

There's a silence. Not awkward, exactly, but charged.

I pull my t-shirt down, making sure my butt and stomach are covered, an old habit, and fish for words.

"You're new here." It's not a question. In a town this size, you know all the regulars by sight. He's not one.

"Is it that obvious?" he asks, amused.

I nod. "No one dresses that nice unless they're going to a wedding or a funeral."

He laughs, a short, sharp sound. "Which do you think it is?"

"Hopefully not the funeral." It comes out more flirty than I intend, which mortifies me instantly. I can't remember the last time I even thought about flirting; it was before I moved here, that's for sure.

He seems to like it, though. "Loki," he says, offering his hand again. This time, I take it.

"Like the Norse god?" I ask, raising an eyebrow.

"Exactly like that." His smile curls, just for a second, into something feral.

"Amethyst," I say. It's a name that often gets twisted and mispronounced, but only those who are close to me get to call me anything else.

"Amethyst," he echoes, savoring the sound. "Pleasure."

The word hangs between us, weighty and a little dangerous. Mystic growls, low and uncertain. Ash, sensing the tension, drops the tennis ball at Loki's feet and wags, as if to break the spell.

Loki bends and scoops up the ball, turning it over in his hands. There's something about the way his fingers move—too smooth, like the joints are triple-lubed or maybe don't have any bones at all.

He offers the ball to Ash, who accepts it with a delighted yip.

"Your dogs have excellent taste," Loki says.

I glance at Mystic, who has wedged herself against my calf, still glaring.

"Only in tennis balls and treats," I say.

He grins, but there's something in his eyes—an edge, a flicker of calculation. "Then I'm honored to make their acquaintance. And yours."

His gaze pins me. It's not predatory, not exactly, but it feels as if he could see everything: the way my hands tremble, the scar behind my left ear, the whole messy history I try to keep folded away.

I'm rattled, but not scared. Not yet.

"Well," I say, taking a step back, "thanks for not flattening me."

He steps aside, sweeping an arm with mock courtesy. "My pleasure."

We stand like that for a heartbeat—me poised to bolt, him perfectly at ease—before the moment breaks.

Mystic jumps up and grabs at the leash I'm holding and begins to tug, eager to do another lap. I let her pull me away, but I can feel his eyes on my back, a weight like static or the promise of thunder.

As I make my way around the fence, I risk a glance over my shoulder. He's still standing there, hands in his pockets, a smile hovering at the corner of his mouth.

The rest of the afternoon passes in a blur. I pretend to watch the dogs, but every time I look up, he's somewhere in my periphery: talking to the old woman with the three-legged lab, helping a little kid untangle his kite string, leaning against the fence with a distant, thoughtful expression.

I tell myself it's a coincidence. I tell myself I'll never see him again.

But by the time I leash up Mystic and Ash and head for home, the hair on my arms hasn't settled, and every step feels like a countdown to our next collision.

The next afternoon, I return to the park. I don't usually come this often, but I felt the urge to, and to my surprise, Loki is there, talking to others in the park. I head for the trail, the dogs at my side.

"Mind if I join you?" Loki asks, just as I reach the trailhead.

"N-no. We're just gonna walk the trail."

He falls into step beside me, and we make small talk as we wind through the woods.

That's when it gets weird. The day is calm—no breeze, not even a whisper—but as Loki passes under the trees, the lowest branches bend toward him, their needles brushing his hair like a benediction. Sunlight dapples his shirt, and the shadows ripple, coiling around his arms before vanishing as quickly as they came.

I stare, sure I'm seeing things, but then I catch it again: the faintest blue-white flicker along his forearm when he tucks a stray strand of hair behind his ear. Runes, or something like them, dancing just beneath the surface.

He must sense me watching because he smiles without turning. "You see it, don't you?" he murmurs, so soft I almost miss it.

My mouth goes dry. "See what?" No way am I admitting to seeing runes... people think I'm crazy enough as it is.

He looks at me, really looks, and for a second, I feel like I'm being dissected, layer by layer. But it's not threatening—it's intimate, almost reverent.

"Nothing," he says finally. "Just a trick of the light."

He moves on, and I follow, not sure if I want to believe him.

We reach the point where the trail turns back on itself, the conversation drifting from mundane (favorite pizza toppings; his is anchovy, the madman) to the existential. He's easy to talk to, but never easy to read. His answers are elliptical, half-truths couched in riddles. I find myself wanting to ask more, to get under the surface, even as every instinct screams that this is not a man you can ever really know.

Ash interrupts by barreling back with a stick the size of a Louisville Slugger, nearly bowling us both over. I laugh, and Loki stoops to scratch behind Ash's ears, murmuring words I don't understand but which the dog clearly does—he drops the stick and sits, eyes wide with adoration.

"Are you a dog whisperer on top of everything else?" I ask, trying to keep my voice casual.

He glances up, the shadow of a smile playing at his lips. "I've always had a knack for animals. They know who's bluffing and who isn't."

I believe it.

We continue making small talk about nothing in particular. He asks about the best places to eat ("Is there anywhere in this town that serves decent coffee?"), the oddest thing I've seen at the park (I tell him about the man who brings his ferret on a leash; he listens like it's the greatest story ever told), and whether I've lived here my whole life.

"No, I mean my family lived in Texas ages ago, but we left when I was a baby. I just moved back six years ago," I say. "East Texas is like gravity—you can escape, but you always get pulled back."

"Any siblings?" he asks, not unkindly, but with a glint of real curiosity.

I hesitate, then shake my head. "Not anymore." Not since that night, the night my family died, but that's not something you talk about with a relative stranger.

He nods, accepting the answer without pushing. His pace slows, and I match him, realizing I'm unconsciously mirroring his stride, the tilt of his head, and the way his hands slide into his pockets and reemerge when he speaks.

Eventually, the sun dips behind the trees, and the temperature drops, a sudden, sharp transition that sets my teeth on edge. The dogs, tired now, flop at my feet and start gnawing on the same stick, tails wagging in opposite directions.

He breaks the silence. "I'd like to see more of the town. I hear the old library is haunted?"

I laugh, relieved. "If by haunted you mean underfunded and in dire need of renovation, then yes."

"Would you show me?" He asks it lightly, but his gaze is intent, pinning me in place.

My first instinct is to deflect, to come up with an excuse. "I'm kinda busy... not sure when I can."

He stares at me for a moment, like he can see what I'd rather keep hidden, but nods.

We lapse into silence again, and I watch the dogs roll and wrestle in the grass. Mystic, ever the disciplinarian, keeps her eyes locked on Loki, as if waiting for him to slip up.

"I should go," I say, but I don't move. I'm rooted, caught in the weird magnetic field of this man who isn't really a stranger but isn't anything else, either. Ash drops the stick at Loki's feet, tail windmilling so hard his whole body shakes. Loki crouches to retrieve it, and as he stands, he holds the stick out to me. Our fingers brush. There's that spark again, stronger this time, a flash of blue-white that arcs between us and leaves my skin tingling.

We both freeze. I stare at my hand; he stares at me. Neither of us says anything about it.

He hands over Ash's leash, his fingers wrapping around mine for just a beat too long.

"Perhaps we'll bump into each other again," he says, his voice low and smooth.

"It's a small town; I think the odds are pretty good," I reply, breathless.

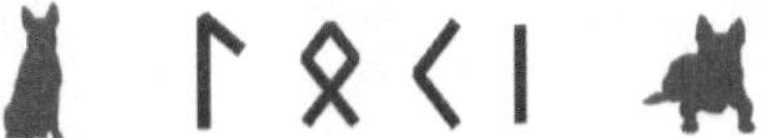

Saturday mornings are for errands and damage control. I wake up late, hair in a purple tangle, and shuffle through a list of small disasters: the dogs have shredded the throw rug, the milk's a day expired, and my last clean shirt has a mysterious coffee stain the size of a possum. I jam everything into a laundry basket and head to Pineridge Market with a handful of coupons and the kind of optimism that never survives contact with a crowded grocery store. I park in the shade and crack the windows, turning on the fans and setting my timer. I know exactly how long the truck will stay cool enough for the dogs to be left.

Mystic and Ash wait in the truck, noses pressed to the glass, watching me march inside. I grab a cart and start with produce, navigating the aisles with the paranoia of someone who expects an ambush from every endcap. Halfway through, I realize I've left my list in the car. I know if I go back, the dogs will go nuts, so I just wing it.

I'm contemplating how many eggs I need when I round the corner of Aisle 3 and plow straight into a solid wall of muscle and wonderfully rich cologne.

Eggs go flying. There's a cartoon moment of panic—dozens of fragile shells tumbling through the air, slow as snowflakes. Somehow, every single one lands unbroken, nesting perfectly in the open carton held by the man I've just rammed into.

Loki.

He stands there, smiling, an unflappable statue in black jeans and a T-shirt that says, "The Future Is Analog." In one hand, he holds the eggs; in the other, a jar of honey with a label written in a language I don't recognize.

"Running your weekend errands solo?" he asks. He saw I'd been reaching for eggs and hands me the carton without a hint of judgment.

"I, uh, yeah," I stammer, clutching the carton like it might bite. "Wasn't expecting to see you here."

He raises the honey, examining it against the fluorescent lights. "I go wherever the universe points me. Today, apparently, it was to the baking aisle."

I try to laugh, but it comes out more like a hiccup. "I thought you were more of a park type."

"Parks don't serve coffee," he says, winking. "And they don't carry the best honey in town."

I glance at the jar and try to decipher the label. "Is that... Finnish? Or maybe Swedish?"

He leans closer, lowering his voice to a stage whisper. "It's from a very small village in the north. Almost impossible to find unless you know exactly where to look."

There's a game here, and for once, I want to play.

"Well, lucky you," I say, regaining a bit of composure. "But if you're baking, you're still going to need eggs."

He considers this, then puts two cartons in his basket. "Excellent point. Would you join me for lunch? I mean, unless you have plans with your canine bodyguards."

His confidence is so unselfconscious it almost feels safe. Almost.

I hesitate, scanning my brain for reasons to say no; none stick. "Okay," I say. "But only if it's somewhere the dogs can come."

He grins, triumphant. "I know just the place."

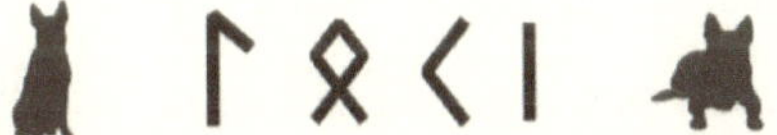

The Blue Acorn Café is a small, strange bistro tucked off the main drag. Its patio is fenced with cedar planks and lit by thousands of tiny bulbs strung between the oaks, giving it the feeling of an outdoor speakeasy for introverts. The tables are weathered wood, each painted a different shade of blue, and the chairs never match. There are more plants than people.

We take a corner table under a sagging umbrella, the dogs lounging at our feet. The waitress brings water for them before she even takes our order. Mystic sniffs the glass, then noses it toward Ash, who laps delicately as if he's the Queen of England.

Loki orders for both of us: lavender lemonade and sweet potato fries to start, then something I can't pronounce for the main. He doesn't ask if I'll like it—just assumes, and weirdly, I do.

Conversation is slow at first. He asks about my job ("office stuff, not worth describing"), my hobbies ("reading, being weird, running the dogs"), and how I like the town ("I don't, but it's mine"). I volley the questions back, but he always answers sideways, never quite giving up the truth.

"You ever get lonely, moving from place to place?" I ask, feeling bold.

He shrugs, swirling his lemonade. "Not really. I find people wherever I go. Or they find me."

"Yeah, but do any of them stick?"

He sets the glass down and leans in, eyes catching the light. "Not until now."

It's so direct that I freeze, unsure if I'm supposed to laugh or run. Instead, I pick at my fries, searching for a safe topic.

Mystic saves me by gently pawing at Loki's shoe, testing him. He rewards her with a fry, which she takes with suspicious slowness, then drops at Ash's feet.

"You have a fan club," I say, relief flickering through me. My mind flashes to other guys Mystic had never seemed to like.

"I'm good with dogs," he replies, not breaking eye contact.

A silence blooms, comfortable this time. The food comes—perfect, of course—and I'm halfway through before I realize I've eaten more than I usually do in two meals.

We talk about the park, about the oddball people who pass through, about the mysteries of East Texas. He tells a story about getting lost on the back roads at dusk, winding up at a cemetery where every headstone is marked with a single word: "WAITING." I shiver at the oddly spooky tale.

"You're not what I expected," I say, and it's true.

He nods, solemn. "Neither are you."

It grows late. The dogs sprawl in the mulch, content. Overhead, the lights blur into constellations. I feel the pulse of possibility in the space between us, both thrilling and terrifying.

He pays, and we walk out together, the night humming with insect song and something less definable. At the edge of the lot, he stops and looks down at me with that same predator's patience.

"I meant what I said. I'd like to see you again, Amethyst."

I swallow, feeling the truth of it in my chest. "Yeah. Me too. But I'm... kinda busy. But I'm sure we'll meet up again."

He smiles, less a flash this time, more a slow, inevitable thing.

The dogs and I pile into the truck. As I drive home, Mystic rests her head on my shoulder from the back seat, a rare display of affection. Ash snores, exhausted by all the new smells and sensations.

I can't stop smiling.

I fall asleep that night with the taste of lavender and honey still clinging, too sweet to trust, on my tongue, and for the first time in years, I look forward to whatever comes next.

Chapter Three

WATCHING AND WAITING

I spend the afternoon in my usual contest with the overgrown patch-work I call a yard. Miss Eliza, the local crazy witchy lady, has sent me various plants over the years since I moved here. I glance over at the dogs, who currently alternate between uprooting lizards and chasing each other in wide, dusty laps, their barks echoing off the faded aluminum of my trailer.

Once the flowerbed is sufficiently de-weeded, I stand and stretch my back, vertebrae popping like knuckles. The dogs barrel over to investigate the carnage. Mystic, always the more dignified of the two, sniffs the up-rooted weeds, then gives me a look equal parts judgment and approval. Ash tries to eat a dandelion head before I shoo him off. "Ain't nobody asked for your opinion," I mutter, swatting a gnat from my nose.

Next, the rosemary. It's gone feral since the rains last month, trailing woody stems in every direction, half of them bruised from Mystic's relent-less patrolling. I fish the rusty garden shears from my back pocket—left there on purpose—and start hacking away, the scent sharp and medicinal in the humid air. My hands ache with the repetition, but I keep at it, pruning until the bush is less a monster and more a shrub. The pile of trimmings on the ground looks like the world's saddest Christmas wreath.

I rake up a drift of fallen pine needles along the fence, more to satisfy my own need for order than because anyone will see it. There's an old chain-link fence at the property line, sagging in the center where a family of possums used to squeeze through. They haven't been around lately. Even the raccoons seem to have better things to do than haunt my yard.

When I finish, I prop the rake against the porch and allow myself a small victory sigh. The dogs collapse in a panting heap by the door, their tongues lolling in perfect synchrony. I'd call them my loyal sidekicks, but the truth is, I'd be lost without them. They're the reason I bother keeping the outside world at bay.

It's then, as I'm tugging off my gloves, that I notice it—a thin seam in the woods where the trees grow a little too straight, the underbrush pressed flat as if something moves there regularly. I squint and realize it's a path, or at least a trail, narrow and deer-worn, fading into shadow where the pines get thickest.

I've lived here for years and never walked that way. I tell myself it's because of ticks, or the mosquitoes, or the sheer number of snake skins I've found under the porch, but the truth is, I avoid the deeper woods out of habit. Childhood superstitions stick, even if you've spent your adult life telling everyone you don't believe in fairy tales.

But the path is different today. There's a strange color to it, like the light bends a little wrong just at the edge of the trees. A golden haze, not quite sunlight, not quite shadow. The sort of glow that makes you think of campfire stories or the way flames look behind closed eyelids. For a moment, I consider leaving it alone—heading in for a cold shower and something to drink, letting the woods do what woods do without my interference. Instead, I find myself stepping forward, curiosity already outweighing caution.

"Stay," I tell the dogs, though I know it won't stick. Mystic plants herself on the bottom porch step, eyes locked on me. Ash feigns disinterest, but I can feel him plotting.

I push through the first screen of undergrowth. The light changes immediately—softens, but also sharpens, every pine needle and strand of spiderweb outlined in fire. It's cooler here, but the air hums with insect song, and the hum soaks into my skin. There's a resinous scent I don't remember from before, sweeter than the rosemary, more like honey dripping on hot metal. I glance over my shoulder; the house is already half-obscured, a mirage floating in a sea of green.

The path winds, zigzagging between root-clustered trees, never wide enough for more than one careful step at a time. My sneakers crunch over old leaf mulch, squelching in spots where the ground is still damp. I keep moving, always certain the next turn will reveal something—anything—worth all the mosquito bites I'm racking up. The light deepens as I go, the amber shifting to orange, then to a color like the inside of a peach.

It's there, past a fallen limb slick with moss, that I see them: markings on the trunks. At first, I mistake them for knots or natural scars, but as I draw closer, the symmetry is impossible to ignore. Shapes like angular Y's, lines intersecting with the precision of a wood-burned brand. Some are topped with three-pronged branches; others curve in a way that reminds me of bow staves or tuning forks. They're not carved, not exactly—the bark isn't cut, but shaded, as if shadow itself inked the lines on.

The markings flicker with pale orange fire whenever I move, the edges glowing and then dimming in time with my heartbeat. I reach out a hand, half-expecting to feel heat, but the bark is just bark. The glow intensifies for a second, then fades, leaving a ghost trace in my vision, like I've stared at a camera flash.

A breeze stirs the needles overhead, and a sound shivers down: faint, silvery, like a handful of glass beads tumbling together. It's not wind chimes—I'd know; I own three sets, all bought during my brief attempt at "witchy chic" home decor—but the sound is eerily similar. I listen, holding my breath, as the chimes repeat. The second time, I realize they coincide with the light: the runes pulse, the sound follows, always when the breeze moves the air. It's impossible, but the impossible seems to have moved in next door and borrowed a cup of sugar.

Something prickles at my temples, cold and electric, and my hands shake as I press them to my face. I can't tell if it's fear or excitement or the slow-dawning certainty that I've seen this before—not just the shapes, but the exact pattern, the sequence of symbols, the way the glow matches the rhythm of my own breath. It's the certainty of déjà vu, the memory of a memory, except I've never seen anything like this in waking life.

Maybe it was a dream. Or a story I half-remember from a library book I once read under the covers, flashlight in hand, determined to find proof that magic was real even after everyone, especially my mother, said it wasn't.

I try to pull away, but my feet root themselves in the mulch, unwilling to budge. The dogs have caught up, silent now, and they press close to my shins, bodies taut as guitar strings. Mystic's fur stands along her neck, and Ash makes a low, uneasy whine. They see it too. Or maybe just me seeing it is enough for them to know something's off.

I draw my phone from my back pocket, hands shaking so badly I nearly drop it. I snap a photo. The screen blanches out, refusing to focus, the shapes on the bark smearing into a band of orange static. The runes, whatever they are, want to be seen but not recorded.

Another gust of wind, another flicker of light and glass-bead chime, and the prickle at my scalp deepens. I force myself to count the symbols—seven, maybe eight, though a few blur at the edge of my sight—and I mouth the pattern under my breath, terrified I'll forget it if I don't.

I don't believe in magic. I don't. But as I stand in the hush between pulses, with the sun leaking out of the sky and the woods closing in behind me, I know I'll dream of these marks tonight. I know I'll trace them in the dirt tomorrow, searching for meaning I have no business finding.

And for the first time in years, I'm not sure if that thought scares me or if it's the only thing that's keeping me together.

I favor the study at dusk. The old house—if you could call this place a house and not a mausoleum for things that refused to die—gathers light in its bones and bleeds it out as shadow. The air inside is thick with the smells of tallow, scorched resin, and that telltale copper tang left by rituals gone sideways. Every book on the shelves is one I've bled for, every candle holder cast in the likeness of a lesser god or a dead rival. Most people would be unnerved. I find it soothing.

The room is half-lit, just enough for the runes on my forearm to catch the glow. Their lines are blacker than midnight, but when I flex my hand, they shimmer, an oil-slick green that glows only for the deserving. Tonight, the ink writhes in anticipation, aware that I'm about to ask it for a favor.

In the center of the room stands the obsidian sphere, nested atop an oak pedestal carved with so many overlapping wardings that the wood should have combusted by now. The sphere is my eye, my memory, my curse. It holds reflections of all the worlds I've left behind, but more importantly, it shows me the things I care to see, provided I feed it the proper sacrifices.

I circle it once, fingers trailing along the grooves in the pedestal, and settle on the battered stool opposite. There's a ritual to this. Everything important in my life is a ritual. I strike a match, let the sulfur scent curl up into my nose, and light the three silver candleholders. The flames gutter, then right themselves, and the shadows in the room dance like they're eager for a story.

I whisper the phrase. Not in English, never in English—it lacks the sharpness, the edge. The old tongue fits better in my mouth, each syllable a promise and a threat: "Við opna veginn milli heima." Open the road between the worlds. My voice is soft, but the room answers back, a low hum in the walls, as if the whole house is breathing with me.

The sphere responds. A pale fog crawls up from its depths, swirling slow at first, then faster as I press my palm to the glass. My skin tingles, the rune on my forearm burning cold, and green fire flickers at my fingertips. I draw a line down the globe's surface, and shadow follows—liquid, alive, more obedient than any hound. I guide it with a thought, willing the vision to show me the woods at the edge of Pine Hollow, and her.

The image forms, clearing in waves like a lake freezing over. I see Amethyst among the pines, her hair a wild purple tangle, her face set in an expression of stubborn skepticism that I find excruciatingly familiar. She moves with the cautious certainty of someone who doesn't yet believe the ground will hold. I can almost hear the dry sarcasm she mutters under her breath as she brushes away low branches, ever the reluctant explorer.

But it's not her face that matters, though I find it more attractive than I should. It's the runes.

They float in the air around her, crackling with violet, sharp as lightning scars. Not random, not noise—she's attracting them, or they're answering her; I can't decide which is more dangerous. The symbols shift and recombine, sometimes wrapping around her head like a crown, sometimes hovering just above her hands. A bindrune forms, delicate and deadly: protection, yes, but also warning. Or perhaps a summoning, if you know the language and how to lie with it.

Her dogs see them, too. They weave at her ankles, spines arched, eyes fixed on the points of brightest light. Whenever she exhales, the marks shimmer more fiercely, as if they breathe with her or hunger for her. That's new. It shouldn't be possible for a mortal, even a stubborn one with her lineage.

I lean closer to the sphere, the surface cooling under my breath. The vision distorts, blurring at the edges, but the focus is clear: something in the woods responds to her. Something older than the words I just spoke.

My jaw clenches, the old worry gnawing at my patience. I'd hoped the magic would settle. I'd hoped she could have a life that wasn't haunted by the curse her bloodline carries. But the forest disagrees. The world disagrees. It's never enough for fate to leave us alone; it must always twist the knife, just to make sure you're paying attention.

I watch her hand reach out, trembling, to touch a mark on the bark. I see the way the light recoils and then surges back, enveloping her fingers. The moment is delicate—she's at the threshold, and on the other side, there are things that would notice her if she crossed it.

I want to warn her, but there's no safe way to do that. Not without drawing even more attention. I settle for memorizing the patterns of the runes, the order in which they appear, the way they knot themselves around her like a net. If there's a message in the sequence, I'll find it.

The room grows colder. The candles lean toward the sphere, their flames almost horizontal, drawn to the drama inside the glass. I withdraw my hand, and the vision fades, the mist receding into the black. I flex my fingers. They're stiff, the nails rimed with green and shadow.

I turn away from the sphere, collecting my thoughts with the precision of someone who knows he's being watched. There are rules, even for me. Especially for me.

If the runes are calling to her, it means she's being marked. If she's being marked, she's no longer just a curiosity but a target. There are others who watch for this sort of thing. Not all of them are as handsome or as morally ambiguous as I am.

I reach for the phone but stop myself. There's time yet. Better to let her think she's still in control, that this is her discovery and not a path I've gently set her on. She's braver than she knows, and she'll need every ounce of that before this is over.

I blow out the candles one by one. The shadows in the room retreat to their corners, sulking. I study the ink on my arm, the runes now dormant but ready to ignite at a moment's notice.

Tomorrow, I'll see her again. Not by the sphere, but in flesh and blood and the reckless spark she brings out in me.

And if anyone else comes looking for her before I do, they'll regret it.

That's a promise I intend to keep.

The woods keep their secrets. They also keep their grudges.

I don't notice the sun has dipped below the treeline until it's almost gone, the sky bruised purple, the pines snapping their needles in the first cool wind since April. My phone says it's barely past seven, but it could be midnight for how the light has drained out of the world.

I'm still standing in front of the marked tree, fingers itching and scalp crawling, when I hear it: a faint clatter, like someone dropped a handful of silverware on stone. It echoes, hollow and metallic, from somewhere deeper in the woods. I tell myself it's just a branch hitting rock, not the old legend of The Pine Walker, but then it happens again—three sharp knocks, spaced too evenly to be random. A moment later comes the chime, high and clear, less wind than wire. Like a bell the size of a sewing thimble, struck by a patient child.

The dogs freeze, heads up, ears pitched forward like they're catching radio signals. Mystic edges closer to me, her hackles up; Ash goes low, tail tucked, a growl fluttering in his throat. Whatever it is, they want no part of it.

The sound repeats, this time with a second noise underneath—rustling leaves, but also something softer, like voices arguing behind a thin wall. The words are impossible to catch, more hiss than language. I back up a step, and the dogs move with me, glued to my legs.

That's when I lose my nerve. I bolt. I don't know if the legend is true, but with everything else happening, I call the dogs and take off.

It's not a graceful retreat. I trip over the fallen limb, scrape my knee in the process, and swear so loud the birds take off from the canopy. The dogs rocket ahead, then race back, urging me along until we burst out of the trees and tumble onto the patchy lawn. I spare one wild glance over my shoulder, half-expecting the woods to spit out a monster or a park ranger or, hell, the ghost of my dead mother. But there's nothing, just the pines, silent and watching.

I sprint to the porch, all dignity lost. The dogs barrel through the open door, and I follow, slamming it shut and twisting the deadbolt so hard I nearly shear it off. For good measure, I drag over the dining chair and wedge it under the knob. It's probably unnecessary, but adrenaline makes you do stupid things. The dogs immediately start their patrol, circling the living room and barking at every creak of the vinyl siding.

Inside, the silence is worse. It's too ordinary. The kitchen hums, the TV blares some rerun, and the fridge whines with the same persistence as my self-doubt. I lean against the counter, heart still hammering, and try to catch my breath.

That's when the questions start.

What the hell did I just see, just hear? Are the runes some kind of message, or just the world's oldest case of pareidolia? Why do I feel like I've touched this magic before, in a life that wasn't mine? My brain wants to rationalize, to chalk it up to stress and sleep deprivation and my lifelong weakness for fantasy novels. But my skin remembers the prickle, the way the marks seemed to breathe with me, the music in the air.

I need answers. Or at least someone else's theory to make my own confusion less lonely.

I grab the laptop and start it up. The Wi-Fi is usually pretty good, even this close to the woods, but tonight it's sluggish as a funeral dirge. The dogs crowd the couch, Mystic staring at the door, Ash curling against my thigh like a weighted blanket.

My stomach does a slow barrel roll as I search for runes. On the first site I visit, I find some of the runes I saw… most seem to mean defense, sanctuary, warding against evil. The more I read, the more certain I am that the trees are trying to warn me, or warn something else about me.

The next site, a small university blog, has illustrations that match what I saw in the woods exactly.

I bookmark the post, then copy the images into a new document, naming it "Delusions" because it feels right.

Last, I fall down the rabbit hole of forums. Most are useless—places for bored teens to invent cryptids and trade ghost stories. But then I find the thread on an East Texas folklore group titled "Twilight Scripts in the Piney Woods?"

The original post is a mess of misspelled words and half-caps, but the details line up: "Weird runes on the trees, only at dusk, dogs won't go near them, air tastes like copper and honey." I scroll through the comments, and one makes me stop; it reads: "Old blood shows the way. If you see the script, you're probably kin. Stay out of the woods at night. They'll notice you."

I reread that last line, the words "they'll notice you" burning themselves into the space behind my eyes.

For a moment, I consider calling someone. But I dismiss the thought: who would I call? Loki? Well, I don't have his number, and what would I say? "Hey, strange man I met a couple of times, am I secretly the chosen one? Is the forest conspiring to kill me, or is my friend Sarah right and I'm crazy?" I chuckle to myself as visions of Buffy the Vampire Slayer flick through my mind, but I brush them off. I'm NOT the chosen one… not possible.

The dogs finally settle, their barks traded for low, uneasy whimpers. I shut the laptop and stare at the ceiling, letting the hum of the house and the steady breathing of my dogs remind me I'm still alive, still safe. Mostly.

I decide, against all sense, that tomorrow I'll go back to the woods. I'll bring a notebook, maybe a camera. I'll walk the path again, trace the runes with my own hand, and prove to myself that it was all a trick of the light. Or that it wasn't, and my life is about to get much, much weirder.

I'm making a list in my head of what to bring when I hear it: a soft knock at the door. Not the wind, not a branch, but the careful rap of knuckles on metal. The sound is almost polite.

Mystic is off the couch in an instant, standing at attention. Ash presses against my knee, trembling. I'm frozen for a second, caught between curiosity and that old, primal dread.

The knock comes again, gentle, insistent. Three times. Exactly like the sound in the woods.

I stand, every nerve on fire, and approach the door. I don't open it, but I press my ear to the thin metal and listen.

There's a voice on the other side, too low to make out. I strain harder. The voice repeats, softer still. It almost sounds like my name.

I don't know whether to laugh, scream, or open the door and find out what's waiting for me. So I do what I always do.

I buy myself one more moment. I stand there, breathing, listening to the woods beyond the walls, and wait for the courage to let the next part happen.

CHAPTER FOUR

WARNINGS AND ADVICE

The next morning comes thick and sweet as syrup, sunlight pouring in through the blinds and pooling across the floor. For a good minute, I let myself pretend I'm not about to make a fool of myself. I tell myself the dogs have more sense than I do, which is a lie, because Ash is currently face-planted on my pillow, snoring like a truck stop regular. Mystic at least keeps one ear cocked toward the window, ready for a squirrel incursion at a moment's notice.

I stretch, muscles popping, and roll out of bed with a groan. Last night's research session still buzzes in my skull: the runes, the way they glowed on the screen, all that talk about bloodlines. I half expect to wake up with them tattooed across my arms. Instead, I wake up with dog hair in my mouth and a pit in my stomach that's probably half existential dread, half hunger.

Breakfast is an afterthought. I shuffle eggs into a pan, toss the shells toward the trash, and miss by a mile. If the universe is trying to tell me something, it's not speaking in any language I know. I get through two bites before the nerves catch up, coiling in my chest like a garden hose left in the sun. I'm supposed to go see Miss Eliza today. Everyone in town jokes she's the town witch. I will admit she's got the folk remedies down to a science. She once gave me a custom blended tea that really helps with headaches.

Eliza said she'd be home after noon, and "come whenever the spirit moves you, sugar," which is how she says "don't be late." I finish the eggs, choke down coffee, and then it's time to get dressed for a visit to the closest thing Pine Hollow has to a local oracle.

The drive across the forest is short, but my thoughts make it a marathon. The trees lean in, gossiping overhead, their needles dark and whispery even in the morning light. Mystic and Ash ride in the backseat, their heads propped between the bars of the old cargo divider, eyes peeled for whatever it is dogs see when they look at a moving world. I talk to them like they're listening. Maybe they are. At this point, I'll take any audience.

The gravel driveway curves in a lazy S, dust rising behind the tires. Miss Eliza's house is a dollhouse gone feral: the wraparound porch sagging just enough to give it character, wind chimes tangled with pine needles, and so many potted plants that the place could probably survive a minor famine. There's a flagstone path from the drive to the porch, and the sun makes it steam like a pie crust fresh out of the oven. I park, and immediately both dogs go on high alert. Mystic's hackles rise like she's been hit with static, and Ash paces a tight figure eight in the backseat.

"You two were fine until we got here," I mutter. "Don't embarrass me in front of the old lady. She'll never let me forget it." I grab their leashes and step out into the thick green quiet.

Miss Eliza meets us halfway up the walk. She looks like someone drew her from a memory: silver hair wild as a dandelion, face barely lined for someone who's probably outlived two husbands and a handful of secrets. Today she wears a dress the color of the night just before it goes dark and a faded shawl that smells faintly of lavender and menthol. Her bare feet are surprisingly nimble as she navigates the choked garden.

"Morning, Amethyst." She never calls me by my last name, never "Ms. Gold" like some folks do, just Amethyst, or "girl," or if she's feeling particularly country, "child." Today it's the latter.

"Hey, Miss Eliza," I say, doing my best not to trip over the dogs, who are now vibrating with a kind of suspicious energy. "You look well."

"I look old," she laughs, and the laugh is a rusty hinge. "But I feel sharp enough to slice bread. Come on, let's get you some tea before you tell me what's chewing at that pretty little mind of yours."

I follow her up the steps, dogs in tow. The porch creaks but holds, and there's a swing at one end with a pillow embroidered with the words "Bless This Mess." Eliza points at it, then disappears into the house.

"Sit," she says, and I do, because no one disobeys Miss Eliza if they want to keep their soul intact. Mystic and Ash sniff every inch of the porch, tails down, steps slow. I try to act casual, picking at the chipped nail polish on my thumb and listening to the sounds of Miss Eliza's kitchen: the tap of a kettle, the rattle of a spoon in a mug, the low, tuneless hum of someone who's seen too much to care what other people think.

She's back in under a minute, carrying a tray with two steaming mugs, a tin of what looks like homemade shortbread, and a tiny jar of creamed honey. She pours with both hands, steady, eyes never leaving me. The mugs are hand-painted, each one different: mine is a deep purple with a run of gold stars around the rim. Her own is green, cracked, and repaired in two places.

"Drink," she says, sliding the mug toward me. "You look like you need fortification."

The first sip scalds my tongue and makes my eyes water, but the taste is so clean and herbal it shocks me into the present. I try to thank her but end up coughing into my sleeve.

"That's real mint, not the powdered stuff," Eliza says, smirking. "Grows right off the porch. Tell me what's eating you, girl."

I take a second to collect myself, inhaling the steam like it might carry away the jitters. "You ever see anything weird in these woods?" I ask, aiming for casual and missing by a country mile.

Miss Eliza's eyes go sharp, fox-bright. "Weird how?"

"Like... lights, or symbols? Maybe... people?" My voice wobbles on the last word, and I hate how it sounds.

Eliza sets her cup down with a thunk. "You got yourself a visitor, didn't you?"

I stare at the porch boards, feeling the flush creep up my neck. "Not sure if you'd call it a visitor. More like... a man. Showed up out of nowhere. The dogs didn't bark. And he—" I stop, not sure how much to say.

Eliza doesn't interrupt, just lets the silence fill up the porch. I watch a wasp thread through the wind chimes, its wings flickering in the sun.

"He was... different," I finally say. "Tall, dark hair, eyes like... I don't know. Not normal. And he said his name was Loki."

At that, Eliza's mouth pinches into a line so thin it might snap. "Loki, you say." She repeats it, as if she's tasting the word for poison.

I rush ahead, words tumbling. "And I know that sounds crazy, but the night before, I saw these... symbols, I guess. They looked like runes, you know, like the Vikings used? They glowed in the dirt. The dogs saw them too, but they weren't scared. Just... alert. And then last night I found the same shapes online. Old Norse stuff. There's a whole forum about it. Some people think it's aliens or the government. Some say it's magic. I don't know what I think."

I stop, realizing I've been talking with my hands the entire time, nearly sloshing tea everywhere. I clamp my fingers tight around the mug and look at Eliza for the first time since I sat down.

She looks at me the way a doctor might look at a stubborn infection. Not unkind, but wary. "You trust your instincts, Amethyst?"

I thought I did. Sometimes. Not always, but I nod, not sure what else to do.

"Good. You're gonna need them." She glances at the woods, then back at me. "There's power in this place. Always has been. Sometimes it's old, and sometimes it's new, wearing an old disguise. I've seen things here that would make your hair curl—though I see yours is doing fine on its own."

I bark out a laugh, sudden and too loud. "That's just the humidity."

Eliza smiles, but it doesn't reach her eyes. "You didn't come here for a hair consultation. You came because you're scared, and you think I might know what to do about it."

I nod again. The dogs whine, and I feel their anxiety in my own bones.

Eliza sits back in her chair, the wood creaking like it might confess something if you pressed hard enough. "You got a good heart, girl, but you're not as clever as you think. Men like that—creatures like that—they don't show up unless they want something."

I flinch because the words cut sharper than I want to admit. I want to tell her that I'm not the kind of woman who falls for handsome strangers, that I've been burned enough times to see through bullshit at a hundred yards. But I think about the way Loki looked at me, the way he said my name, and I know I'm lying. After all, I had been fooled twice before. It's why I haven't dated in eight years. I want to be smart, but I'm not sure I am.

"I don't think he wants anything from me," I say, soft as moss. "He just... appeared. It was like he already knew me."

"Maybe he did," Eliza says. She pours more tea, even though I've barely touched mine. "Sometimes the world turns in a way that brings people together for a reason. You don't have to know the reason. You just have to decide if you're going to run from it or run toward it."

I pick at the edge of my mug, watching the glaze shimmer where the sun hits it. "I don't know what to do."

"You don't have to do anything yet," Eliza says, and this time her smile is gentle, grandmotherly. "Just don't be a fool. And don't trust every sweet word that drips from a handsome mouth. Most of them are lies or worse."

I think of the night before: the heat in my chest, the way Loki's smile felt like a dare, and the sudden, desperate hope that maybe, just maybe, I could be someone's magic for a change. The urge to confess everything—to tell Eliza how much I wanted it to be real, how scared I was that I'd mess it up—burns so bright it almost blinds me.

Instead, I say, "The tea's good. Thank you."

Eliza cackles, the sound bouncing off the porch and out into the waiting woods. "You're welcome, child. Now finish your drink and help me weed the lemon balm. There's nothing like honest work to keep your head from floating off into the clouds."

I nod, set the mug down, and watch the steam curl away into the warm air. The dogs settle finally, their tension easing as if the house itself has given them permission to relax. Maybe I'm imagining it, but the porch feels safer now, like the worst of the storm has passed.

For now.

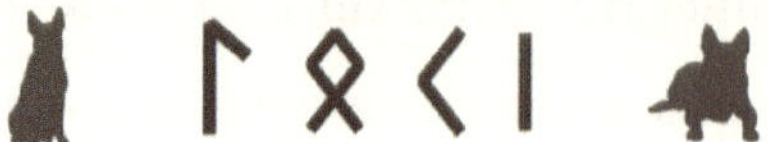

Turns out, weeding lemon balm is as meditative as therapy but with more dirt and fewer uncomfortable silences. Miss Eliza keeps a trowel holstered in her apron like a gunslinger, and the second we finish the porch tea, she's elbow-deep in the planter boxes, muttering to herself about snails and "the damn heat." I follow her lead, hands in the soil, my own thoughts loose and slippery.

When we finish, she waves me toward the side door and shuffles ahead. The inside of her cottage is even stranger than the porch: a riot of old photographs, shelves bursting with yellowed paperbacks, glass jars stuffed with dried flowers, and, unless I'm seeing things, a pair of actual raccoon skulls. The air is thick with incense and sun-warmed dust. There's a living room, technically, but it's more like a museum curated by a hoarder with a witch's aesthetic. Mystic and Ash are hesitant at first, but after a quick perimeter sweep, they curl up on a faded rag rug by the wood stove.

Eliza plops onto the couch and gestures for me to take the mismatched armchair. "You want more tea, or maybe something stronger?" She winks. I shake my head, and she laughs, then reaches for a tin of ginger snaps on the coffee table.

My eyes wander to her bookshelf. Most of the spines are sun-bleached, but a few stand out, bold with Nordic runes or heavy with red wax seals. There's a collection of odd stones—some shiny, some dull, all crammed into an old tobacco tin—and right above it, pride of place, a gold brooch shaped like two snakes twining around a circle. It looks ancient and expensive, and also like something you'd wear to a séance.

"So, Loki," Eliza says, and her tone is so matter-of-fact it nearly sends the ginger snap down the wrong pipe. "You said he had strange eyes?"

I nod. "Green, but not normal green. More like—" I falter, realizing how ridiculous it sounds. "More like a cat, but on fire. He didn't seem like he... fit here. He was too... confident. Too calm."

Eliza plucks at the hem of her skirt, gaze fixed on the middle distance. "They never act like they're supposed to. That's how they get you."

She tips her head, her crow's feet crinkled in perpetual skepticism. "You feel drawn to him?"

"Yeah," I admit, the word tasting like surrender. "But I don't trust it. I've been the butt of enough jokes to know when I'm being set up for a punchline."

Eliza snorts. "You want the truth, or something easier?"

I hesitate, then say, "The truth."

She leans forward, elbows on knees, hands clasped. "There's stories as old as time about gods and monsters coming down to walk with mortals. Sometimes they just want to watch. Sometimes they want to stir things up. Most times, they're bored and looking for trouble." She flicks her eyes toward the dogs, then out the window, where the late sun throws tree shadows across the yard. "But the ones you really gotta watch for are the ones who want to feel."

"Feel?" I echo. People had said since the first day I moved here that Ms. Eliza was a little crazy. The kids called her a witch. The adults just shook their heads and said she was just... different. Hearing her now, I get it. She talks like gods are real and come here all the time.

She nods. "You ever hear the old tales about the trickster gods? Never satisfied, always hungry. They show up, and everything changes. Could be a blessing, could be a curse, but it's always a storm. Usually, folks get swept up and spit out somewhere new."

I think about the wild, unsteady way my heart reacted to Loki. How a stranger could walk out of the woods, and suddenly I'm the center of his attention, like the rest of the world's a backdrop, and I'm the only thing in focus. It's terrifying, but it's also the first time I've felt... seen. And isn't that what everyone wants, deep down?

"You're telling me I should stay away," I say, trying to sound cool, but it comes out more... disappointed.

Eliza shakes her head. "I'm saying, don't close the door so tight you can't let anything in. But don't leave it wide open for whatever's knocking, either."

There's a quiet then, the air thick with what she isn't saying.

She finally moves to the bookshelf, fingers skimming the spines before she pulls down a slim volume. The cover is black, the title in what I assume is Old Norse. She flips to a marked page and hands it over.

"Read this," she says, "out loud if you can."

I stumble through the words—half vowels, half consonants, all impossible. "I don't know what it means," I say, embarrassed.

"Roughly?" Eliza says, settling back into the couch. "It means, 'If you seek the stranger, you seek yourself. If you trust the shadow, you dance with the dark.'"

I think about this, the echo of the words in my chest. "Is it a warning?"

"Or a prophecy. Or a joke. That's the thing about old stories: sometimes the endings change depending on who's telling it."

There's a scratching at the window, a sound like fingernails on glass, and both dogs snap to attention. Mystic rises, hackles high, while Ash gives a low, uneasy whine. Eliza's eyes flick to the window, then to me.

"You ever wonder why you see things that other folks don't?" she asks, her voice low. "Why the runes, the lights, why you don't seem to fit?"

I nod, not trusting myself to speak, not sure how she knew those things. I mean, I mentioned the runes... but the rest of it... how could she know?

"You're marked, whether you know it or not." She says it like she's telling me I have spinach in my teeth, nothing more or less. "Some people are just born closer to the cracks in the world. You can patch them, or you can fall through."

There's another movement outside, this time heavier—like a body brushing the outer wall. The dogs growl, synchronized and sharp. I move to get up, but Eliza holds up a hand.

"Let him look," she says. "He's just making sure you're paying attention."

I frown, wondering what she meant by that. The air chills, and I realize for the first time that I might actually be in danger, or at least in the kind of story where people don't always make it to the last page. But I don't want to leave, not yet. Not with the way Eliza's looking at me, like she's waiting to see what I'll do.

She returns to her chair, rummages in a nearby basket. "Know that the runes... they are helpful, but can be costly," she says it like I should know what she's talking about, and pulls out a pendant: a smooth, dark stone set in wire, strung on a thin black cord. She holds it out, palm up.

"Take it," she says. "For protection. Or luck. Or just because it's pretty. Doesn't matter what you believe, as long as you believe something."

I accept it, the stone warm from her touch. "Thank you," I say, though it feels inadequate.

She smiles, and this time it's real. "Don't mention it. Now go home before it gets dark. The pines aren't as friendly after sunset."

"If I see him again," I say, "what should I do?"

Eliza thinks for a long moment, her gaze gone soft with memory. "Ask him what he wants. And listen to your heart, not just your head. Sometimes the heart knows before the rest of you catches up."

I nod, the words settling heavy in my chest. I stand and start for the door.

Behind me, Eliza murmurs, "Careful, child. Some storms are worth weathering, but only if you're brave enough to come out the other side."

I slip the pendant over my head and tuck it under my shirt.

Dusk slinks up on the world like a thief, softening the edges of the yard and painting the trees blacker than the inside of a locked closet. The dogs stop just off the porch and look back at me.

"Thank you, really," I say, and I mean it. The pendant is a solid warmth at my throat, a little anchor against the weirdness.

Eliza gives a half-shrug, half-hug, patting my shoulder like she's testing for loose screws. "Don't mention it, child. Just remember what I said. Men whose eyes change with their moods aren't to be trifled with, no matter how good they look in the sunlight."

I bark out a laugh, nerves leaking into the sound. "He's not exactly my type, but I'll keep my distance." Guys who looked that good were never that interested in me.

She fixes me with a look that says liar, but lets it go. "Drive safe. And keep your porch light on tonight. Just in case."

I nod, but before I can turn away, she leans in and whispers, "If you hear knocking, wait until morning. Nothing good ever comes to a lonely girl after dark." I nod again, my heart banging like a trapped cricket, and hustle the dogs toward the car.

But the dogs have other ideas. They freeze on the path, eyes locked on the biggest pine tree at the corner of the yard. Mystic's fur stands up in a bristled ridge; Ash lets out a low, almost conversational growl. I follow their gaze, but all I see is trunk and shadow, branches swaying in the lazy breeze.

"Get in, you goofs," I mutter. They move, but it's like they're walking through thick mud, every step a reluctant surrender.

I load them up, slam the door, and only then do I let myself glance back. Nothing moves at the tree line, but my skin prickles like I'm being watched through a two-way mirror. I shake it off and slide into the driver's seat, the old Ford shuddering to life beneath me.

Backing out, I check the rearview and catch a glimpse of Miss Eliza, framed by the porch light. She's not waving, not moving at all. Just watching the treeline.

Halfway down the drive, I swear I saw a rabbit or something dart in front of me. I hit the brakes. Not hard, just enough to make the seatbelt bite. There's a pulse of cold, a breath that doesn't belong to the world. For a second, I think I see something—a shadow unfurling near the big pine, denser and darker than anything the night should allow. It ripples, almost human-shaped, then snaps back like a trick of the eyes.

The urge to floor it is strong, but instead, I put the car in park and step out. The dogs lose their minds, barking and lunging at the windows, but I walk around the car to see if I can see anything. I'm all goosebumps and dumb courage.

Nothing. Not a footstep, not a whisper. Just the wind in the chimes and the distant hum of frogs. I take a few deep breaths, tell myself I'm losing it, and turn to leave.

I head back to the driver's side, and that's when I trip—just a half-step, just enough to make me feel stupid. My hand shoots out, and for the tiniest sliver of time, I swear I feel fingers on my wrist. Not rough, not cold. Gentle, but real. When I yank my hand back, there's nothing there. But the air smells sharp, like ozone before a storm.

Shaken, I scurry back to the car. As I pull away, I see Miss Eliza still standing on her porch, eyes fixed not on me but on the tree line. Her mouth moves; it almost looks like she's saying something to that big pine.

A shiver runs through me that has nothing to do with the night air. I drive, headlights cutting tunnels through the pines, dogs whining low in the back seat. At every bend of the road, I expect to see someone—something—waiting.

But the forest is empty. Just me, the dogs, and a new understanding that I'm not the only thing haunted by this place.

When I get home, I fumble with the key, rush inside, and lock every door behind me. The dogs curl up by my feet, their tension slowly bleeding away. I check the porch light twice before turning in.

That night, I dream of green-gold eyes and shadows that speak in riddles. I wake up certain of only one thing:

He'll be back.

And I'll be waiting.

CHAPTER FIVE

DIGITAL CONNECTION

Most of the world wakes up to an alarm, a sunrise, or the sound of a rooster if you're in the right flavor of Texas. I wake to the dual percussion of Mystic and Ash flinging themselves at the bedroom door, their barks already at code red. I drag myself from the shrapnel field of my dreams—half runes, half the memory of someone's hands in my hair—and let the dogs herd me down the hallway with the same fervor they'd use to pen a wayward cow.

It's a Tuesday, which means "business casual" in my work-from-home universe. For me, that translates to a dog-haired T-shirt advertising a defunct roller derby league and the only yoga pants I own that aren't see-through in the butt. My home office is wedged between my craft table and my sewing table, the desk squeezed so tight you'd think I was planning to eject myself with a trebuchet the second my shift is over. Mystic immediately parks under the desk, eyes up and alert. Ash patrols the carpet perimeter, nails clicking out Morse code for "danger, boss, danger."

And my shift begins; someone screams about a router, someone else asks if we offer "elderly discounts," and can I send her a birthday card. Through it all, Mystic and Ash alternate between snoring and sudden outbreaks of war-drum barking at the window, which makes me extremely thankful for my noise-canceling microphone. I wish I could take a picture of their faces when a squirrel crosses the yard—pure murderous intent—but my phone is already at ten percent, and the day's just started.

Third call in, I nearly pour water on my keyboard when the screen blips and a new ticket appears: ***'INBOUND: LOKI (PRIORITY).'*** All caps, flagged in red, and with no callback number. For a half-second, I wonder if some hacker's spoofing the system or if it's my own subconscious screwing with me because I thought about him last night before bed.

I hover the mouse over "Accept." My heart does a dumb little stutter. Mystic whines and noses my knee. I click.

Video call. Not standard protocol. The connection's good, zero latency, which means he's either in a Google data center or some ancient lair with better fiber than I've ever had. The image opens on a panel of dark wood antiques, oil paintings framed in gold leaf, and a single lit candle beside what looks like a bust of Julius Caesar, except the head's got horns.

I brace myself, wondering if this is a prank, a deepfake, or maybe a nervous breakdown.

"Amethyst Gold," he says, his voice low and rich, with a cadence that makes every syllable seem like it's meant to be savored. He's dressed in a black button-down, open at the throat, sleeves rolled up to reveal a lattice of tattoos on his arms—runes, I realize, like the ones from the woods. His hair is back in a loose, slightly messy knot. His face is distractingly sharp, all angles and curves that seem deliberately designed to make mortals question their life choices.

I clear my throat. "You do know this is for technical support, right? I can troubleshoot your internet, but I'm fresh out of exorcisms or whatever you need."

He smiles. Not the practiced, soulless grin I'm used to from the charming sociopaths that call in, but something softer, knowing. "No exorcism needed, Amethyst. I was hoping for a personal connection."

The dogs both perk up at the sound of his voice, ears locked forward, heads cocked in perfect unison. I could've sworn they recognized him. Or maybe it's just the frequency he uses—a resonance that cuts through the static of the day and leaves you feeling exposed.

I try to maintain control of the call. "Well, if you're calling about your account, I'll need your customer ID number." My tone is dry, bordering on a desert.

"Ah, but I was under the impression you already know who I am." He leans forward, elbows on what must be the world's most expensive desk. The candlelight flickers against his skin, making the runes on his arm glow pale silver.

I take a swallow of soda, now officially flat and undrinkable. "Look, I'm not really supposed to do video calls, and you're not even in the system. How'd you get my work line?"

He shrugs. "It's a talent. Also, I thought it might be fun."

I don't want to let him rattle me, but the longer he looks at me—like he's reading my birth chart and browsing my browser history all at once—the harder it gets to remember that this is just a call. Just another stranger. Nothing special.

"So, Loki," I say, purposefully making it sound like an alias, "what can I do for you today?"

He grins, a flash of teeth. "You could start by telling me about your morning. It looks like it's been eventful."

I blink. Is he monitoring my webcam? Or did he catch the tiny slip of desperation in my voice from earlier? "If you want to talk about internet service outages, I can get you a supervisor," I shoot back.

He laughs, a smooth, dark sound that settles between my ribs. "I admire your boundaries. They're almost impressive."

A flicker—just a nanosecond—in his eyes, a pulse of gold. Then it's gone. Maybe the light, maybe my own nerves.

I try to ignore the shiver running down my spine. "Fine, you want to chat, let's chat. Got a favorite Norse myth? Or are you just appropriating the look for clout?"

He steeples his fingers, the tattoos shifting as he moves. "I like the one where the gods try to bind the wolf Fenrir, and it takes every trick in their arsenal to do it. The wolf only loses because he trusted someone who promised not to hurt him."

My heart stutters as that comment triggers a memory of what happened just before I picked up and moved here. I was living in Tennessee and had been set up on a date by Sarah. She told me she had met him at a conference. Things got weird quickly. Turns out Sarah had set up a dating profile, and in the end, he went all cyber stalker on me. When he threatened Mystic and me, I disappeared. I eye the video call, and part of me is terrified it might be happening again, but something about him... it doesn't feel that scary.

I pull myself back to the conversation and ask, "What's your take on customer service? You seem the type to have opinions."

He leans back, amusement twisting his mouth. "It's all about power and illusion, isn't it? The illusion of choice. The dance between what you can give and what you can withhold. It's a sort of magic, in a way."

I laugh despite myself. "Well, my 'magic' is getting screamed at by grandmas who want free HBO. Not exactly the stuff of legend."

"Don't sell yourself short, Amethyst. Every legend needs someone to keep the gods humble." He picks up the candle, cradling it like a precious thing. The flame wavers, grows for a second, then resumes its normal shape. "Have you found the runes yet?"

I freeze. "What do you mean, 'found'?"

"You've seen them." He says it like he's reminding me of something, not asking.

For a second, I can't breathe. Mystic pushes her nose against my calf, grounding me, reminding me that at least one living being in this room is real.

"I—" The word sticks. I don't want to give him the satisfaction. But I also want to know what he means, more than I want to keep my pride. "Yeah. I saw them. What the hell is going on? How do you know about that?"

His smile softens as he sets down the candle, now closer to the bust with horns. The wax pools, the scent—probably beeswax, or maybe something richer—seems to reach through the screen. "They're a message. Or a warning. Or a door, if you're willing to open it. Most people ignore them. You didn't."

I roll my eyes. "Well, I tried, but the dogs make it... hard to ignore."

His smile softens, a private sort of approval. "Animals have always been better at these things."

I want to keep the conversation flippant, but my curiosity's getting the better of me. "Why me? I'm not exactly special. Hell, I barely scraped through a college mythology elective, and I used to want to open a bookstore because I wanted to read all the fantasy and mythology books. But I don't know anything about that stuff."

He shakes his head. "You're different. You've survived things that would have broken others. Most people, given what you've lost, would be a mess. Or cruel. You're neither."

There's a silence, but not an awkward one. More like a breath before a leap.

I don't want to talk about what I've lost. I don't want to go there, not with this relative stranger. So I deflect. "You sound like you're recruiting me for a cult. Or an MLM."

He laughs, softer now, but still with that edge of delight. "Nothing so sinister. I just enjoy your company."

My cheeks warm. The absurdity of blushing over a video call is not lost on me.

"Is that why you showed up on my porch the other night?" I blurt. "Because you were bored and wanted to scare the shit out of me?"

His eyes narrow, the gold flickering again. "I didn't show up on your porch. What happened?" His hands clutched at the desk, and he leaned forward, his eyes flashing with something like... concern.

"Just... noises. I thought I heard three knocks on my front door."

"Tell me you did not open the door."

I hesitate a moment and swallow. "No. No, I didn't. I just... ignored it."

"Good. Don't answer the door and don't reply to... voices in the woods."

There's an earnestness to him that unnerves me more than any threat could. I bite my lip and wonder who had been on my porch. "I know better than that," I try to remember if I had been like the dumb girls in the horror movies, the ones who hear the noise in the creepy house and ask who's there. I don't think I did... God, I hope I didn't.

Mystic whines louder, pawing at my ankle. I give her a head scratch, not trusting myself to look directly at the camera.

"So now what?" I ask, my voice smaller than I want it to be. "Am I supposed to decode the runes? Is there a quest?" I know I shouldn't be talking about this kind of thing on a supposed work call, but I can't help it.

He shrugs, one corner of his mouth tilting upward. "Maybe. Or maybe you're just supposed to keep living, one day at a time. Sometimes that's enough."

That hits me harder than expected. I almost want to end the video chat. Instead, I pivot. "You ever wish you could change things that you did... or said?"

He grins, white teeth and something dangerous. "Many things."

I don't know why, but I told him how my parents and brother had died in a car wreck. I had been at my high school graduation party. My family had been driving home. I hadn't said I loved them.

Loki listens, really listens, the way most men pretend to but never do.

I like how he never pities me, even when I mention my parents, or my brother, or the endless string of holidays spent alone. There's something magnetic about it, like he knows all my wounds but refuses to let me wallow.

The call software pings a warning: *'SESSION LIMIT: 5 MINUTES REMAINING.'*

He looks at the camera. For the first time, I see uncertainty flicker in his face. "May I call you again?"

It's a simple question, but the weight of it lodges deep in my chest.

"Yeah," I say, surprising us both. "You can call."

The screen glitches for half a second, and I catch a fleeting overlay: gold runes spiraling from his forearm up to the base of his neck, glowing with the same light I'd seen in the woods. Then it's gone.

He sees my surprise and offers a crooked, rueful smile. "Till later then."

"Thank you for calling. I hope I was able to solve all your issues," I reply, finally acting like I'm on a work call.

The session ends. The window winks out, leaving me staring at my own reflection in the black monitor. Mystic and Ash crowd around, pressing their bodies to my legs, as if worried I might vanish next.

I lean back in my chair and exhale, feeling the weight of the conversation settle in every bone. For the first time in a long while, I want the day to hurry up and finish. I want to see him again.

In the short break between calls, I notice the faint pattern of runes etched into the condensation on my tumbler.

I run my thumb across them. They dissolve instantly, but the feeling lingers.

There's a knock at the window. I turn, but nothing's there. Just the pale blur of my own face and two sets of dog eyes watching, waiting for the next miracle.

Or maybe, the next disaster.

Hard to tell the difference sometimes.

I spend the rest of the day pretending to work, my brain instead doing wind sprints through every detail of that video call. Mystic and Ash orbit me with renewed vigilance, as if they know the boundaries of our world just got a little more porous. Every time a shadow flickers on the trailer wall or a cloud passes in front of the sun, they let loose with a volley of warning barks—just in case the eldritch horror from the neighbor's shed tries to eat us before supper.

I try to distract myself with petty drama from the company Slack—some upper management kerfuffle about time theft and badge-in/badge-out metrics. I click through the drama, not really reading. My mind's already chasing runes and ancient wolves and the sound of Loki's voice saying my name like it's something precious.

When five o'clock hits, I close the laptop with a finality that feels like it should echo. I think about wine, but I'm still haunted by the flat taste of this morning's soda. Instead, I drink water straight from the tap and watch the last of the sunlight melt through the kitchen blinds.

I'm not used to this—the hope, the anticipation. I spent most of my adult life waiting for disappointment; it always comes, so this tightrope between anxiety and wanting is new. I stare at the fridge and dare it to offer up some sign, some cosmic instruction manual for not screwing up your one shot at happiness. The fridge does not answer. Mystic, however, does—she noses my leg, then plants herself in the center of the linoleum, clearly ready for dinner.

I'm halfway through feeding the dogs when my phone vibrates against the countertop.

No number. No name. Just "Unknown Caller."

My first thought is scam, my second is disaster, my third is that somehow Loki has hacked the telecommunications grid just to mess with me, which, based on this morning's performance, seems par for the course.

I thumb the screen to answer. "Hello?"

A moment's static, and then, "Good evening, Amethyst." His voice is low, velvet-wrapped mischief. "Did I catch you at a bad time?"

I nearly drop the phone in the dog food. "You caught me at dog feeding time, but I suppose that's not a state secret."

He laughs, and I feel it in my teeth. "I'm calling to invite you to dinner."

I process that for a second. "Dinner. Like, tonight?"

"If you're free," he says, and I can hear the smirk in his voice. "I thought seven o'clock. There's a place in town I believe you'll like."

I glance down at my stained T-shirt and remember my laundry is still in the dryer. My heart flips, then sinks, then flips again. "You make a habit of giving short notice?"

"Only when the outcome is uncertain," he replies, then lets the silence hang.

I want to say no, to play it cool, to avoid looking desperate, but instead I hear myself say, "Yeah. Sure. Dinner."

"Wonderful. I'll text you the address." He pauses. "And Amethyst?"

"Yeah?"

"I can't wait to see you," he says, and this time it doesn't feel like a line or a trick. It just feels honest.

He hangs up. I stare at the phone, the shimmer of his words still echoing. Then the text comes through, just an address—no name, no instructions, just coordinates for the brave or the foolish. I nearly text Sarah and ask her if she was trying to play matchmaker again. She promised she wouldn't, not after the time she set up a dating profile and pretended to be me, then set me up on a date with the guy. She said she did it because he was perfect on paper, but I'd have never given him a chance. I shudder at the memory of the stalker. I was safe. It had been eight years. He wasn't going to find me. This wasn't another of those setups. I really, really hoped it wasn't one of those setups.

Mystic and Ash have finished eating. They watch me, heads tilted, as if they're wondering which end of the world we'll be encountering tonight.

I march to the bathroom and stare at myself in the mirror. My hair is a mess of purple coils, and my eyeliner has migrated halfway to my temples.

I look exactly like the girl who grew up on comic books, then romance novels and energy drinks, who once decorated her locker with her favorite vampire. I do not look like the kind of girl who gets asked to dinner by men who were named after mythological gods.

I splash water on my face and dig through the closet for something that says, "I'm not trying too hard" but also, "I am not a disaster." I settle on black skinny jeans, a faded T-shirt with a silver moon on it, and the one denim jacket I own that isn't covered in old dog hair. I debate makeup and decide on just a smear of lip gloss. I want to look like myself, even if "myself" is an acquired taste.

By the time I finish, it's half past six. The sun's bleeding out through the pines, the world painted in amber and blue. I toss the last of my anxiety in the trash, leash up the dogs, and walk them down the drive. I pause before the mailbox, take a long breath, and imagine for a second that all the rules of fate are about to be rewritten, and I immediately feel stupid for the thought.

Mystic and Ash sniff the air, then stare back at me, as if to say, "Are you sure you're ready for this?"

I'm not, but that's never stopped me before.

I pile back into the trailer, towel off the mud from Ash's legs, and make a final pass at my hair in the hallway mirror. It's as good as it gets. My hands shake a little, but only in the way they do when something big is about to happen.

The dogs settle into their beds as I grab my keys, already resigned to a quiet evening of napping and low-level vigilance. I give them both a scratch behind the ears. "Don't wait up," I tell them, then add, "I won't be late."

They don't respond, but their eyes follow me all the way to the door.

Outside, the last of the day's light catches in the treetops, the air crisp and full of the promise of something new. I lock up, breathe deep, and head to the car. As I slide into the driver's seat, I check my phone one last time just to make sure the address is real, that I haven't imagined all of it.

It's still there, bold and undeniable.

Tonight, I'm having dinner with the man Ms. Eliza called a trickster.

And if the world tilts on its axis, I can't say I wasn't warned.

The Gilded Owl is the kind of place that feels like it shouldn't exist in Pine Hollow, or maybe anywhere south or east of Dallas. The sign is hand-painted, the sidewalk cracked just enough to let a stripe of moss creep along the edge, and the front windows glow with the hush of a thousand miniature suns. I've driven by it a hundred times, always assuming it was too expensive, too romantic, or just too much for someone like me.

I step inside at exactly 7:03, three minutes late, because I read somewhere that's the magic number for not seeming too eager. The air is warm with garlic and rosemary and something darker, like rich coffee or burnt sugar. I spot him immediately: Loki, already standing beside a two-top near the window, one hand resting on the back of a wrought-iron chair. His shirt tonight is deep green, the shade of old bottle glass, and it sets off his eyes in a way that feels unfair to all the other eyes in the room.

The table is set with linen napkins folded into little crowns, and in the center is a bud vase holding a single violet. It's ridiculous and beautiful, and I almost back out before I remember the promise I made to myself at the mailbox.

He spots me, and for a second, the whole room feels still, like we're the only two people in it. His smile is gentle and inviting, but with that familiar twist at the edges. "You came," he says, as if he wasn't entirely sure I would.

I shrug, suddenly bashful. "Free food. I'm not made of stone."

He laughs, then pulls out my chair in a move so smooth I almost trip over my own feet getting to it. As I settle in, I realize how close we are—less than a hand's width apart. I glance up to find him already watching me, elbows resting on the table, fingers woven loosely together. It's intimate but not in a way that makes me want to run. In fact, it's comforting.

We order quickly. The waiter is a college kid with tragic facial hair and a black apron two sizes too small. I go for the trout—pan-seared, with lemon-dill butter and a glass of water. Loki chooses the lamb tagine and, at the waiter's suggestion, a bottle of Malbec.

As the waiter leaves, I notice the room is full of couples and two-tops, all arranged in a quiet, conversational orbit. A jazz pianist in the corner fills the spaces between words with a melody that sounds familiar, though I can't name it. Everything is soft: the lighting, the clink of glass, the little bursts of laughter from the other tables. I feel like an extra in a movie, watching the leads from a safe distance—except the lead is me, and the only script I've got is the panic scrawling itself across my pulse.

"So," he says, resting his chin on his hands, "how are the hounds?"

I blink. "Mystic and Ash? Good. Confused, mostly. I think they can't imagine why I left the house so late."

There's a moment of easy silence. He studies me, but not in a predatory way; it's more like he's savoring the sight of me, cataloging all the details for later. It should be creepy. It's not.

He breaks the silence first. "You seem... different tonight."

I raise an eyebrow. "Different good or different bad?"

"Good," he says, and the word lands like a warm hand on my shoulder. "You seem lighter."

I laugh, surprised. "You mean less like someone waiting for the universe to step on her?"

"Exactly that," he agrees, nodding solemnly.

Our waiter returns with the wine, pours a taste for Loki, who sips and nods like he's been doing it for centuries. I watch the ritual, suddenly self-conscious, and when the glass is offered to me, I shake my head. "I don't really drink wine," I confess. "I mean, I'll try it, but I usually go for things that taste like juice boxes for adults."

He smirks. "You want to try?"

I take the tiniest sip. It tastes like velvet and cherries and something sharp, maybe regret. "Not bad," I admit, "but I'd rather have a soda."

He laughs, and I realize he really likes it when I'm honest. He tops off his glass, then sets it aside, giving me his full attention.

"Tell me something true," he says.

I flinch. Not because I'm afraid of truth, but because the last person who asked for it only used it as ammunition.

I fish for a safe answer. "I used to compete in dog sports—rally, agility, scent work, that kind of thing. I was pretty good before life decided to eat all my savings and the transmission on my truck."

He looks genuinely impressed. "You have the hands for it," he says, then immediately looks embarrassed. "Sorry. That sounded less weird in my head."

"No, I get it," I say. "You can tell a lot about someone from how they move or how they talk to animals."

He leans back, considering. "You're not afraid of much, are you?"

"Not anymore," I say, surprising myself.

Our food arrives all at once—a riot of scent and color. My trout is perfect, skin crisped to a deep gold, the lemon butter pooling around it like a halo. Loki's lamb is a mountain of savory steam, studded with dried apricots and almonds. He raises his fork in a silent toast; I do the same, and for a moment, it feels like we're part of some ancient feast, two royals in exile sharing the spoils of a lesser world.

The conversation is easy—lighter than air but with the density of something real. We talk about books, and I admit to my love of trashy supernatural romance novels. He counters with an anecdote about a famous poet who owed him money and somehow makes it sound plausible. We talk about mythology, which he seems to know with the casualness of someone who lived it.

I ask, "Do you think the real Loki, assuming there is one, ever gets tired of being the bad guy in all the stories?"

His expression shifts just a little. "Someone has to play the villain," he says, and there's a sadness to it I haven't seen before. "But it's rarely the whole truth."

I think about that. "Maybe he's just misunderstood."

He holds my gaze, his eyes flashing with...something, surprise maybe, before he replies, "Maybe."

For a while, we just eat. The silence is comfortable—the kind where you don't have to fill it because the presence of someone is enough. Every so often, I catch him watching me, and every time I do, his eyes pulse with gold, like there's a secret message behind them.

Eventually, he reaches across the table, resting his hand close enough to mine that the heat of his skin radiates. I don't pull away. Instead, I let my fingers inch forward, closer, until they brush his knuckles. The contact is electric—not a shock, exactly, but a jolt of recognition, like two wires finally making a circuit.

He smiles, softer now. "Thank you," he says, and I don't know what for, but I believe he means it.

The jazz pianist winds down, and the restaurant empties out, couples melting into the dusk. I don't want to leave, not yet. I want to stay in this pocket of warmth and light, where nothing bad has ever happened and nothing bad ever will.

Loki signals for the check, and the waiter brings it with a flourish, like he's delivering a state secret. Loki signs without looking, then stands and offers me his hand.

I take it. I don't even hesitate.

Outside, the air is cool and sweet, the sky spangled with stars. He walks me to my truck, the silence between us thick with possibility.

Before I get in, he leans close, close enough that I can feel his breath. "Can I see you again?" he asks, his voice barely above a whisper.

I nod, too breathless to speak.

He grins, a wild, beautiful thing, and for a second, I wonder if he'll kiss me. But instead, he just brushes a strand of hair behind my ear and steps away, the perfect gentleman or the perfect monster.

I watch him walk back toward the restaurant; my eyes must be playing tricks on me. His figure blurs at the edges, as if the world can't decide if he's really there.

In the truck, I sit for a long time, hands trembling, pulse running wild. I watch the restaurant's windows glow against the night, and for the first time in forever, I feel like I belong to something—someone.

I drive home with the windows down, letting the wind carry away the last shreds of fear.

When I open the trailer door, Mystic and Ash greet me with a wag and a whine, as if they already know everything. I drop to my knees and bury my face in their fur, laughing and crying and, for once, not caring which is which.

Tonight, the world did not end. Instead, it began.

And somewhere in the woods, the runes are waiting.

But for now, I am happy to wait with them.

Chapter Six

STORM WARNING

It starts with the air—the way it thickens, heavy as wet velvet, before the first thunder ever shudders the ground. I see it in the dogs, too. Mystic's hackles are up, her nose flaring as if she could inhale the whole sky. Ash is less subtle: tail low, muscles taut, whining through his teeth every few steps, like the world itself has turned stranger than usual. I'm no less jittery, my mind still humming from last night's dinner, from the feeling of Loki's gaze on me like I was something he could own. It should have faded by now, the adrenaline, but it hasn't.

We walk the path behind my trailer, needles crunching under my old sneakers, the pines so close they crowd out the light. There's no breeze, not really, but the treetops shiver with secrets, needles sifting down in clumps like rain that forgot how to fall. Every few yards, I glance up, as if I'll catch the sky doing something it shouldn't. I'm not sure what I'm expecting—another spectral shape at the edge of vision, maybe, or a trick of the light that spells my name in runes across the trunks.

The clouds roll in with a purpose. They don't just drift—they hunt, low and dark and layered so thick the day goes blue at the edges. I almost turn back twice, the nerves scraping my insides raw, but the dogs have energy to burn, and the promise of a storm always made me restless. We move deeper under the boughs, away from the dull glow of the trailer security lamp, until the world feels carved out of shadow and resin and old, cold wind.

Thunder rumbles—not above, but somewhere inside the woods, as if the sound itself is stalking us. I feel it through the soles of my feet, a vibration that shakes the smallest bones in my ears. Mystic stops dead and leans hard on the leash, her eyes slitted toward the trees to our left. I follow her gaze, every inch of skin on high alert, but there's nothing. No, not nothing. A prickle of movement, almost too fast to see, like the forest had blinked and then pretended nothing happened. Tiny little bells sound in the distance.

"Let's keep moving," I mutter, voice low, mostly for my own benefit.

The dogs don't listen. Ash plants himself between me and the brush, paws spread, tail straight out. Mystic starts a low, rolling growl that tells me she's not bluffing. My scalp tightens as I scan the dark, my heart rabbiting in my chest. I'm about to bolt when a shape steps from behind a trunk on the opposite side of the trail—not lurking, not skulking, but simply appearing with the casual arrogance of a man who's never needed to be afraid.

Loki is taller than I remembered, or maybe it's the way he carries himself, like he's always on the edge of turning into something else. His hair's unbound, wind-tossed, dark as the clouds rolling in overhead. He's wearing a dark green jacket, the color almost lost in the gloom, and there's a smear of something—sap, maybe, or blood—on the sleeve. His hands are bare, fingers long and restless.

He doesn't startle when Ash barks, just cocks his head and waits for the silence to return. The dogs snap to attention but don't lunge, don't even growl anymore. They look at him like he's an old, uncomfortable memory they don't want to remember.

"You again," I say, and I hate how unsteady my voice sounds.

He shrugs, his smile thin and wry. "I was just in the neighborhood."

My heart rate doubles. "Did you—are you following me?"

A flicker of hurt, or mock hurt, passes over his eyes. "I prefer to think of it as fate." He glances at the sky, then at me, and something inside his expression sharpens, becomes dangerous. "Storm's coming in fast. Thought you might appreciate the company."

I glance at the sky. It's true—the clouds have gone from menacing to outright furious, swirling tight and low with a pressure that has my eardrums squealing. The pines start to sway, the upper branches clattering together in a way that's more warning than music.

"Is it always like this with you?" I ask. "You just... show up, and things go psycho?"

He doesn't answer, just steps closer, closing the gap between us with predatory grace. The dogs shift out of his way, then circle back to flank me. I'm trapped, but not really—he's not threatening, not exactly, just... present. So present I can barely remember the air before he arrived.

He studies my face with an intensity that should feel violating, but instead makes my skin sing. His eyes are green, shot through with gold, and for one second, as the first drops of rain hiss down through the canopy, they glow—actually glow—like the ember at the end of a cigarette.

"Why do you keep showing up?" I ask, the words tumbling out before I can decide if I want them to.

A shrug, half-amused. "I like the way you look at the world." He glances at my dogs, then at my hands. "And you're fun when you're frightened."

I want to be angry, but the storm is coming so fast now I don't have time for the luxury. I glare at him, and the rain sluices down the pine needles, drumming so loudly I have to raise my voice. "We need to head back."

He nods. "You go ahead. I'll walk with you."

It's not a question, and somehow I know it's not a threat. The dogs are still hyper-alert, but they don't bark anymore. I tug their leashes, but Loki falls in beside me, his steps light and perfectly in sync. We start down the path, feet sinking in the sudden mud, my pulse racing against the beat of the rain.

For half a minute, neither of us speaks. The storm is so loud it swallows all the words I might have said. My mind spins—last night, the stories he told, the way he made me feel like I was the only person in the world, and then vanished like smoke. It's not normal, none of it, and the more I think about it, the less real it feels.

The first lightning flash is close enough to bleach the path to white, and the thunder follows instantly, splitting the air with a crack so sharp it makes my bones ring. I flinch. Loki doesn't. He just turns his face up to the sky and lets the rain wash over him. For a second, I'm convinced he's not human at all, but some kind of spirit wearing a man's skin.

We're almost to the turnoff for my trailer when it happens. Lightning hits a pine less than fifty yards ahead, the trunk exploding in a shower of sparks and splinters. I scream, the dogs yelp, and Loki grabs my shoulder so fast I barely register the movement.

"Stay back," he says, and his voice isn't human anymore—it's doubled, weirdly resonant, like there's a second voice echoing under the first.

The top third of the pine shears off, spins once, and lands directly in our path. A shower of needles rains down, stinging my face and arms. The dogs cower, whining, and I drop to a crouch with them. Loki stands his ground, hands out at his sides. He looks like he's waiting for an attack.

For a split second, time slows. I see everything: the rain caught in perfect beads on his eyelashes, the green-gold flare of his eyes, the way the fallen branch is still crackling with static. I'm afraid, but it's not the usual kind of fear. It's sharper, cleaner, and electric.

The storm pulses, and so does the tension between us. My skin is humming, my thoughts are chaos. The air tastes like metal, and Loki's presence is so heavy it feels like gravity itself is bending around him.

Another boom—another flash. The second tree goes up, but this time the branch snaps directly above us, a thick, jagged limb twisting down toward my head.

I don't scream this time. There's no time.

I just look up and watch the branch fall, the world narrowing to the curve of its descent and the way Loki's body tenses, ready.

And then everything stops.

In the moment before the branch hits, I feel a shift in the world. Time slows—not in the way mortals feel in an adrenaline rush, but truly, measurably slows, each droplet of rain frozen in place. Her eyes are wide and bright, reflecting the blue-white bolt of sky, the iridescence of a thousand overlapping afterimages. It's almost beautiful how perfectly paralyzed she is, how much raw want and terror are written on her face.

I move. Faster than breath. The old blood thrums in my veins, a hunger to act, to intervene, to show her that reality is a thing I can break and remake at will. I don't bother with subtlety—there's no time for it. My arm shoots out, sleeve tearing, and the runes that run from wrist to elbow erupt in green-gold fire. The heat of it is real, the power raw and hungry, and for one unguarded moment, I let her see exactly what I am.

The branch halts. Not just slows—stops, in mid-air, as if the laws of motion themselves have forgotten what comes next. Rain pours down its length, beads up on a shimmer of light I can barely hold steady. I flex my fingers, the binding rune burning at the center of my palm, and for a heartbeat, I let the magic soak the world in color and noise.

The dogs bark, a frantic, echoing alarm that makes the air itself tremble. Amethyst is still locked in place, every muscle tight, her face painted with a splash of rain and the sick, electric glow of the runes. She looks at me, and for the first time since I arrived in this realm, I see it—the moment a human realizes there is something older, stranger, and infinitely more dangerous standing at her side.

She doesn't run. She doesn't even scream. Just stands there, breath locked in her chest, skin gleaming with cold sweat and water, her whole body strung out between fight and flight and the paralyzing inability to do either.

I turn my wrist, redirecting the force, and the branch—still crackling with static—veers left, smashing into the muddy trail with a dull, sodden thud. Chips of bark and pine cones scatter, ricocheting off our legs. The rain fills in the silence, a white noise that drowns the panic for just a second.

Her chest heaves. She lets out a sharp, rattling exhale, as if she's just remembered how to breathe. The dogs go silent, pressed against her thighs, their hackles flat now, their ears slicked back. They know better than to challenge the magic in the air.

My hand drops to my side, the runes fading but still visible, an afterimage of power that will take hours to cool. I look at her, and she looks back, purple hair plastered to her cheeks, eyes ringed with disbelief and something else—something like hunger.

I should say something. Anything. A joke, a threat, a warning. But the words curdle in my throat, and all I can do is stare, letting her see me as I am, as I've always been: a thing that should never have walked so close to humanity.

For a second, the whole world is just us. The ruined tree, the ragged edge of the trail, the raw, rain-soaked distance between her pulse and mine.

And for the first time in a very long time, I wish I could be someone else.

The world goes silent for a long, shivering second. The rain thins to a drizzle, and the wind softens, leaving only the smolder of ozone and the rapid thump of my own heart. I stand in the wreckage of the trail, the ruined tree at my feet, and look at him—the man who just stopped the laws of physics with a flick of his hand, like he could unmake the world and put it back together however he pleased.

Loki steps back, the runes on his skin dimming to ghostly outlines, fading into the memory of what just happened. His face is shuttered now, all the wild light and intent drained away, replaced with a kind of bleak, practiced calm. He wipes a streak of rain from his face, not meeting my eyes.

"You should be more careful where you walk during storms," he says. His voice is flat, almost bored, as if nothing out of the ordinary just occurred.

I stare at him, dumbfounded, the words echoing in my head like a punchline to a joke I don't understand. My fingers are shaking, adrenaline still burning in every limb, but I force myself to take a step closer. Mystic and Ash whine, crowding behind my knees, but I don't care—I need answers, and I want them now.

"What was that?" I demand, my voice thin and breaking. "What did you just do?"

He doesn't move, doesn't flinch, just stands there like a statue carved out of storm clouds. "Nothing you need to worry about."

I shake my head, furious. "Don't you dare give me that. I saw what you did. You stopped it. You made it—" I fumble for words, for logic, for anything that makes sense. "You made it stop in midair. That's not possible."

He glances at me then, just a flick of his eyes, but it's enough to make my breath catch. They're still glowing faintly, pupils slit like a cat's, and the way he looks at me is equal parts hunger and regret.

"It's safer if you forget," he says. "You don't want to know."

My skin is buzzing, every inch of me alive with questions and fear. "Too late. I already do."

He lets out a bitter laugh, so quiet I almost miss it. "That's the problem, Amethyst. You always want to know."

Something in me cracks—the part that wants to pretend, to play normal, to walk home and forget that anything ever happened. I lunge forward, meaning to grab his arm, to shake the truth out of him, but he steps back. Not out of fear. Out of mercy.

His voice is soft now, almost apologetic. "Go home. Please."

The rain starts up again, heavier this time, drowning out any last words I might try to say. He turns, shoulders hunched, and walks off the trail, vanishing into the pines with a grace that doesn't belong to any normal man.

I stand there, numb, the dogs pressed so close I can feel their heartbeats pounding through my jeans. The lightning's gone, the thunder a distant memory, but the aftermath hums in the air like a secret I can't let go of.

The walk back is a blur. The storm dies almost as fast as it started, the woods returning to their damp, sullen quiet. Mystic and Ash are jumpy, every snap of twig a reason to bark, every shadow a thing to distrust. I keep looking over my shoulder, but there's nothing. No Loki. No explanation. Just the ache of questions piling up behind my ribs.

By the time we make it to the trailer, I'm drenched and shaking, not from cold but from the realization that nothing in my life will ever be normal again.

Inside, the lights are too bright, the TV too loud, the dogs too restless. I towel them off, ignoring the way my hands won't steady, and watch them circle the living room, searching for something that isn't there. I want to scream, to throw something, to demand an answer from the universe. But instead, I curl up on the couch, blanket tight around my shoulders, and stare at the door, half-expecting him to walk through it, half-hoping he never does.

I know what I saw. I know what he is.

And I know, with a bone-deep certainty, that this was just the beginning.

From the edge of her property, I watch. There is nothing subtle about it: the sharp ache in my hands, the way my nails dig half-moons into my palms, the measured breaths that do nothing to slow the creature inside me. I should leave. I should be gone by now, vanished into the borderlands where I belong. But I am not gone. I am here, crouched in the wet mulch beyond her fence, watching the only person who has ever looked at me like I am real and not a story best left untold.

Amethyst is wrapped in a blanket, feet propped on the porch rail, head bowed over the bright, traitorous light of her phone. Her hair is still damp from the storm, a wild mess of plum and blackberry that glows faintly in the last light of evening. The dogs circle her restlessly, unable to settle, tails low and eyes locked on the shadows where I kneel.

She doesn't see me, but I see her. I see everything. The way her shoulders hunch, as if the cold is inside her bones; the way her thumb scrolls back and forth through messages, hoping for a sign; the way her lips press together when she thinks she is alone. Even now, after what happened on the trail, she wants to believe in something gentle. It is the most dangerous thing about her.

Twilight thickens. The sun dies in increments, and the air goes brittle with a hush that has nothing to do with wind. I sense it before it happens: the shimmer, the ripple, the moment when all the color drains from the world except for one impossible, luminous green. It begins at the edge of her porch, a tendril of energy that snakes through the dog's water bowl and up the porch post, branching out into a latticework of lines so fine they look painted by breath alone.

She stands up, the blanket falling to her knees, and stares as the symbols take shape—burning, fading, then returning brighter than before. The runes spiral over the boards, up the screen door, around the threshold in a pattern older than words. Each one a warning. Each one a story written for those who are never meant to understand.

The dogs bark, frantic now, their bodies rigid with the urge to defend and the certainty they cannot. Amethyst hushes them, her voice shaking. She steps closer to the edge, arms tight to her chest, and squints at the nearest glowing mark. I see her lips move as she sounds out the old shapes, her mind scraping against the memory of the internet rabbit hole she'd fallen into just days before.

DANGER. DECEIT. BEWARE.

I taste the flavor of those words on the back of my tongue, sharp as acid. I want to break the spell, to dash it from her sight, but it is not for me to decide. The runes are sentient, alive with the need to be seen, to be heeded. I am both their creator and their captive.

My phone vibrates in my pocket, a digital whine against the ancient hum of magic. I ignore it, watching as Amethyst backs away, one foot catching on the rail. She almost falls, but the dogs nudge her upright, their panic now a low, keening whimper. I watch her face—searching, disbelieving, desperate for a meaning that does not end in fear.

I want to tell her it's okay. I want to tell her it was all a trick, a show, something she can forget. But I don't have the words, and even if I did, it would be a lie.

My thumb hovers over the screen of my phone. I type, erase, type again, the message as fragile and lethal as a knife balanced on a needle's tip. In the end, I settle for the truth, or the nearest thing to it:

'I'm sorry. Stay away from me.'

I hit send. Across the yard, her phone pings. She jerks, reads, and for a moment her face is blank. Then she folds the phone to her heart, bending double as if the wind has knocked her flat.

The runes pulse brighter, searing the last light from the evening. I see their meaning reflected in her eyes: the certainty of pain, the promise of loss, the lure of something so close to love it terrifies us both.

I turn away. I force myself to move, feet silent in the soft black dirt, body stitched together with the remnants of my old, practiced arrogance. I do not look back. I do not let myself want.

But the runes keep burning, long after the sun has set, and in their green-gold glare, I see her silhouette frozen at the edge of the porch, alone and stubborn and incandescent with possibility.

In the end, I know it is only a matter of time before she comes looking.

Chapter Seven

SEEKING COUNSEL

The kitchen table feels sticky under my forearms, the laminate never quite losing the last decade's worth of spilled syrup and dog drool. Mystic and Ash are tangled in a defensive coil under my chair, their bodies pressed so close to me I'd have to peel them off. My phone glows at the edge of my plate—a half-eaten blueberry muffin stares back, a small crime scene of crumbs—and I can't look away from it. It's barely past nine, but the sky's gone weird again, a marbled light leaking through the blinds, catching every speck of dust in an amber haze.

The urge to call Sarah is a physical thing, a pulse behind my eyes, but I hover for three full minutes before hitting the button. Maybe she's busy. Maybe she'll pick up and everything that happened yesterday will seem like a hallucination, the afterburn of some unmedicated sleep spiral. Maybe she'll think I'm losing it, and that possibility terrifies me even more than what I saw in the woods.

The phone rings once, twice, and she answers, her voice already caffeinated, already slicing through my defenses. "Amethyst Gold, you sound like you're about to have a panic attack. Are you okay? Are the dogs okay?"

I look down. Mystic's left ear flicks in time with Sarah's voice; Ash lets out a burble of concern. "I'm fine. They're fine. They're—they're actually really calm this morning. I just—are you at home?"

Sarah sighs in that way she does when she's got three things going and doesn't want to be on the phone but is too well-trained by her therapist's code of ethics to say so. "I have a client in fifteen, but yes, I'm here. What's up? And don't give me the 'nothing' routine, Ame, I can hear your pulse in your voice."

I force a laugh, then immediately hate the way it sounds. "You remember that guy? The one I told you about at the park, Loki?" I keep my tone light, as if I'm sharing a crush, not a cosmic incident.

Sarah doesn't miss a beat. "The one with the serial killer name. Yes, I remember. What about him?"

"He did something. Something I can't explain. And you know me, I don't even believe in, like, horoscopes or past lives or anything, but..." My voice thins. I want to hang up. I want her to listen. "I saw him do something impossible."

The silence on the line is brittle and white-hot. Finally, Sarah asks, "What do you mean, 'impossible'? He juggle a car? Levitate a barista?"

I can't help the nervous laugh that shakes loose. "He stopped a tree, Sarah. Like, not with his bare hands. It just... stopped. There was this storm—one of those freak Texas ones, out of nowhere, and I was on the trail with the dogs. Lightning hit this old pine, and the branch should've—" I replay it in my mind, the green-gold shimmer of runes under his skin, the way time itself seemed to hiccup. "It should've taken me out. But it just... hung there. Like someone hit pause on a movie. And then he dropped it off to the side like it was nothing."

"Ame, honey, this doesn't sound right," she says, instantly falling into her clinical voice. "Men who can do impossible things are either charlatans or dangerous. Or both."

I flinch at the word dangerous. It clangs against my ribs, more warning than diagnosis. "He didn't hurt me. He saved me. And then he just—" I struggle to describe the way Loki had looked at me, equal parts terror and longing, like he was the one in danger. "He left. Said it was a mistake. Told me to stay away from him."

Sarah is silent for a long, loaded second, as if she's running through every possible DSM diagnosis before speaking. "Amethyst, have you been sleeping?"

I press my forehead to the table, close my eyes against the jagged brightness behind my eyelids. "Not really, no."

"Okay. Listen to me. You're isolated, your work is a mess—"

"I'm not isolated and my job's not a mess."

"—and you're letting yourself get attached to someone you barely know. Ame, you do this every time. You jump into things. You—" Sarah's voice softens. "You want to believe in magic so badly, you make it up."

The accusation lands, cold and mean, even if I know she means well. "I didn't make it up, Sarah. Mystic and Ash saw it, too. They freaked out—"

"Dogs sense anxiety. You know that. It's probably feedback from you."

I sit up, anger threading through my fear. "I'm not losing my mind."

"No, but you're not being rational. You're in a dinky little town, alone, and your first instinct is to trust a stranger over your own judgment. Ame, I love you, but this isn't you. You're not this—" Sarah gropes for the word and settles on, "—gullible."

"I am not gullible." I bite off each word, the memory of Loki's face vivid and close. "You didn't see what I saw."

Sarah sighs, the breath scraping the edge of the phone's mic. "Let's say, for argument's sake, you're not hallucinating. Maybe he's some kind of... illusionist. There are people on TikTok who can make it look like they can bend spoons with their minds."

I want to scream. I want to reach through the phone and shake her until she gets it. "He's not a TikTok magician, Sarah. There was something about it—about him—that was real. More real than anything I've ever felt. And I know how that sounds."

My hands are shaking. Mystic shoves her nose under my elbow, demanding contact, and I let her. "I can't explain it, but it happened."

Sarah's voice takes on that hard, maternal edge. "Okay. Let's break this down. First, this guy appears out of nowhere. Then, you start seeing strange lights and shadows in your woods. Now, he's performing magic tricks? This isn't romantic; it's terrifying. You don't know what he's after. Maybe it's money, maybe it's—hell, I don't know, a cult initiation?"

I snort at that, but my stomach turns. "He doesn't want anything from me. He's actually tried to push me away."

"That's even worse!" Sarah's voice goes up an octave. "Am, you're describing a textbook manipulator. Classic trauma bonding: rescue you from danger, then disappear so you'll chase him. I'm telling you, it's a play."

I lean my head back, eyes tracking the lines on the ceiling as if the right answer might be written there. "If it is, it's a damn convincing one."

"You need to stay away from him until you know what's really going on," Sarah says, her voice flattening into command.

I want to agree. I want to say, Sure, I'll block his number and delete all my memories and just—pretend none of it happened. But I can't. "It's not that simple," I whisper.

Sarah lets the silence stretch, then softens. "Ame. I'm worried about you. This is how bad things start. You see the best in people, even when they're standing in front of you with a bloody knife and a signed confession."

A laugh bursts out of me, a sharp, unwanted thing. "He didn't stab anyone, Sarah. Unless you count my sense of reality."

Sarah relents, just a hair. "Just promise me you'll be careful. And that you'll call the second anything seems off. Not in three days, not after another storm, but right then. Can you do that?"

I nod, forgetting she can't see me. "Yeah. I promise."

She takes a slow, therapist breath. "Thank you. Now, when are you going to come to Dallas? You really need to get out of that town. It's not good for you."

I stare at the far wall, where runes have flickered. "The town is fine. It is good for me, just because you don't like small towns. I need to figure out these runes...."

Sarah clicks her tongue. "You mean the pareidolia thing? Like how people see faces in burnt toast?"

"No, it's not pareidolia. I'm not seeing faces.... it's more like writing." I close my eyes and see the marks, the spiky lines and Y-shapes, the way they pulsed when Loki was near. "Sometimes they hurt to look at. Sometimes I feel like I could read them if I just looked long enough."

Sarah hums a noncommittal sound. "Could be your brain's way of processing stress."

Maybe she's right. Maybe I'm imprinting meaning onto static, onto shadows and dust. But then why do the dogs react? Why did Loki flinch, that first time, as if the symbols themselves were a threat?

As if to prove the point, Mystic jerks upright, hackles prickling. Ash goes rigid, tail a warning flag, and both stare at the kitchen window with the singular, uncanny focus dogs reserve for things humans can't see.

I twist in my chair, my heart beating a tattoo in my throat. There—etched on the condensation of the glass, as if traced by a finger dipped in fog—is a single rune, bigger than any I've seen before. A spear of light, bisected by jagged branches, like a tree on fire. The sun hits it, and for a moment it glows, purple and sharp as a bruise.

I drop the phone. I can still hear Sarah's voice, tinny and alarmed, calling my name. But I don't move. The rune changes, grows, other lines budding off until the shape looks like an insect, then a word, then—impossibly—I recognize it from the charts I'd obsessed over last night: Ragnarok. The end of everything.

Mystic barks once, sharp and warning, and the mark dissolves into a haze of moisture.

I pick up the phone, my hands shaking so badly I nearly drop it again. "Sarah?"

"Ame? Are you okay? You went silent, and then there was barking—"

"I'm fine," I say, the lie bitter on my tongue. "It's just—"

"Did you see another symbol?" She sounds concerned.

"Yeah," I whisper, staring at the window. "Yeah, I did."

Sarah's voice is softer now, edged with fear. "Ame. Promise me you won't go outside. Not today. Not until you hear from me. Okay?"

I nod, still watching the window, the afterimage of the rune burned into my vision. "Okay," I say. "I promise."

Sarah hesitates, then says, "I love you, Am. No matter how crazy this gets."

"I love you too," I say, though the words feel strange and hollow, like they're meant for another version of me.

I hang up and set the phone down. Mystic and Ash have retreated to my feet, eyes fixed on the window, and I slide to the floor beside them. I wrap my arms around both dogs, feeling the tremor of their anxiety in my bones.

On the other side of the glass, the world is motionless, washed in the thin light of an ordinary day. But I know better. I know the runes will come again, and that when they do, there will be no pretending it's not real. There will be no going back.

Not for me. Not for any of us.

I hang up from the phone call with Amethyst, my hands shaking. She's losing it. The isolation in that small town is making her delusional, and now she's involved with someone calling himself "Loki" who's supposedly performing magic tricks.

I quickly reschedule my next appointment and start researching. After twenty minutes of digging through paranormal message boards—exactly the kind Amethyst would frequent—I find a mention of something called "Division," a group that supposedly helps people who think supernatural phenomena are real.

When I comment asking for contact information, most users warn me away. But CSOD99 sends a private message with a link, then immediately leaves the chat.

The website is sparse and professional—just a contact form. I don't hesitate.

My friend has been isolated in a rural Texas community for six years. She's now involved with a potentially dangerous individual who calls himself 'Loki' and claims to cause supernatural phenomena. I believe she's being manipulated and is experiencing psychological distress.

I include everything: Amethyst's address, phone number, and a description of the trailer. Everything they might need to find her and get her the help she clearly needs.

Above the town, on a rooftop forgotten by pigeons and the weekly gutter man, I stand with my face tilted to the sky. The morning sun fights to burn off a cloud that has no business being here; the rest of the county is awash in blue, but over my head, the world curdles to gunmetal. My black hair whips in a wind that ignores every flag and treetop except for the sovereign patch of roof beneath my feet.

I close my eyes and let the pulse of my own unease trickle down my spine: guilt, hunger, a longing that stings like lemon on a knife wound. I want—what? The right word doesn't exist. I want to want less, or more precisely, want not to care, but the feeling roots inside me, feral and unyielding.

Thunder grumbles, soft but petulant. My fist clenches, and a line of cold runs from the base of my skull through both arms into my fingers. The runes on my forearms—hidden today by starched cuffs and a silk jacket—crawl with light that only I can see. The storm responds, darkening in concentric circles, the air so charged it tastes of burnt sugar.

I see the street below as a painting in reverse: everyone a little too sharp, colors acid-bright, movement both frantic and sluggish. A couple out for an early walk pauses at the crosswalk, the man's hat flipping off his head as the wind shifts. A school bus driver looks up, knuckles white on the wheel, and guns it through a yellow light. And there—at the edge of the block—a woman wrestles her Great Dane toward a patch of grass, her face scrunching as she tugs her coat tight against a chill only she seems to feel.

I breathe in through my teeth. I try to think of Amethyst's face, the impossible play of violet and defiance and hope that haunted me all night. Instead, the memory of the tree branch—split, hanging in the air like a guillotine held by a trembling hand—slides over my thoughts and paralyzes me with the knowledge that I failed her, even in saving her. I have always been my own undoing, but this time, the stakes are different.

"Control yourself," I say, the words stripped raw and quiet. My breath curls in the air, visible even in June. The wind howls louder, and with it comes a sudden, violent hail—pebbles of ice that explode against the roof, the air, the concrete below. The sound is so loud it becomes silence.

People run for cover. The Great Dane barks, then cowers; the woman whirls and looks up, right at me. I duck behind the parapet, cursing my own carelessness, but not before I see the recognition—no, not recognition, but a wild, animal terror—on her face.

The runes blaze now, and I feel my shape blur at the edges, the way it always does when my magic spills beyond my own boundaries. The air turns glassy; the world slows to a syrupy crawl. Fog rolls in from nowhere, licking the ground and blurring the street, the houses, the bodies. A frost spreads in a perfect circle around the building, three houses deep, leaving crystalline daggers on mailbox flags and window-panes. My breath is hoarfrost.

Then, as suddenly as it arrived, the hail stops. Silence thuds in my eardrums. The fog burns off in a spiral, sucked up by the hungry storm overhead, and the sky begins to forget it was ever angry at all.

A faint noise, like chalk on stone, draws my attention to the chimney. Something moves in the grout between bricks—a glimmer, then a flare, as a symbol carves itself into the mortar with impossible speed. The mark glows, brighter than sunlight, a Twilight Rune visible even in the daylight. The lines shift and multiply, weaving through Norse shapes older than the town itself, until they settle into two simple words:

Midgard's heart.

I stare at it, the ache in my chest replaced by a hollow that is nearly relief. Midgard: Earth. The mortal realm. And, I suppose, the mortals within it—the stubborn, wild, irrational creatures I have always loved. That I have always hated and never understood. Her.

I place a hand on the brick, feeling the rune's heat through the skin, into bone. I understand now. This world is her anchor, and I must be hers, or nothing at all. The storm inside me doesn't abate, but I pull it tighter, refusing to let it pour into the world unless I choose.

Below, the woman and her dog have vanished into a side street. The air is clear, the temperature normal. Life resumes its stupid, beautiful momentum.

I lean my forehead against the chimney, fingers tracing the last sparks of the rune as it fades. I whisper, "I will not lose you."

The wind dies, leaving only the smell of summer rain, and somewhere in the distance, a bell rings. I stand alone on the rooftop, but the loneliness is a choice now, and the feeling that follows is no longer despair but resolve.

I will find her again. And this time, I will not run.

The air is thick with mosquitoes and intention. I walk the edge of my property, boots squishing in yesterday's runoff, and Mystic and Ash move with the low, predatory focus of wolves half-remembering their wild ancestors. Every ten yards, one or both dogs will pause, heads swinging in synchrony, and their gaze fixes on nothing—until I get close, and the nothing becomes something, and the something becomes a glimmer of runes, alive for a heartbeat, then gone.

The first time it happens, I'm ready. I've got my phone out, camera set to 'burst,' finger trembling over the shutter. The symbol is simple, a Y with two extra arms like a child's drawing of a splay-handed tree. Mystic barks once, sharp and questioning, and I snap eight blurry frames before the rune dissolves into bark dust and the next breath of wind. I scroll through the pictures—nothing. Even in the best shot, all I see is the bark, no sign of what's burned into my retinas.

I keep walking. The dogs range ahead, Ash bounding in idiot loops while Mystic tracks with the patience of a cop on stakeout. I follow the fence line, feeling watched, though I know that there's no one for miles. The rural silence is total except for the pant of dog breath and the slap of my boots on wet earth.

A text comes in, startling me with its juddering vibration. I glance down and see Sarah's name, followed by the preview:

'This is what I was talking about—BE CAREFUL.'

She's sent three links, all flagged in red:

'Gaslighting Tactics Used by Narcissists'

'How to Spot a Conman'

'Dangerous Personalities: When to Trust Your Gut.'

I close the phone. I don't need the reminders. I trust Sarah, I do, but her voice in my head today is just another run of static, a warning that's impossible to obey. If Loki wanted to hurt me, he'd have done it already. Instead, he saved me. And then pushed me away.

The dogs circle a thicket near the back acreage, noses low, hackles up. Mystic stops, paws at a pile of leaves, and whines. I crouch beside her, ruffling the coarse fur of her neck. "What is it, girl?"

She doesn't answer, of course. But as I lean in, I see it: a rune, drawn not on the trunk of the oak but traced in the layer of pollen and dirt that coats the fence rail. This one is a spiral, ringed with spikes, almost like a sun or a cyclone. I reach out and touch it. The pattern is cool and slick beneath my fingertip, as if someone painted it with dew.

The instant my skin makes contact, something zaps through me—like static, but with meaning, a wordless download straight to the hindbrain. I jerk back, startled, and check my finger. For the first time, the mark doesn't fade. Instead, it glows a dull purple against the pink of my palm, not ink but light itself.

I try to take a picture, but the camera refuses to focus. The mark shudders on my skin, then crawls up my lifeline, stretching toward my thumb like it's mapping the future. It doesn't hurt, exactly, but it tingles in a way that feels like it should. I stare, mesmerized.

Ash circles me, tail low, whining as if I'm suddenly speaking a language he doesn't understand. I sit in the grass, back against the fence, and try to breathe normally. The mark lingers, bright and insistent. From the charts I found online, the closest match is a Norse bindrune, usually meaning fate, or sometimes destiny, depending on who you ask.

I close my hand into a fist, trying to hold the meaning in place. "Is this what you want?" I ask the air, unsure if I'm talking to the universe or myself. I close my eyes, feeling a bit dizzy. I slowly open them and look up.

The sky is perfectly clear. There are birds overhead, a vulture circling high and three crows picking at something in the neighbor's field. The dogs fall silent, as if the world itself is waiting for my decision.

I think of Sarah's warnings, her certainty that men like Loki only bring ruin. I think of every bad decision I've made, how they always start with the hope that this time will be different. I think of the way Loki looked at me—not like prey, but like I was the only thing anchoring him to this world.

The rune starts to fade, but not all at once. It pulses, brighter for a moment, and then dims. I breathe out, and as I do, the wind changes. It picks up, hard enough to rattle the fence and send the dogs skittering for cover. I look up, and the sun is blotted out by a cloud that came from nowhere, black as oil and shaped like a spiral. Rain spits down in sudden, fat drops, so localized that the rest of the horizon stays blue and bright.

Within seconds, I am soaked. The cold stings, but I don't run for shelter. Instead, I stand up, hair plastered to my scalp, and lift my palm to the sky, daring the storm to take the last of the runes with it.

The dogs press close, both shivering but refusing to break formation. The rain intensifies, and the world shrinks to a tunnel of water and wind and the memory of his voice.

I see him—not in front of me, but behind my eyelids—a flicker of black hair and impossible green, a smile that's equal parts promise and warning. I feel the electric pull, the unspoken dare. I haven't felt like this... ever.

Sarah's voice is in my head: "Stay away from him until you know what's really going on." But what if what's going on is the only thing that's ever felt real?

The storm ends as suddenly as it began. My clothes stick to me, heavy with water and the weight of decision. The rune is gone, but the feeling isn't. I open my hand and watch the last drops run off my fingers.

Ash shakes, spraying water everywhere. Mystic sits, as if waiting for instructions.

I take out my phone, thumb hovering over Loki's contact. For a moment, I hesitate, then type:

I saw the sign. I'm not afraid.

Good lord, I feel like I'm going crazy. This can't be real. I'm just seeing things. I delete the message and shake my head.

I walk back toward the house, the dogs at my side.

If the world is ending, I think, at least I won't have to go through it alone.

CHAPTER EIGHT

DANCE OF REVELATION

If I had a dollar for every time I swore I'd never go to one of these things again, I could probably buy this whole new house and more land. The way the string lanterns hang between the pine trees, swaying in the bug-thick air, makes the whole place look like a crime scene that got redecorated by the PTA. My purple t-shirt clings to me, damp with that special brand of late-spring Texas sweat, and I'm regretting the decision to wear yoga pants with no pockets. Every time I try to relax, the waistband rolls down, and I'm yanking it back up like a nervous tic.

I can hear Mystic and Ash whining from my back seat—parked just beyond the vendor row in the deepest shade, windows rolled down, battery fans going full blast, their heads sticking out like the world's least subtle surveillance crew—but I promised myself I'd try to be normal for one night. So I brave the gauntlet: tables draped with handmade soaps, wind chimes, tie-dye, and vendors barking about kettle corn or locally sourced honey as if it's the antidote to death itself.

The caramel apple booth is a sticky mecca of kids with painted faces and parents in cargo shorts. I grab a sample slice, the sugar and tartness blasting my tongue, and try to focus on anything except how exposed I feel. Every stranger's glance feels like a dare, and I'm ready to take the L and retreat to the parking lot when I see him.

He's across the square, standing perfectly still under a canopy of paper lanterns. Black-on-black clothes, boots that cost more than my last three rent checks, and this aura like a dark river cutting through the crowd. He's not even pretending to browse; he's just watching. Every time someone gets within three feet, they edge away like he's got a sign that says DO NOT TOUCH—HAZARDOUS MATERIALS.

I tell myself I could just walk away. That I should. But the moment his eyes meet mine, everything inside me flips over. My stomach goes weightless, and my mouth fills up with the taste of panic. He looks at me like he's been waiting hours, maybe days, and he doesn't blink. I can't tell if he's mad or hungry or something worse. The last thing he said—Stay away from me—punches through my brain like a shotgun blast. So why am I still standing here, hands clenched so tight I leave half-moon dents in my palms?

He starts to walk. Not fast. Every step is measured, like he's giving me time to bolt. I should bolt. It would be the smart thing to do. But my feet are stuck, rooted in pine needles and regret, and every step he takes eats up the distance between us like a countdown.

Someone jostles me from behind, a woman with a knit scarf and three kids in tow. "Sorry, hon," she says, then gives me a double take. "You okay? You look like you seen a ghost."

"Something like that," I say, my voice hoarse. I swallow hard and glance around for an exit strategy. The crowds are too thick; the only way out is forward. Towards him.

The closer he gets, the more the world narrows, the sounds of the festival collapsing into muffled static. The only thing in focus is the cut of his jaw, the glint in his eyes, the faint shimmer of green-gold under the lanterns that makes his gaze look radioactive. He's beautiful in that way wild animals are beautiful—right up to the second they decide to eat you.

He's five feet away now. I feel every molecule of air between us vibrate. I try to remember how to breathe, how to smile, how to do anything except stare back like a deer about to become someone's dinner.

His lips part, just a fraction. I can almost hear the words he's going to say, the apology or the threat or the warning. Instead, he just stands there, close enough for me to see the pulse in his throat, the way his fingers flex and release at his sides.

My jaw sets. If I'm going to get vaporized by a Norse god in the middle of a community fundraiser, at least I'll go down with some dignity. I square my shoulders, look him dead in the eye, and say, "You here for the funnel cakes or the existential dread?"

His smile, when it comes, is small and sharp. "I hear the caramel apples are to die for."

A laugh snorts out of me before I can stop it. Tension breaks, but only a little. I'm still bracing for disaster, but now there's something almost—almost—funny about the whole situation.

We stand like that for a second. Long enough for it to get weird. The festival noise creeps back in around the edges: kids screaming, a band warming up on the makeshift stage. I realize I haven't moved. I realize, with a hot twist of embarrassment, that I don't want to.

He leans in, just enough for his voice to thread through the din. "You look...well." The pause before 'well' is almost a question.

"Define well," I say. I mean it to be a joke, but it comes out raw, my voice barely holding steady.

He studies me, a scan from hair to shoes that makes my skin prickle. "Alive," he says, and it's not a compliment; it's a statement of fact. Like he's relieved but doesn't trust it to last.

I want to touch him. I want to punch him. I want to ask him what the hell is happening to me, to us, to this whole freak show of a town. Instead, I settle for glaring. "You told me to stay away."

He doesn't flinch. "I did."

"Doesn't seem like you're following your own advice."

He tilts his head, a little wolfish. "That's never been my strong suit."

My laugh is shaky, but real. "What is your strong suit, then?"

The smile drops off his face like a mask falling away. "Finding people who shouldn't be lost."

My breath catches. For a second, I'm thirteen again, waiting for someone to come find me after the accident, after my family disappeared into that yawning blank. Nobody ever did. Until now, maybe.

I look away, blinking hard. There's a banner overhead that reads "ANNUAL PINE HOLLOW FESTIVAL: ALL ARE WELCOME!" in Comic Sans. The absurdity helps. "So what now?" I ask, my voice small.

He doesn't answer. Instead, he reaches out—slow, so slow I could stop him if I wanted to. His hand hovers over my shoulder, not quite touching. "Are you afraid?" he asks, softer than before.

I think about lying, but I don't have it in me tonight. "I'm terrified."

He nods. "Good. You should be."

The words are a warning and a comfort, somehow both at once. I let the silence stretch. I'm not sure what else to say. I'm not sure I could say anything if I tried.

He steps back, just a fraction, like he's giving me the choice to stay or to run. My heart thunders so loud I'm sure he can hear it. I wonder if anyone else can.

My phone buzzes in my pocket. I ignore it.

He waits, patient as the night.

And I realize, with a dizzy lurch, that I'm done running. Maybe for good.

She's the axis around which this whole feverish event spins. I see it in the way her pulse flares along her jaw, the way she bites the inside of her cheek when she thinks no one's watching. She should have run, but she stands her ground—chest out, chin up, ready to bite or to bleed; she hasn't decided which. I sidle through the lantern-lit corridor of tents, an easy predator. The ground is slick with pine needles and spilled beer, the air thick with barbecue smoke and the old, stubborn Texas humidity.

She flicks her gaze past me, feigning indifference, but every nerve on her body's edge is tuned to my frequency. The edge of her purple shirt catches the breeze, and I want to see how quickly I can tangle her up in it, or in me. I let the crowd nudge me closer. My smile is for her alone.

"Small-town festivals have a certain charm," I say, voice pitched low enough that it's a secret just for us.

She snorts, tossing a purple curl over her shoulder. "If you're into cover bands and caramel apples." But there's heat in her words; she wants me to keep up, to push.

"Is that what brought you here?" I ask, letting my tone linger on her.

She shrugs, a quick flash of self-mockery. "I thought the apple would bite back."

I laugh, short and real, and she flinches like she wasn't expecting me to have the capacity for it. "What if I said I came for the company?"

She rolls her eyes, but her cheeks go rose-petal red. "You're full of shit," she says, then tacks on, "but you wear it well."

I steer us past a booth stacked with ugly pottery, my hand brushing her forearm. She doesn't pull away, even when I let my fingers rest at the small of her back. I feel her shudder, the war inside her as loud as a thunderclap. It's intoxicating.

"You don't seem like the festival type," she says, shooting me a look that's half challenge, half plea.

"Maybe I'm not," I say. "Maybe I go where the interesting people are." I squeeze, just a little, and she melts and stiffens at the same time. I could break her in half, or heal her, or both.

We cross into the main square, a logjam of bodies and bad lighting. The band onstage is midway through "Take Me Home, Country Roads," and it's so earnestly off-key I want to hug the entire population of Pine Hollow for trying so hard. She spots a tent with handmade journals and makes a beeline for it. I follow, basking in the way she glances over her shoulder, like she's checking for monsters and hoping to find one.

The vendor is a hunched old woman who looks like she's been grown from the same soil as the trees. She ignores me, locking eyes with Amethyst instead.

"These are beautiful," Amethyst says, picking up a journal bound in raw, buttery leather. "Wish I had anything worth writing in them."

The old woman's mouth quirks up. "What makes you think you don't?"

Amethyst goes still, then sets the book down like it might explode. "What about you?" she says, turning to me. "Ever keep a diary?"

"Not for a long time," I say. "I find it's better to live in the moment."

She shakes her head, but she's smiling now, soft around the edges. "You're dangerous," she says, and this time it's not a warning; it's a confession.

The band behind us shifts gears, the clumsy twang of the banjo giving way to a slow, haunted ballad. All around, couples link up and sway, lantern light casting double shadows that look like ghosts holding each other in the dark. I take her hand—cool, almost trembling in mine.

"Dance with me," I say, not a question.

She hesitates. The world drops to a hush, as if waiting for her verdict.

"I don't dance," she says, but lets me tug her into the open anyway.

We join the moving spiral, her hips stiff, her hands gripping my shoulders like a lifeline. I lean in, letting my breath tickle her ear.

"Are you afraid I'll step on your toes?" I murmur.

She snorts again, but her lips are right up against my throat. "You'd probably take the whole foot."

I draw her closer, savoring how quickly the boundaries fall away. There are hundreds of eyes on us, but none of them matter. For a second, I can see the future, can see her in my arms a thousand years from now, the world different but this moment the same.

I lose the thread of the song. Doesn't matter. I set my own rhythm, guiding her through the movements until she trusts me enough to loosen her grip. The air around us vibrates, the scent of rain and sun-warmed skin and sweet resin. I feel her heart pounding, wild and terrified.

"You're shaking," I say, not unkindly.

"I don't like crowds," she says, but her body tells a different story.

"Should I get rid of them?" I offer, half-joking.

She laughs, and the sound is so bright I want to bottle it. "You wouldn't."

I do. I let a little of myself out—a flicker of intent, a flex of ancient will—and time seems to slow. The music echoes, stretched and syrupy, the dancers around us blurring to a standstill. The lanterns burn hotter, casting green-gold halos. I look down at her, and she's staring back, her eyes huge.

"What's happening?" she whispers.

"Nothing you don't want," I promise.

She shakes her head, but she doesn't let go. "You're not real."

"Neither are you," I say, and I mean it. "You're better."

The song warps and warbles, a glass bead rolling across a marble floor, and my eyes flare. I can't help it. The runes glow beneath my skin, green and gold and white-hot, and I see the reflection of them in her pupils.

Someone gasps, just outside the circle.

"Did you see—?" a voice mutters.

"His eyes. Jesus, are those contacts?"

"Is that a trick?"

There's a ripple in the crowd. Phones come out. I smile and bow, dipping Amethyst as if we're on stage. She's breathless and dazed, her hair a wild halo. For a heartbeat, I want to kiss her in front of all these strangers—to show her that the world is as weird and beautiful as she ever dared to hope.

But I don't. Not yet.

Instead, I whisper, "Would you like to get out of here?"

She looks up at me, and for the first time tonight, she's not afraid.

"Yeah," she says. "Lead the way."

We slip out of the circle, the music snapping back to normal speed, the crowd surging in behind us like a tide. She keeps my hand in hers, and I keep thinking about how easy it would be to vanish with her forever.

But tonight, I'm content to walk through the pine needles, the lanterns, the echoes of a festival that will never quite forget what it just saw.

For one perfect, deranged second, I feel like the main character in a book that's about to get yanked off the library shelf. I stare up at him, at the way his eyes seem to burn through the lantern haze, at the cut-glass angles of his jaw and the faint smirk he wears like a battle medal. My pulse is a runaway train. I feel my hands curl, fists at first, and then I just—fuck it—grab the front of his shirt and haul myself up onto my tiptoes.

I don't know if I'm going to punch him or kiss him, not until my lips are on his, and by then it's way too late. The world tilts. His arms come around me, hard, catching me like I'm about to float away. For a terrifying instant, I think he'll push me off, but instead, he lifts me, just enough that my toes barely graze the dirt. The kiss is everything I didn't want to admit I'd been craving—hungry and wild, sweet at the edges. I bury my hands in his hair, softer than it looks, and there's a low sound at the back of his throat like he's been holding his breath for centuries.

And that's when it happens.

The whole festival flickers. The air gets hot, sharp, and all the shadows bend in weird directions. The paper lanterns overhead explode into orbs—real orbs, not cheap electric bulbs, burning with their own impossible light. The tacky wooden stalls dissolve into towering pavilions made of gold and bone, banners whipping in a wind that wasn't there before. The crowd freezes, every person a living statue: a vendor with cider caught mid-pour, a kid with her tongue outstretched for cotton candy, the local band's fiddler with both hands in the air. All their faces turned, eyes wide and glassy, staring straight at us.

I can smell ozone and pine sap and something old, like burnt honey or the end of summer. The music keeps playing, but it's warped—notes overlapping, doubling back, building into a low, dangerous hum that makes my teeth ache.

Loki's skin is burning under my hands. Not hot, exactly, but bright—like he's made of stars or something even older. I pull back, gasping, and he's staring at me, shocked and not shocked, like he's been waiting his whole life for this exact disaster.

I look down and see a ripple spread out from our feet, warping the ground, the grass turning blue and silver and then back again. All around us, people are caught mid-motion, half-wrapped in the old world and the new. For a second, the whole damn universe balances on the tip of my tongue.

I could stay like this forever. I could die like this, and it would be fine.

But then the crack comes. Not a sound, exactly, but a feeling—a pressure drop, a sledgehammer to the solar plexus. The pavilions shatter back into tents, the orbs pop into nothing, the smell of magic collapses under the weight of cheap beer and funnel cakes. The band misses a beat, and everyone stirs, blinking and muttering, as if they all woke from the same fever dream.

I'm still clinging to him. He's still holding me. My face is wet, and I don't know if it's sweat or tears or what. I don't care.

He lets me down slowly, hands lingering at my waist. His smile is gone, replaced with this look of awe and terror that makes him seem almost—almost—human.

I take a step back, then another. My whole body is shaking, but I keep my eyes locked on his, daring him to make sense of any of this.

He doesn't try. Instead, he just watches me, like he's afraid I'll vanish if he blinks.

Maybe I will.

The crowd starts moving again, a tide of people who have no idea what just happened or maybe they do; maybe they'll all go home tonight and lie awake wondering what it means to see gods walking in the daylight. I push through them, past the cider booth, past the bandstand, past the entire pathetic, glorious mess of Pine Hollow's one-night masquerade. No one stops me. No one can.

I don't look back.

Not even when I know, with a weird, impossible certainty, that he's still watching.

The command tent stinks of melted plastic and microwaved leftovers. I hover near the entrance, invisible as the draft that shudders the canvas every time a breeze slips through Pine Hollow. The Division is the same everywhere: folding tables, fluorescent tubes so bright you can see the afterimage even when you close your eyes, paper maps layered with so many colored lines the topography looks like a fever chart.

Two agents sit shoulder-to-shoulder on battered camp chairs, eyes glued to the synchronized glow of their tablets. Agent Carter is a stork of a woman, all tendon and grim focus, her ponytail so tight it looks painted on. Warrick is younger, the kind who still says "Ma'am" to Carter even when she's not listening. Both have the signature Division complexion—skin gone pale from years under artificial light and nothing left of trust but the reflex to double-check every fact.

Carter runs the loop for the third time. The festival footage is mostly crowd noise and pointless meandering, but when the timestamp hits 21:17, every screen in the tent goes blue-white with a pulse that's visible through closed eyelids. She taps the screen as the feed stutters: wooden stalls blur to gold, every onlooker flash-frozen in mid-motion, and at the dead center of the anomaly, a purple-haired woman and a man in black, locked together like figures on a Grecian urn. Warrick mutters "Jesus," then snaps back to typing, fingers trembling.

"Run it again," Carter says, monotone. "Frame-by-frame, digital and thermal." She pauses. "And find out who they are."

Warrick lines up the sliders. There's a sick thrill in watching the transformation pixel by pixel—first the lanterns erupt, then the local wildlife in the grass flattens and whimpers, then the vendors go slack-jawed, pupils blown so wide there's barely any white. On the thermal overlay, Loki is a radiant green-gold blot, Amethyst a dull, trembling echo.

"High thaumic signature," Carter says. She taps a stylus against her teeth, never breaking rhythm. "That's your culprit, right there."

Warrick nods, tongue wetting his upper lip. "What about her?"

The question hangs, heavier than the heat in the tent. Carter doesn't answer immediately. Instead, she pulls up the secondary feed: a drone-eye view of the festival. The moment the surge starts, a five-meter radius around the pair goes grayscale. Even the air seems to freeze, the cloud of funnel cake grease and cigarette smoke halting mid-drift.

"She's the constant," Carter says. "Same as at the park and the March incident at the library. Every time, she's in the frame."

Warrick pulls up a new window, the search bar already loaded. "Name?"

"Amethyst Gold," Carter says after pulling up the town records.

"Pets?"

"Two. Mystic and Ash. Registered to her current address."

He types. The system returns a DMV photo—a bad one, all wild hair and glare. Next to it, a vet's file with the cattle dogs' faces, eyes luminous even in black and white.

The generator rumbles, drowning out the folk tune still leaking in from the festival's dying hours. Carter cross-references Amethyst's purple shirt and yoga pants against every piece of footage they've got, using a facial recognition overlay that paints her face with a neon grid.

It takes less than thirty seconds for the system to spit out the answer: "Anomaly confirmed. Amethyst Gold, female, forty-five, residing—" the address is redacted, but Carter and Warrick don't need it. They know.

Warrick glances up, eyes ringed with exhaustion. "So what now?"

Carter shrugs, a movement so small it could be a tic. "We log it, escalate to Tier Four, and wait for instructions. She's the first one in decades to make it this far without a containment flag."

Outside, the music starts up again—louder, messier, a last gasp of normal before curfew. I watch the agents work, the weight of a thousand years settling on their hunched shoulders, and I wonder what they'd do if they knew they were only the latest in a line of bureaucrats doomed to miss the point.

Carter locks her screen and stands. "You on dogs tonight or me?"

Warrick gives a rueful grin. "You. They bit through my last riot shield."

Carter laughs, a real sound, but then the moment's gone and she's back to business. "Pack up. We move at dawn."

Chapter Nine

AFTERMATH

The morning after the festival, I pace my trailer like a caged tiger hopped up on off-brand energy drinks, which—spoiler alert—absolutely tracks with the number of said drinks I slammed after last night's fiasco. Mystic and Ash trail me with military precision, their herding dog DNA dialed to eleven, blue-gray fur bristling with every click of my slippers against the scarred linoleum. Ash's tail swishes so hard it slaps the paneling. Mystic keeps cutting in front of me with the commitment of a Secret Service agent determined to take a bullet for her incompetent charge.

The trailer smells like dog farts and stubborn hope. I catch my reflection in the microwave's grease-streaked glass: purple hair mashed into a knot on top of my head, dark circles under my eyes that could double as war paint. My t-shirt says "Zero Chill Club," which would be funnier if it weren't so goddamn accurate.

"Y'all see what you did?" I ask the dogs, dropping my voice into the gravelly tone I used to discipline toddlers back when I worked at the library daycare. "Got us both banned from polite society and probably flagged on some government watch list for public display of...what, exactly? Spontaneous mythological combustion?" Even though I know the dogs had nothing to do with it.

Ash yips, as if in agreement. Mystic just huffs, her attention glued to the window, where the sun claws up through the dense pine. It's humid as a boiled egg out there, but the inside of the trailer feels like a pressure cooker left too long. Maybe it's just me, crammed so full of adrenaline and shame and unresolved lust that the very walls are about to pop off the cinder blocks.

I make a lap, passing the kitchen counter and giving my abandoned can of Coke a dirty look. The can, half-drained and sweating onto a stack of unopened bills, glares right back. A silent judge, unimpressed by my attempt to drown last night's insanity in cheap sugar and caffeine.

Last night's insanity. Oh, gods.

It's all still there, strung out in high-def replay behind my eyelids: the music, the scent of kettle corn and candied apples, the lanterns bobbing on invisible strings. The way Loki—I'm not even going to pretend he's anything but Loki now—walked through that crowd like he owned the concept of "being looked at." The feel of his hand, cold and weirdly familiar, when he pulled me onto the dance floor. The flash of the world coming apart in color and sound, his eyes glowing that impossible green-gold, his lips on mine.

And then the magic—actual, literal, what-the-fuck magic. Reality bent, and everyone saw it. I'm not special, not delusional. I am, however, the only one who ran screaming into the night with the dogs and left behind a hundred slack-jawed maybe witnesses and a trickster god standing in the middle of a temporary Asgard.

I round the couch, stub my toe on the wobbly coffee table, and curse Loki's entire family tree. Mystic and Ash trade a look—at least I'm not the only one who thinks he's trouble, right?—and then Ash launches himself onto the couch, circles three times, and plants his butt firmly in the "sentry" position, nose aimed at the door.

"What, you think he's coming back?" I ask. The idea sends a bolt of panic through me, but also a low, traitorous thrill. "He probably has a line of exes stretching from here to Valhalla. The man's a professional risk."

The clock says it's not even eight yet, but my brain's running on fumes and spite. I snag a donut from the box on the counter (purchased during my post-midnight shame spiral at the all-night gas station, thank you very much) and gnaw the edge while I scrounge my laptop from the pile of unfolded laundry in the corner. The screen wakes with a friendly "don't you dare" hum. Emails from my boss, the usual scams, one from Sarah with the subject line "WTF, Amethyst?!!" and seventeen exclamation points.

I don't open it. Not yet.

Instead, I search "public magical event Pine Hollow Texas" just to see if anyone's spinning a cover story. No hits yet, but it's only a matter of time. TMZ probably has a drone on the way. I'm about to dig for the local news station when a crackling, high-pitched yip makes me look up.

Mystic is standing at the sliding door, nose pressed to the glass. Her hackles are up, which is not unusual, but what's weird is the low, constant growl in her throat. I peer past her and scan the yard. Nothing. Just the same tangle of pine and underbrush, dew shining on the old tire swing.

Then the air shifts—literally—and for a split second, I smell... ozone? Like the charged smell after a thunderstorm. The hair on my arms stands straight up. A familiar cold dread slithers down my spine.

The kitchen lights strobe, off-on-off, and suddenly the walls of the trailer flare with jagged shapes—runes, I realize, like the ones from my research but more alive, burning purple and green and moving across the paneling in angry, slashing bursts.

I scream. The dogs lose their minds. Mystic throws her whole body at the door, barking like she means to kill a god. Ash launches off the couch and starts biting at the flickering runes on the wall, his teeth snapping at empty air. The whole thing lasts maybe five seconds before the lights settle, the runes vanish, and I'm left crouched behind the kitchen island, clutching a steak knife and a donut.

I should be more scared, but it's not the first time the universe has tried to mess with me, so I just shout, "Fuck off! We're closed!" into the static air.

Mystic turns and stares at me, tongue lolling, tail wagging in satisfaction. Ash does a perimeter check of the whole trailer, nose to ground, before coming to sit next to me at the kitchen island. His butt lands with a thump. I scratch his ear, trying to get my heart rate out of the "imminent heart attack" range.

My phone buzzes, face down on the table. Sarah, again. I thumb the call to speaker and hope she can't hear how rattled I sound.

"Ame? What happened last night? You were supposed to call me after the festival."

"I'm alive," I say, and then immediately regret the melodrama. "The festival was... memorable."

"Memorable," Sarah repeats, in that dry, therapist-in-training voice that means she's about to interrogate me for my own good. "Let me guess, you ignored everything I told you and... kissed the guy in front of the entire town."

I roll my eyes and reluctantly tell her a whitewashed version of what happened.

Sarah groaned, "So you kissed and the sky exploded? Then you ran like the devil was after you."

"He probably was," I mutter. I can hear her typing, probably taking notes for some kind of intervention.

"So, was it worth it?" she asks, and I imagine her squinting at the phone, her mouth pursed in concern, judgment, and genuine affection. "Was he worth the drama?"

I don't know how to answer. I still taste the ozone, still feel the crackle of his hands on my skin, the weird gravity of being seen, known, and wanted by someone who isn't supposed to exist. I want to say yes, but the truth is I have no idea. The risks are... not quantifiable.

"Ask me after I get the runes off my goddamn walls," I say. "And after I eat the entire contents of my fridge."

"You really need to come—"

"No," I say, softer. "I'm fine. Got the dogs. Got my steak knife."

She makes a skeptical noise but lets it go. "Okay. But text me if you see, I don't know, flying ravens or a dude in a horned helmet. Seriously."

I roll my eyes and promise I will, and hang up before she can psychoanalyze me into a corner. The room is still too bright, so I pull the curtains and drop onto the floor with the dogs. They curl around me, damp noses pressed to my hands, their breathing slow and steady.

It's only when I close my eyes that I let myself admit I'm not angry, not really. I'm scared, sure. But underneath it is a wild joy, a rush of having lived through something impossible, something bigger than myself and all my little worries. I laugh, a sound too loud for the little trailer, and Ash perks up like he's just heard a treat bag open.

"Don't look at me like that," I tell him. "I'm allowed to have a crisis. It's called being a 'grownup'."

Mystic grumbles, then settles her head on my lap. I lean back and stare at the ceiling, waiting for the next shoe—or world—to drop. Maybe it will be Loki himself, knocking at my door. Maybe it'll be another magic light show. Maybe it'll just be me and the dogs and this weird, lovely terror for the rest of my days.

I can live with that.

Night creeps up before I know it. Mystic takes up her post as a furry blockade between me and the front door, and Ash positions himself at the window, eyes tracking every shadow with a vigilance that would put any security system to shame. I toss them treats, but they don't touch them. Not even the peanut butter ones. That's how you know it's serious.

I brush my teeth, tie my hair into a slightly less tragic bun, and let myself slide under the comforter with the TV on low. My last thought before sleep is that I'm living in a haunted dog fortress, protected by two genetically engineered wolf-dogs and an attitude problem.

Honestly? It's the safest I've ever felt.

It's twilight in the pines, that liminal hour when the world's still holding its breath and every shadow moves like it's got somewhere better to be. I cut through the woods at a speed that would put most woodland predators to shame, feet silent and cloak slick with the day's humidity, runes flickering on my forearms like a warning sign for whatever idiot god might be reckless enough to try following me.

I'm not running, exactly. "Running" is for those without a backup plan or a misplaced sense of superiority. This is more of a tactical withdrawal, emphasis on "tactical." Last night's circus at the festival left a crater in my composure that even I can't patch with sarcasm. I haven't had a slip like that since the Fall, and it's not a thing you talk about in polite trickster society. Not unless you want to be dog-piled by every vengeful spirit and bored demigod on the continent.

The trees thin, and Miss Eliza's cottage emerges from the green like a memory I'd rather not revisit. It has been a long time since I came here; Eliza is not quite mortal; she's been touched by the gods. She doesn't tend to talk about that, and we immortal beings tend to use caution when interacting with her. No one wants to piss her off, or the god who still protects her. As I draw close, the wind chimes clatter in a language older than words. The air's thick with burning sage and some home brew that smells suspiciously like black currant and cloves. She's on the porch, of course, waiting for me, smoke curling from her cigarette in a spiral as precise as a mathematician's fever dream.

"You're late," she says, which is funny since I've never once arrived on time in her presence. I kick off my boots with a practiced flick and take the steps two at a time, careful not to let the runes show unless I want them to. I don't, but they do anyway. They pulse with a greasy blue-green light just under the skin, right where the veins should be. Eliza's eyes narrow, the blue gone icy and sharp.

"I brought you a present," I say, because I know she hates small talk. I toss a half-crushed packet of licorice tea onto the table next to her ashtray. It's a peace offering of sorts, or a warning shot, depending on her mood.

She's not buying it. "Sit," she orders, and I do, because there's no upside to pissing off the only other supernatural in Pine Hollow with a century of dirt on everyone.

There's a silence. It lasts just long enough to make me want to gnaw off a finger. Then, "It's about the girl, isn't it?"

I should deny it, keep that secret from everyone. I should pull a face and go all bluster, but my brain is still half-baked from last night's magic meltdown, and my tongue betrays me. "You saw the display?" I ask, knowing damn well she did.

"I always see." She sucks on the cigarette, exhaling smoke that somehow forms the Old Norse symbol for "idiot" before dissipating. "You've been sloppy."

The accusation lands, heavy and accurate. "It wasn't supposed to go that far," I admit. "Was just trying to have a bit of fun. Blend in. Maybe... learn something." The last part's a mistake. I never admit to "learning" things. It's unbecoming of my brand.

She snorts. "Fun? You nearly popped the boundary. Every ghost in a hundred-mile radius woke up with a hard-on last night."

I wince. "That's a mental image I could have lived without."

She leans back, chair creaking. Her gaze is surgical, stripping away any cleverness I might be clinging to. "So, which is it? You botched the spell, or she's got you in a chokehold?"

This is the part I've been dreading. I crack my knuckles, wishing I could make a rune appear to let me off the hook. No such luck. "I think," I say, the words like glass in my mouth, "it's the latter."

She doesn't look surprised. She never does. "You always had a thing for mortals," she says, softer now. "But this one—she's different?"

I nod. The silence stretches. The forest is so quiet you can hear the chimes argue in the breeze.

"She's different," I say, and it comes out more desperate than I'd like. "I've had flings, sure, but this one gets under the skin. Literally." I hold up my arm. The runes respond, brightening like a toddler at the sight of candy. "Never lost control before. Not like that."

Eliza considers this. She flicks her cigarette into a chipped mug and studies me the way a biologist studies a doomed lab rat. "Gods don't lose control, Loki. Not unless they want to." That isn't true, and she knows it, but it is what we tell ourselves.

I want to argue, but the words die. She's not wrong. "Maybe I wanted to. I don't know. Feels like everything's more dangerous, more alive, when she's around." I laugh, sharp and mean. "It's pathetic."

"Why'd you come to me?"

"You're the only one here who... understands," I say. "And you know how this stuff works." I gesture to the air, the forest, the edges of the world that she patrols with her dusty charms and evil eye collection.

She stands, slow and deliberate, and the chair makes a sound like old bones. She steps closer, her face close enough that I can see every spider-web of time at the corners of her mouth. "Listen to me, you sad sack of mythology. The last time you got tangled up with a mortal, you started a war and nearly got yourself obliterated."

"That was a thousand years ago," I protest.

"Try again, kid. It's never more than yesterday for your kind."

She reaches into her shirt and pulls out a necklace I'd never noticed before, a knot of silver wire threaded with a lump of amber and a tiny scrap of bone. She presses it into my palm, and the runes on my skin ripple, then settle, like a dog curling up to sleep.

"What's this?" I ask, instantly suspicious.

"Protection. From yourself, mostly." She tightens her hand around mine, the grip iron. "You love her, don't you?"

I jerk back like she's burned me. "Love is a mortal disease," I say. "I don't catch those." But I'm not sure that's true, not anymore.

She gives me the smile reserved for the truly damned. "You're already sick, Loki. You came to me hoping I'd talk you out of it or put her in a box where you couldn't reach her. But that's not how this ends. You know better."

I swallow hard. "How does it end, then?"

"With a choice. Same as always."

A crow calls out from somewhere in the trees. The wind picks up, and the runes on my arm start a low, resentful flicker.

Eliza taps the necklace still clutched in my hand. "You can put it on and try to be mortal. Live a little, die a little, suffer and rejoice and lose her in the end like all the rest. Or you can do what you always do and let the chaos win. Hurt her before she hurts you. Leave nothing but ashes." Something in how she says it tells me that last choice would be the most dangerous.

The words are a punch to the gut. "That's it?"

"That's always it," she says. "You want a future with her? Earn it. Otherwise, get out of her life before you ruin it." She turns away, the topic closed.

I sit on the porch a while after she goes inside. The necklace is heavy, warm even in the cooling air. I could leave it here. I could go back to the city, drown myself in whiskey and lies, and forget all about her. But I won't.

I wrap the chain around my hand, let the amber settle against the runes, and feel the pulse of something dangerously close to hope.

Tomorrow, I'll see her again. Tomorrow, I'll decide.

For tonight, the choice is enough.

I am surprised when my phone rings. It's an unknown number, and I nearly ignore it. "Hello?" I answer cautiously.

"Sarah Mitchell?" a stern woman's voice barks.

"Who is this?"

"You contacted us about your friend."

"Oh! Division! I didn't expect a call so quickly. Yes, she's having delusions. She won't accept help. I've been trying to get her out of that backwater town for years. I'm really worried about her. She's imagining this guy is using magic, and she's seeing lights—"

"Would this be in Pine Hollow, Texas?" the woman asks.

"Uhm... yes. Why—"

"What is your friend's name?"

"Amethyst. Amethyst Gold."

There is silence on the other end of the line. "Sarah, we will be contacting you again. We need to do a little investigating. You can call this number if you hear anything more."

Chapter Ten

MARKED

The temperature is only ninety-three, but the sun drills through the sky like it's hunting for brain cells. I'm about six minutes away from heatstroke and one ugly public episode of "local woman found dead in pajamas and Crocs, clutching a weed whacker." My hair, which started the day as a plausible messy bun, has become a damp, purple puffball that repels gravity and basic dignity. I sweat in places I didn't know could sweat, but at least the dogs are living their best life: Ash sprints in manic arcs around the yard, tongue slapping side to side, while Mystic patrols the edge of the property like a bouncer who failed upward.

The only thing louder than my yard tools is the dull roar of the pine woods, the constant chorus of insects that somehow gets worse every summer. Every ten minutes, Mystic freezes, nose in the air, and stares into the shadows between the trees like she's expecting a serial killer or the Amazon delivery guy, which in her mind are equally dangerous.

I'm halfway through untangling a cluster of greenbriar from the porch steps when Mystic's hackles go up, her whole body vibrating with a low, seismic rumble. Ash brakes hard, paws skidding in the gravel, and joins her at the invisible perimeter. My first thought is possum. Second is deer. Third is "oh hell."

He's back.

I glance down, try to smooth my hair and fail spectacularly. I wipe my forehead with the hem of my shirt, which does nothing for my dignity, and grab the closest weapon—a plastic garden trowel—because apparently I am a twelve-year-old child.

The world quiets. Even the cicadas shut up.

And then, like he's been there the whole time, Loki walks out of the tree line.

He's not dressed for the heat. Black jeans, black boots, black button-down shirt with the sleeves rolled to the elbow. His hair is tied back, but not neatly—strands have come loose and stick to the line of his throat. He walks as if gravity's a rumor, moving faster than a man should but never seeming to hurry.

The dogs don't bark. They stand there, side by side, tails low and eyes locked. Not afraid, not even wary, just... waiting. He gives them a nod, like he's acknowledging equals, and Mystic's tail gives a single, grudging thump. Ash just pants, tongue lolling, eyes wild.

I clutch my trowel, fingers slippery with sunscreen and nervous energy. "You know," I say, "most people knock."

He stops at the edge of the driveway, hands in his pockets, and gives me a slow, up-and-down once-over. "You looked busy," he says. "Didn't want to interrupt your—" he gestures at the pile of half-dead weeds and old campaign yard signs I'm using as mulch, "—landscaping."

I scowl. "If you're here to critique my gardening, you're at least a week late. I already lost to the dandelions."

He smiles, crooked and infuriating. "I'm here to see you."

The words hit like a punch to the solar plexus, and I can't tell if it's panic or something meaner, sweeter. I set the trowel down and try to act like a functioning adult. "You could have called."

His mouth twitches. "I assumed you blocked my number."

Fair. I hadn't, but it was a fair assumption.

I dig my toes into the gravel and wipe my palms on my yoga pants, which makes black streaks across my thighs. "So what, you just show up and hope I'm not armed?"

He raises a brow. "Statistically, most Americans are always armed. I took my chances."

The dogs have relaxed, but now they're flanking me, one on each side. I scratch Mystic's ears with trembling fingers and try to decide if I'm going to let this get weird, or if it's already there.

I open my mouth to ask the question I've been chewing on since the festival—What the fuck was that?—but instead, what comes out is, "You want a Coke? It's hot as hell."

He shrugs, then follows me up the steps, boots making no sound on the old wood. The porch sags under our combined weight, but he doesn't seem to notice. The dogs crowd around his legs, noses working, and he gives each a gentle pat on the head. Mystic goes stiff, then leans in, as if she's forgotten she's supposed to be the tough one.

Inside, the air is marginally cooler, the air conditioner chugging along like a dying animal; I really need to replace it. Maybe next payday. I grab two sodas from the fridge, wipe the condensation on my shirt, and hand one over. His fingers brush mine, just for a second. It's enough to short-circuit my brain.

We stand in the kitchen. I don't invite him to sit, and he doesn't try. There's an awkward silence, the kind that would last forever if someone didn't break it.

"So," I say. "You want to explain what happened at the festival, or should we just agree to never speak of it again?"

He leans against the counter, arms crossed, every inch of him a lesson in how to own a room. "I'd rather talk about now," he says.

I laugh, high and weird. "Now is just like then, except with less funnel cake and more regret."

He stares at me, eyes narrowed, and for a second I think he might actually be mad. But then he says, "I didn't mean to scare you."

That pulls me up short. I set my soda down and cross my arms, a weak imitation of his stance. "I wasn't scared," I lie. "I was... surprised. And maybe a little pissed off."

He looks at me, really looks, like he's cataloging every micro-expression and storing it for later. "You're a terrible liar."

"Guess I'm out of practice," I say, and try to laugh it off.

He doesn't let me. "Who hurt you?"

The question is so blunt, so out of nowhere, I almost choke. I think about telling him to fuck off. Instead, I look down at the scar on my forearm, the one from the glass lamp my ex threw at me during what the police called a "domestic disturbance." I think about the stalker in Tennessee, the one who kept showing up outside my job until I moved states and changed my number. I think about the years I spent convincing myself I was hard to love, that wanting anything made you a target.

I shrug, because it's easier than talking. "What makes you think someone hurt me?"

He doesn't blink. "I know the signs. And you never look at me the same way twice."

I can't decide if that's supposed to be romantic or terrifying, so I just say, "Maybe you're hard to look at."

He smiles, but there are no teeth in it. "That's not it."

The silence threatens to swallow us again, so I do what I always do: I change the subject. "Look, I need to run to town. The dogs are almost out of food, and I'm low on... everything. You want to come, or are you just going to lurk around my property like a sexy cryptid?"

He tilts his head. "You think I'm sexy?"

Oh, fuck me. "I think you're a pain in the ass. But you clean up nice."

He grins, wider this time, and I want to punch him and kiss him in the same breath. "I'll ride with you," he says.

I grab my keys and the dogs' leashes, trying not to notice the way his eyes follow me. Outside, the heat has gone from oppressive to personal, the sun low and angry. The dogs jump into the backseat with practiced ease, and Loki holds the driver's side door open for me like it's 1952. I blush, and I'm a little upset with myself that I did. I slide in, and he shuts it.

He walks around the truck and climbs in. He slides in close enough that I can smell him—smoke and pine and something sharp, like ozone. I start the engine, and for a moment we just sit there, the AC blowing stale air, neither of us willing to make the first move.

"Town it is," I say, and pull onto the dirt road, the trailer shrinking behind us.

As we drive, he stares straight ahead, but his hand drums a tattoo on the console, fingers moving with restless energy. I want to ask him what's wrong, but instead, I just keep driving, eyes on the road, pretending I can't feel the heat radiating from his skin.

We don't talk. Not yet.

But I know, with a certainty that makes my stomach flip, that we will.

There's only one road into Pine Hollow, and it passes straight through the center of town like a vein you can't hide. The hardware store sits at the heart of it—halfway between the ancient post office and a taco stand that only operates on odd-numbered days. I pull up to Henderson's, and before I even kill the engine, the dogs are barking at the parade of smells rolling off the building. In the summer, it's a chemical soup: grass seed, tractor grease, cigarettes, and an underlayer of dried-out garden snakes they always forget to clean out of the bug zappers.

I tug the leash, and Ash launches himself into the gravel lot, dragging Mystic (and me) behind. Loki hangs back for a second, like he's testing the air for traps, then slides out of the car with that elastic, too-smooth grace. He squints at the sun and buttons his shirt up one more snap, which would be weird on anyone else, but on him, it just looks intentional.

Mr. Henderson—Mr. H to everyone under seventy—waits behind the counter, thick arms crossed over his "Ask Me About My Screwdrivers" T-shirt. He's as much a fixture as the rusty nail bins or the row of haunted-looking snow shovels that have never, not once, seen snow.

"Amethyst!" he calls, voice booming across the store. "You're looking—" he pauses, clocking my sweat-and-mud situation, "—well, you're looking like you've been busy."

I resist the urge to salute. "Just trying to keep the local weeds from forming a union."

He laughs, a sound that's equal parts cough and chainsaw. "That's what I like about you. Always ready with a comeback, even when you're losing."

Mystic and Ash rush up for their ritual dog treats, and Mr. H obliges, scratching behind their ears with a tenderness that would get him banned from most biker bars. Loki stays just inside the doorway, arms at his sides, eyes darting around the aisles like he's memorizing escape routes. The only other people in the store are two old men from the VFW and a mom with a kid who's busy finger-painting rude words into the dust on a bag of peat moss.

"Glad you're here," Mr. H says, lowering his voice a notch. "Strangest thing Saturday night. Power cut out right as I was counting the till, but only for a minute. All the bulbs went blue, and the radio started playing backward. My old man always said that meant a cold front was coming, but the air never moved. Not even a breeze."

I nod, like I haven't heard three versions of this story already. "Was probably a power surge. Or a solar flare. Or, you know, the rapture."

Mr. H chortles, then leans closer. "You didn't see anything weird out at your place, did you?"

Before I can answer, the VFW guys start arguing over by the seed display. "I'm telling you, Walt, my eyes aren't what they used to be, but I saw it. Lights, like you wouldn't believe. Looked like the whole damn sky was doing Morse code."

Walt grunts. "My daddy always said weird lights meant the Pine Walker was stirring."

His buddy makes a scoffing noise, but it dies fast. The words just hang there: Pine Walker.

I shoot a look at Mr. H, who shrugs. "Old story," he mutters. "Every county's got a monster."

"I thought that was just a campfire thing," I say, then immediately regret it.

He gives me a look that says, "Not as campfire as you'd think." Then, louder: "What can I help you with today, Amethyst?"

I recite my list—pet-safe weed killer, zip ties, a hose nozzle, and whatever they have in the way of dog-safe ant bait. Mr. H scribbles it all down, then nods at Loki. "And your friend?"

I hesitate, half-expecting Loki to fake a Scandinavian accent or drop some obscure request for wolf's-bane. Instead, he just says, "I'm good, thank you," with a warmth that might actually fool someone who hadn't watched him nearly glitch reality in front of a hundred people last weekend.

Mr. H grins, but there's something off about it. He's clocked Loki, maybe even recognizes him from the festival. Or maybe it's the way Loki stands, like he's not quite attached to the floor.

The mom and her kid check out, but as they do, the cash register fritzes—first a high-pitched whine, then a flurry of weird, random numbers. The screen flashes, then dies. For a second, I see something on the glass—a shape, a rune, bright enough to make me flinch.

The kid laughs. "Cool glitch, mister!"

Mr. H grumbles, thumps the register, and it resets with a noise that sounds suspiciously like a sigh. The mom mutters something about "mercury in retrograde" and hustles out, kid trailing behind.

I walk the aisles, Loki trailing close, picking up odd bits and stacking them in a basket. At one point, I glance at the dust on a bag of fertilizer and see a pattern—another rune, just for a second, before I wipe it away. The air smells faintly of ozone, and I wonder if I'm the only one who notices.

As I check out, Mr. H leans in, voice barely above a whisper. "Honey, you sure you're alright? You look… tired. More tired than usual." He glances at Loki, then at the dogs, then back at me.

I force a smile. "I'm fine. Just a weird week."

He slips an extra pack of batteries and a heavy-duty flashlight onto the pile, no charge. "Just in case. Power's still flickering. You let me know if you need anything, you hear?"

"I hear," I say.

He bags up my stuff, double-knots the dog treats, and hands it over with a look that's equal parts concern and conspiracy. "You take care. Maybe stay close to home until the weirdness blows over."

I nod, but the words stick. "Will do."

On the way out, Loki catches my arm, just a brush of fingers, and says, "You have people here. They care about you."

I snort. "Yeah, the way you care about a loose wire. Or a stray dog."

He doesn't answer, just smiles with that look that means he knows more than he should. The dogs pile into the truck, shedding fur and dignity all over the backseat. I load the bags, feeling the weight of every glance from inside the store.

As we pull out, I see Mr. H watching from the window, one hand on the counter, eyes narrowed. It's not suspicion, exactly. It's more like he's bracing for the next storm.

I can't blame him. I feel it too.

We drive away, the sun now a deep red smear behind the trees, and the world feels smaller and more dangerous than it did this morning.

But at least I have extra batteries.

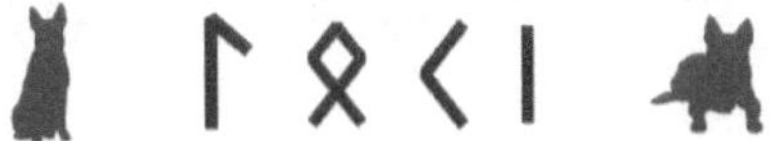

The Pineridge Market is a social trauma generator even on a good day. The doors whoosh open, and the blast of manufactured air hits me full in the face, the scent of citrus floor cleaner barely masking the undertone of meat cooler and despair. Mystic and Ash do a practiced "stay" in the shade while Loki and I head inside, grabbing a cart that squeals with every fourth rotation.

Inside, the noise is worse than the heat: babies wailing, pop country on the speakers, and the relentless drone of every human in a thirty-mile radius doing their shopping at the same damn time. I haven't even made it to the dog food aisle when I catch the first whisper.

"—I'm telling you, it was her. The purple-haired one. She was right there when it happened—"

"—my nephew says he saw her eyes go all crazy, like those deep-sea fish—"

"—and that's not even the first time. I heard she—"

I round the corner and the two women from the pharmacy pretend to study vitamins, but their necks turn in unison, tracking me like I'm a tornado warning. I nod, polite, and they smile with the rictus of people who will never, ever buy anything I'm selling.

Loki follows, hands in pockets, looking more relaxed than I've ever seen him. "You're popular," he murmurs.

"Yeah, I'm running for Queen of the Apocalypse," I say, loading dog food and some snacks for me into the cart. "Want to be my campaign manager?"

He grins, but his eyes flick past me, scanning every face. I get the feeling he's reading the room like a chessboard, memorizing who's likely to bolt and who's likely to form a mob.

I try to be quick, grabbing something quick for dinner. When we reach the checkout, the lines are long and slow and packed with the kind of retirees who think six feet of personal space is a tool of the devil. In front of me, a woman with a pyramid of canned beans keeps sneaking glances over her shoulder, like she's worried I'll rearrange her chakras if she blinks.

"Did you see the lights?" she whispers to the checker.

The checker, a guy my age with tragic facial piercings, nods. "Freaked my cat out so bad he hid under the fridge for two days. I heard it was some kind of chemical leak."

The woman shakes her head. "No, it was her. She's marked."

I snort, just loud enough for her to hear. "Marked for what? Double-coupon Tuesdays?"

She goes crimson but doesn't back down. "My great-grandma used to say the Pine Walker marks the ones it wants. My nephew saw—"

I cut her off. "Your nephew needs less Reddit."

The checker tries not to smile, but it's a losing battle. He starts scanning my stuff, but the register flickers, then dies, then comes back with a high-pitched squeal that makes the hair on my arms stand up. The scanner makes a weird symbol—almost a rune—then flashes blue.

He glances up, suddenly nervous. "Sorry, miss, system's a little weird today. We've had techs out twice."

I look behind me. The line is backing up, and people are whispering even louder now. I see a phone pointed at me—someone's recording, probably hoping I'll start levitating or shooting lightning from my eyes.

Loki shifts his weight, close enough to touch, and says, "Want me to cause a distraction?"

I shake my head. "If you start juggling chainsaws or chanting in Latin, they'll burn down the store. Let's just get out of here."

The checker bags my stuff by hand, then hands over the receipt. "You have a good day, ma'am," he says, but the look in his eyes is pure "please don't haunt my dreams."

I push the cart out, Loki walking beside me, the world suddenly sharper and more hostile than when we walked in.

I untie the dogs from the shady place by the door. They greet us like we've been gone a month. I crank the truck, load them in the back seat, and toss them a treat. Then I start to load the bags, hands shaking harder than I want to admit.

Loki picks up the bag of dog food and drops it in the bed of the truck and leans against it, watching me. "Does it bother you? Being the center of all this?"

"Would it bother you?" I ask.

He shrugs. "I've always liked the attention."

I close the door. "Well, I don't. I just want to be left alone."

He studies me, then nods, accepting that answer, and we both get in the truck.

As we drive away, I see the pharmacy women outside, heads together, still staring after us. For a second, I think I see the reflection of a rune in the glass behind them, bright and cold as a winter star.

Maybe it's just the sun.

But I don't believe that, not for a second.

We cut across the feed store parking lot, and I remember I still need gas, or I'll be hoofing it home in the dark, with nothing but two dogs and a cosmic punchline for company. The station is empty except for an old man and his grandson, who always gives me a discount on beef jerky if I let him scratch behind Mystic's ears. Tonight, though, they both watch us pull in with a gravity that makes the air go heavy.

Loki offers to pump, which would normally make me suspicious, but the need to hide in the blessed cold of the station is stronger than my pride. I slip inside, the bell announcing my arrival to the ancient, yellow-lit world of Cool Ranch Doritos and lottery displays.

The kid at the counter—barely sixteen, face a patchwork of acne and determination—nods to me. "Hey, Miss Amethyst. You okay out there? Saw the commotion at the market."

I shrug. "Just need gas and a sugar rush."

He grins, but it dies fast when the old man comes out from the back, wiping his hands on a dish towel so old it's more holes than cloth. His eyes, normally clouded, go sharp when they land on me.

"Evenin', Miz Gold," he says, voice thick as honey and twice as slow. "Haven't seen signs like this since I was a boy. 'Course, back then, we knew to stay inside."

I half-laugh, trying to shake off the chill. "Signs? Like weird weather, or—"

He cuts me off with a look. "Like the Walker. Folks don't talk about it now, but when things go sideways—when the sky turns colors and animals quit making noise—you keep the porch light off and pray it passes over."

The kid shifts behind the counter, uncomfortable. "Grandpa, c'mon, that's just stories."

Grandpa shakes his head. "You don't remember. I do." His gaze flicks to the window, where Loki stands beside the dogs, head tilted toward the woods like he hears a tune no one else can. "Walker only comes out when there's something it wants. Or someone."

I try to smile, but my face won't cooperate. "Well, I'm just here for gas, so I'll be out of your hair in a minute."

He softens, just a little. "Not your fault, child. None of this is ever the fault of the marked."

It feels like a curse and a benediction.

I pay, grab a couple of candy bars for the road, and meet Loki outside.

He's got a look on his face I can't read—a mix of triumph and regret, like he just watched his favorite movie and remembered how it ends. "They know," he says, not a question.

"They all do," I reply. "But it's not just me, is it?"

He shakes his head. "No. But you're the focus. You always have been."

I'm not sure I want to know what he means. We pile into the car, and the dogs curl up tight, as if they can smell what's coming.

The only place left to eat in Pine Hollow after eight p.m. is the Diner, a squat rectangle of cinder block and neon that smells like syrup and burnt bacon grease even from the parking lot. I almost drive past, but my stomach rebels at the thought of another night's sleep ruined by low blood sugar and higher anxiety.

Inside, the crowd is down to the regulars—four off-duty cops in the corner, a pair of local teens sharing fries, and a booth of retirees who have been here so long the vinyl is molded to their butts. The woman at the counter, Ruby, gives me a tired wave and sets out a menu without asking what I want. She's one of the few people in town who's never judged me, at least not to my face. And they ignore when I bring the dogs in. Maybe they assume they are service dogs; I don't know and I don't care.

We sit in a corner booth, Loki across from me, the dogs curled under the table like a pair of bodyguards. The fluorescent lights flicker, and the air is thick with the hum of too many conversations overlapping, none of them interesting enough to listen to but all of them impossible to ignore.

I order pancakes, eggs, and extra sausage. Loki just says, "Coffee. Black." He drums his fingers on the table, tapping out a pattern I almost recognize but can't place.

We're not even halfway through the first awkward silence when the room goes weird. It starts with the windows—runic shapes, clear as day, etching themselves into the condensation. Not subtle, not hidden. Everyone sees it.

The retirees freeze, forks in midair. The teens drop their phones. One of the cops stands, hand on his belt like he's going to draw on the supernatural.

Then the lights go dead, plunging the whole diner into an electric blue gloom. The only illumination is from the runes, which glow like embers and throw long, warped shadows across the linoleum.

The dogs whine, hackles up.

The silence stretches so long I almost forget to breathe.

Then, one by one, every screen in the building—phones, register, the old CRT TV over the counter—flickers to life, showing the same impossible symbol: a spiral ringed with spikes, the exact mark I saw on my hand that morning. It pulses, then resolves into a word I don't know how to read, but it still hits me with the force of a freight train.

Survival.

Ruby yelps, drops a plate, and the crash snaps the room back to reality. The lights stutter on, the runes vanish, and the room explodes in noise.

"Did you see that—"

"—not possible, not possible—"

"—call the sheriff—"

Loki sits back, arms folded, like he's just watched a fireworks show and is waiting for the finale. The retirees bolt, muttering about the end times. The teens follow, nearly knocking over a table in their rush.

I sit, staring at my hands, which are shaking so badly I can't hold my fork.

Ruby approaches, face pale. "You alright, sugar?" she asks. But her eyes flick to Loki, then back to me, and she flinches when our fingers almost touch.

"I'm fine," I say, voice thinner than I want.

She sets down the check, hands trembling, and whispers, "You oughta get out of town for a while, Amethyst. Just till things calm down."

I want to laugh, but the urge dies quick. "Yeah," I say. "Maybe I will."

Loki stands, leaving cash on the table. He looks at Ruby, and for a second she meets his gaze, but then her eyes slide away like they can't bear the sight of him.

We walk out into the night, the parking lot empty, the town's neon reflecting off the low cloud cover in sickly, supernatural hues.

"You did that, didn't you?" I say, once the door swings shut behind us.

He shrugs. "We did it. Energy's been building for days. Your presence draws it in, amplifies it."

"Why me?"

He looks at me, and there's actual pain in it, real as bone. "Because you see it. You always have."

I want to scream, or punch him, or drag him to the ground and demand he make the world normal again. But all I can do is stand there, heart beating so loud I'm surprised the whole town doesn't hear it.

The drive home is silent. Not tense, not angry—just empty, like every word has already been spoken and there's nothing left but aftermath.

As we pull onto my road, Loki says, "It won't stop now. Not for a while."

"Then what do I do?" I ask.

He doesn't answer, but his hand finds mine, and for the first time all night, I feel something like hope.

Not much. But enough.

The road to my place is just two ruts in the clay and a thousand years of bad decisions. We drive it slow, the only sound the tires crunching over gravel and the breathless pant of the dogs in back, who have gone from feral to funereal in the space of half an hour.

The world feels wrong. The woods to either side crowd the headlights, the branches clawing at the car like they want to peel off the paint and get to the marrow underneath. The air is so thick I can't even taste my own fear over it, and my hands ache from gripping the wheel too tight.

I pull up to the trailer, engine ticking down, and just sit for a second. Loki makes no move to leave. The dogs wait, silent, not even a whine from Mystic, who usually tap-dances on the backseat when we come home late.

I kill the lights, and for the first time, I see it: a slow, ghostly glow deep in the woods, not moonlight, not the neighbor's porch lamp, but something colder, bluer, and so steady it has to be watching us.

"You see that?" I ask.

Loki nods, face unreadable. "They're coming. Sooner than I thought."

"Who?" I say, but I know. The Walker. Something even scarier? The whole damn town with torches and hashtags? Take your pick.

He turns to me, eyes flat and real. "This level of activity—what happened at the diner—someone will have noticed. Someone with teeth."

"Great," I say. "So we just... wait? Hide?"

He laughs, but it's empty. "You're not the hiding kind."

I want to deny it, to tell him he doesn't know me. I used to be one who didn't hide, but now... I sigh. I don't have a comeback.

We unload in silence, moving like fugitives. The dogs slink inside and park themselves in the hallway, facing the door. I dump the groceries on the counter, not caring if the eggs crack, not caring about anything except the feeling that there are eyes on me from every wall, every window, every flick of shadow in the room.

Loki stands in the living room, hands loose at his sides, head cocked like he's waiting for instructions from God. Or whatever god he still believes in. I look at him, and something inside me cracks, the last veneer of normality flaking off and leaving only the raw, needy thing underneath.

"Why did you come back?" I ask, the words small but sharp.

He takes a step closer, and I realize he's shaking, just a little, like it costs him to stand still. "Because you're the only thing in this world I want to be real."

He means it. I can feel it, the way a tuning fork knows when it's found its frequency. I should be scared, but I'm not. Not of him.

I close the gap, grab the front of his shirt in both fists. "Show me," I say, and then I'm kissing him, hard and messy, teeth knocking together, lips bruised and open.

He responds like a man who's spent a century starving. His hands go to my hair, my back, pulling me in so close it hurts, and the hurt feels like a prayer.

We stumble to the couch, knocking over a lamp, and I hear the dogs reposition, as if giving us privacy out of sheer embarrassment. I laugh into his mouth, and he laughs back, a low rumble that vibrates through my bones.

I have to admit, the man can kiss. This time it's not just a simple kiss. His lips trail across my cheek and down my neck, making me shiver.

He bites my neck, not hard, just enough to mark me, and I let him. My nails rake his back, and he groans, low and dark, and says my name in a way no one ever has—like it's a password or a curse.

He pulls back and brushes his fingers over my face. I blush and glance down. I feel like I need to say ...something, but I have no clue what to say. I bury my face in his chest, breathing him in, letting his heartbeat sync up with mine.

We curl up on the couch. He traces the line of my collarbone, the gesture gentle and so out of character I almost cry.

"We don't have much time," he says, his voice a whisper.

"What do you mean?" I reply, pulling him closer.

Later, when the world has settled to a hush and the dogs are asleep at our feet, I ask, "Is it always like this with you? The chaos?"

He smiles, lazy and satisfied, and I see a glint of gold in his eyes. "Only when I'm lucky."

I shake my head. "You're trouble."

He shrugs, unbothered. "You like trouble."

And damn it, he's right... when it's shaped like him.

The headlights pass over the windows, the blue glow recedes. I see people getting lost and turning around in my drive all the time, so I think nothing of it.

For a little while, the world is just two people on a couch, clinging to each other like it's the only thing that matters.

Maybe it is.

I wake up hours later, the sky outside bleached to the pre-dawn gray that makes everything feel possible and impossible at once. Loki is asleep, arm draped over my waist, hair wild and beautiful. For a minute, I just watch him, memorizing the shape of his mouth, the way he sighs when I shift against him.

Then I hear it: a car door, soft and deliberate.

I slip off the couch, careful not to wake him, and go to the window. There's a black SUV parked at the end of my drive, headlights off. A man and woman stand beside it, both dressed like they mean business. The woman holds a tablet, and she looks like she's scanning my house.

I shiver, but not from the cold.

I pad back to the living room, crouch by Loki's head, and whisper, "Someone is out there."

He opens his eyes, fully awake, and for the first time I see fear in him. Not much, but enough. He gets up, and by the time we reach the window, they are gone.

"Maybe they were just... lost?" I say, knowing that isn't true.

Loki looks at me like I should know better. "Well, they are gone... for now," I mutter.

CHAPTER ELEVEN

SIEGE

Twelve hours after every screen in Pine Hollow's diner had displayed the same impossible symbol, the first black SUV rolled into the woods. Agent Mercer's team was setting up a perimeter around the source. The footage from inside the restaurant had been classified within minutes of upload.

The trailer is a quarter mile further down, out of sight behind the rise, but it doesn't take a genius to know these people didn't come for the view.

Four agents spill from the SUVs, each of them clad in tailored blue-black, the sort of suit that says, "I have a badge and also a black budget." Even their shoes are shined to a weaponized gleam, which is impressive in a world full of red dirt and pine needles. They gather at the tailgate, the biggest of the four opening the hatch with the confidence of a man who's never been denied.

Agent Mercer, the leader, has her hair cut so close to her scalp it looks like it was painted on, but there's nothing soft about her. The rest of the team stands with their hands behind their backs, like they're waiting to be called to the firing line. Mercer wields a tablet with a custom-molded grip and a screen that glows blue, saturated with satellite overlays and pulsing with little dots that probably mark every living thing for five miles.

They start unpacking equipment with a weird choreography, each piece nested in dense black foam, each device flashing or beeping like it's eager to get to work: EMF meters, thermal imagers, boxy cameras with lens clusters like insect eyes.

"The anomalies have been increasing in frequency," Mercer says, voice flat and unhurried. She stabs a finger at the tablet. "Last week we had two spikes in this sector. Three more in the last forty-eight hours. Whatever's happening, it doesn't fit any of the existing parameters."

The second-in-command, a heavyset man with a jaw like a shovel blade, nods as if he's been waiting all his life for something that doesn't fit. "What's the nearest projection?"

Mercer doesn't look up. "Four hundred meters, due southeast. Adjacent to the civilian's residence. Readings are aberrant—extremely high variance, no baseline correlation. Teams will deploy in pairs. We sweep and log, no intervention unless absolutely necessary." She hands the tablet to the next in line, a woman with steel-rimmed glasses, then starts distributing equipment, including a holster with a compact sidearm that looks nothing like standard issue, unless you're in a sci-fi movie.

Rodriguez finally finds his voice. "What exactly are we looking for, ma'am?" His question hangs in the air, breathless, like he's hoping the answer will be "just a test, don't worry."

Mercer fixes him with the kind of look that could pickle a frog. "Unusual light patterns. Electromagnetic surges. Shadow markings—locals call them 'Twilight Runes.' Anything that deviates from standard field behavior." She doles out the last of the devices and checks her own scanner, which hums and warbles as she calibrates it against the wind.

Mercer splits them into pairs, sending Rodriguez and the jawline guy north, while she and Glasses Woman cut east along the tree line. They move in silence, save for the wet crunch of pine needles and the periodic burble of a walkie. Their equipment pings and chirps, little digital birdsong, and sometimes there's a flash of blue when one of the meters registers something interesting.

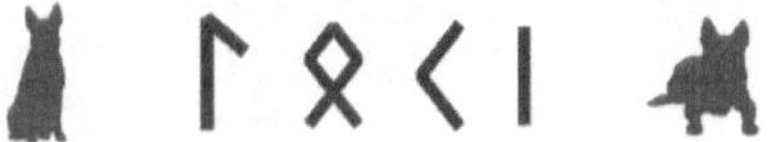

I'm sitting at the kitchen table like it's just another Tuesday, hands cupped around a mug of tea that's been cold so long it tastes like regret. Ever since Loki left, the dogs won't stop circling, like someone or something is prowling around out there. Mystic posts up at the north window, nose pressed hard to the screen, body quivering every time she catches movement in the yard. Ash takes the southern flank, growling low at a patch of trees he's always hated, eyes never blinking. I can't decide if their paranoia is making mine worse, or if it's the only reason I'm not running out there with a baseball bat and a flashlight.

My phone buzzes against the Formica, screen lighting up the corner of the table. The text is from Loki.

'Don't go outside. We have visitors.'

I get up and pace to the window, careful to keep my head low so whoever is out there doesn't catch a reflection. Sure enough, I can see shadows moving at the edge of my property, ducking in and out of the trees with weird little instruments.

Mystic abandons her watch post and presses against my thigh, making this pitiful whine she never uses unless she's dead scared. I try to pet her, but my hand's shaking so badly I can't.

"It's okay, babies," I whisper, my voice the kind of lie you use on toddlers when the storm's right overhead. "We're safe in here." I hope she believes it more than I do.

I text Loki back:

'Who are they?'

I want to ask how he knows that. Where he is?

No response. I set the phone on the windowsill, where it makes a tiny clack against the pane, and peek out again.

The dogs pace the floor, matching each other's stride, their bodies always between me and the door. The hair on Ash's back stands up in a ridge, and Mystic's ears flick every time the agents make a new noise. I reach for the old baseball bat I keep by the stove, not because I think it'll help, but because I'd rather be nervous and armed than just nervous.

The air in the trailer feels heavy, thick with the kind of anticipation that usually precedes a tornado warning. I stare at the phone, willing Loki to answer, but it just sits there, black and silent, like it's decided to betray me along with everything else.

Then, out of nowhere, both dogs lose their minds—barking, snapping, throwing themselves at the door. It's not the kind of bark they use for squirrels or stray possums. This is the bark they saved for that one time a coyote got at the chickens, the bark that says something alive and danger-ous is right outside the threshold.

I grip the bat, breath frozen, and stare at the patch of darkness just beyond the porch light, heart punching holes in my chest. The agents are out there, sure. But the dogs aren't barking at them.

There's something else in the woods.

The first thing I notice is the drop in temperature. Not the kind that comes with nightfall, but a sudden, bone-deep chill that makes the air feel sharp and metallic. The dogs sense it too, tails stiff, bodies vibrating with the urge to chase or run or both. Mystic's lips pull back in a snarl.

There's a figure between the pines, tall and lean. He moves with a liquid grace, and even from here, I know it's him: Loki. He doesn't walk so much as glide, his body rippling at the edges, like he's not quite committed to being all the way solid. I press my palm to the glass, breath fogging the pane, and watch.

From where I stand at the window, I can see how Loki cocks his head, studying the agent like a cat studies a trapped bird. He lifts his sleeve—barely, just enough—and I see the runes light, practically burning through his skin, pulsing with a light that's both green and not green, a color I can't name. He murmurs something, too quiet for the agents or me to catch, but the sound travels through the air and turns the shadows feral.

The darkness thickens around one of them, and for a second, he's lost in it, waving his scanner like a lifeline. Then, from the brush, a coyote bolts—huge, gaunt, with eyes that burn like embers. The agent yelps and falls back, stumbling over a root as the animal blurs past him, disappearing into the undergrowth. The scanner clatters to the ground, forgotten.

Inside, the dogs lose their shit. They bark and howl, noses to the door, desperate to join the chase. I grab their collars, knuckles white, and try to drag them back. "No," I hiss, "not tonight, not now," but I can barely hold them. My heart is right there with them, slamming against my ribs.

My phone buzzes again, and I snatch it up. The message is from Loki, clipped and clinical:

'Government agents. Supernatural division. Stay inside.'

I want to text back something clever, something snarky, about Mulder from The X-Files, but my hands are shaking too hard. He can't be serious; there isn't really a supernatural division… is there? I just watch as Loki keeps pace with the agents from the shadow line, never breaking cover. When they try to regroup, he stretches out his hand, palm down, and the air distorts—ripples, bends, and then goes dead still. The agents start arguing, then split up, their voices rising in confusion.

The cold in the house deepens, and for a second, I wonder if Loki's doing it on purpose, a kind of signal flare meant only for me. The dogs settle, just for a heartbeat, and Mystic stares at the window like she can see him standing there, waiting.

I stare, too, and in the darkness, I see the faint outline of a face—pale, sharp, eyes burning with that impossible green-gold. He nods once, like he knows I'm watching. Then he's gone, melting into the night as if he'd never been.

I check the phone again, but there's nothing more from Loki. I want to believe the worst is over, but I know better. This is just the prelude. The real show hasn't even started yet.

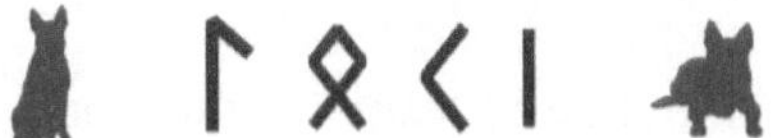

The leader and her partner—a big guy with a scar on his chin—are the first to break the line. They move in slow, deliberate steps, their scanners lit up with pulsing LED arrays that strobe blue and then red every few feet. The moment they hit the edge of my property, I feel it; I don't understand how, but it's like a static charge popping through the soles of my feet and up my spine. The dogs feel it too: Mystic's hackles bristle again, and Ash lets out a sound halfway between a growl and a whimper. The agents aren't even bothering to be quiet; I can hear them. I really need to get this trailer better insulated.

"Mercer, we've got something," the partner says, his voice so clear in the night I almost answer him myself. Mercer stops, reading the tablet, and then bends to snap photos of the ground where the grass seems to shimmer with a wet, silvery gleam. The effect isn't just a trick of the light. It pulses, like the ground itself is breathing.

They are close enough I can hear them from inside.

Mercer points and says, "Look at this. Right here." Her voice is less clinical now, more... reverent? I press my head to the glass and watch as she kneels, careful, and angles her flashlight along the dirt. Symbols crawl up through the dead grass—curling, twisting marks that rearrange themselves every time she moves her head. The runes. My breath sticks in my throat.

She reaches for one, slow as you please, but the air around her hand ripples, like a stone thrown into a still pond. She hesitates, then tries again.

This time, her glove frosts over, a spidery filigree of ice racing from her fingertips to her wrist.

Mercer doesn't even flinch. She leans in, eyes locked on the shifting symbol, and presses the shutter on her phone over and over, as if one of the pictures will give her a clue. Then her radio crackles, sharp enough to make me jump, and they are close enough I can hear their radios from inside.

"Rodriguez to command. We have movement on the west edge. Large animal—possible coyote, but it's acting wrong. Equipment malfunctioning, visual interference, requesting protocol update." His voice is tight, an octave higher than before, like he's trying not to squeal like a kid.

Mercer straightens, shakes the frost from her glove, and keys her mic. "Maintain visual. Don't engage. Set up perimeter and monitor for escalation."

Inside, the dogs start to pace again, faster, the tension winding tighter with each lap. I run a hand through my hair, trying to remember if I ever learned what you're supposed to do when government agents surround your house and start talking to the ground. I snort and shake my head.

Mercer stands at the edge of the lawn, hands on her hips, and scans the house with that cold, implacable stare. For a second, our eyes meet—I swear she can see me, even though the light's against her. She doesn't smile, doesn't wave, just turns and starts talking to her partner in low, fast bursts.

Whatever they're doing out there, it's not just observation anymore. It's containment. They are containing me.

The pressure in the air builds, like the charge before a lightning strike, and I can almost hear the runes humming beneath the soil. I close my eyes and breathe deep, steady, grounding myself with the heartbeat of the dogs at my feet.

This is it. The standoff.

And I have no idea which side I'm supposed to be rooting for.

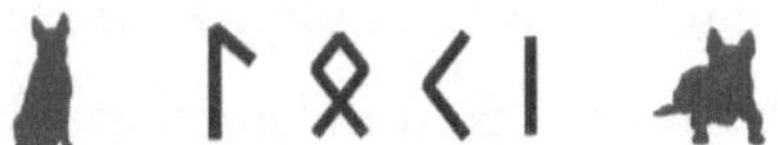

Dusk slides in like a velvet trap, the sky bleeding from peach to violet while the air grows heavy and slow. I can't remember the last time I was so aware of a sunset, but tonight every second counts. The agents are jittery as squirrels, pacing their perimeter, double-checking every cable and spike, voices rising in short bursts over their radios. The dogs are restless, tails flagging, ears trained on the windows, as if they're waiting for a signal only they can hear.

It starts with a flicker. I catch it in the far corner of the yard, just where the property line drops toward the creek: a thread of blue-green light, thin as fishing line, weaving through the weeds. It brightens, writhes, then pops into a knot of runes that hover inches above the ground, rotating like a lazy coin. My breath snags—no amount of denial can make this look normal. It's not a trick of the light. The runes are moving... alive.

The agents see it too. Mercer shouts, "Visual! Visual!" and her team converges, meters and tablets at the ready. The lights on their devices go berserk, strobing and alarms wailing in chorus. Mercer yells, "Every piece of equipment is seizing up—screens are frozen, needles spiking." One of the agents swears and yanks his glove off, shaking his fingers like a hot wire bit him. Another smacks her scanner against her thigh, but the screen is black.

Inside the trailer, the air takes on a weird, ozone tang, sharp and sweet at the same time. The runes crawl over the yellowed windows, painting the whole living room in neon ghost light. My shadow stretches long across the wall, shot through with streaks of blue-green, and for a second it's like I'm watching someone else live my life, a puppet on a haunted stage.

The runes multiply, gathering speed and number. They ring the house in a perfect circle, each new symbol locking into place with a tiny pop and a flare of light. The circle completes with a suddenness that knocks the air out of my lungs—like the last number of a combination lock clicking home.

The agents panic. They scramble for the SUVs, radios blaring static; nothing works. One tries to jump the line into my yard, but the moment his boot hits the glowing grass, he's thrown backward, skidding through the pine needles and landing hard against a stump. The runes don't even blink.

Then Loki appears. He steps out from behind a pine the size of a mini-van, hands in his pockets like he's just out for an evening stroll. His eyes burn green-gold, and when he looks at me—really looks at me—I feel it all the way to my bones. He walks toward the house, unhurried, and the runes part for him, bending inward like grass in a high wind.

He reaches the steps and pauses. For a second, everything is silent—the agents frozen, the dogs quiet, even the runes holding their breath. Then he crosses the threshold, and the whole world explodes.

The runes shoot upward, forming a dome of light around the house. Everything from the forest to the house. The sound is a long, rolling thunder that rattles the dishes in the cupboard and makes my ears ring. The dome pulses, then settles, the runes rippling across its surface like water in a pond. It's fifteen feet high if it's an inch, and so bright I have to squint to see Loki standing just outside the front door.

Inside the dome, it's quiet again. The dogs settle at my feet, still but alert, eyes glued to the man on the porch. I want to move, to say something, but

I can't. The sight of him—the realness of him, here, now—is almost too much. He knocks once, light as a whisper.

The agent, I think it was Rodriguez, makes a rookie mistake. Maybe it's fear, maybe it's ego, but he barrels straight at the glowing edge of the dome, arms pumping, face set like he's about to tackle a linebacker. The moment he hits the runes, he's picked up and tossed—literally tossed—ten feet backward, spinning in the air before slamming into a pine with a crack I feel all the way up my spine. He drops, limp, and lies still for a few heartbeats before rolling over and groaning.

The other agents don't take it well. Two of them draw sidearms, sweeping the dome like they're expecting it to fall to a few rounds of jacketed lead. Mercer barks orders, her voice tight and brittle, but her hands never stop moving—she's already unclipped a weird, gun-shaped device from her belt, something with a glass coil and a blue diode that pulses in sync with the runes outside.

Loki steps up to the door and knocks once. I yank it open before he can knock again. Up close, he looks tired—lines at the corners of his eyes, hair wind-tangled, but his gaze is steady and weirdly gentle. He doesn't smile, but his eyes are kind. "May I come in?" he asks, his voice low and warm.

"What the hell is happening?" I demand, grabbing his sleeve and hauling him inside before Mercer's team can draw a bead on him. The dogs circle his legs, sniffing with the same cautious reverence they reserve for thunderstorms, then plant themselves at his feet, tails wagging slowly.

He closes the door with a careful click. "The runes have recognized the threat. They're protecting you—and, incidentally, me. No one else can cross the barrier now. Not unless..." He trails off, and I don't like the look that flickers across his face.

"Not unless what?" I ask, already dreading the answer.

He shrugs, and his hand finds mine—cool and sure, like a grounding wire. "Not unless someone on the inside wants out badly enough to break the seal. Or unless the agents outside find a way to disrupt the pattern. But that's... unlikely."

Outside, Mercer's team is regrouping. I hear the low, frantic buzz of radios, catch the flash of their tactical lights as they sweep the dome, searching for a weakness. Rodriguez staggers upright, supported by his partner, and they both glare at the runes as if they're personally insulted by the laws of physics.

Loki watches them with detached interest, like he's observing lab mice. "They'll call for backup," he says, "but it won't matter. The runes are self-sustaining now."

I pull my hand away, more out of habit than distrust. "So we're just... stuck? What happens if they start shooting?"

He grins, just a flicker of the old mischief. "Then you'll have some very angry local law enforcement in your yard, and the government will have a lot of paperwork to fill out. But don't worry. The dome is bulletproof, at least for now."

Mystic settles next to Loki's boot, tail thumping. Ash leans against my thigh, warm and solid, and I realize my hands have stopped shaking.

Through the window, I watch Mercer pace the edge of the dome, barking into her radio, waving her arms as if sheer force of will can break the barrier. The other agents set up more equipment, this time pointed at the dome itself, sensors blinking and spinning. It's almost funny, if you ignore the part where I'm trapped in a force field with someone I'm beginning to think is a literal god and a team of armed feds outside.

I turn to Loki. "You owe me a real explanation. And a stiff drink."

He nods, and for a second, I think I see something like pride in his eyes. "Ask anything," he says. "You've earned it."

I make tea instead, the old routine calming my nerves. The dome hums, the agents shout, the dogs relax at our feet, and Loki stands in my kitchen like he's always belonged there.

Outside, the lights and voices intensify. Mercer's calling in the cavalry.

Inside, I just want to know what comes next.

By midnight, the world outside my trailer glows with the harsh, un-natural light of government-issue floodlights. The agents have ringed the dome with portable generators and halogens, every inch of the barrier lit up so bright it throws the shadows of every pine needle a mile. The dome itself pulses in time with the runes, the symbols swelling and contracting, sometimes so bright I have to shield my eyes. Inside, it's twilight all the time, with the shadows bending in odd directions and the air humming just above the threshold of hearing.

Loki stands beside me at the window, hands folded behind his back, chin lifted like he's admiring a work of art. His reflection in the glass is uncanny—every few seconds, the smooth lines of his face sharpen, the angles grow more severe, and his eyes flash that impossible, molten gold. It's like the boundary between real and unreal is wearing thin, and he's not bothering to hold it together for my sake.

The dogs press against my legs, their bodies hot and solid, a living reassurance. Mystic watches Loki, unblinking, while Ash alternates between me and the door, torn between two loyalties. I rest a hand on each of their heads, feeling the way their hearts hammer, steady and determined.

"They won't give up easily," Loki says, not bothering to hide the admiration in his tone. "I suppose I should be flattered. It's been centuries since anyone put this much effort into stopping me."

I snort, unable to stop the smile that creeps up. "You're the only god I know who treats a siege like a fan convention."

He grins, but his gaze is glued to the line of agents outside. I watch Mercer direct the setup, her silhouette crisp and implacable. She moves her team with the precision of a chess master, every pawn in its place, every gambit calculated.

"Who are they?" I ask, keeping my voice low. The question isn't just for me; I think the dogs want to know, too.

Loki tilts his head, eyes narrowing as Mercer points at the dome and sketches out a new perimeter on her tablet. "A division of the federal government. Their purpose is to identify, contain, and exploit supernatural phenomena. Officially, they don't exist. Unofficially, they've been tracking me—and, by extension, you—for months."

"Me?" The word tastes bitter, like bad medicine. "What do they want with me?"

He turns to face me, expression softening. "They don't want you. Not really. They want me. But you're what they think is the cause. You're the incentive. If they can convince you to cooperate—or use you as bait—they think they can get what they want."

"And what's that? Your autograph? A backstage pass to Ragnarok?"

He laughs, sharp and bright, and the sound makes the runes on the dome pulse faster, the whole barrier flickering with a thousand reflected smiles. "No. They want control. Of the magic, the knowledge, the possibility of a world not bound by their rules."

Outside, Mercer finishes a call and steps up to the edge of the dome, so close I can make out the lines of her jaw, the chill of her expression. She raises a megaphone—old school, which I guess is all that works now that the electronics are dead—and calls out:

"Amethyst Gold! This is Agent Mercer. We know you're inside. We're not here to hurt you. Please, come out and talk."

I glance at Loki. "Should I?"

He shakes his head, a hint of real worry flickering in his eyes. "Not yet. If they get you outside, they'll take you apart. Piece by piece. They're not interested in the truth, only in power."

"Great," I mutter, dropping the curtain. "So I'm a hostage in my own house."

Loki touches my arm, gentle. "You're not a hostage. You're the only person here who gets to choose what happens next."

The words stick with me. I watch Mercer pull her team back, setting up tents and workstations, preparing for a siege. The runes along the dome throb, brighter with every moment. The dogs settle, finally, as if they know the worst is over—at least for now.

I sit at the kitchen table, Loki across from me, and we drink coffee in silence while the world outside transforms into something neither of us quite understands. Every so often, the dome shudders, and the trailer shakes, but inside it's warm, safe, almost normal.

"We're not getting out, are we?" I ask, tracing a finger down the side of my mug.

Loki smiles, slow and sure. "Not unless you want to."

I lean back, the exhaustion hitting me all at once. The dogs nap under the table, breathing in sync, and I watch the light from the runes shimmer on the ceiling, wondering what the hell I'm supposed to do.

Outside, Mercer continues to set up her command post. Beyond that, the woods are dark and deep, full of things waiting to wake. Inside, it's just me, Loki, and the dogs, caught in a story bigger than either of us ever wanted.

But for now, that's enough.

The siege has begun, and I'm ready for it.

Chapter Twelve

GOD OF LIES, GOD OF LOVE

The kitchen clock has been stuck at 2:23 for as long as I can remember, but tonight the hands are pulsing. Every time the runic light outside flickers, the second hand jitters forward, then slides back like it's being pulled by regret. I stand barefoot on the sticky linoleum, Mystic and Ash bracketing my shins like a matched set of haunted sentries, and stare at the runes plastered across the window. It's like living inside a planetarium, if the constellations were designed by someone with a grudge against geometry.

The Division agents have moved their vehicles back, but they're still visible: silhouettes clustered around the blue glare of their weird tech, heads bent, arms gesturing. I can almost hear the hiss of walkie-talkies, the slosh of thermos coffee, the cursing when another gadget shorts out. They look so normal, so human, until the runes fire up and all their shadows scatter like cockroaches.

Loki is doing his own impression of a corpse, except more beautiful. He sits ramrod straight in the battered kitchen chair, hands loose in his lap, head tipped to the ceiling. His eyes are closed, but I know from the tension in his jaw that he's not asleep—if anything, he's deeper awake than I've ever seen anyone. The runes outside crawl across his cheekbones, map their way up his throat, tinting the hollows under his eyes in a way that makes him look both ancient and twelve years old.

I sip my coffee—cold, because the microwave is a casualty of the magic surge—and try to ignore the tickle of panic crawling up my spine. I've survived hurricanes, tornadoes, my own family's funeral, but this is a different kind of storm. This is the waiting part, the part where the sky goes green and the air smells like copper and you don't know if you should take cover or stand on the porch and dare the lightning.

The barrier holds. I don't know how, or why, or for how long. The runes keep changing. Each time I look, the pattern's different, more complicated, less like something I could doodle on a napkin and more like the work of a calculus demon. Mystic paces the room, nails clicking, then wedges her nose under Loki's limp hand. Ash is more direct: he hops onto the banquette, leans in, and breathes in Loki's hair, as if memorizing the scent for when it's gone.

I can't take the silence. "You look like you're about to host a séance," I say, my voice wobbling on the landing between joke and plea.

Loki doesn't open his eyes. "You say that as if it's a new experience for me."

It's a good line. If I weren't so keyed up, I'd laugh. Instead, I wrap my hands around my mug and say, "The Division's got drones up. They're aiming some kind of antenna at the trailer. Looks like an electric bug zapper for monsters."

Loki's mouth quirks, but it's not amusement. "They're hoping to disrupt the boundary. It's a pointless gesture. The runes are older than any of their machines."

"Yeah, well, you ever seen what happens when a Texan gets told 'no' by a lock? Give it five minutes and they're coming through the goddamn drywall." I huff out a breath, setting the coffee down so hard it splashes the counter. "I need you to tell me we're not going to die tonight."

He opens his eyes, and for the first time, I realize he's been holding back. The runes outside don't just reflect in his eyes—they're replicated, in miniature, burning and shifting in the green-gold of his irises. It's both the hottest and scariest thing I've ever seen, and I've watched every episode of American Horror Story.

"We're not going to die tonight," he says. "At least, not in any way you've died before."

"That's not—" I start, then bite down. It's as much reassurance as anyone ever gets from him.

He shifts in the chair, flexes his hands as if testing the pull of invisible strings. The dogs go still, noses in the air, hackles up.

Loki looks at me, not with the usual playful mockery, but with something closer to regret. "If you want to leave, you should do it now. Once the barrier fails, it will be... unpleasant."

"Yeah, I can see how going outside to greet the murder-SWAT would be a huge upgrade." I slap the counter with both palms, the sound echoing in the magic-thick air. "If you know something, say it. Don't make me drag it out of you like some fourth-grade science project."

He doesn't flinch. "You're right. I haven't been honest with you."

"Well, duh." My voice is sharp, but the fear underneath tastes like blood. "But you could start now."

He stands, and for a second I'm irrationally angry— I can't name why, maybe because he seems taller, and his presence fills the room until there's no air left for me. Mystic and Ash flatten their ears, but neither barks. Loki steps toward me, and for the first time since this all started, I consider that maybe Sarah was right: maybe I should be afraid of him, not just for him.

He stops a pace away. "The barrier is holding for now. Every time I use the runes, every time I let the magic run through me, it takes something."

I look at him, really look, and see the shudder in his fingers, the strain in his shoulders. "So why do it?"

He smiles, not kindly. "Because it's the only way to keep you alive."

I roll my eyes, but my hands are shaking. "Jesus, you're dramatic."

He lifts a hand, palm up. It's trembling, just a little. "You wanted the truth."

I reach out before I can think better of it, wrap my fingers around his. The shock is instant—a jolt, not of pain, but of electricity, like every nerve in my body has been switched from off to on. For a second the world blurs, the runes outside blurring into a river of neon. When my vision clears, Loki is kneeling, forehead pressed to the back of my hand, and the dogs are whimpering in harmony.

I try to yank my hand back, but he's holding it gently, as if it's something fragile and worth protecting.

"I can't keep hiding," he says, voice muffled. "Not from you."

The lights outside surge, then falter. The runes stutter, the barrier going ragged at the edges. The kitchen clock rolls forward five seconds, then sticks again.

Loki lets go. He straightens, and for a moment I see something flicker behind his eyes—something old, and bitter, and tired of pretending. "It's time," he says, "for you to know too."

He steps back, spreading his arms. The runes on his skin flare, climbing up his wrists, spiraling across his shoulders, painting themselves into the lines of his collarbones. He grows, not just in height but in presence, until I feel myself shrinking, my own self a paper cutout compared to him.

His hair is longer now, tangled around his face, and his eyes are nothing human. The tattoos are alive, moving in fractal loops, radiating power so intense the air in the kitchen ripples. When he speaks, it's with two voices: one the Loki I know, the other a deeper, more resonant echo.

"I am Loki, of Asgard. Born of chaos, breaker of fates, bringer of storms. I have hidden among mortals because I thought it would spare them. I have failed at that, as I have failed at most things."

I'm pinned in place, too scared to run but too fascinated to look away. I think: This is it. This is how people go mad, staring at something they know can't exist, but it does, and it wants something from you.

Loki bows his head. The tattoos subside, settling into faint blue-green lines under the skin. His voice drops to a whisper. "If you wish to hate me, I will understand. But I will not lie to you again."

The silence in the kitchen is absolute. Even the clock has given up.

I, after a long, wild minute, snort. "I don't hate you... I just thought you were trying to prank me."

He blinks, startled.

"I mean, God of Chaos?" I'm laughing, because if I don't, I'll scream. "All this time I thought you were... I don't know, crazy? An alien?"

A slow grin spreads across his face, and for a moment he's just Loki again—the one who flirts with disaster and looks damn good doing it. "I have been called worse."

I take a shaky step forward, closing the gap between us. "So what now? You gonna turn into a snake or something?"

He shakes his head. "Only if you ask nicely."

I punch him in the shoulder. "Stop..."

The runes outside flicker again, but this time I'm not scared. Not as much. I look at him, and he looks at me, and there's a truce in the air, fragile as glass but real.

Outside, the agents are packing up the gear that doesn't work anymore. The world is still spinning, but for the first time, I feel like I've got a hand on the wheel.

Inside, the kitchen clock starts ticking forward again, one second at a time.

For a solid minute, I just stand there, hands locked behind my back, as if the only thing holding my body together is the pressure of my own knuckles. The world has not ended, but it's been whittled down to the size of my trailer, which is now home to one recently outed god and a pair of traumatized cattle dogs who want nothing more than to crawl inside my rib cage and set up camp.

Loki watches me with a sidelong glance, reading my expression with the hunger of a man who's never quite trusted mirrors. His tattoos recede, leaving pale skin and the suggestion of veins too blue to be human, but the air around him is still buckling, a heat haze of possibility. It's hard to look at him straight on. Hard to know which part is the mask and which part is the actual, literal face of Chaos.

I lean against the fridge. The old magnet collection—half of them promotional, the other half scavenged from truck stops—jostle to the floor, and I let them fall. The kitchen feels even smaller now. I clear my throat. "Can you... show me what you are? I mean, is this what you really look like?"

Loki's mouth twitches.

I shrug, trying for blasé but missing by a mile. "I mean, you told me you were the God of Chaos. Show me."

There's a split second where I think he might actually refuse. Then he bows, flourishes a hand, and the world hiccups.

He's standing on the other side of the kitchen. No—he's still in front of me, but also behind, and also lounging on top of the refrigerator with his ankles crossed, watching the room like a bored cat. Three Lokis, each more real than the last, each flickering with a slightly different afterimage.

I blink. The Loki behind me says, "You wanted to see?"

The one on the fridge says, "Don't worry, I'm house-trained."

The one in front of me smiles, all teeth. "But that's only the first layer."

He becomes a shadow, then a wolf, shaggy and huge, the color of midnight and the crackle of distant thunder. Mystic and Ash yelp, retreating behind my legs, but the wolf doesn't snarl. It sits, head cocked, tongue lolling, waiting for my reaction.

I gape, and then, because this is apparently my coping strategy, I laugh. "Okay, that's new."

The wolf's fur ripples, then shivers itself back into Loki, who's now wearing a T-shirt I definitely recognize as my own (purple, stretched out at the collar, logo faded to near oblivion). "You stole my shirt," I say.

"It looked better on me," Loki counters. There's pride in his voice, and something else—relief? Fear? I can't tell, but it's genuine.

He snaps his fingers, and now he's a raven, glossy and iridescent, hopping along the back of the sofa. He caws, wings beating, then explodes into a cloud of feathers that rematerialize into a dozen miniature Lokis, each one perched somewhere in the room: the windowsill, the sink, the rim of my coffee mug.

"Oh my god," I say, pinching the bridge of my nose. "You're like if David Bowie and a plague of frogs had a baby."

The real Loki—the one with the most gravity, the one looking at me like I'm the only fixed star—gathers all his illusions back into himself with a gesture. For a heartbeat, the air's so thick with ozone my hair stands up. Then it settles, and there's only him, breathing hard, like it took actual effort.

I exhale. "So that's what you've been hiding."

He nods, slow. "Do you believe me now?"

I shrug, but it's a helpless gesture. "I don't know what I believe, but I believe you."

Outside, there's a commotion. The Division's backup has arrived: a new set of headlights, a fresh cadre of silhouettes fanning out along the runic perimeter. They move differently this time—more cautious, more respectful, as if the trailer has become a holy relic or a bomb on a hair trigger.

Loki moves to the window, stares out. His shoulders tense. The runes are flickering faster, the patterns growing more complex, and for the first time I see the strain. His knuckles are white on the frame, and the tattoos on his wrists are smoldering, pulsing with each heartbeat.

"They're going to try and break through again," he says.

"Will it work?" I ask.

He looks at me. "Not if I hold the line."

I step up beside him, close enough to feel the shimmer of his power. Mystic and Ash press in, flanking me, their bodies vibrating with nervous energy.

"What happens if you don't?" I say, voice barely above a whisper.

He doesn't answer. Instead, he reaches for my hand, the contact light but charged. The tattoos flare, then retreat, as if bowing to my touch.

"You're a lot to take in," I say, "but I've seen weirder."

He laughs, and it's the first honest sound in the room since the reveal. "That's why I like you."

I roll my eyes. "Please. I'm just the only girl on your Tinder who hasn't blocked you yet." I know full well I've never even downloaded that app.

He grins. "Not true. Most of them are dead."

It's so morbid I almost spit coffee, but the dogs' whine brings me back to the present.

Loki turns back to the window. "They're recalibrating. If they get desperate, they'll bring in something bigger. I can buy us time, but—" He glances at me. "But there's a price."

I wait, arms crossed. "There's always a price. What is it this time?"

He gestures at the runes, at himself. "If I push too hard, I lose control."

"And that's bad?" I prompt.

He looks at me, eyes very green and very old. "It's worse than you can imagine."

There's a long silence. Outside, the agents are setting up some kind of tripod, angling it at the runic barrier. Inside, the air is thick with anticipation.

I walk to the table, pick up my mug, and down the dregs. "You know what? Fuck it. If you're gonna go nuclear, do it in here."

Loki blinks. "Are you certain?"

I smirk, but my hands are shaking. "Let's give them a real show."

He nods, and this time when the tattoos flare, they don't stop at his wrists. They spiral up his arms, over his shoulders, across his jaw, illuminating every angle of him until he's more light than flesh. The runes on the windows echo, pulsing in synchrony, and the room hums—a frequency so deep it's felt, not heard.

Outside, the agents are backing up. The tripod starts to spark, then erupts in a shower of blue flame. The men and women scatter, ducking behind the vehicles as the runes arch up and over the trailer, forming a dome that crackles with living energy.

Loki lifts his hands, and the runes on his skin detach, swirling into the air like a school of phosphorescent fish. They join the barrier, thickening it, reinforcing it, until nothing of the outside world is visible except the flicker of lightning and the distant howl of wind.

Inside, the temperature drops. I hug myself, teeth chattering, but I can't look away from the spectacle. Loki's no longer just a man—he's a force, a storm in a suit, and I'm the only thing grounding him.

I move to him, press my hand to his cheek. The tattoos flare, then settle.

He looks at me, voice cracking around the edges. "I can't hold this forever."

I shrug. "Just long enough for them to get bored."

He laughs, but it's tired. "You are truly relentless."

I smile, and it's genuine. "That's why you like me."

The runes outside begin to slow, stabilizing. The agents retreat, their vehicles reversing down the road, the last of the gear abandoned in the brush. It's just us now—Loki, me, and the dogs—cocooned in a world that doesn't belong to anyone else.

Loki slumps against the window, shoulders heaving. "It's done. For now."

I sit next to him, shoulder to shoulder. Mystic and Ash wedge themselves in, making a warm tangle of limbs and fur.

For a long time, neither of us says anything. The world is quiet, save for the soft thump of Mystic's tail and the distant, grateful whine of Ash.

Then Loki speaks, so softly I almost miss it. "I'm sorry."

I turn to him, and for the first time see the fear behind the bravado. "What for?"

He shrugs. "For bringing you into this. For being what I am."

I lean my head on his shoulder, close my eyes. "You didn't bring me anywhere. I came. And if you ever try to apologize for existing again, I will slap the god right out of you."

He laughs, and the sound is full of wonder.

I grin, eyes still shut. "You're an idiot."

He wraps his arm around me, careful, tentative. "You have no idea."

The runes outside burn a little brighter, then fade to a soft glow. The world is still, the agents are gone, and for the first time since any of this started, I feel like the storm has passed. Or maybe, I think, the storm is just getting started. But at least now I've got someone to ride it out with.

Loki squeezes my hand. "We have time," he says.

I nod. "We do."

And in the silence, we both believe it.

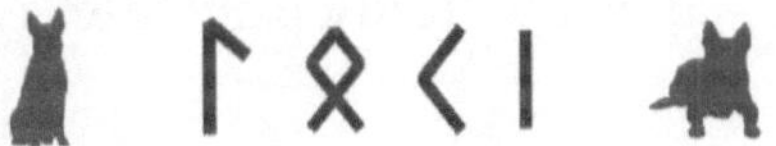

I've never been good at silence. Now, with the agents driven off and the runes on the windows flickering in post-coital exhaustion, the silence is as loud as a screaming match. I stand in the kitchen doorway, my hands clenched in the hem of my shirt, and stare at Loki as if he might vanish if I look away too long. Mystic and Ash have collapsed on the banquette, heads pillowed together, their breath syncopated with the pulse of the runes. It would be cozy if not for the lingering ozone and the afterimage of a dozen Lokis still pirouetting in my mind.

The trailer is too small for avoidance, and even if it wasn't, I would have no idea where to run. I don't want to run. But the thing vibrating in my chest isn't just anticipation anymore—it's a wild tangle of want and terror, a hunger with edges that make my hands shake.

Loki's standing at the window, shoulders tensed, as if expecting the agents to rematerialize and demand an encore. He's more himself now, more solid, but the runes still whisper along his wrists and neck, soft blue-green threads that move in time with his pulse. I study the sharpness of his jaw, the set of his mouth, the way he's careful not to turn his back on me, not to let me out of his peripheral vision.

I step into the living room, then hesitate halfway across. My feet feel rooted to the linoleum. What am I doing? What am I even thinking?

"Hey," I say, softer than I mean to, my voice barely carrying across the small space.

He turns. The tattoos on his face are fading, but there's a glow in his eyes that makes my knees want to give out—and also makes me want to bolt for the door. "Hey," he answers, like we're just picking up a conversation from the middle.

I force myself to take another step, then another, until I'm close enough to see the faint stubble on his chin, the flecks of not-quite-human gold in the green of his eyes. My heart's hammering so hard I'm sure he can hear it.

"You okay?" I ask, because it's what you're supposed to say when someone's just saved your life with sorcery and trauma. And because I need to say something before I lose my nerve entirely.

He shrugs, a little helpless. "You're the one who had a run-in with the gods."

I'm not sure if he means himself or the runes, or the actual divine presence in the air. I don't care. I take a breath, searching for words that won't make me sound like a complete idiot. But before I can speak, he does.

"Amethyst," he says, his voice rough around the edges. "I need you to know—" He stops, runs a hand through his hair, looking suddenly vulnerable in a way that has nothing to do with magic. "I think I'm falling in love with you."

I freeze. Not the poetic kind, the literal, all-systems-locking-down kind. The words hit me like a physical force, and for a moment I can't breathe, can't think, can't do anything but stare at him.

Panic floods through me immediately. "You don't—you can't—" I'm backing up, hands raised like I can ward off the words. "You barely know me. And I'm just—I'm nobody special. You're a literal god, and I'm just some woman in a trailer who can barely keep her life together."

"Stop." His voice is soft but firm, and he reaches for me slowly, like I'm a spooked animal. "Don't run from this."

I'm pressed against the wall now, my heart hammering, every instinct screaming at me to flee. "This is insane. You know that, right? This whole thing is completely insane. You don't know what you're saying."

He takes another step toward me, palms up, non-threatening. "I know exactly what I'm saying. And I know it's terrifying. But that doesn't make it less true."

The way he's looking at me—like I'm something precious and fragile and worth protecting—makes my chest tight with emotions I don't know how to name. No one, EVER looked at me like that. Not once.

He stops just out of reach. "I'm not asking you to say it back. I just needed you to know."

I stare at him, torn between wanting to run and wanting to close the distance between us. "I—" I start, then stop, swallow hard. "I'm scared."

"Of me?"

"Of this. Of feeling…" I gesture helplessly between us. "Of wanting something I can't have."

"What makes you think you can't have it?"

I let out a bitter laugh. "Come on. Look at you. Look at me. This doesn't make sense."

He moves closer, slow and careful. "The best things rarely do."

I let out a shaky breath, studying his face. "You really mean it? What you said?"

"Every word."

Something tight in my chest loosens, just a fraction. "I'm not sure of anything. I'm terrified. But I—" I push off the wall, taking a tentative step toward him. "I want this. I want you. Even if it's the stupidest thing I've ever done."

Relief washes over his face, but he still doesn't move closer. "We don't have to—"

"Don't," I interrupt, taking a tentative step toward him. "Don't talk me out of it. I'll do that all by myself if you give me half a second."

He reaches for me then, slow and careful, palms hovering an inch from my arms as if afraid he'll break something. When I don't pull away, he draws me in, so gentle I almost start crying.

"I just—" his voice cracks, "—I want to do it right."

I pull his face down to mine, kissing him with all the ferocity I've spent my life trying to subdue, trying to drown out the voice in my head that's listing all the reasons this is a terrible idea. He tastes like static and summer storms, like the moment before rain hits dust. He's trembling, and it takes me a minute to realize I am too.

"I don't know what I'm doing," I whisper against his mouth.

"Neither do I," he admits, and while I don't believe him, somehow that makes it better.

The room tilts, just a little, and I drag him toward the narrow hallway, knocking over a pile of books and a dog bed in the process. But I stop at the hallway entrance, sudden doubt flooding through me.

"What if—" I start.

"What if what?"

"What if I'm terrible at this? What if I disappoint you? What if—"

He cups my face in his hands, forcing me to meet his eyes. "Impossible."

"You don't know that."

"I know you," he says simply. "That's enough."

Mystic and Ash follow us down the hall, ears cocked in canine curiosity, but when I open the door to my bedroom, they seem to sense the change in atmosphere. Mystic noses the threshold, then sits, content to guard the perimeter.

Loki stands in the doorway, eyes wide and hesitant. The uncertainty in his expression matches my own, and somehow that steadies me.

"I don't—" he starts.

I cut him off. "Don't say it's dangerous, or you'll break the mood. What's left of it, anyway."

He nods, laughs, and it's the most human sound I've ever heard from him. "Understood."

I reach for his hand, then hesitate. "Are you sure about this? About me?"

Instead of answering, he steps into the room and closes the door behind him. The space feels impossibly small, the bed looming like a question neither of us knows how to answer.

"We can stop," he says quietly. "Anytime. Just say the word."

I nod, not trusting my voice. Then, before I can second-guess myself into paralysis, I step back toward the bed, and he follows.

For a long, charged minute, neither of us moves. My heart is beating so hard I'm sure he can feel it. He lifts his hands toward my face, then hesitates, fingers hovering inches from my skin.

"Is this—can I—?" he starts.

I nod, not trusting my voice. When he finally cups my face in his hands, his touch is so light I wonder if I'm dreaming it. The runes flicker along his fingers, trailing warmth everywhere he touches, and I can't help the small gasp that escapes.

He freezes. "Did I hurt you?"

"No," I whisper. "It's just—the magic. I can feel it."

He starts to pull back, but I catch his wrists. "Don't stop. It's not bad, just... different."

I shiver, but not from cold. The silence stretches between us, heavy with uncertainty. I want to say something clever, something to deflate the tension, but my mouth is dry and my thoughts are scattered. Finally, I force out the truth: "I've never done this before."

He goes absolutely still, hands freezing on my face. "What?"

Heat floods my cheeks and I can't meet his gaze. "I mean, not with a god. Or anyone. Ever." The words come out in a rush, embarrassment making my voice small.

His hands drop to my shoulders, gripping gently. "Amethyst—"

Panic rises in my throat. "If you're going to change your mind, just say so now. Don't make me—"

"No." His voice is firm, but gentle. "That's not—" He takes a shaky breath. "No one's ever wanted me for me. Not like this. Not knowing what I am."

I manage to look at him then, see the vulnerability written across his features. "Loki, you saved my life. You seem to actually want to know me. How could I not want you?"

Something shifts in his expression—relief, maybe, or wonder. When he kisses me this time, it's softer, slower, like he's afraid I might disappear. His hands move hesitantly—down my back, then up again, never quite settling.

"Tell me if you want me to stop," he murmurs against my lips.

His lips capture mine with a fervent urgency, and I find myself responding instantly to the fiery heat burning between us. "I will," I promise, though I can't fathom wanting him to. The anticipation of the unknown ignites a restless need deep within me.

His fingers find the hem of my shirt, but he pauses. "Can I—?"

"Yes." The word comes out breathless.

He pulls my shirt over my head with careful deliberation, and I'm suddenly hyper-aware of everything: the cool air on my skin, the way his eyes widen, the nervous flutter in my stomach. I resist the urge to cover myself as my nipples tighten in response to the sudden exposure.

"You're shaking," he observes softly, caressing my breasts as his thumb brushes over my now hard nipples.

"So are you," I point out, and he laughs—a nervous, breathy sound.

"Terrified," he admits.

"That makes two of us."

He traces his mouth down my throat, pausing at my pulse point. "Your heart is racing."

"Yeah," I whisper, pressing my palm to his chest, "so is yours." The tattoos shimmer under my touch, and he draws in a sharp breath.

"The runes—they react to you," he says, wonder in his voice.

"Is that normal?"

"Nothing about this is normal." He pulls back to look at me, searching my face. "Are you sure? We can stop anytime."

I wrap my arms around his neck, pulling him closer. "I'm sure. Scared, but sure."

"I don't want to hurt you."

"You won't." I hope I sound more confident than I feel.

He kisses me again, deeper this time, and his hands begin wandering with a mission; fingers gripping at my hips before slipping around to cup my ass cheeks firmly. But with every new touch or change in pressure, he stops, studying my face for any hint of discomfort.

When his fingers unbutton my jeans and work their way down my legs slowly and reverently, he pauses before slipping between my thighs. I fight the urge to hide my exposed sex from his gaze.

"You're perfect," he breathes, and it sounds like a prayer.

"I'm not—"

"You are." He slides his fingers over my wet folds, gently teasing my clit, causing me to gasp at the sensations he's stirring within me. "Tell me what you like. What feels good."

"I don't know," I admit, embarrassed. "I told you, I've never—"

"Then we'll learn together." His smile is gentle, patient. "Just tell me how this feels."

He touches me more deliberately now, gliding two fingers inside me as his thumb continues to circle my clit. When I arch into his touch and moan, he does it again, more firmly. He reads my responses like a map to buried treasure.

"Good?" he asks, his voice rough with lust.

"Yes," I manage, my head spinning. "Don't stop."

He explores each inch of my body with reverent attention—nipping at my collarbone, sucking on my nipples—learning what makes me sigh and squirm. When I finally come undone under his touch, he watches in fascination, as if witnessing something sacred.

"Was that—are you okay?" he asks, the vulnerability in his voice endearing.

I laugh, breathless. "More than okay."

As he begins removing his own clothes—peeling them away to reveal the sculpted muscles beneath—his hands shake with nervous energy. "I should warn you," he says hesitantly, "when the magic takes over and I lose control ... things can get intense."

"Define intense."

He gestures at the runes dancing across his skin. "The last time I was with someone ... I accidentally set their bed on fire."

Despite everything, I snort with laughter. "Good thing I need a new mattress."

He grins, some of the tension leaving his shoulders. When he's finally naked, the runes on his skin flare so bright I have to blink. He's beautiful in a way that makes my chest tight—lean and strong, every line of him perfect and impossible.

"Now I'm really intimidated," I whisper.

"You and me both," he says, settling between my thighs. But he doesn't move to penetrate me yet. Instead, he looks at me with an expression of soft uncertainty. "Last chance to change your mind."

"I'm not changing my mind." I reach up to cup his face. "But maybe ... go slow?"

"As slow as you need." He leans down to kiss me, gentle and reassuring. "If anything hurts or you want to stop, just tell me."

"I will."

He aligns himself at my entrance, and I tense involuntarily as he presses against me. He stills immediately.

"Breathe," he murmurs. "Just breathe."

I do, forcing myself to relax. He waits until I nod before pressing forward again—so slowly it's almost torturous. The stretch burns but isn't unbearable.

"Okay?" he asks, his voice strained with the effort of holding back.

"Okay," I manage.

He moves carefully inside me, matching my pace and watching my face for any sign of pain. When I finally adjust, the discomfort fades into something else entirely—pleasure that begins as a slow burn before building wondrously.

I wrap my legs around him tighter and whisper urgently, "You can move."

He thrusts into me, each motion controlled and deliberate yet filled with passion. The entire room seems to come alive as the magic builds between us—runes swirling from the walls, engulfing us in an otherworldly glow.

"I can't—" he gasps. "The magic—"

"Let go," I tell him, surprising myself. "I trust you."

When he finally surrenders to the magic and lets himself shatter—the God of Chaos giving in to his most primal desires—he says my name like it's the only word that matters. The runes explode around us, filling the air with an impossible light that matches the crescendo of our pleasure as we reach our climax together.

We collapse afterward into a tangle of sheets, sweat, and residual enchantment. The room still pulses with soft light as the storm outside refuses to calm.

"Are you okay?" he asks, his voice hoarse. "Did I hurt you?"

I curl against his side, exhausted and exhilarated. "I'm ... perfect."

He laughs, the sound vibrating through his chest. "You are. You really are."

For the first time in my life, I actually believe it might be true.

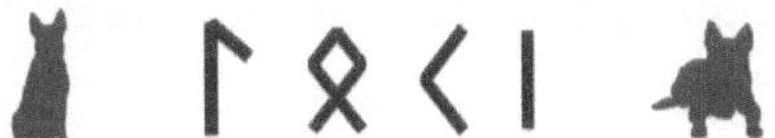

I wake to the sound of thunder. Not the far-off, lazy kind that purrs in the distance, but the immediate, just-above-your-roof kind—raw and intimate, rattling the bones of the trailer until the window frames threaten to shake loose. It's still dark, but the world outside is lit in flashes: green, then blue, then something that isn't a color, exactly, but a kind of living brilliance that makes my nerves hum. For a split second, I wonder if I've died and this is the afterlife—me, buried in cheap sheets with the world ending outside—but then Loki shifts beside me, his arm tightening around my waist, and I know it's real.

I lift my head, just enough to see the ceiling. The runes are still there, brighter than before, swirling in slow constellations above the bed. They drift and merge, break apart, form new patterns that make me think of star charts or the tangled lines of my own life. Loki is sprawled on his back, hair spread over the pillow, breathing slow and even. In sleep, he looks ... normal, almost gentle. The tattoos on his chest and shoulders are alive, rising and falling with each breath, painting his skin in a language I don't understand but desperately want to learn.

I nestle back down, tracing my fingers over the blue-green lines on his ribs. He shivers, then opens his eyes. They're softer now—less fire, more river.

"Morning," I whisper, even though it's definitely not.

He smiles, pulls me closer. "It's two in the morning."

"Still counts." I stretch, every muscle protesting, every inch of my skin alive with leftover magic. "Did you mean to do the light show?"

He glances up at the ceiling, then back at me, sheepish. "Not really. Side effect."

I laugh, low and close to his ear. "You're like a human Tesla coil."

He brushes my hair out of my face and kisses my forehead. "You're not exactly grounding yourself."

The storm outside rages on, louder now. The trailer groans, but the bed is a cocoon of warmth and shared gravity. Mystic and Ash are curled up in the corner, two tight blue-gray commas, asleep at last. Through the bedroom window, I can see flashes of light arching between the trees, runes burning into the bark with each strike. The world's been rewritten, and I'm not even sure who's doing the editing anymore.

I prop myself on an elbow and look down at him. "You really didn't know it would be like this?"

He shakes his head. "You're ... more than I expected. More than I knew how to hope for."

I want to make a joke, deflect it, but the look on his face is pure, undiluted awe, and I don't want to ruin it. I let myself rest in the silence, letting the thunder fill the space where words would be.

After a while, Loki sighs, the sound deep and almost sad. "We can't stay here forever, you know."

I grin. "We've got at least until the next utility bill comes due."

He laughs, and it's warm, the storm outside temporarily less important. "The Division will be back."

I shrug. "Let them. You saw what we did to their last 'containment protocol.'" I touch his jaw, gentle. "We'll figure it out."

He closes his eyes and leans into my hand. "You say that a lot."

"It's usually true."

I kiss him, slow and lingering, then roll onto my back, staring up at the rune constellations. "What are they saying?" I ask. "The runes. Do you know?"

He's quiet for a long time. "They're ... singing, I think. It's not language, not really. More like memory."

I close my eyes and listen. For a moment, I hear it—the low hum, the pulse, the sense of being held in place by something bigger than fear. It's almost like music, and I let it wash over me, let it blend with the feel of Loki's body against mine and the distant, steady heartbeat of the dogs on the floor.

We stay like that, tangled together, the storm howling outside, the room bathed in the gentle light of runes. I want to ask what comes next, want to plan for the inevitable disaster, but right now, I'm content to let tomorrow wait.

The runes overhead shift, spelling something I can almost read. I squint, then laugh, and Loki looks up, curious.

"What is it?"

I gesture. "Pretty sure that one says 'DANGER' and the other says 'DECEIT.' You've got a real sense of humor, you know that?"

He grins, wicked. "Takes one to know one."

I press my face into his neck, breathe him in. He wraps me tighter, as if he could keep me safe just by holding on.

The storm outside reaches its peak, the wind shrieking, lightning carving new glyphs into the sky. But inside, the world is small and warm and bright. I close my eyes, letting myself drift.

For the first time in my life, I feel like I belong.

Tomorrow, the agents will regroup. Tomorrow, the runes will fade, and the world will try to go back to what it was. But tonight, in this battered trailer at the end of the world, I have everything I've ever wanted: a bed, a storm, a pair of loyal dogs, and the most impossible man in the universe.

I hold him close, listen to the song of the runes, and fall asleep knowing—really knowing—that morning is coming.

And for once, I can't wait to see it.

My phone rings, an unknown number, so I scramble to answer it. "This is Sarah."

"Ms. Mitchell, my name is Agent Mercer. Would you be willing to help us to ... help your friend, Amethyst Gold?"

"Yes, of course," I respond. I contacted them because I want to help her. I wanted professionals with experience with this kind of thing. "What do you need?"

"There are ... several things we need. We will have an agent at your place in about twenty minutes. We would like you to come to one of our bases."

"Sure... I will do whatever it takes to help her."

Chapter Thirteen

BETRAYAL

I never realized how much useless shit I owned until it was time to run. My hands are a blur, snatching things I think we might need: dog treats from the bin, every roll of toilet paper in the bathroom closet. The trailer still smells like last night's panic: sweat, fear, dog breath, and the tang of ozone that means Loki's magic is on a bender again.

He's standing dead center in the living room, eyes locked on a single point in the air. The mug of cold coffee I left on the table is floating a few inches above its ring of condensation, trembling like it's afraid of heights. Around him, little things keep glitching: a coaster melting into the wood grain, the zipper on my overnight bag shuttling itself open and closed, the dogs' metal bowls bending in and out of shape as if made of taffy.

I'm packing my life into Walmart bags and dog-eared backpacks, every movement a dare to the universe: Come and get me, I fucking dare you.

Mystic and Ash follow me from room to room, tails down, noses glued to my calves. They know something's wrong. Mystic keeps barking at the bathroom mirror, like she expects it to answer. Ash has wedged himself under the kitchen table and won't come out even when I shake the box of Milk-Bones at him.

Loki watches the chaos, arms folded, face stuck between amusement and pure, undiluted terror. He's wearing an old oversized t-shirt, the one with "SURVIVOR" on the back, and it looks both hilarious and sad on him. The runes on his wrists blink in and out like malfunctioning Christmas lights, some so bright they leave afterimages in my eyes.

"Are you sure you want to bring the fondue set?" he asks, nodding at the bright red pot I've just crammed into a laundry basket.

"Yes... no... I don't know," I snap, shoving in a box of instant ramen for good measure.

He shrugs, and the air around his head wobbles, distorting his hair into a purple-black halo. "Of course."

I try to focus; I really do, but the whole place feels like it's closing in. Every time I zip a bag, I hear engines outside, see shadows moving in the corners. I check the window for the third time in ten minutes—nothing but the trees and the battered blue mailbox at the end of the drive.

I stuff some towels in with the rest, burying my mom's wedding ring at the bottom just in case. I'll sell it for gas money if I have to.

My phone rings, piercing the panic with an obnoxious "Eye of the Tiger" that Sarah insisted on setting as her ringtone. I nearly drop it twice before hitting accept.

"Ame? You okay?" Sarah's voice is sweet tea with a shot of bourbon, soothing but sharp. I realize too late that my hands are shaking.

"Yeah, yeah, just—busy." I jam the phone between my shoulder and chin, using both hands to wrangle the duct tape around the box of dog food. "What's up?"

Sarah doesn't answer right away, which is not like her. I can hear wind on the other end, maybe a car. "I saw the news. Something about a chemical spill near your place?"

"Yep," I say. "Evacuating now." I had seen the news; Division had arranged for the news to report our area had a tanker truck spill, not far from my place. I figured I'd just play along.

She lets out a hiss. "Shit. How bad is it?"

I glance at Loki, who's now levitating a ballpoint pen just to show off. "Not great. We're leaving tonight."

"Where are you going?" Sarah's tone is casual, but I've known her since college; she's worried. I love her for it, but it makes my head itch.

"No clue. Maybe north, maybe west. I hear Oklahoma is nice this time of year." I say it loud enough for Loki to hear; he rolls his eyes and mouths, "Oklahoma?" like it's the worst idea in the world.

Sarah's voice gets even softer. "Ame, can you put me on speaker?"

I sigh and do it, balancing the phone on top of the ramen box. "You're live," I announce.

"Hey, Loki," Sarah says, and the way she says it is not a question.

He raises a hand to the phone, and the pen drops from midair, clattering on the countertop. "Hello, Sarah."

There's a pause, and I can almost feel the static traveling between them. Mystic, sensing the shift, presses her muzzle against my thigh, whimpering.

"Listen," Sarah says. "You guys need a safe place to go that will take the dogs. I got options. One is my cousin's place outside Tyler—nobody goes there, not even her. Or you could stay at my dad's hunting cabin. It's got power, water, and nobody knows it exists except me and a very confused tax assessor."

Loki's face goes tight. He nods at the phone, like Sarah can see him. "Thank you. That's—generous."

Sarah keeps talking, rapid-fire now. "Ame, honey, just text me when you're out of town, okay? I want to know you're safe. Be careful."

"I will," I say, softer than I mean to.

She drops her voice to a whisper. "Are you sure about this guy? I read some things—"

Loki snorts. I glare at him, then at the phone. "I'm sure. He is not a problem. Now drop it," I say, and instantly regret it.

Sarah is silent for a heartbeat. "Okay. Call me if you need anything. Seriously, anything."

I mumble a thank you and kill the call. The room feels twenty degrees colder.

Loki turns away, pacing, running his fingers over the floating mug, which now rotates like a planet on a lazy axis. "You trust her?" he says finally.

"She's my best friend," I say, too defensive. "I've known her since college."

He makes a face. "Maybe. People change when they're afraid. Or when someone offers them answers."

The words sting more than I want to admit. I start shoving bags toward the door, one after another, like if I keep moving, I won't have to think about it.

"Where's the leash?" I mutter, patting my pockets. Mystic answers by producing it from underneath her ass, grabbing it with her mouth and handing it up to me while wagging her tail as if the world isn't ending.

Loki crouches to help with the bags, his face inches from mine. I expect him to make a joke, to lighten the mood, but he doesn't. Instead, he says, "You're a good person, Amethyst. I hope you stay that way."

I look at him, really look. There's a sadness behind his eyes that makes me want to break something. "Don't start with the goodbyes," I say. "You're not dying. You're coming with."

He stands, the runes on his hands flickering in sympathy. "Of course."

I want to say more, but my throat is closing up. Instead, I kneel by Ash, tucking his favorite toy in the side pocket of my duffel. Mystic nuzzles me, licking a trail of snot and drool across my cheek. I laugh, choking on tears I refuse to let out.

"Good pups," I say. "We're all set."

We pile the bags by the door, the mountain of possessions as pathetic as it is essential. Loki moves to the window, peering through the curtain. His shoulders are tight, posture all nerves and muscle.

"What's wrong?" I ask, but I already know.

"They're close," he says. "We need to go. Now."

I don't argue. I grab the dogs, the bags, the keys, and hustle out the door into the semi-dark morning. Loki hovers behind me, one hand on my shoulder, the other pressed to his own chest, as if he's keeping something inside from spilling out.

The trailer slams shut behind us, the echo ricocheting down the empty road. The wind smells like burnt electricity, and the trees on the far side of the clearing bend away from the sun.

We're running, and we don't even know what we're running from. But for the first time, I think we might have a chance.

If only for a little while.

The sky has turned the color of boiled denim by the time we finish stuffing the last duffel bag into the bed of my pickup. The engine protests when I crank it, coughing up a cloud of blue smoke, but it finally settles into a lumpy idle that rattles my teeth. Mystic and Ash are already in the cab, panting in the stifling air, their bodies vibrating with a tension I can't name.

Loki is scanning the treeline, runes under his skin flickering so fast they look like strobe lights. He's got his hand on my shoulder, but the way he's squeezing says he's not comforting me; he's grounding himself, using me as an anchor so he doesn't come unspooled and float away.

"We good?" I say, glancing over my shoulder at the trailer, every window dark. It looks abandoned, like we've already been gone for months. I wonder if we'll ever come back, or if the place will rot into the dirt without us.

He doesn't answer, just tilts his head toward the county road. "Move," he says, urgent and low. "They're coming."

And then I hear it: tires on gravel, the whine of high-performance engines, a sound that doesn't belong out here except in movies where the FBI shows up to ruin everyone's day. Two, three, maybe four black SUVs explode out of the treeline, headlights off, each one piloted by a figure in black tactical gear. They swing into the clearing with terrifying precision, boxing in the pickup before I can even slam it into reverse.

Mystic goes berserk, throwing herself at the window and barking so hard her voice cracks. Ash loses his mind, claws raking the dash, growling deep and ugly. I fumble with the door, but Loki yanks me back, hand clamped on my arm like a vice.

The first SUV screeches to a halt so close to the pickup it scrapes paint. The doors open in unison, agents boiling out: helmets, body armor, mirrored visors, and weapons that look military but also... wrong, like someone let a medieval torture fan design the next generation of AR-15.

The lead agent—a woman, Mercer, I'm sure of it, just from the way she moves—takes a step forward, then peels off her helmet in a fluid motion. Her hair is buzzed to the scalp, face sharp enough to cut glass. I recognize her instantly.

The woman from the woods, from the surveillance, from every bad dream since this started.

But she's not the first one to speak.

From the second SUV, Sarah emerges. Her hair is pulled tight, her face bare of makeup, wearing a zip-up fleece I gave her for Christmas three years ago. She looks at me, eyes rimmed in red, and my entire chest hollows out. I want to shout at her, to call her every name I know, but all I can manage is a thin, "Sarah? No... Why?"

She can't meet my gaze. "I'm sorry, Ame. It's for your own protection."

Loki steps between me and the advancing agents, his body language so un-Loki—tight, defensive, no trace of swagger or irony. "Get back in the truck," he hisses, but I'm glued to the dirt.

Mercer raises a gloved hand, palm out. "Amethyst Gold. Please surrender the entity and come with us. No one has to get hurt."

I laugh. It's a horrible, strangled noise. My gaze is glued to my supposed best friend. "You're kidding, right? You brought the whole X-Files after me?"

No one laughs. Instead, one of the agents pops the trunk on their SUV and pulls out something that looks like a cross between a cattle prod and a church relic—brass, studded with crystal, runes crawling across its surface in sickly blue light.

Loki's voice goes guttural, layered with something I've only ever heard in nightmares. "Get. In. The. Truck."

I backpedal, hands up. The dogs are going full Cujo now, howling at the glass. My finger finds the door handle, and I yank it open just as an agent fires the device. A bolt of blue energy crackles over Loki's head, shattering the rearview mirror and leaving a smoking gouge in the pickup's paint.

He wheels on me, face wild. "Hold on," he says, then grabs my wrist and closes his eyes.

The world goes sideways. There's a moment—maybe a second, maybe a century—where everything turns inside out: colors swap places, sounds invert, my body lifts off the ground. For a blissful heartbeat, I'm sure we're gone, teleported to some safe haven in the Twilight Runes' protection.

But we're not.

Instead, we slam back into reality exactly where we started, only now Loki's breath is coming in short, painful gasps. The runes on his arms have turned the color of old bruises, and sweat beads on his forehead. He looks at me, eyes wide with terror.

"They're using binding sigils," he says, voice barely above a whisper. "My own magic—turned against me."

The agents are closing in, weapons up, every movement coordinated and practiced. Sarah stands behind them, her face twisted with something halfway between guilt and relief.

Mercer advances, voice cold and practiced. "Loki, you are under arrest for violation of the Magnus Accord and unlawful presence in the temporal continuum. You are to surrender yourself immediately for transport and containment. Do not resist."

Loki spits on the ground, the spittle sizzling as it hits the dirt. "Come and get me."

I don't know what to do. My hands are shaking so badly I nearly drop the keys. I look at Sarah, but she won't meet my eyes. She did it again. Thinks she knows what's best for me. This is worse than the stalker she set me up with, and he almost killed me and Mystic.

The first agent lunges for Loki with the runic device, but before it can connect, Mystic explodes out of the passenger side window, teeth bared, launching herself at the agent's arm. The device clatters to the ground, short-circuiting in a burst of sparks. Ash is right behind her, barking so ferociously he nearly scares himself.

Loki grabs my hand, pulling me behind the truck. "We have to go," he says, but his legs are jelly. He's not going anywhere fast.

Mercer and her team regroup, drawing strange-looking pistols that glow with the same blue energy as the runes. "You have one more chance," she says. "Do not make us escalate."

I clutch Loki's hand, feeling the pulse under his skin slow and stutter. For the first time, he looks truly afraid.

"I can't get us out," he says, his voice breaking. "They've boxed me in. Completely."

The dogs are circling us, hackles up, teeth bared. Mystic lunges at the nearest agent, who swings a baton and clips her on the ribs. I scream. She yelps, stumbles, but recovers, more enraged than hurt.

Mercer signals. Three agents move in at once, one firing a net that expands midair, shimmering with runes. It lands on Loki, who screams—a sound raw enough to strip paint. He collapses, the net constricting around him, blue light crawling up his arms and legs.

I throw myself onto the net, trying to tear it free, but it burns my hands, the sensation like dry ice and electric shock all at once. I scream, but they don't stop.

Another agent levels a pistol at my head. "Don't move," he snaps.

Sarah finally steps forward, arms out. "Ame, please, stop—don't make them hurt you."

I'm crying now, ugly and loud. "You did this," I spit. "You fucking did this. AGAIN! You went behind my back, AGAIN!!"

Sarah's lip trembles. "I'm sorry. You stopped answering my calls. You wouldn't listen to reason. I was losing you, Ame. I couldn't just watch you disappear into... whatever this is."

Loki writhes on the ground, his eyes rolling back. The dogs whine, circling, powerless.

Mercer gestures, and the agents drag Loki toward the SUV, net and all. I try to follow, but Sarah catches me, holding me tight despite my flailing, my cursing, my promise that I will never, ever forgive her.

"I had to," she whispers, tears streaming. "You don't know what is real; this guy is dangerous."

I struggle and then sag, every bone in my body turning to ash. I watch as they get Loki next to the SUV, the blue light leaking from the net staining the glass.

Mercer turns to me, her face unreadable. "We'll be in touch, Ms. Gold. Stay here, and you won't be harmed."

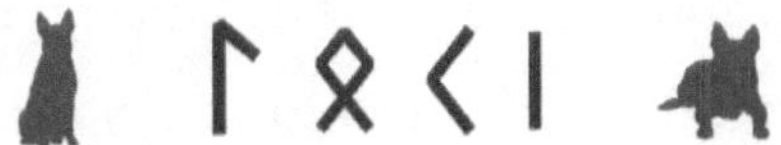

It's funny how quickly a day can go from apocalyptic to worse.

One second I'm drowning in the empty silence, staring at Loki's limp body wrapped in that damned net. The next, everything explodes: gunshots, barking, the scream of metal, and the rattle of energy so intense it makes my bones hum.

I hear Loki's voice, strange and layered—a dozen voices packed into one. "Stay back!" he roars.

The next instant, green lightning splits the air. It arcs from Loki's outstretched hand, ripping through the net that holds him, then leaps to the nearest agent, slamming him into the side of an SUV with a sound like a dropped watermelon. The smell of ozone is sharp enough to sting my eyes. A second arc lashes out, tossing another agent into the dirt, armor smoking.

Loki's on his knees, hands locked behind his head, runes crawling up his face like ivy. His power is ugly now, wild, bending the air in jagged lines. He tries to stand, but an agent clubs him in the side with a weapon that looks like a taser built by a psychopath. Loki jerks, howls, but doesn't fall.

I shove against Sarah, god, I hate her. I run. No plan, just running. There's a shovel propped by the trailer's side, half-buried in the red dirt from when I tried to fix the fence last spring. I grab it with both hands and charge the nearest agent. He sees me, but too late—I swing for his knee. The impact vibrates up my arms, rattling my teeth. He crumples, howling, baton skittering out of his hand.

Mystic is a blur, launching herself at another agent's calf. She latches on, teeth buried deep, and the man howls, kicking, but she won't let go. Ash circles, barking, darting in to nip at any exposed flesh. For a moment, it looks like we might actually have a shot.

Then Sarah's voice cuts through the chaos, sharp and desperate. "Ame, stop! You're making it worse!"

I turn, shovel raised, blood pounding in my ears. "Worse? This can't get worse and it's your fucking fault!! You think this is help?"

She's crying, her eyes wide and wet, mouth twisted in grief. "They promised you'd be safe if—if I helped—please, just stop, Ame, please—"

Behind her, two agents wrestle Loki to the ground, one driving a knee into his spine while the other jams something onto his wrist: a band of metal, studded with tiny, shifting runes. The instant it locks, the light under his skin dies. All of it. He goes limp, gasping, his face drained of all color.

He lifts his head, eyes locking on mine, and there's no magic left in them—just a flat, animal panic. He mouths something, but I can't hear it over the noise. I can't read his lips either.

I rush forward, shovel raised, but another agent intercepts me, bear-hugging me from behind. My ribs creak under the pressure. I drop the shovel and flail, trying to elbow him, but he's twice my size and wrapped in body armor. The only thing I can do is scream.

Mystic yelps. I turn in time to see her kicked aside by a boot, rolling twice before scrambling upright, tail tucked. Ash is faring better, keeping low and nipping at ankles, but the agents are too many, too well trained. "Don't hurt them!!"

Sarah rushes to me, trying to wedge herself between me and the agent holding me down. "Let her go! She's not dangerous!"

The agent ignores her. Instead, he shoves me to the ground, pinning my wrists behind my back. My face hits the dirt, and I taste blood. I try to twist, to see Loki, but there's a boot in my shoulder.

Through the blur of bodies, I see the agents hauling Loki to his feet. He can barely stand; he sags between two men, his head lolling. They frog-march him to the SUV, open the door, and slam him inside like a sack of trash.

"No!" I scream, my throat shredded.

Sarah is sobbing now, clutching my hand, repeating, "I'm sorry, I'm so sorry, I didn't know—"

I want to bite her. I want to tear her fucking face off. Instead, I jerk my chin up and spit blood at her feet.

"They're going to kill him," I say, my voice raw.

Sarah shakes her head, hair wild. "No. No, they promised. It's just containment. Just—until they can figure out how to fix it."

"Fix what?" I snarl. "He's not broken!"

The agents aren't listening. One by one, they load up, slamming doors, weapons still trained on us even as the engines rumble to life. The lead agent—Mercer—gives Sarah a look, then me.

"Stay put," she says, like I'm a dog. "Don't try to follow."

Mystic crawls to my side, licking the blood from my cheek. Ash presses in close, whining, eyes fixed on the departing SUVs. I hug them both, digging my fingers into their fur until it hurts.

The agents release me, and I collapse, face in my hands, dogs pressed tight against my body.

Sarah kneels beside me, still babbling apologies, but I don't hear her. I can't. There's a hole in my chest where Loki used to be, and the only thing left is the throb of old magic, fading, fading, until it's gone. "Get away from me, you backstabbing bitch!"

For a long time, I don't move. The dogs don't move. Sarah sobs into her sleeve, and I just kneel there, empty.

They took him.

They took everything.

And I'm not sure if I'll ever get it back.

I can't move. Not because the agents are still here—they're packing up, watching me and talking low, loading the last evidence into the back of the SUVs like they're hauling groceries. Not because Sarah is clutching my arm, whispering frantic apologies in my ear. But because there's nothing left to move for. Not even the satisfaction I'd feel if I punched her in her backstabbing face.

Mystic and Ash press against me, their bodies rigid, heads cocked. I bury my face in their fur, breathing in their warm, animal stink. My mind is empty. Burned out. I stare at the patch of earth where they knocked Loki down, where the ground is still scorched from his last, desperate spark.

I want to scream, but there's no air left in my lungs.

Something in the air changes. It starts with the dogs—they both lift their heads at the same time, ears high, noses twitching. The hairs on my arms stand straight up, and my teeth start to chatter, even though it's not cold.

Sarah must feel it too because she goes still, the rhythm of her breath flattening into a hush. The agents—six, maybe seven still out in the open—pause, hands on their gear, eyes scanning the tree line.

For a heartbeat, nothing happens.

Then, just above the dirt, the Twilight Runes ignite. Not as a trick of light, not as hallucination or memory, but physically there, hanging in the air. They blaze in daylight, blue and gold and purple, lines of script crawling over each other, folding and unfolding, a language so old my brain trips trying to read it.

The nearest agent swears, drawing a weapon, but the gun jams instantly, the safety welded shut by a creeping web of blue sigils.

"What the hell is this?" Mercer demands, backing up a step.

The runes ripple, then rush together, a tornado of light coiling around my legs and torso. I try to scramble backward, but I can't—I'm paralyzed, stuck to the earth. The runes snake up my body, cold and hot at the same time, and I feel every scar, every bruise, every old hurt mapped out in burning lines.

Sarah lets go of me, scrambling back. "Ame? What's happening to you?"

I open my mouth to answer, but nothing comes out. My skin is buzzing, the sensation so intense I think my bones might shatter from the inside. I look down, and the runes are fusing to my arms, wrapping around my wrists, painting my fingers in intricate, moving tattoos.

One of the agents tries to intervene, lunging forward, but the runes arc off my skin, blasting him backward. He hits the side of the SUV and slumps, groaning.

The runes climb higher, wreathing my throat and jaw. I gasp, but the air tastes different—sharper, sweeter, full of electricity and ozone. My hair floats up, purple strands standing on end, and when I look at my reflection in the window of the pickup, my eyes are glowing.

Not a trick of light.

Glowing.

Mercer signals her team, voice frantic. "Get the net! Restrain her—now!"

Three agents converge on me, two with the rune-web net, one with a taser. But the net fizzles, unraveling before it even touches my body, the runes eating through the mesh like acid. The taser never even makes contact—the wires arc away, pulled by the swirling energy now orbiting me in tight, glowing rings.

Sarah stumbles back, hands over her mouth. "Ame, you're—I don't—"

I stand up, not by choice, but because the runes haul me to my feet like a marionette. I'm taller than I've ever felt, my body light, every cell fizzing with borrowed power. I try to step forward, and the runes respond, parting the air, shoving the nearest agent aside like he's made of foam.

I hear a car door slam. I look over, and as the SUV is thrown into gear, there's Loki, face pressed against the SUV window, blood on his mouth. His eyes are huge, stunned, but there's something else there: pride.

It looks like he's saying, 'They've chosen you. Of course they have.' And then the SUV is flying out of the yard.

The agents hesitate now, caught between fear and orders. I feel the runes tighten, coiling around my chest, and suddenly I understand. I know what they want, what they are. It's knowledge, but also hunger—ancient, endless, alive.

Mercer tries one more time, voice trembling. "Amethyst, let us help you. We can control it—contain it—"

The runes answer for me. I raise my hand, and a rush of light slams into her, sending her sprawling across the hood of her own SUV. The rest of the agents scatter, yelling, ducking behind vehicles.

I walk, slow and measured, toward the vacant spot where the SUV once stood, its tires having kicked up a cloud of dust as it sped away with Loki inside. The runes beneath my feet still carve symbols into the ground with every step, burning the grass, melting the gravel, their energy sizzling in the air. Mystic and Ash follow at my heels, tails high, their eyes reflecting the same purple fire that blazes in mine, a testament to the power coursing through us.

Sarah stands at the edge of the clearing, paralyzed, staring at the space the vehicle occupied just moments ago. "Ame," she says, voice tiny and quivering. "What are you?"

I stop, feeling the runes swirl around me, their ancient language whispering secrets. I'm searching for the right word, one that sits on the tip of my tongue, ancient and impossible, yet elusive to English expression. Instead, I just smile, teeth sharp and bright, a promise of defiance.

"A survivor," I say, the words hanging in the electrified air.

Sarah's face crumples, but I don't care. I don't want her close, don't want her apologies, don't want to feel the gravity of her regret pulling at my body like a tide. I turn, runes spiraling up my arms, and fix her with a look so sharp I can practically see it slice the hope out of her eyes.

"Go, Sarah." My voice is not my voice. It's doubled, echoed, alive with something that doesn't care for second chances. "Get out. Don't come back. I never want to see you again."

She nods, stumbling over her own feet as she backs away, then runs—full tilt—into the treeline, sobbing. The sound of her flight is brittle leaves and snapping twigs. Part of me wants to feel sorry, but the runes won't let me. They hum with a new certainty, a new coldness, and it's easier than I thought it would be to let the last scrap of our friendship burn to ash.

Another agent tries to play hero. He ducks behind the pickup, thinking the steel and glass will save him, then barrels at me with the runic net stretched wide. I see his face through the mesh—eyes wild, mouth set in a line that probably looks good on performance reviews—and for a heartbeat, I almost pity him. Almost.

He lunges, net first. The moment it makes contact, the runes on my body flare, brighter than a welding arc, and the net disintegrates. Not a slow burn, not a sizzle, but a full-body detonation—purple fire, geometry, the smell of fried copper. The agent screams, drops the frame, and falls to his knees, clutching his face. Mystic moves in, teeth bared, a low growl vibrating the air. The agent scrambles backward, hands up, and vanishes into the shadows at the edge of the yard.

The rest of the agents retreat, slinking behind their vehicles, every eye fixed on me like I'm a wild animal they don't have a cage for yet. I stand alone in the middle of the clearing, haloed in the afterglow of living language, my hair whipping in the wind, the dogs flanking me. My skin crawls with power. My body feels like a live wire, every nerve ending doubled and tripled, the world filtered through a lens of impossible clarity.

For a long moment, no one moves. The birds are silent. The wind, too.

Then, from somewhere deep in the woods, I hear the distant wail of sirens. Not local—these are too low, too measured, the kind of sirens that mean someone called in a favor at the highest possible level. The Division won't stop. Not for me, not for Loki, not for the trail of runes now burning themselves into every patch of dirt I cross.

Mystic whines, nudges my hand with her nose. The runes pulse, gentle for once, and I drop to my knees, hugging her tight. Ash butts in, tail wagging, tongue lolling, and the pressure in my chest breaks just enough for me to breathe.

But I know what I have to do. I can feel it in the runes, carved into the marrow of who I am. I have to get Loki back. He's alive—I'm sure of it, as sure as I am that the sun will rise tomorrow—but he's not safe, not while Mercer is running the show.

The runes agree, flickering across my vision, drawing a map only I can see.

I stand, brushing the dirt off my knees. I look back at the trailer—our little shipwreck, battered and empty—and for a second, I almost wish I could go inside, lock the door, and pretend the world is still one where magic stays on the page and best friends don't sell you out for your own good. But that world is gone.

It's survivor time.

The runes seem to erect a wall around the agents. I sling my go-bag over one shoulder, leash the dogs, and start walking. The agents watch, weapons twitching, but none of them dare to follow, not that they could. One tries to shout after me, but the runes cut him off, the words freezing in his throat. I smile, a sharp, mean thing, and keep going. The world outside the perimeter is colder, less charged, but the runes stay with me, twisting up my arms and around my throat in patterns I'll never be able to erase.

The dogs break into a run, and I run with them, the woods blurring past in a smear of pine needles and possibility. The runes spark with every stride, leaving marks on the trees and rocks, a trail only I can read. I run until the air shreds my lungs, until the world tilts and the sky turns the color of old bruises. I run until I find the road, and the runes point the way north.

There is only one person who might have any idea how to help me: Miss Eliza. The runes flare, and I have a feeling they are making sure the Division can't track me as I plunge into the woods without looking back.

CHAPTER FOURTEEN

THE PRISONER OF MIDGARD

Wakefulness comes as a punishment.

I snap into existence with a body clamped flat and cold, every muscle locked at full extension. For a moment, the world is nothing but staccato pulses—light, darkness, light—each flash harsher than the last, each shadow smothering as a burial shroud. The first sound that registers is the keening whine of electronics, pitched to torment, and then the drag of my own ragged breath, hissing through clenched teeth. My face itches with sweat. My mouth tastes of old pennies and bile.

I'm flat on my back, strapped into a cradle of surgical steel. The ceiling above me is pure white, seamless and luminous—no seams, no bolts, no easy way out. The air reeks of disinfectant so sharp it burns the soft tissue behind my nose. They have not even given me the dignity of a pillow.

Restraints at the neck, biceps, wrists, thighs, ankles. Each band etched in runic script so old it predates any alphabet humans have ever known. They burn on contact, not with fire, but with the icy clarity of self-loathing. I struggle, reflexive, but the bands only constrict, tightening until my pulse sings in my temples and my hands go numb. There's no point in screaming. The cell, if it even merits such a term, is designed to absorb sound and light, to deny the prisoner the comfort of echoes or shadows or anything like hope.

I try to shift, to command the space, to become insubstantial. Nothing. The trick does not work here. Instead, every cell in my body is mapped, indexed, and pinned like a moth to velvet. The suppression is not only physical; it's metaphysical, a weaving of material and meaning. These bastards have learned to trap the parts of me that aren't even supposed to be real.

Panic is new. I almost relish it.

There are voices beyond the glass. They keep it dark on their side, but my eyes are built for all spectra. They cannot hide from me, not truly. Three figures: two in full hazmat, one in a tailored suit, mouth blurred behind a medical mask but eyes sharp and cold and very, very awake. They move like surgeons, or maybe more like undertakers. The suited one consults a slate tablet, scrolling through readings with one finger, never glancing up.

I could tell them so much about themselves from the way they stand, the way they try to become invisible in a room made for observing me.

Instead, I focus inward, testing the boundaries. The runes on the restraints twist and snake with my attempts, tightening if I so much as think about shifting my shape. I try to extend my senses beyond the table, reaching for the faintest trickle of magic—something, anything—but as soon as the thought forms, pain shreds it, white-hot and electrical. I nearly bite my tongue in half.

Fine. Mortal rules, then. Mortal answers.

The two in hazmat suits let themselves in through a negative-pressure lock, moving with that slow, deliberate caution reserved for bomb squads or viral outbreak teams. They do not speak to me. They check the runes, shine UV flashlights over my skin, and scan the pattern of tattoos along my forearms and neck as if searching for something new.

The taller one produces a syringe as thick as a candle. "Specimen ready for draw," it says, voice genderless, modulated to strip out accent or inflection.

A needle that big is not necessary. It's just for theater.

They angle for the vein inside my elbow—how clinical, how cliché—and drive the needle home. Pain, of course, but the surprise is not the sharpness. The surprise is that I feel it at all.

No anesthetic, no glamour, no healing factor ready to erase the insult. The blood is slow to fill the vial. I watch, fascinated, as the color transitions from the familiar blue of home to the ugly, oxygenated red of this world. I want to sneer. I cannot move my face enough to do it.

"Levels are stable," the short one reports. "Suppression is holding at 98 percent. Subject remains at baseline."

They switch arms. I grit my teeth, tasting more blood.

The suited one, the observer, clears their throat and steps up to the glass. "You're awake," it says. No name. No title. Just that flat, American vowel. "Good. We have a lot of work to do."

I try to speak. It takes two tries before my mouth cooperates. "You're going to die here," I rasp, and mean every word.

The observer ignores the threat. "You understand your situation, yes?"

I flick my gaze around, as much as the restraints allow. "This is a very expensive hole you've put me in."

"It's a containment facility," the observer says. "Purpose-built." They flick a glance at the tablet, then back to me. "We've been tracking your kind for years. But you're the first to let us study you this closely."

The scientists—no, the jailers—begin attaching leads to my chest and temples, fastening adhesive pads, securing sensors along my jaw and over the pulse points on my throat. Every contact point is another burn, another snarl of pain, but I don't let them hear it. They're measuring every variable: heart rate, oxygen, hormone levels. I realize, dimly, that the rate is not just for show. My body is genuinely panicking. Some part of me is closer to death than I have ever been before.

The observer watches, hands clasped behind their back. "You have no rights," they say, clinically. "No protections under any Geneva or Helsinki accords. The entity known as Loki is not considered a sovereign being. Our protocols allow for unrestricted study."

"That's a mistake," I manage. The pain is building now, layer upon layer. "You think you can contain what you don't understand?"

The observer's eyes crinkle, the only smile I will ever get from them. "That's the point of this exercise."

I see the second needle coming. This one glows with a sick blue light, the liquid inside thicker than mercury. The label on the injector says only: PHASE III.

They plunge it into my thigh, slow and deliberate.

This time I scream. I can feel the runes ignite, not just on the restraints but in my bones. Every nerve ending lights up, each one vying to outdo the others in creative misery. The pain is old, cosmic, the kind that could drive planets mad. My vision whites out, then comes back in time to see the hazmat duo step away, hands moving in practiced, impersonal synchrony.

The observer leans in. "The runes in your bonds are genuine," they say, as if to a recalcitrant child. "Carved from a splinter of the Yggdrasil. Enhanced with twenty-first-century science. If you attempt to shift, the field will triple. If you attempt to exit your physical form, the runes will turn it to vapor."

I laugh, though it's mostly a cough. "You really have no idea who I am, do you?"

"We have a dossier," the observer says. "Several, actually." They tap the tablet and swipe through images—police sketches, security footage, old woodcut prints from a previous life. "But none of that matters now. Here, you are just data. A living experiment."

The pain is spreading now, a colony of suffering setting up in my gut, radiating out to every joint and tendon. I am sweating. Shivering. I realize, with a jolt of disgust, that I am hungry. That I am thirsty. That I could, perhaps, be broken. The idea is obscene.

"Why?" I ask, my voice thin as ice. "What do you hope to learn?"

"Everything," the observer says. "What you are. What you can do. What else is out there." Their eyes go shark-like, empty of anything but process. "And, of course, how to kill you if necessary."

One of the hazmat duo wheels in a cart of instruments, all gleaming steel and glass and digital readouts. They arrange the tools in neat rows, prepping for the next phase. The other one busies itself with a rolling ultrasound, pressing the head against my ribs and narrating the results in clinical monotone.

I try, once more, to shift my form, to become anything but this. The pain is immediate and staggering—every synapse clamped tight by a power older than gods. My vision splits into negative and color, and I am forced back into myself.

"Don't bother," the observer says, not unkind. "No one escapes here. Not you, not the ones before you, not even the hybrids."

I let my eyes go dead. "How long do you plan to keep me?"

"As long as it takes," the observer says. "You're a resource, not a guest."

The pain does not abate. It cycles, peaks and troughs, always threatening to tip me into blackout. I think about the centuries I've spent in comfort and pleasure, the chase of sensation. I think about how every cage is a lesson and how much I always hated the learning.

The hazmat duo finish their prep. One produces a bone saw—not because they need to, but because they want me to see it—and holds it up for the observer's nod.

"Ready to begin?" the observer asks, and for a heartbeat, I almost admire their commitment to the part.

I meet their eyes. "You will regret this."

The observer taps the glass, a parent putting a child to bed. "We already do."

They dial up the runes. The pain blooms anew, red and unrelenting. My scream this time is silent, only the arch of my back betraying me. The world fuzzes at the edges, then collapses into a tunnel. I see faces from all my lives, all my escapes, all my victories. I see the impossible girl and her impossible dogs. I see myself, as I was, as I am, as I will never be again.

They cut. They sample. They measure everything.

The lights go white.

When I next surface, I am alone, sweat-soaked and shivering, the taste of blood still fresh on my tongue. The restraints have been adjusted, a fresh set of runes now inked into the flesh at my wrists. I am weak. I am afraid. I am, for the first time, something like mortal.

But this is not the end.

They may have built a perfect cage, but they have not learned the first rule of gods or monsters:

Nothing is inevitable, and everything can be undone.

I lie back, memorize the pattern of light and pain, and begin to plan my escape.

They don't let me sleep, but sleep happens anyway. In the cracks between procedure and pain, I slip into a half-dream, a fevered twilight that tastes of ice water, old coins, and ammonia. The lights above my cell never dim; they change hue in a way that's supposed to simulate day and night, but it only makes the passage of time more unreal. I exist in a wash of artificial blue, punctuated by the bright white of the procedure lamp and the occasional red of my own blood, spattered on the medical-grade vinyl.

At first, the hallucinations are manageable—static, noise, the jumpy replay of the last moments before capture, like a security tape stuck on loop. But as the chemicals pile up, the boundaries start to slip. Shadows move in the corners of the cell, making faces. Sometimes the faces belong to strangers, but mostly they belong to the dead.

They come in order of intimacy. First, the small-time marks—the marks, the men and women I used, cheated, and manipulated into whatever game seemed interesting that century. Their faces hover just out of reach, each one mouthing the word "why," or sometimes nothing at all. Some wear suits, some wear skinsuits of blood and rot, but all of them fix me with eyes that will not blink.

After the marks, the warriors and the gods come. Odin, in particular, is impossible to shake. He sits cross-legged at the end of the table, picking at his nails, every so often glancing up with the kind of bone-deep disappointment that doesn't require words. His eye patch is gone, and the empty socket weeps a slow, steady trail of black. He says, "I told you, Loki, they'll never stop coming," and then, "You were always the most dangerous to yourself."

Freya visits, too, resplendent in her swan cloak, feathers slick with something that's not quite water. She leans over me, her face so close I can feel the phantom chill of her breath. "You're not even trying to escape," she hisses. "What would the old you say?" Her nails are claws, and they leave tracks in the air above my face, but never break the skin.

Sometimes my mother appears, but she never stays long. Her hair is black, her eyes like bottomless wells, and when she speaks, it's only to say, "You're not finished." Then she's gone, and I'm alone with the others.

The dead do not stop coming. They press in, crowding the cell, until the air is thick with their judgments and their rot and their terrible, unblinking eyes. I hate them. I love them. I miss them more than I can bear.

Eventually, the hallucinations congeal into something more vivid. Amethyst appears—not as a ghost, not as an accusation, but as herself. At first, she's a whisper, a shimmer of purple light sliding up the wall to pool under the gurney. Then she's there, standing at the foot of the table, hands on her hips, dressed in those battered yoga pants and the shirt with the faded superhero logo. Her hair is down, a curtain of violet in the fluorescent dark.

She is more real than the others. She's solid. She smells like wet dog and coffee and fear.

"Hi," she says, her voice breaking just a little.

"You're not supposed to be here," I tell her.

She shrugs. "Neither are you."

I try to laugh, but the sound sticks in my throat. "You're a hallucination," I say.

She grins. "Then you finally get to see what's been happening on my end."

She moves closer. I flinch, expecting the restraints to flare, but they don't. Her hand hovers over my forehead, and when she touches me it's—warm. Human. I want to reach up, to cup her hand in mine, but I can't even twitch my fingers.

"You look terrible," she says.

"You should see the other guy," I manage.

She snorts, but her eyes are wet. "Why do you do this?"

"Do what?"

"Take the hit," she says. "You could have run. You could have left me there. Instead, you're..." She gestures at the table, the IVs, the bruises. "...this."

For a moment, I can't answer. Then I say, "Maybe I finally found something worth being caught for."

She rolls her eyes, but she doesn't pull away. "Don't get sappy now," she says. "You need to hold on. I'm coming for you."

I blink. "That's not safe. They—these people—"

"They don't know who they're messing with," she says. "Just hold on, okay? I'll figure it out. I always do."

Her fingers trail down my cheek, and the light in the cell goes purple for a moment, soft and complete. Then she's gone. No fade-out, no goodbye, just an empty space where hope had been.

The pain comes back, sharp and precise, carving me down to the bone. But it doesn't matter. Not as much. I let the other ghosts come, let Odin and Freya and the endless parade of dead crowd the cell with their accusations. I let them talk. I let them watch.

But I listen only for her.

I hold on.

I hold on.

I hold on.

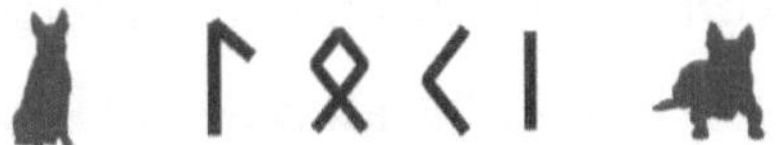

The briefing room is buried five levels below ground, shielded against every signal known to man or myth. No windows, just the hum of filtered air and the radiance of ceiling panels locked on "afternoon" twenty-four hours a day. Three agents sit around a steel table, their faces puckered by exhaustion, the glare bouncing off their foreheads like an interrogation spotlight.

Mercer runs the debrief with a surgeon's detachment. Every file is lined up along the table's edge: printed surveillance photos, genealogical charts, forensic lab reports, and a series of blurry images annotated with red Sharpie and something that looks suspiciously like old blood. At the center of the table, projected in sickly blue, is a photograph of Amethyst Gold, age seventeen, from her high school yearbook. Next to it is a faded black-and-white photo of her grandmother, the resemblance uncanny save for the hair.

The wall behind Mercer is wallpapered with sigil photographs: Norse runes, old and new, captured by satellite or from boots on the ground, every symbol annotated with what the Division's linguists think it might mean. The symbols in the old photos are less precise, more organic, but the experts say that only means they're more authentic.

"Start from the top," Mercer orders, not looking up from the notes.

Rodriguez, still sporting a gauze dressing on his jaw from the field, clears his throat. "Target: Amethyst Gold. Subject displays anomalous resilience to Class Two entities, with evidence of untrained rune affinity."

Keller, the eldest, leans forward, hands clasped like a priest. "Run the maternal line back four generations. Every female shows up in at least one supernatural incident report. The grandmother—Ruby Mae Davies—was investigated in '54 for suspected cult activity. The case was closed, but the file mentions the same symbol as the one we found on the trailer site."

He taps the table, bringing up a side-by-side of the trailer's bark-burned runes and a photo of a hand-carved wooden amulet from the old evidence room. The match is obvious, even to the untrained eye.

"Coincidence?" Mercer asks, sharp.

Keller shakes his head. "Statistically impossible. The pattern repeats every generation."

Lee, the tech, speaks up without looking away from her tablet. "There's something else. The ocular anomaly. The purple pigmentation in Gold's irises isn't a known mutation. It's not even in the database. The only other samples we found were in old crime scene photos from Iceland, dated to the early 1900s. No living relatives, but the DNA markers line up."

"How?" Rodriguez asks, the word trailing uncertainty.

"Nobody knows," Lee says. "But every time it shows up, there's a spike in supernatural event reports. Like a warning flare."

Mercer considers this. "What about the runes themselves? Any change in the pattern?"

Lee scrolls through several satellite overlays. "They're shifting. We saw new symbols after the breach. Some of them weren't even in the database. It's like the language is evolving in real time."

Mercer sits back, arms folded. "So she's not just a victim. She's a conduit. Or maybe a catalyst."

Keller snorts. "Or a bomb."

A silence hangs, thick and unsatisfying.

Finally, Mercer turns to the photo of Amethyst's grandmother, blown up to twice life-size. In the background of the photo is a bookshelf, and on the top shelf is a battered, rune-carved box. The shape of it is almost identical to the one the lab found embedded in the trailer wall.

"Get me everything on Ruby Mae Davies," Mercer says. "Not just Division files. Medical, financial, even church records. And send someone to the site in Louisiana—her line moved there in the '60s. I want to know if the pattern held."

Rodriguez nods and scribbles notes.

Mercer flicks the files off the projector, leaving the room in blank, humming light. "We're running out of time," she says. "The runes have never changed this fast. If Loki's involved, it's only going to get worse."

"Do we escalate?" Keller asks.

Mercer's jaw tightens. "Not yet. But keep the suppression ready. And move Gold up to Red Priority. She's not what she thinks she is."

The agents gather their files, eyes a little wider than when they started.

Amethyst Gold's face glows on the empty screen, eyes bright as bruises.

Outside, somewhere in the dark, the runes are already rewriting the world.

Chapter Fifteen

PREPARING THE RESCUE

I hit the gravel road with my lungs on fire and my dogs already outpacing me, Mystic bulleting ahead and Ash sticking close enough to trip me with every panicked stride. The pines on the Thornwick property start whispering the second I cross onto their soil—no exaggeration, the trees literally murmur under their breath, runes crawling up the bark like phosphorescent lichen. If I wasn't already in a dead sprint, I'd stand there gawking, maybe get myself eaten by whatever decided to wake up in the woods tonight.

The dogs zero in on the porch like it's a lighthouse. I drag up behind them, wheezing, shirt stuck to my back with sweat, knees gone to jelly. The first step creaks under my weight—then the whole porch sighs, as if disappointed I even made it this far.

Eliza's already waiting. She's got a hurricane lantern dangling from her fist, the light a jaundiced ring that barely dents the black. She's in what I'm pretty sure are pajamas—ragged plaid pants and a men's undershirt, sleeves rolled over sinewy biceps—but the wild white mane of her hair makes her look a hundred times more witchy than any robe or cloak ever could. She eyes me up and down, one eyebrow cocked, then tips her chin toward the pines.

"So what did the Division do this time?" she says, voice all gravel and cigarettes.

"You know about the Division?" I ask, and she gives me a look that tells me I'm an idiot. I manage a laugh, which is really more of a bark. "It wasn't my fault, exactly."

She shrugs, no sympathy. "If I thought it was a tornado, I'd already be in the root cellar. You bring that chaos with you, girl."

Mystic's already wormed her way between Eliza's feet, tail wagging so hard it rocks the lantern. Ash just circles, hackles up, eyes never leaving the treeline.

I open my mouth to explain I didn't start it, but Eliza cuts me off with a flick of her hand. "Inside. We're not feeding the mosquitoes—or anything else—tonight."

The door groans as she shoves it open, letting out a draft of air that smells like dried sage and gun oil. I shut the door behind me and lean against it, letting my heart slow enough to keep from stroking out.

Eliza sets the lantern on a battered side table and surveys me, arms folded. "You look like hell," she observes, which is probably the closest she'll ever get to expressing concern.

"Been a rough week," I say. "The Division showed up at my place. Not just watching. Full perimeter, night-vision, weird gadgets. And they brought backup."

She snorts. "Feds always bring backup when they're scared. Means whatever's after you is worse than they are." She gestures at a sagging loveseat, covered in three blankets. "Sit. I'll get the whiskey."

I collapse onto the couch, letting my head fall back. Mystic hops up beside me, tucks her nose under my arm, and sighs like she's been running for days. Ash stands guard at the window, watching the woods with the patience of a predator.

Eliza clatters around the kitchen, pouring a pair of shots. She returns, hands me one, and sinks into an ancient recliner that wheezes under her weight.

We sit in silence for a minute, the only sounds the tick of the lantern and the distant, restless wind in the pines. I study the runes on my arms, still glowing faint purple. They pulse when I think about the agents, the net, the sound of Loki screaming.

Eliza takes a sip, then sets her glass on the armrest. "Alright," she says, "tell me everything. Don't leave out the weird stuff."

I do. I tell her about Loki, about the Division's new toys, about Sarah selling me out, about the way the runes fused to my skin and set me on fire from the inside. How they... took control of my body. I tell her about the dogs, about Loki's last look through the SUV window, about the taste of blood in my mouth as they dragged him away. I even tell her about the voice that wasn't my voice, the way I told Sarah to get gone and meant it with my whole soul.

Eliza listens, stone-faced. She doesn't interrupt, not once. When I finish, she sits back and closes her eyes, breathing slow.

"Well," she says, "you did a number on the woods. The pines on the north side are glowing like Christmas, and the whole ridge smells of ozone and old magic. Never seen it burn that hot this far south."

I rub my hands together, still trembling. "Sorry. Should I, like, pay for damages or something?"

She cackles, long and low. "Honey, the Division's been trying to shut this place down for fifty years. If you nuked a few trees, that's a net gain for the home team." She leans forward, elbows on knees. "But those runes—what you're describing—it's not just Chaos. It's old, old binding. Loki's work, but also something else."

I shiver. "You think I'm infected?"

She shakes her head. "Not infected. Chosen, maybe. Or unlucky. Or both."

We drink. I cough at the burn of the alcohol and try to absorb that. Chosen isn't a word I've ever liked. It sounds too much like "volunteered for the meat grinder."

Eliza stands, stretches her arms over her head, and grins at my wince when her spine cracks like a gunshot. "Let's see the damage," she says, nodding at my arms.

I pull up my sleeve. The runes crawl from my wrist to my elbow, deep purple, almost bruised in places. They move when you look straight at them, but if you look away, they freeze—like they're pretending to be just another bad tattoo.

Eliza runs a finger over the script, not gentle, and the runes flare hot under her touch. She mutters something in what I recognize as Old Norse, then snorts. "That's a first. Never seen them answer back like that. You're not just marked, Amethyst. You're a conduit. Not even your grandmother had this."

I stare at her like she's nuts. My grandmother? I had never met the woman. I knew nothing really about my family. Mom told me my grandma died when I was a baby. We had no pictures, no heirlooms, nothing. Yet the woman who the town says is crazy... knew her? But somehow I think the conduit thing might be more pressing.

I don't want to ask, but I do anyway. "A conduit for what?"

She fixes me with a look so sharp it could skin a cat. "For him. For whatever the hell Loki's trying to do, and for whatever the Division wants to stop. You're the link."

I bite my lip. "So what do I do?"

Eliza's answer is instant. "You get strong. You learn what those runes can do. And you don't let anyone—feds, gods, or otherwise—turn you into their pawn."

I nod, but it's mostly for show. Inside, I'm still unraveling.

Eliza moves to the window, peering through the warped glass at the woods beyond. The pines pulse with ghostly light, every trunk etched in runes, every needle humming with secret language. She seems satisfied with whatever she sees.

"You mentioned my grandmother... like you knew her." I blink. "I thought—she died before I was born."

Eliza laughs. "I did know her. She was my closest friend. She died, yes. But not before giving the Division the worst headache of their miserable careers." She comes back to the chair, sits, and leans in close. "Ruby Mae Davies. Real piece of work. She was doing rune work in the war, before the feds even had a word for it. Your mother didn't want anything to do with this, and the runes never called her. Your grandmother made me promise I would not be the one who brought you in. You would come on your own if you came at all. Your mother... well, your mother never had the gift. That's why they moved around so much when you were little—she was trying to keep you away from places where the old magic runs strong. She did what she could to make sure you didn't have to choose this."

"Tell me about my grandmother," I say, voice cracking.

Eliza grins. "Brave, and a little nuts. Like you."

I let myself laugh, just once.

The dogs have finally relaxed. Mystic is curled up on my lap, snoring, and Ash has parked himself at the door, tail wagging in his sleep. I wish I could feel that safe.

Eliza pours us another round, this one smaller. "Here's what you do," she says. "You stay here tonight. You rest. You let the runes settle. In the morning, we'll see what's what."

I want to argue, to ask more questions, but the weight of the night and the whiskey conspire to glue me to the couch. I nod, once.

Eliza stands, stretches, and heads for the hallway. She pauses at the threshold, backlit by the lantern.

"One more thing," she says, not turning around. "If you want to survive what's coming, you need to decide if you're fighting for yourself, or for him." She lets that hang, then vanishes down the hallway, her bare feet silent on the warped floorboards.

I stare at the ceiling, counting the cracks and water stains. Outside, the pines pulse with rune-fire, every flicker a heartbeat I can't ignore. I scratch Mystic behind the ears, watch her sigh in her sleep, and try to remember a time when I believed in happy endings.

I don't find one.

But I do find hope, thin and sour and stubborn as a weed.

I clutch it close and let the runes sing me to sleep.

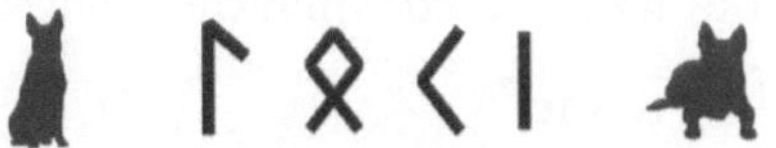

Sunrise at Miss Eliza's is a joke—there's too much forest, too many curtains, and the house itself seems to repel natural light like a bad memory. I wake up on the couch with Mystic's head pinning my thigh and Ash's paws wedged under my chin, both of them dead asleep and radiating the kind of dog heat that's supposed to be comforting but just makes me sweat through my T-shirt. I peel myself out from under them and tiptoe down the hallway, making a beeline for the back room Eliza calls the library.

The "library" is really just a glorified hoarder's nest—wall-to-wall bookcases, every shelf double-stacked, with the overflow piled in dangerous columns around the ancient braided rug. Miss Eliza is there with a box. She pulls out a journal and points to a faded diagram of spiraling symbols. "This is your grandmother's."

She hands me the journal and a box of other things on the clear spot on the floor.

My hands shake when I open the journal, a little black book with my grandmother's initials stamped in gold. The paper smells like dust and vanilla and time. The entries are short, weird, and often illegible, but some things pop out: lists of names I don't recognize, sketches of symbols I definitely do, and, in one margin, a crude drawing of a wolf with a forked tongue.

Eliza is silent for a moment, then begins, "The runes aren't yours to command, child. They're older than your bloodline, older than this forest. Your family's gift isn't making them—it's understanding them."

I think back to how they had reacted when the Division took Loki. "But I can feel them responding to me."

"Feel, yes. That's safe. It's when you try to MAKE them do what you want that the trouble starts." Eliza's voice goes grim. "Your grandmother learned that the hard way."

"What happened?"

"She tried to force them to protect the whole county during that bad storm in '73. Found her three days later; she couldn't remember her own name for a week. The runes had burned out half her mind." She flips through pages, showing progressively shakier handwriting. "Took her two years before she could light a candle with magic again. Never did get back to full strength."

I stare at the journal, at the evidence of my grandmother's decline. "What's the alternative?"

"Learn patience. Use them sparingly. Work WITH them, not against them." Eliza's finger traces the faded runes on the page. "And never, ever try to control the big ones alone. That's what partners are for."

"Partners?"

"Your grandmother never had one. But you..." Eliza glances toward the window. "You might be luckier than the rest of us." I assume she's talking about the dogs. Can they help me?

Ash materializes at my knee, yawning, then collapses in a heap like he's been awake all night. Mystic sniffs the box, circles, and curls up with her tail over her nose. I get the sense they don't want to be awake for what comes next.

In the bottom of the box, there is a small wooden box that has a trick latch, the kind that requires a weird pressure and a twist. I fumble with it until my thumb slips, and the thing springs open, nearly launching the contents into my lap. Inside: a bundle of letters, a dried bouquet of something that might have been heather or just East Texas weeds, and a tarnished silver locket that's heavier than it looks.

The locket is engraved with the same pattern as the runes on my arms. I can feel the pulse in my thumb as I brush it, like it's alive. I hold it up to the dust-smeared window, trying to make sense of the markings, and for a second the whole world slows. The light glints off the metal, and the runes on my skin flare to life, a line of heat running from the hollow of my throat to the tip of my pinky. I yelp and nearly drop the thing.

Ash's ears go up. Mystic growls, low and annoyed.

I dig a thumbnail into the locket's seam. It doesn't want to open, but I force it anyway. Inside: a tiny, curled scrap of parchment, covered in ink so faded it's more stain than symbol. I squint, then trace the first few lines. It's Norse, or something like it—thick, blocky strokes that match the ones on my arms.

The runes respond, flickering, then settling into a steady glow. My pulse is racing. I breathe through it, in and out, and try not to imagine the Division's lab techs taking apart my DNA like a jigsaw puzzle.

I didn't realize Miss Eliza had left the room; she's silent as a banshee. She returns and she's got two mugs in hand, steam rising.

"Good," she says, kicking aside a pile of books to sit cross-legged across from me. "You found it."

I hold up the locket, shaking a little. "What the hell is this?"

She sips her tea, eyes never leaving mine. "It's a reminder. Your grandmother's way of making sure you'd never forget who you were, even if the world did its best to make you forget."

She gestures at the locket, at the journals, at the photos. "Ruby Mae was a guardian. The runes—your bloodline—they're not just for show. They're a chain. A lock. Sometimes a key."

I blink, hands trembling. "Guardians of what?"

Eliza shrugs. "Artifacts, mostly. Knowledge. Sometimes people. Sometimes things that should never leave Asgard, let alone end up in East Texas." She leans in, voice dropping. "The Division thinks they're studying you, controlling you, but what they're really doing is protecting themselves. From what you carry."

The words hit like a sledgehammer. I look down at the locket, then at my hands, where the runes have faded to a faint, bruise-colored stain.

A shadow crosses the window—just a crow, or maybe something else. I hear bells... so I'm guessing something else. Ash's head snaps up, and Mystic growls again, this time with real menace.

I tuck the locket into my palm, feeling the cold weight of it. "So what do I do?"

Eliza smiles, sharp and a little sad. "You decide if you're going to fight the runes or learn how to use them. Because if you don't, the Division will. Or worse—he will."

She means Loki, but she doesn't say it out loud. I don't think she has to. I also know that I trust Loki. He would never hurt me. He wouldn't push me to do anything I didn't want to.

The room feels smaller, the ceiling lower, the air thick with history and old secrets. I want to cry, or punch something, or run until the world falls away. But the dogs are calm now, and the runes are quiet, and for the first time in forever, I know what I am.

Not a weapon. Not a monster. Not a pawn.

A lock. Maybe a key.

I can work with that.

Time is a poorly kept secret in the cell. The Division's architects, in their wisdom, left out clocks, calendars, and every other hint of passing days, but their little oversight has never troubled me. I've spent too many centuries counting hours by pain, by hunger, by the rhythms of my own decay. Here, it's easy: one pulse for every second the runes bite into my wrists, another for the way the light flickers when I remember something I'd rather forget.

I'm alone, of course. They don't post guards inside the viewing window anymore. Even the bravest agents only watch from behind layers of glass and layers of runes, as if I might rise up and bite through the wall with my teeth. I like that. I like knowing they're scared. It helps keep the cold out.

The first ghost appears in the corner, near the seam where the ceiling meets the cinder block. She's early, but I'm not surprised. The Division's chemists have been dosing me with ever more creative compounds, each one a bespoke little torture: one makes my thoughts run slow as syrup, another lights up my nerves like festival lanterns. The newest cocktail is a hallucinogen, or maybe it's just old-fashioned guilt.

She's beautiful, the first one—tall, golden, elegant in the way of Asgardian court women. I know her by the set of her jaw, the line of her brow. She's wearing the same blue silk she wore the night we ruined her wedding feast, but it's spattered with black and the train has been chewed to ribbons. Her hands are clasped so tight the knuckles go white.

"Hello, Ingrid," I say, and my voice is steadier than I expect.

She glides toward me, feet not quite touching the floor. I can't smell her perfume, not through the chemical haze, but I remember it: lilac, and something sharp underneath. She stops a pace away, tilts her head, and lets her mouth curl in a smile so thin it could slice me open.

"You're smaller than I remember," she says.

I flash her my best wolfish grin, the one that always worked on her when we were alive. "Time shrinks all things."

She ignores the jab. "Why did you leave me there?" she asks, voice soft as dying embers.

"Because I had to," I say, and for once I mean it. "They'd have killed us both."

Ingrid's eyes never leave mine. "You never intended to stay. You never intended to save anyone but yourself."

She's right, and we both know it. The runes on my wrists pulse in agreement, sending a jolt up my forearm that makes my teeth ache.

"You were always good at making pain look like a choice," she whispers, then fades to nothing, a curl of blue silk in the air.

The second ghost doesn't wait for the first to clear. He's huge, even hunched under the low ceiling, arms banded with scars. A Jötunn, my old kin. His eyes are small, dark, and so full of disappointment it almost makes me laugh. Almost.

"Gunnar," I say, not bothering to sit up.

He circles the bench, slow as a bear in winter. "You lied to me," he rumbles.

"Everyone lies," I reply, "especially to themselves."

He grabs my chin in one spectral hand, forcing me to look up. His fingers pass through my skin but the chill remains, an ice that sets my nerves crackling. "You said we would be free," Gunnar says. "But you brought us here to be caged."

He's not wrong, either. I want to say I regret it, but the words won't come. The runes twist tighter, carving fresh pain into my bones.

Gunnar lets go, steps back. "You're not the only one who can't change." He vanishes, but the chill lingers, icing my breath.

The parade picks up speed. Next is the king—mortal, old, eyes clouded by war and wine. He's wearing the same dented crown I once convinced him would make him immortal. He laughs, a wheezing cough, and wags a finger at me.

"You promised me eternity," he says.

I can't help but smile. "You're still here, aren't you?"

He laughs again, the sound turning into a wet rattle. "Only because I can't leave." He steps forward, his face inches from mine. "You are nothing but a voice in the dark, Loki. You were never meant to be real."

He collapses at my feet, and the floor drinks him in.

They come faster now. All the betrayals, all the seductions, every mark and every monster I ever used, abandoned, or outfoxed. Their accusations blur together: You used me. You broke your word. You watched the world burn and called it justice. Each voice is a knife; each face is a mirror. My hands shake on the bench. I dig my nails into my palms, trying to feel something besides regret.

The runes on my arms are burning now, a fever so hot I think I might melt. I don't cry out—I never do—but the air tastes of ash and metal. The ghosts don't care. They press in, crowding the cell, their hands reaching, their eyes full of old wounds.

One of them is smaller than the rest. I don't recognize her at first. She's a child, maybe seven or eight, dressed in rags and clutching a ragged scrap of paper in both fists. Her hair is black, her eyes wide as the night.

I stare at her, heart stumbling. "No," I say, and it comes out as a whisper.

She steps forward, holding out the paper. "You promised," she says.

I try to turn away, but the runes clamp down, locking me in place. The girl is at my knees now, her face inches from mine. Her breath smells of earth and smoke and endings.

"You promised I would be safe," she says.

I can't answer. I can't even breathe. The ghosts behind her close in, their voices rising in a tide of accusation.

I fall off the bench, knees hitting the tile. The pain is sharp, but I welcome it. The girl's eyes never leave mine.

"I'm sorry," I whisper. "I never meant for you to suffer."

She leans in, places a cold, spectral kiss on my forehead, and disappears.

The cell is empty again. The lights buzz overhead, harsh and flat. My wrists are bleeding where the runes have cut through skin. I curl up on the floor, the cool tile against my cheek, and let the pain wash over me.

For a long time, I don't move. I let the ghosts come and go, let the runes burn and fade. I let the guilt settle in, heavy and endless. I think about Amethyst, about her laugh, about the way she looked at me and saw through every mask I ever wore. I think about the promises I never kept, the ones I wish I'd made.

The Division thinks they've beaten me. They think this cell is a prison. They have no idea.

This is just the beginning.

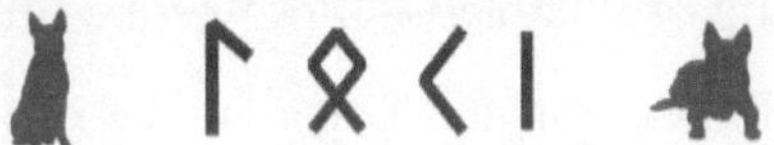

The attic smells like petrichor and scorched newsprint, every square inch packed with memories that have either been sanitized or set on fire. I stand in front of a mirror older than most Texas towns, toes curling in the dust, the family locket heavy against my throat. The runes on my arms smolder in the half-light, every pulse a reminder that I am not alone in here, not even in my own body.

Miss Eliza prowls the perimeter, setting out candles and drawing chalk marks on the ancient pine floorboards. She doesn't believe in "ambiance," she says, but some things require a little old-fashioned theater. Mystic and

Ash are on the landing, watching through the banister, every hackle up and vibrating.

"Ready?" Eliza asks, voice pitched low, as if there might be Division mics hiding in the insulation.

I'm not, but I nod anyway. "What's the worst that could happen?" I joke.

She gives me a look that makes it clear she's thought about that, and it's not a short list.

"Start with your breathing," she says, settling onto a milk crate. "Focus on the locket. Let the runes do what they want."

I inhale, slow and shaky. The locket is cold, the metal buzzing with a heartbeat I know isn't mine. I touch it, thumb brushing the engraved lines, and the runes on my skin flare to life—purple and gold, flickering along my veins. In the mirror, the effect is even more pronounced. I look like someone set my DNA on fire.

Eliza murmurs a string of syllables—Old Norse, guttural and impossible. She's said before that language is key, that the runes respond to the music of memory and blood. I repeat after her, mouth stumbling on the consonants, and the air thickens, turns syrupy.

The runes shift. They climb my arms, up my neck, across my collarbones. It's like being tattooed from the inside out, a hot, living needle dragging power through every nerve.

"Good," Eliza says, softer now. "Don't fight it. Let the memory happen."

The first flash is Loki, as always. Not the wounded wolf from the SUV window, but the man I first met: tall, smiling, eyes full of jokes he hasn't told yet. He stands behind my reflection in the mirror, arms crossed, a little amused, a little wary. The runes on his arms are the same as mine, only brighter—green-gold, alive.

I want to turn around, to grab him, but I know better. I meet his eyes in the glass.

"I can feel you," I whisper.

The runes pulse, as if in answer.

Another flash: the Division's cell, cold and white, Loki on a bench with wrists bound in iron and runes. He looks up, startled, as if I've called his name across an impossible gulf. His mouth moves, but I can't hear it—just the shape of my name, the surprise and relief in his eyes.

The vision snaps back to the attic. I'm sweating, heart pounding, the runes on my skin throbbing with every heartbeat. Eliza hands me a towel, but her face is serious.

"Did you reach him?" she asks.

I nod. "He's alive. He's hurting."

She sits back, crosses her arms. "That's good. That means the link is working. But you need to be careful—if the Division's watching, they'll see you coming a mile away."

I laugh, a little wild. "They already do."

Eliza's expression softens, just for a second. "You care about him," she says, like she's diagnosing a disease.

I look away, then back at the mirror. "I love him," I say, the words unfamiliar and sharp. "Despite everything he is."

The admission hangs in the attic, vibrating in the air. Even the dogs go still.

Eliza lets out a breath. "That's your choice. But remember: your bloodline was meant to guard against chaos, not be swept up in it."

I meet her gaze. "Maybe it's time for a new tradition."

She barks a laugh. "Spoken like a true Davies woman."

"What killed my grandmother?"

"The runes. Eventually, they burn you out from the inside. Unless..." She pauses.

"Unless what?"

"Unless you find a way to share the load." Eliza's eyes flick toward the mirror. "That's why partners matter. The magic doesn't have to consume just one person."

"You mean... Loki."

Eliza didn't look happy, exactly, but she nodded.

I close my eyes, the locket burning against my skin. I reach for the connection, for the thread of power that links me to Loki. It's easier now—the runes want to help, to guide, to bind us together.

In the Division cell, Loki's head snaps up. I see him, not just as a memory, but as he is now: bruised, battered, eyes haunted by the ghosts of a thousand mistakes. He smiles, just a little, and the runes on his arms blaze in time with mine.

"I'm coming for you," I say, voice steady.

He nods, and the ghosts behind him retreat, just for a moment.

The vision fades, but the power remains. I open my eyes. The attic is brighter, the dust motes swirling in patterns that echo the runes on my skin.

Eliza stands, hands on hips, looking me over like she's not sure if she should hug me or lock me in a salt circle. "You're ready," she says. "Or as ready as you'll ever be."

Mystic and Ash race up the stairs, tails wagging, and press their bodies against my legs. The runes fade to a dull glow, but I know they're waiting, just under the surface.

I grip the locket, feel the cold certainty settle in my bones.

He's waiting, too.

The ghosts are gone, but they don't leave the cell empty. Their absence is just a different kind of haunting: the silence thick, the aftertaste of old accusations fermenting in the air. I pace, bare feet scuffing the tile, counting the steps it would take to cross the cell at a dead run if the runes ever slipped, if the field ever flickered. They won't. That's the point.

For the first time in a long time, I have no plan. No escape route, no clever con, no new mask to slip over the mess I've made of my own face. Just me, the runes, and the words they carved into my bones.

I stop at the glass, lean in, and study my reflection. The Division polishes this wall to a shine—another tactic, meant to turn my own image into a torment. It works. The face I see is pale, jaw sharp with hunger, eyes ringed in black. But behind it, like a ghost, shimmer all the other faces I've worn: the courtier, the monster, the trickster, the king, the woman in a thousand different skins. None of them look happy. None of them look free.

"Was any of it real?" I ask, quiet, so the microphones don't have to work for it. "Or am I just the sum of every lie?"

The glass doesn't answer, but the runes on my wrists pulse, a silent drumbeat. I remember the ghosts—especially the little girl, the one I failed most. I close my eyes, wanting to forget, but another face swims up: Amethyst, standing in the woods with her hair on fire and her arms glowing with impossible power.

She believed me. Even when she shouldn't have.

A door hisses open down the hall. The Division likes to make an entrance. This time it's just a guard, a low-grade flunky in Kevlar and a helmet two sizes too big. He walks past the cell without looking in, but then—just before the window's out of sight—he turns, grins, and taps a finger on the glass.

"Your girlfriend's not coming for you, freak," he says, and his breath fogs the window. "No one even knows you're here."

I bare my teeth, but the threat falls flat. The guard moves on, heels clicking in perfect military time.

For a second, I want to rage, to scream, to claw at the wall until the runes slice my hands to ribbons. But that's the old instinct: to break things, to break myself, to spit on the cage just for the pleasure of making someone clean it. I almost give in. Almost.

Instead, I laugh. Quiet, but real.

Because even now, I can feel her. The link is faint, a trickle of power threading through the runes, but it's there: a warmth under the skin, a voice under the noise. She's searching for me. She hasn't given up.

"She already has," I whisper, and this time the words are not a threat but a promise.

I sit on the floor, cross-legged, palms pressed to the tile. I close my eyes, breathe deep, and start to gather what's left of my strength. The runes fight back at first, like hungry animals, but I coax them, whisper to them, make bargains only I understand.

I am not running anymore.

If she comes, I will be ready.

I will be worthy.

The power builds, slow but steady, pooling in the hollow of my chest.

Outside, the guard's footsteps fade, replaced by the whine of the lights and the hiss of recycled air.

I smile. Not the old smile, but a new one.

Let them come.

Miss Eliza's kitchen looks like the aftermath of a tornado and a murder trial. Every inch of the Formica is covered in papers, hand-drawn maps, Sharpie diagrams, and the kind of annotations only a paranoid insomniac could love. The dogs are at my feet, restless, their eyes gleaming purple whenever the runes spark under my skin. It's still dark out, but the horizon behind the black trees has gone the color of bruised peaches. We don't have much time.

Eliza stalks the perimeter, cigarette smoldering, mug of chicory coffee gripped in her left fist like a talisman. She's pulled her wild hair into a braid so tight it looks like it could garrote a man. She hasn't said much in the last hour. I think she's trying not to.

I run through the plan again, tracing the route from the service road to the Division's back entrance, the one that's supposed to be camouflaged as a storm water maintenance facility. It's not perfect, but the runes in my head light up whenever I look at this path, and I trust them more than any Google Earth.

"You sure you want to do this?" Eliza says, finally. She doesn't look up from the mug.

I shrug, careful not to show how bad my hands are shaking. "Not even a little bit. But it's not like the universe gave me a return policy."

Ash noses my backpack, already packed: a half-empty first aid kit, some protein bars, and the locket, which I've looped around the zipper. Mystic paces, circles, then sits at the door, ears flicked to whatever's waiting out there.

Eliza sighs, then yanks open the old floor vent next to the stove. She fishes around inside, cursing, then pulls out a battered leather sheath and a glass vial stoppered with wax. She slaps them on the counter in front of me.

"This is old shit," she says. "Family stuff. Don't break it unless you're planning to make it count."

I unsheathe the dagger. The blade is etched all over with runes, but these aren't the Division's fancy laser-cut sigils. They're hand-carved, and the edges bite deep enough that I can feel the weight of every ancestor who ever bled for this family. The grip fits perfectly in my palm.

The vial is worse. The liquid inside glows—literally, like a million fireflies trapped in a jar. It's star-bright and thick as syrup. I hold it up to the kitchen light, and the whole room dims for a second.

"What is it?" I ask.

Eliza shrugs, and for once her face looks old. "Best guess? Concentrated runic resonance. Your grandmother used it once when the feds tried to burn us out. She said it made her strong enough to hold the line for three days. After, she slept for a week and said she never dreamed again."

I tuck the dagger and the vial into my pack, careful not to clink them together. "Any side effects?"

Eliza laughs, harsh. "Only the usual: insanity, temporary blindness, risk of spontaneous combustion." She points at the dogs. "If you start acting weird, they'll know before you do."

I pet both their heads, heart thumping.

We go through the plan one more time. The runes seem eager now, like they're ready to flex. Every time I focus on the Division's coordinates, I get a rush of cold certainty, the kind of confidence that isn't really mine but fits anyway.

When the first light starts to seep over the horizon, Eliza pours us both a finger of whiskey. "For the road," she says. "And for whatever happens after."

We clink glasses. The whiskey burns, but it's nothing compared to the fear. I still can't imagine how the Division hasn't found me, then I glance around... I'm guessing this place is warded out the wazoo.

I catch my reflection in the kitchen window, and for a second, I don't recognize myself. The eyes staring back are purple, but flecked through with gold. My hair is wild, and my face has lost every trace of the old shyness. I look fierce. Or maybe just desperate.

Eliza notices. "You look ready," she says.

I roll the locket in my palm, feeling the cold metal hum. "What if he's not worth it?" I ask, voice cracking. "What if all those centuries of chaos and manipulation are who he truly is?"

Eliza snuffs her cigarette, grinds it to ash. "You'll find out. But if you run now, you'll never know. That's the real curse."

I snap the locket around my neck, shouldering the pack. The runes on my arms flare, in sync with my heartbeat.

The dogs whine, eager. I kneel and hug them, hard.

Eliza gives me a look that's almost tender. "Go," she says. "Before I change my mind and lock you in the root cellar."

I grin, a real grin for the first time in weeks.

I step outside, the morning cold and sharp, the sky streaked with purple and gold. Eliza loaned me her beat-up truck. The dogs leap ahead, Ash baying, Mystic a silent blur as they race to the truck.

I open the door, and the dogs leap in. I climb in and crank the motor; it takes a moment, but it turns over. I put it in gear and pull out.

Whatever happens next, I'll face it.

And if I have to burn the world to save him, so be it.

CHAPTER SIXTEEN

THE RESCUE MISSION

The Division's so-called "containment facility" isn't on any map, not even the ones Miss Eliza keeps in her cigarette tin. I find it by smell: fresh asphalt, burnt ozone, chain-link still off-gassing that metallic tang from being hastily unrolled. The closer I get, the more the runes along my arms come alive, crawling under the skin like snakes with an agenda. Even the dogs are twitchy—Ash whimpers in his sleep, paws paddling, and Mystic stares out the windshield, hackles up, tail flagging like she expects the trees to shoot back.

I park the truck in a drainage ditch a quarter mile out, kill the lights, and watch the blank concrete bunker squat behind a double fence and a strip of parking lot wide enough for a helicopter to land. There's no one at the gate. Just a camera the size of a toddler's head and a sign that says "AUTHORIZED PERSONNEL ONLY" in eight languages, English first and boldest.

I'm not authorized, but I'm pissed, and I have backup.

Miss Eliza's words float up, cold as the morning air: The runes want to help, to guide, to bind us together. She never said anything about them liking to show off, but that's obvious now—the more I focus, the more the symbols on my arms pulse, all purple and gold, like someone wired my veins into a rave.

I dig the locket out of my shirt, thumb the seam until it cuts a groove in my skin. The dagger's heavier than I expect when I pull it from my pack, the leather grip still sticky from decades of attic sweat. I run the blade along my left forearm, just above the throb of my pulse, and whisper the words Eliza drilled into me: "Ek biðja þik, eldri."

The runes flare, and for one exquisite moment, the pain in my arm turns to light.

I draw the first glyph in the air with the tip of the knife. The symbol hangs, smoking, then flickers and twists as if it's got somewhere better to be. I don't let it go. I trace a second glyph, then a third, until there's a whole ring of script orbiting my wrist. The wind picks up, curling the smoke into a braid, and suddenly the dogs are alert—ears high, every muscle tense, as if something out there is barking back.

The camera on the fence twitches, zooms, and the parking lot erupts in halogen glare. I see my own shadow on the ground, huge and ragged, arms upraised and shaking. The first two glyphs twist together, then burst into purple flame, licking along my fingers without burning. The feeling is beyond pain—it's pure electricity, every cell howling, every thought whittled down to a single obsession: get inside, get to Loki, get the fuck out before the Division figures out how to turn me into a wall sconce.

The flames crawling up my arms flicker as a warning, not a question. The perimeter's bristling with Division boys in navy-on-navy tactical gear, their faces the color of spoiled milk behind the face shields. I'm so high on adrenaline I don't even realize I'm running until my sneakers pound the pavement and the camera's red LED splits in two, slagged by a whip of fire that lashes from my wrist and licks it clean off the post.

A siren starts howling, the kind that wakes up all the crows for a mile. I duck behind the truck's wheel well just as a cluster of guards bails from the bunker, weapons drawn, every one of them tracking my location like they've been briefed on my high school gym stats.

Mystic and Ash move as one. Mystic, bold and silent, charges the gap between the two nearest guards, fangs flashing. Ash takes the other side, tail straight, barking so loud it's almost funny. I snap up and get a look at the gate: it's chained, but the links are cheap aluminum—just for show. I clench the dagger and point it at the lock. "Open," I hiss, not even bothering with Norse.

The glyphs on the blade flare white-hot. The padlock melts into a puddle of nothing, spattering the boots of the nearest guard. He jumps, and Mystic's jaws close around his calf, dragging him to the ground with the efficiency of a dog born to make things that weigh hundreds of pounds more than them do what they want. The other guards hesitate, then one gets bold and comes for me, brandishing some kind of cattle prod on steroids.

I don't think, just react: purple fire spits from my palm, hitting him center mass. The flames don't burn flesh, not exactly—they burn the spaces in between, the little whispers of matter the world keeps for itself. He screams, drops the prod, and sprints for the tree line, smoldering from the inside out.

I keep moving, the dogs at my heels. The pull toward Loki isn't a direction; it's a tidal force: a hot ache in my chest that yanks me every time I consider veering off-mission. I make the turn for the bunker door, but it's already open—someone in there is either expecting me or has figured out that the usual "stay inside until it's over" policy is about to get them roasted.

Inside, the place is a fever dream of federal budgets. Every surface is steel or some kind of carbon fiber, and there are runes everywhere—etched in the door frames, painted in spirals around the light fixtures, even tattooed on the arms of the agents who make the mistake of getting between me and my next checkpoint. One gets a good look at me and tries to run a net gun, but the dogs take him out before he gets a shot off. The net discharges on the ground, strobing blue-white, making the runes on my skin twitch like they're pissed at the competition.

I press my back against the cold wall, chest heaving. The runes on my arms are pulsing so brightly they hurt to look at, and there's a taste like copper pennies coating my tongue. Mystic limps slightly—the tranq dart grazed her shoulder—but her eyes are still blazing with that otherworldly light.

"How much deeper?" I whisper to the empty hallway, knowing the answer will be "too deep" no matter what.

Ash noses my hand, leaving a smear of something dark on my palm. Not his blood—theirs. The thought should horrify me, but all I feel is a cold satisfaction. They took him. They hurt him. Every agent between me and Loki is just an obstacle to remove.

The facility stretches ahead, a maze of steel and fluorescent lights. I can feel him somewhere below, like a compass needle pulled toward magnetic north. But I can also feel how much the runes have already taken from me—the tremor in my hands, the way my vision blurs at the edges.

I touch the locket at my throat. Still warm. Still humming with power.

"Okay," I breathe. "Let's finish this."

Corridors blur. My hands are bleeding now—either from the knife or from the raw energy it's channeling—but I can't stop to look. There's a shadow at the edge of my vision, the memory of Loki's voice: "Don't run from this." I can't tell if it's encouragement or a warning.

The pull leads me to a stairwell. I take the steps two at a time, boots skidding on the treads, and Mystic barrels past me to snap at the heel of an agent two landings below. There's a hiss, a jolt, and Mystic yelps—just once—before shaking it off and trotting on, unharmed. Whatever they're packing, the runes are burning through it. And the runes are keeping my dogs just as safe as they are keeping me.

Basement level: colder, the air recycled and gritty. The walls close in, but the magic doesn't care. Every new hallway, every locked door, the glyphs on my arm twist and mutter to each other, plotting. When I reach a thick steel blast door, I put my hand to the plate. It's cold—so cold it should have numbed me instantly, but the fire in my blood just laughs. The runes crawl down my wrist, form a line, and sink into the seam around the door.

I mutter the words Eliza taught me: "Ek opna þik." The whole fucking door shivers, then pops open with a sound like a cannon shot. For a split second, the dogs and I are bathed in pure white light.

On the other side: six more guards, three of them already pointing the rune-web nets. The lead agent, a woman with all the warmth of a corpse, raises her hand. "Amethyst Gold," she says, as if I'm at a DMV and not breaking into a classified facility. "Stand down and you won't be harmed."

"Sure," I say, "just as soon as you show me where you keep the ancient gods."

Her jaw sets. "We're authorized to use lethal force."

"Good luck with that," I say, and duck as Mystic launches herself at the woman's legs.

They fire the nets. I slash the dagger upward, and the glyphs detonate: purple fire meets the blue mesh midair, and the net vaporizes. The dogs take down another guard. Ash gets clipped by a tranquilizer, but it only slows him. The rest of the guards hesitate, then one bolts for the exit.

The lead agent—Mercer, I recognize her now—draws a sidearm. I don't see her fire, but I hear the whine of a bullet skimming past my ear. I drop, roll, and come up with the dagger pointed right at her throat. I have never made a move like that in my life. These runes are something else.

"Back up," I snarl, and she does. The rest are either unconscious or gone.

At the end of the hall, there's a glass wall—thick, nearly a foot—and beyond it, Loki.

He's chained upright, arms spread, legs braced in manacles that glow like uranium. His skin's gone waxy, the runes on his body black as dried blood. For a moment, I think he's dead, but then his head jerks up, and his eyes—green, dull, still so fucking Loki—lock on mine.

The sight of him stops me cold. This isn't the man who caught a falling tree branch with magic, who made the world bend around his will. This is what they've reduced him to—broken, drained, barely holding on. The rage that fills me is clean and sharp, like breathing liquid fire.

I run to the glass, slap my palm against it. "Loki," I say. My voice cracks. "I'm here. What did they do to you?" The words come out as a whisper, but they carry all the fury I can't scream.

He blinks, slow. "You shouldn't be," he whispers, voice hoarse as death. "They'll—"

"Like hell." I press my palm harder against the glass. "I'm getting you out of here." I try the handle, but it's locked down tight. The runes on the barrier pulse, almost mocking me. "Don't suppose you can do your usual trick?"

His lips curl in a faint smile. "Not with these," he says, rattling the manacles. "Yggdrasil root. Division's getting clever."

"Let's see if they planned for crazy," I mutter and press the locket to the seam.

The runes on my skin flare, the purple fire coiling into a tight spiral. The glass begins to melt, not drip, but run—as if the world's been tilted and now the laws of physics are following my rules instead of theirs. I cut a circle with the dagger and slam my shoulder through. It's hot, and it stings, but I don't care. I make a ragged opening and crawl through, almost face-planting onto the tile.

Loki's shackled to the wall by a latticework of runes, each one twisting in on itself, a fractal of containment. "You're glowing," he says, his voice faintly amused.

"Shut up," I say and start sawing at the first manacle with the dagger.

The rune script fights me—every cut I make, it tries to heal, like I'm carving a tattoo into a hydra. I think about what Eliza said: Don't fight the runes. Use them.

I take a breath. Let the magic take over.

The runes on my arms reach for the ones on the manacle, and for a second, the two sets of symbols talk. It's more feeling than sound—a kind of pressure, a debate, a negotiation. The manacle flares, tries to resist, then buckles. The lock splits. I pull the first shackle off and toss it.

"Neat trick," Loki says. He tries to stand, but his legs won't hold him.

I have to stop, hands shaking so badly I nearly drop the dagger. The runes are eating through me like acid, each cut costing more than the last. Sweat drips into my eyes, and I can taste blood where I've bitten through my tongue.

"The next one's going to hurt," I warn him.

"More than this?" He rattles the remaining shackles weakly.

I meet his eyes. "More than anything we've done before."

He nods, understanding. "Then do it quickly."

I move to the next shackle. It's easier now that I know how. The rune on my palm bites into the metal, and the manacle falls away. Two more to go. The flame on my arms is so bright it's like having a sun inside my skull.

The glass wall shatters behind us. Mercer's back, pistol in hand, and she's not fucking around this time.

"Step away," she says, her voice shaking with something halfway between terror and awe.

Loki looks at me. "You have to go. You can still—"

"I'm not leaving you here," I snarl and rip off the last shackle.

For a split second, everything stops. Loki stands, unchained. The runes on his arms go from black to blinding gold, a flare so intense it swallows the world.

Mercer fires. The bullet hits me in the shoulder, a hot punch that sends me to my knees. The runes don't like that. They go wild, leaking fire from every pore.

Loki doesn't run. He turns to Mercer, and the look on his face is so old, so infinite, that she forgets to fire again. The runes on his skin stretch, snake, and leap for her, wrapping her hand and wrist, yanking the gun away.

He grabs my arm, pulling me to my feet. "Can you walk?"

I nod, even though I'm not sure. The bullet hurts, but the runes burn it away, cauterizing the wound in a rush of purple light.

He pulls me through the glass into the corridor. "We have to go," he says. His voice is stronger now, but it's layered, not just human—there's a thread of something old and hungry underneath.

We stagger together, his arm around my waist, both of us bleeding and shaking. I can feel his power returning, but it's wild now, uncontained. The runes on his arms burn so bright they leave afterimages.

"Are you still you?" I ask because I need to know.

He stops, looks at me with eyes that are more gold than green. "Ask me again when we're safe."

It's not reassuring, but it's honest. I'll take honest over comforting any day.

I glance back. Mercer's on the ground, clutching her wrist. The gun is gone, melted into a puddle. Mystic and Ash are in the hall, both dogs barking like there's a bear behind every door.

We run. The alarms have shifted tone—no longer just a warning, but a surrender. The whole place shakes as the wards on the walls fail one by one, overpowered by the raw magic spilling from the two of us. Every step, every turn, the dogs lead the way, their eyes lit with the same purple fire.

We reach the upper corridor, the way out. The guards we pass don't even try to stop us; they see the runes and the fire, and they back away, stunned. At the exit, the steel door that took a platoon to close is already sagging open, bent from the inside.

We stagger out into the predawn, Loki's arm around my waist, both of us limping and bloodied and too spent to laugh.

I look up at him, his eyes alive with gold and green and the promise of every bad idea I ever wanted to try. "You okay?" I ask.

He grins, baring his teeth. "Never better."

Then he kisses me, right there in the parking lot, the world still burning behind us. And even with the pain, even with the taste of blood and ozone in the air, it feels like the first true thing I've ever done.

The dogs circle, tails wagging. The sky goes gold at the edge, the first line of sun breaking through the trees. We're alive.

We're free.

The kiss in the parking lot is the world's worst timing. Or the best, depending on whether you're measuring by Hollywood or body count. I feel Loki's lips—cool, hungry, the taste of copper and smoke—and then the wind rushes in, carrying the sirens and the shouts and the unmistakable sound of more Division boots swarming the surface. My body wants to melt against him, but the adrenaline is too high. My shoulder aches where the bullet grazed it, but the runes are still working, skin knitting over as they drink in the pain and spit it back as power.

He pulls away, eyes blazing, the gold-flecked green so inhuman I have to look away. "They're coming," he says, and in his voice, I can hear the old echo, the God of Lies and Surprises, the thing the Division built this whole place to contain. He lets go of me, but only enough to get me moving.

We book it toward the tree line. The dogs are already there—Ash first, then Mystic—making a wedge through the tall grass, tails slicing a path of resistance and defiance. I'm half a step behind Loki, and for the first time since this nightmare started, I feel the familiar lurch of hope: we did it. We're out. We're alive.

But the universe hates a clean getaway.

The moment we hit the ditch and roll for cover, the world goes blue with floodlights. Four, five, maybe six black SUVs converge from the road. Out come the agents, not the rookies this time but the clean-up crew—the ones who don't flinch, who don't bother with body armor because they know the last line of defense is the one that gets a raise. Mercer is with them, her wrist already bandaged, her face set in that stone-cold "I told you so" glare that makes me want to punch her teeth in.

"Stay down," Loki says, but I'm already up, knifing the locket from under my shirt and thumbing it so hard I split my thumbnail. The glyphs on my forearm are glowing again, but different: not wild, not angry, but clear and steady, like they're finally listening instead of arguing.

Mercer shouts an order. The agents advance, guns up, no hesitation. Someone in the back has a compact launcher—it looks like a leaf blower but with binding sigils stenciled up the handle.

Loki doesn't hide. He steps into the open, arms out, and for a half-second I wonder if he's giving up, if he's going to let them haul him off for another round of vivisection. But then I see the muscles in his neck tighten, the tattoos along his spine ignite, and the world goes off-axis.

It's not a roar, exactly. Not a sound at all, but a pressure wave that flattens the grass and punches the air from my lungs. Every Division agent within fifty feet staggers; some fall. Mystic and Ash drop to their bellies and whimper, but they keep their eyes on me, waiting for my move.

The launcher guy gets off a shot—a net that glows with the color of migraine and chemical fire. Loki swats it out of the air with his bare hand, the net vaporizing to motes as it crosses the force field of green-gold lightning now arcing from his fingertips. The rest of the agents open fire, but every bullet melts or bends or is deflected in a way that makes me realize I've never, not once, seen true power until now.

But the energy's eating him alive. He's shuddering, sweat pouring, every line of his body held together by willpower and rage. The runes on my arms answer—purple and gold, brighter with every heartbeat.

It hits me all at once: it's not just him that's the conduit. It's both of us. We're two nodes on a circuit, and with every step I take toward him, the circuit completes, power building, magic layering itself in feedback until it's ready to burn down the universe—or at least the entire county.

"Loki!" I scream, and the sound is both mine and not mine, doubled and trebled by every ghost and ancestor who ever lived through a night like this.

He turns. "Now!" he shouts, his voice booming with more than human lungs.

I leap to him, hands outstretched. The runes meet, purple flame crashing into green lightning. The backlash nearly knocks me out, but I hold the locket tight, forcing the magic through it, shaping it as best I can.

We're a beacon now. The sky above us splits, a seam of color that's not color at all, just pure intention made visible. The agents drop their weapons and back away, some crawling, some just staring with the horror of people who've never believed in gods until they met one and realized belief wasn't required.

The world goes slow, syrupy, the sounds flattening to a dull throb. Loki grabs my waist with one arm, the other bracing my hand against his chest. "Hold on," he says, and this time it's not a metaphor.

The power surges. I feel every nerve ending fire in sequence; my body is not just mine anymore but a channel, a fuse about to blow. The locket burns so hot I think it will brand my palm for life. The Division agents are screaming, but the sound is miles away.

We detonate.

I don't have better words. There's a moment—no, an eternity—where everything is white and noise and acceleration, and I am everywhere and nowhere. I see the structure of the facility from above, every wall and lock and sensor mapped in my head as if I built it. I see Loki as he truly is—beautiful, terrifying, not even remotely human, every part of him alive with story and hunger and the need to break every rule. I see myself, small but not weak, fierce in a way I never let myself believe, every flaw now etched into a legend. I see Mystic and Ash, blue-lit and huge, guardians of some lost cosmic flock.

When the world slams back together, we're in the smoking crater that used to be the Division's pride and joy. Concrete is shattered, fence posts twisted into metallic vines, the bunker now a memory and a warning.

Loki is on his knees, face pale, eyes sunken but burning with that impossible green. I'm next to him, the locket still fused to my hand, the runes on my arms flickering like tired fireflies. My legs won't hold me, but I don't care.

The dogs are the first to recover. Ash licks my face, and Mystic barks once and nudges Loki's shoulder as if to say, "Get your shit together, Dad."

I laugh, then cough, then realize I'm laughing and crying at the same time, tears hot and weirdly sweet.

Loki drags himself upright and puts a hand on my shoulder. "Told you," he rasps. "Never better."

Behind us, the remains of the agents are picking themselves up. Mercer stands at the edge of the blast radius, eyes huge, face slack. She doesn't try to approach, just watches as we get to our feet and stagger for the woods.

"What now?" I say, my voice shaking with the aftershock of power.

Loki shrugs, then grins. "Run?"

I can't help it—I laugh again. "That's your plan?"

He pulls me close, arm around my waist, and whispers in my ear, "It's worked so far."

We limp toward the trees, the dogs circling, the world still ringing with what we just did. I know it's not over—never is—but for the first time, I think maybe it could be.

When we're almost to the cover of the pines, Loki stops and turns to look back at the burning wreckage. I follow his gaze. The runes on my arms glow just once, and I get the sense they're not angry anymore. Sated, maybe. Proud.

He squeezes my hand, and I look up at him. "You did good," he says. His voice is soft, for once. "Better than anyone before you."

I want to say something profound, something to capture what it's like to stand on the edge of the world and find out you're braver than you ever knew. But I'm too tired, too raw, too busy holding myself together.

So instead, I say, "Next time you get kidnapped, can we maybe do it somewhere cooler?"

He laughs, and for a second, the woods aren't so scary.

We melt into the shadows, the four of us—one god, two dogs, and whatever I am—leaving behind the old world and walking toward whatever comes next.

It's then that I hear an explosion, and I turn around to see the rest of the Division compound collapsing.

CHAPTER SEVENTEEN

RAGNARÖK IN EAST TEXAS

The explosion should have been the end of it—one final blaze to seal whatever the Division had been hiding. But as the flames reach deeper into the bunker's core, I realize we haven't ended anything. We've just ripped open a door that was meant to stay locked. I'm still shaking, blood sticky on my arm, the acrid taste of ozone and cordite fighting for space in my mouth. Loki leans heavily on me, but it's not weakness; it's the way a sapling leans in a tornado, using me as a windbreak.

Mystic and Ash are at my heels, fur bristling, their chests heaving like bellows. Ash has a gash on his snout, but he ignores it. Mystic keeps glancing back at the trees, as if she's waiting for something even worse to drop out of the sky.

For a second, there's just the roaring crackle of fire, the hiss of burning plastic, and the slow shuffle of my heart learning to beat again. Then the world shudders, a seismic hiccup that rattles my teeth and threatens to fold the ground in half. It's not just an explosion this time; it's something deeper, older, like the earth's own alarm clock is going off and nobody remembered to hit "snooze."

I turn to Loki, but he's already moving, his face screwed up in a way that's equal parts fear and rage.

"What did you do?" I say, only half-joking.

He grins, but it doesn't reach his eyes. "I think we broke the battery. And everything it was holding together." A pause. "Sorry?" I could help but laugh quietly.

Another shudder. This one comes with sound—a low, basso rumble that's not quite thunder, but not quite anything else, either. The trees around us start to vibrate, pine needles shivering off in drifts. For a heartbeat, the woods are brighter than daylight, the fire lighting up the trunks in insane orange stripes.

Then the ground splits.

Not wide, not like a Hollywood earthquake, but enough. A seam tears through the clay and red dirt, shooting from the bunker's grave and slithering toward us. The dogs backpedal, tails between their legs but not running. I don't run either, partly because there's nowhere left to go, and partly because I'm too tired to outrun my own mistakes.

The first creature pulls itself out of the gap like a nightmare learning to walk. It's long and lithe, a thing that used to be a person maybe, but now is just a slick black skeleton, hunched over and stuttering like a stop-motion monster. Its eyes are perfect spheres of white. It flickers, catches sight of us, then bolts into the trees at impossible speed.

"Well, shit," I mutter. "That's definitely not in any of the fairy tales."

It's only the beginning.

The seam keeps burping up more. Some scuttle on too many legs, others pour like liquid shadow between the trees, and a few drift overhead, leaving trails of glittering ash that smell like old graves and broken promises. One is the size of a refrigerator, made entirely out of teeth. Another skitters forward on needle-thin legs, a child's head bobbing at its center, the face slack and dreaming, eyes rolled back to show only white as it staggers into the underbrush. After the first dozen, I lose count.

Some of the things head away from us, straight for the trees. But others—ones that smell more like magic than monster—turn toward us, drawn by the only two living, breathing, bleeding targets in range.

The dogs growl in stereo, the sound low and dire. Mystic bares her teeth, hackles so high she looks twice her usual size. Ash huddles closer, eyes darting from me to the creatures and back. He's scared, but he's also bracing for a fight.

"We have to stop them before they reach town," I say, trying to make my voice sound less like a plea and more like a plan.

Loki's eyes are pure green fire now, no human left in them. "We will," he says and grabs my hand.

His palm is fever-hot, but his grip is steady. Our fingers mesh, and something clicks in the air—like a circuit closing or a spell finishing the last line of its incantation.

The Twilight Runes ignite.

They start at the base of every pine tree, crawling up the trunks in spirals of violet, then leap from branch to branch, knitting the woods together in a web of living light. The symbols are old, older than Norse, older than words. They burn with the color of bruised orchids and lightning. For a moment, the whole forest is alive with script, runes chasing each other up and down the bark, flickering like warning lights on a doomed spaceship.

The creatures hesitate. Some shy away from the flare, burrowing into the ground or darting for shadows. But others—the hungriest, the smartest, the ones that know exactly what they want—push through the pain and keep coming.

The wards hold, barely. The purple light thickens into a wall between us and the swarm. I can feel it in my teeth, a buzz that's almost music, almost memory. The runes on my arms answer, burning hotter, the lines twisting to match the ones on the trees. The effort sends needles of ice through my skull. My hands shake, fingertips gone·numb, but I hold on. Loki's grip anchors me, keeps me from dissolving into the magic entirely.

But the wards aren't enough. They flicker at the edges, gaps yawning open for a split second before snapping shut. The creatures test every weak point, slamming into the barrier, clawing at the lines, biting and gnashing and wailing in languages I can almost understand.

"It's not going to hold," I say, panic crowding out any leftover hope.

Loki squeezes my hand. "It doesn't have to," he says, his voice gone weird and doubled. "We just need to buy time. Or get creative."

The next thing to hit the barrier is a shapeshifter, its form blurring through a dozen animals before settling on something like a wolf with too many eyes. It howls, a sound that warps the air, and for a second the runes stutter, the wall going transparent. On the other side, the crowd thickens: spirits in human shapes, walking through trees like they're mist; shadow-things that crawl upside down on the branches; a dozen minor gods with halos of sparks around their skulls, all fighting for a way through.

The Division bunker finally gives up the ghost. There's a muffled boom, and a new column of flame punches a hole in the night. The shockwave knocks loose a wave of pine cones, raining them down on our heads.

Loki doesn't even flinch. "We can't fight them all," he says. "But maybe we can cheat."

I laugh, which surprises us both. "That's your plan? Cheat?"

He grins, teeth bright against the dark. "Always worked for me before."

Ash yelps—a warning, not pain. Mystic throws herself at the barrier, snapping at a spirit that's wormed halfway through a seam in the runes.

Her jaws close on nothing, but the act buys us a heartbeat. I can feel the wall falter, then surge back twice as strong, like it's feeding off our fear, our will to stand our ground.

The creatures keep coming. The minor gods are the worst. They move slowly, but every time one gets close, the barrier bends, runes melting like sugar. One locks eyes with me, and it's like being stared at by an x-ray, every secret on display.

"They're going for the town," I realize, the words leaking out in a gasp. "If we break, if the wards go down, they'll slaughter everyone."

Loki nods, solemn for once. "That's why we don't break," he says. "Not now."

He shifts his grip, pulling me closer. The runes on his arms and chest are alive, crawling, multiplying. The marks on my own skin burn in sympathy, spreading up my neck, over my jaw. I don't fight it. For the first time, I let the runes take over, let the magic shape me instead of the other way around.

The forest becomes a cathedral of light, every pine a pillar, every rune a stained-glass window. The creatures outside the wall wail and rage, but they can't get through—not yet. Not while we're holding the line.

Mystic and Ash flank us, shoulders squared, teeth bared. The dogs are more than dogs now. I can see it in their eyes—something old, something loyal, something that remembers the first time a human asked a wolf to sit and the wolf decided to say yes.

Loki looks at me, and for a second we're not in the woods, not in a fight, not even in danger. We're just two people, hand in hand, standing against the dark.

"Ready?" he asks.

"Never been more ready," I say.

He laughs, low and fierce, and the sound tips the balance.

The runes flare, the barrier thickens, and the world's oldest magic finds a new foothold.

It won't last. We both know it. But for now, it's enough.

We stand together, the last line of defense between the wild and the world.

And for once, I'm not afraid.

Let the monsters come.

For ten seconds, maybe less, the wall holds.

Then something slams into it hard enough to make my teeth chatter, the runes on the pines flaring so bright they throw afterimages on my retinas. Mystic and Ash are already at the line, barking so loud it cuts through the monster screech like a tornado siren. I reach for their collars—instinct, habit, muscle memory from a hundred walks in the park—and I nearly lose my hand.

The dogs aren't dogs anymore.

I mean, they are, technically—fur, teeth, tails—but their bodies are stretching, swelling, bones creaking as they double and then triple in size. The fur ripples, patterns shifting under the skin, and the runes I've seen on my own arms burn themselves into their coats in bands of blue-white fire. Mystic's eyes go full floodlight, pupils swallowed by a glow that makes her look like she's lit from the inside. Ash's hackles stand so high it's like he's wearing a mane.

The change is so sudden, so violent, that I stumble back, falling on my ass in the pine needles. Loki catches me with one hand, steady as a rock, his own eyes flicking from the horde to the transforming dogs and back again.

He whistles, low and impressed. "Divine guardians," he says, his voice gone thick with awe. "I've seen it in stories, but never in a bloodline this pure."

The words barely register. Mystic and Ash charge the barrier, smashing through a seam in the wards. Where the purple light falters, their bodies fill the gap, jaws snapping at anything stupid enough to get close. Mystic grabs the shapeshifter by the throat, her jaws closing like a vise. The creature tries to slither out, but she shakes it hard, and the thing's neck snaps with a sound like a tree branch breaking in winter.

Ash takes on two shadow-things at once, pinning one with his paw and slamming the other against a tree trunk. The first one goes limp, dissolving into a smear of cold fog. The second one puts up more of a fight, wriggling and screaming, but Ash clamps down and shakes until it splits apart, the pieces wriggling off into the underbrush.

The rest of the horde hesitates.

And then all hell breaks loose.

A minor god—slender, with skin like hammered gold and eyes burning orange—pushes through the wall of runes, arms outstretched. "Siblings!" it shouts, and the voice rattles my bones, "the old world is dead! Follow me—"

Mystic barrels into it at full tilt, tackling it to the ground. The minor god is strong, but not strong enough. She holds it by the throat, jaws just short of crushing, daring it to move.

Meanwhile, the shapeshifters regroup, their forms less human now, more like dogs themselves—only way too many legs and faces like wax masks melting under a lamp. They come for me in a wave, teeth bared, claws scrabbling for purchase.

I freeze. Not because I'm scared (okay, maybe a little), but because for the first time in my life, the runes are running the show. I lift my hands, and the air between my palms buzzes with power, a purple mist that hardens into a shield right as the first shapeshifter lunges. It hits the shield, rebounds, and goes sprawling.

I blink, stunned. "Did you see that?" I shout.

Loki is already working. He steps in front of me, one hand raised, the other curling around my waist. The runes on his arms blaze to life, emerald fire licking from his fingertips. He hurls a bolt of green lightning at the minor god trying to wiggle out of Mystic's grasp, the energy slamming into its chest and pinning it to the dirt. The smell of burnt ozone fills the air, sharp and chemical and alive.

The god screams, but the dogs hold it down. The shapeshifters try again, three of them piling up on my shield, but the barrier holds. I can feel the drain, though—a sucking, slurping hunger, like the runes are feeding off me even as they keep me safe.

Loki pivots, another bolt ready. "The runes respond to you!" he shouts over the chaos. "Your magic and mine—they're different but complementary!"

"Don't stop talking dirty," I yell back, just because it makes him laugh.

Another god—this one smaller, with black glass eyes and a mouth that stretches wider than it should—slinks along the edge of the wards, looking for a way around. Ash intercepts, body-checking it so hard the thing bounces off a tree and lands in a heap. He circles it, snarling, and the god cowers, covering its head with spindly arms.

I risk a glance back at the town. In the distance, I can see lights—porch lights, streetlamps, the steady throb of civilization. The thought of any of these things making it past us and into the heart of my world—the hardware store, the church, the gas station with the best barbecue in three counties—makes my blood run cold.

"Loki!" I say, panic tightening my voice. "They're going to try to flank us—use the trees to get around!"

He nods, understanding at once. "Then we don't give them the chance." He pulls me close, his hand finding mine, and together we drive the energy forward, the runes on the trees swelling to double thickness, then triple, the purple light so strong it bleaches the world of every other color.

The horde wails, the sound echoing through the woods in a pitch so high it almost shatters the shield. Mystic and Ash redouble their efforts, Mystic snapping at anything that moves, Ash covering the line with a wide, menacing sweep. Where they walk, the runes seem to follow, strengthening, knitting together.

One of the spirits—half a head, half a tangle of arms—slips through a gap and comes straight at me, howling with a voice that's all hunger and cold. I almost falter, but the runes in my hands answer, forming a latticework of energy that catches the spirit mid-flight and grinds it to a halt.

I think, Go away, and it does—shredded into nothing by the mesh.

Shredding spirits with pure thought should terrify me, but all I feel is relief.

More creatures try, but the pattern's clear: we hold the line, the dogs clean up anything that slips through, Loki blasts the heavy hitters, and I patch the holes with runic duct tape.

It's working. For now.

I risk a glance at Loki, his face slick with sweat, every muscle taut with effort. "How long can we keep this up?" I ask.

He shrugs, grinning through the exhaustion. "Long enough for the world to catch up, or long enough to burn out. Either way, we go down swinging."

The next wave is bigger, louder, and more desperate. The minor gods are learning, coordinating their attacks, testing for weak spots. Mystic yelps—just once, but it's enough to send a spike of terror through my heart. She staggers, a gash leaking spectral blood down her shoulder, but she doesn't fall. She clamps down on the nearest monster and rips it clear in half.

The creatures waver, sensing the shift. For a second, they pull back, regrouping in a loose circle just outside the brightest runes. Some of them are scared. Some are just smart. The rest—well, there's always another idiot ready to throw itself at a lost cause.

Loki's grip tightens around my waist. "They'll try something new," he says, eyes locked on the horde. "They always do."

"We'll be ready," I say, surprising us both.

The purple light flickers, but it's not failing; it's condensing, sharpening, focusing into a beam that slices through the night, drawing a line between the living and whatever those things are, between what belongs here and what doesn't.

The dogs pace the line, their eyes burning, their jaws slick with monster ichor. I want to hug them, but I know better. Right now, they're soldiers.

So are we.

The horde shifts, preparing for one last assault. I brace, gather every scrap of willpower I've got, and let the runes do their work.

This is what I am now.

This is what we are.

Bring it.

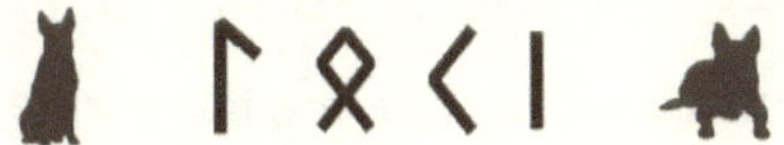

It's not a wave. It's not even a flood.

It's a siege, and we're the last fucking castle on the map.

The monsters regroup, moving in patterns that are almost military—probing, feinting, looking for holes in the wards. The minor gods are at the front, tossing spirits and shapeshifters like cannon fodder. Burning ozone coats my throat like metallic honey, sweet and sharp and wrong, stinging my eyes. Even the pines are sweating sap, the bark slick with resin as the runes work overtime.

I wipe sweat from my face, barely keeping the purple mesh up as a trio of shadow-hounds slam against it. My vision's narrowing; I'm seeing the world through a tunnel lined in runes and lit by the strobe of magical afterburn.

Loki's at my back, every muscle cabled and tense. His runes glow a sickly, gorgeous green, the light roiling just under his skin like bioluminescence gone feral. He hurls magic with both hands—bolts of chaos, razor-thin slashes of fire, traps that snag spirits and twist them into knots of energy. It's beautiful, but it's also sloppy, the way a lightning storm is beautiful right up to the moment it sets your house on fire.

Mystic and Ash, gigantic and glowing, are still holding the line. But even they're starting to flag. Mystic has a limp now, favoring her left foreleg, and Ash's tongue is lolling, his breath coming in ragged pants. They snarl and fight and throw themselves at anything that breaches, but it's clear: we're running out of time.

Something's got to give.

A six-armed thing—spider legs, human torso, face like a melting doll—pushes through the wards. It's fast, too fast for the dogs to intercept. It goes straight for Loki and me, arms out, fingers tipped with claws the size of steak knives.

Loki whips around and throws a bolt of green flame. The thing shrugs it off, absorbs it, and grows another arm.

It laughs, a sound like a bag of gravel getting shaken out on concrete. "Trickster," it hisses, "your time is—"

Mystic tackles it from the side, the impact driving it into a tree so hard the trunk splinters. She bites down, but the thing's flesh is rubbery and resistant. It whips around, claws raking Mystic's flank and drawing a spray of light—not blood, but something colder. Ash jumps in, latching onto the thing's ankle, and together they wrestle it to the ground.

I need to help, but the runes on my arms are pulsing out of sync, half my power shunting to the shield, half wasted fighting itself.

"We need something stronger," I say, the words clawing their way out through my clenched teeth.

Loki's voice is a snarl: "I know."

He reaches behind, gropes for my hand, and I grab him. The world contracts to the heat of his skin, the shock of his grip, and the wild, burning surge that passes between us. For a split second, we're fused—like plugging two high-voltage wires together and hoping the house doesn't burn down before the lights come on.

"Let me channel through you," he says, and it's not a suggestion. It's a plea.

I nod, not trusting myself to speak.

The connection is instant and total. His chaos, my structure, merging into something that's neither and both. The green lightning of his power twines with the purple fire of mine, swirling up our arms and into the runes on the trees, the ground, even the air itself. Every symbol in the forest lights up, a chain reaction racing from pine to pine, bark to branch, root to root.

The creatures sense it. Some turn to flee, but most are too deep in bloodlust to care.

The next wave hits—and this time, we hit back.

I throw my arm forward, palm open, and the blended power blasts out in a ribbon of fire and light. It carves through the oncoming horde, vaporizing the first row of shapeshifters and setting the minor gods on their heels. The ones that survive are stunned, blinking, uncertain for the first time.

Loki laughs, wild and triumphant, and the sound is infectious. "They've never faced this before!" he yells. "Not in any world!"

I grip his hand tighter, pouring every ounce of fear and anger and love into the magic. The runes on the pines twist, then lock together, forming a lattice so dense it's like a cage of living, breathing crystal. The monsters slam into it, bounce off; some dissolve, some explode in sprays of raw magic.

But the barrier holds.

Mystic and Ash sense the change. They pace the perimeter, massive bodies reinforcing the weakest points. Wherever a creature looks like it might push through, the dogs are there—snarling, biting, bracing the wall with the full weight of their new forms. Their eyes burn with pride, with joy, with a kind of vindication that goes all the way back to the first wolf who decided to guard a human campfire.

The horde is breaking. You can see it in their movements, the panic setting in as they realize they're not the hunters anymore. The minor gods try to rally—two of them link hands, chanting in a language that hurts my ears—but Loki cuts them off with a word. It's not English, or Norse, or anything I've heard before. It's raw, primordial, a syllable that rings like a sword on an anvil.

The gods disintegrate, their bodies coming apart at the seams, the energy sucking back into the runes on the trees.

The world shudders, then goes silent.

For a heartbeat, I think I'm deaf. Then I realize: the monsters are gone. The only sounds left are my own ragged breathing, Loki's, and the soft whimpering of the dogs as they collapse to the ground, spent.

But something's wrong. The retreat feels too easy, too clean. In the sudden quiet, I catch a whisper of movement—not fleeing, but regrouping. Waiting.

"It's not over," I breathe.

Loki follows my gaze to the tree line, where shadows pool thicker than they should. "No," he agrees. "But we've bought time. And sometimes that's enough."

I drop to my knees, the runes on my arms fading from blinding light to a soft, dull ache. My vision blurs at the edges, black spots dancing like flies. The runes are drinking from me—not just energy, but something deeper. Memory, maybe. The taste of my first kiss. The sound of my mother's laugh. Small prices for keeping the world intact.

Loki drops beside me, his face split by the biggest, stupidest grin I've ever seen. "You did it," he says, eyes wide with something like adoration.

"We did it," I correct, too tired to snark.

He leans in, forehead resting against mine, both of us too exhausted to care how ridiculous we look. The runes are still glowing, but now they pulse in time with our heartbeats, slow and steady, like they're learning how to rest for the first time in centuries.

Mystic and Ash crawl over, sandwiching us in a wall of fur and muscle and unconditional love. Their bodies are already shrinking, the runes receding into their coats, but the eyes—they keep the glow.

For a long minute, none of us say anything. We just breathe and listen to the world recalibrate around us.

Finally, Loki speaks. "That was…"

He trails off, either lost for words or too proud to admit he's never seen anything like it.

"Divine chaos meets mortal compassion," I say, the phrase popping into my head unbidden. "A power neither of us could wield alone."

He laughs, then groans, clutching his ribs. "You always did have a way with words."

I roll my eyes, but I'm smiling, too. "You're not so bad yourself, trickster."

We sit there, surrounded by the dogs, the dead monsters, and the thick, sweet scent of pine. The world feels lighter. Not healed, exactly, but on its way.

Loki tilts my chin up, his eyes searching mine. "What happens now?"

I glance at the barrier, still humming with power, the runes settling into a new pattern. "We keep watch," I say. "Guard the line. Make sure nothing like this ever happens again."

He nods, solemn. "A new tradition, then."

I want to say yes, but the word sticks in my throat. Instead, I lean into him, letting the quiet speak for me.

Mystic nuzzles my hand, Ash curls around my feet, and above us, the pines stand tall—no longer trembling, no longer afraid.

The runes hold.

So do we.

For the first time, I believe in happy endings.

And if the universe disagrees, it can come and get us.

Together.

CHAPTER EIGHTEEN

PROTECTING PINE HOLLOW

The world's gone weirdly silent. Not the ordinary country hush, not the lull of cicadas and wind, but a hush so deep it feels like the town itself is holding its breath, waiting for the next bad thing to land. Maybe it's the ozone tang still lingering on my tongue, or the way the storm clouds keep crowding closer, massing in walls too dark for late afternoon. Or maybe it's just that for the first time in my life, I know what waits in the shadows, and it's not afraid of me anymore.

Pine Hollow looks abandoned. Not a car in motion, not a porch light on. The sky is bruised purple and orange, that apocalypse sunset you only see in movies or in the five minutes before a tornado eats your house. Every window we pass is shuttered, every mailbox battered flat, like the town's already declared defeat and is just waiting for the post-game report.

I'm running on fumes. My legs ache, the runes on my arms are still tender from overdrive, and I'm almost positive my heart is skipping beats just to keep things interesting. But it's not like I'm in charge of this convoy. That's the dogs' job.

Mystic is leading, a blue streak in the rain-slick street, tail high and hackles up. She's not just on alert—she's in full battle mode, every muscle rigid, every footfall exact. Ash follows close behind, growling deep and steady, his fur so puffed he looks like he's trying to double as a throw pillow. They don't bark unless they see something, and right now they're barking at everything: the water tower, the empty Tastee Freez, even the potholes that have been here since before I was born.

I shoot a look at Loki. He's got that pissed-off, scared-to-show-it expression that means things are bad, but he won't say how bad unless I make him. The runes on his arms have faded, but there's a new gleam in his eyes—a green-gold shine that wasn't there before the Division knocked us around. He walks like he owns the world, but there's a shake in his hand when he reaches up to brush a wet lock of hair from his face.

"What are they seeing?" I say, but it's less a question and more a way to break the quiet before it breaks me.

He shakes his head, scanning the shadows. "Not sure. The lines are fraying. The boundary's weaker than I thought. There's...something feeding on it." He grins, but it's the kind of grin you wear at a funeral. "We don't have much time."

I don't ask how much. I already know.

The dogs take a hard left at the corner of Main and 5th, making a beeline for the water tower.

"Of course they're heading for the tower," Loki mutters, following their lead. "Every town has a focal point—the place where the barriers are thinnest. Pine Hollow just happens to advertise theirs with a giant steel middle finger."

I used to think of it as a joke—Pine Hollow's one claim to fame, if you count a rusty phallic landmark and some spray-painted curse words as fame. But tonight it looks different. The steel glints even in the gloom, and the air around it is alive, a halo of static that makes my hair float up off my scalp.

The ground under my feet hums, faint at first, then sharper, like a phone set to vibrate and jammed under your skin. Every step forward, it gets worse. The sidewalks are spider-webbed with fresh cracks. The asphalt's buckled, curling up in strips as if the road's trying to peel itself away from whatever's coming.

Ash loses it first. He stops in the middle of the road and lets out a bark so loud it rings off the houses, echoing back like a dare. Mystic joins in, and the two of them start circling, barking at the base of the tower like there's a squirrel made of nightmares hiding inside.

I reach for my phone, mostly out of habit. The screen's black. Not dead, not even on the fritz—just totally black, like the power's been sucked out by a magnet the size of Texas. I glance at Loki. He raises an eyebrow, his own phone dead in his palm.

"It's starting," he says. He doesn't sound surprised. He sounds tired.

"I'd make a joke about cell service," I say, "but I'm kind of running out of jokes."

He smirks, just a little. "You'll think of one when you need it."

There's a beat where neither of us moves, the dogs pacing and whining at our knees. I can feel the hunger in the air now—a pull, low and mean, coming from the tower and whatever's gnawing at the edge of the world behind it. My guts twist. My head starts to buzz, that familiar pre-migraine tickle; I guess that means the runes want something, and they're going to get it.

The dogs snap back to attention, both sets of eyes locked on me.

I'm supposed to know what to do next. Only I don't.

My hands start to shake, but I fumble for the bottle anyway—the one Miss Eliza packed in the bottom of my bag, wrapped in three layers of newspaper and a note that just says, "For the breach. Don't fuck it up." I wish I'd gotten better instructions. Or at least a recipe for an easier life.

The bottle is old, glass gone cloudy, and the stuff inside glows faint blue. The cap is stuck, but I crack it loose with the corner of the water tower's base because subtlety is for people whose bones aren't currently singing with unspeakable magic.

Loki's right behind me, a hand on my shoulder. It should be comforting, but instead it's a reminder: if I fuck up, he'll have to clean it up, and we both know how that ends.

"You don't have to," he says, and for the first time in all the chaos, he sounds like he means it.

I laugh, shaky and sour. "You want to take over?"

He just shakes his head, the green in his eyes flickering. "You're stronger than you think, Amethyst." He leans in, forehead brushing mine, his hand never leaving my shoulder. "You always were."

I stare at the bottle, at the little blue spark trying to crawl out of the glass. "I don't know if I can do this again," I say, my voice so low I almost hope he doesn't hear.

But he does. "You can," he says. "You will."

I uncork the bottle. The smell is sweet and sharp, like old licorice and the air before a lightning strike. I tilt it back and swallow. The liquid burns—first my tongue, then my throat, then my guts—but it's not a real burn. It's the feeling of every cell waking up, a thousand nerves screaming at once, every memory I ever tried to forget jumping up to take a bow.

The runes on my arms ignite. Not just a glow, but full-on wildfire, leaping from skin to air to the metal legs of the water tower. My heart stutters, then pounds hard enough to rattle my ribs.

The world is gone. There are only the runes, the dogs, the blue fire, and the sound of my own voice as I start to scream.

Except it's not a scream.

It's a chant, the old words, the ones from the locket, from the blood, from the dark places in the attic and the stories nobody wanted to write down. My voice rises, the runes coil around me, and the air shreds itself into whorls of blue and gold and pure, raw intent.

The pain is beautiful. The fear is gone.

I look at Loki. His eyes are wide, not scared, just awed, like he's never seen anything so alive.

"We don't have much time," he repeats, but there's hope in it this time, like maybe, just maybe, we do.

The dogs howl. The world howls with them.

And I step into the storm.

The water tower is ground zero for all the laws of physics I ever pretended to understand. The space around it warps, the light bends, and the world gets thin, like there's only the thickness of plastic wrap worth of reality left between Pine Hollow and the screaming dimension on the other side.

I can see the rift from halfway down the block. It's not a metaphor anymore, not just magic or crazy talk. It's real, jagged, and ugly, a tear in the night that pulses every time my heart does. The edges shimmer, sometimes blue, sometimes that angry Division white, sometimes pure, hungry black. The inside's worse: a roil of shadow and movement, flashes of bone and teeth and things that know how to hate.

Ash is the first to reach it. He doesn't even slow down—just charges into a pack of things that spilled out of the rift and are busy trying to eat the world, one piece at a time. The things are small, at least compared to the gods and monsters we fought earlier, but they're fast and sharp, and there are too damn many of them.

Ash snaps one in half with his jaws, then whips around and slams another into the asphalt hard enough to leave a wet smear. Mystic is right behind him, moving with a precision that is almost not canine at all. She grabs two by the neck, shakes until they go limp, then drops them and moves on. I watch her for a second—really watch her—and I realize she's not even angry. She's focused, calm. Like this is what she was made for.

"Don't get distracted," Loki says, but he's smiling a little, pride leaking through the mask.

"Wasn't planning to," I say, but my eyes keep drifting back to the dogs. I'm not sure if I should be proud or terrified.

The rift coughs up something bigger—a child's idea of a snake, all jaw and tongue and flailing claws. It hisses, then lunges. Mystic and Ash double-team it, Mystic going for the eyes while Ash rips into the soft underbelly. It screams, a sound like feedback through a million-watt amp, and thrashes so hard it takes out a chunk of the chain-link fence. Ash gets thrown, hits the ground, rolls, and is up again in half a heartbeat.

I grip the hilt of the dagger. The blade is cool, but the runes etched along its length pulse, humming in rhythm with the ones on my arm. I don't know what I'm supposed to do with it—stab the rift? Carve a sigil in the ground? Sacrifice something and hope for the best?—but I know this: Eliza didn't send me with it for decoration.

Loki's runes are lit up now, a full-body shimmer that makes him look like he's cut from gemstone instead of meat and bone. The green in his eyes is back, but it's not alone; gold and black swirl through it, fractal and fierce. He keeps glancing at the rift, then at me, then at the rift again, like he's solving an equation he really, really hates.

The ground shakes. Not a little this time, not a warning, but a full-on tremor that makes the water tower groan and tilt six inches off plumb. From the heart of the rift, something pushes—a hand, or maybe a claw, or maybe just a shadow pretending to be one. It hits the edge of the tear, then recoils, pissed and confused.

The Twilight Runes spiral around the base of the tower, coiling up the legs like angry snakes, then leap from steel to air, making a kind of fence around the wound in reality. For a second, the rift hesitates, the things inside pressing up against the light, searching for a weakness.

Loki steps up beside me, close enough to touch, his arm warm and buzzing with energy.

"We have to seal it," I say. My voice is steady, but the rest of me is cold. "Before whatever's inside figures out how to get past the wards."

He hesitates. It's not much—just a second, just a flicker—but it's enough. "If we do," he says, "it might take everything. Us. The dogs. The runes. All of it."

I can feel his fear, not just for the world, but for us. For the power, the connection, the thing that's kept us alive and together even when everything else fell apart.

I look at him, really look, and realize this is the first time he's ever asked for permission.

"It's okay," I say, and I mean it. "I'd rather lose all of it than watch this world go to hell."

He closes his eyes, just for a second, and when he opens them, the old Loki is back: arrogant, wild, a little bit in love with the end of the world.

"Alright," he says. "We do it together."

The rift pulses again, and the world tries to fold itself in half. The dogs howl, but they're not scared—they're calling the power, calling the runes, calling us.

I grab Loki's hand. The dagger in my other hand flares, the runes along the blade igniting in a corona of purple and white.

The air is so thick with magic I can barely breathe. Every rune in the town, every symbol I've ever seen or drawn or dreamed, is awake and staring at us.

We start the chant. I don't know the words until I say them, but my mouth remembers. Old Norse, or maybe something older, something that doesn't need words at all. Loki's voice is right behind mine, weaving in and out, sometimes an echo, sometimes a harmony, sometimes a growl so deep it rattles the fillings in my teeth.

The rift hates it. It shivers, the edges bleeding light, the things inside wailing and clawing at the boundary. The world blurs. The dogs are beside us now, bigger than ever, their eyes pure flame, their bodies outlined in shifting runes that move faster than I can track.

I raise the dagger, pointing it at the center of the wound.

Loki raises his free hand, palm out, fingers spread.

The runes on our arms stretch, reach, merge. The energy is so strong it makes my bones ache, my vision go white at the edges.

The chant gets louder, and the rift gets smaller. Every word is a punch, every line a nail in the coffin of whatever's on the other side. The smaller monsters try to rush us, but the dogs take them down, fast and efficient. Ash wades through a pile of them, jaws snapping, eyes never leaving mine. Mystic holds the line at my side, her body a wall of heat and power.

The rift is closing, but it's fighting back. A scream rips out of it, not a voice, but a feeling—regret, anger, a promise to come back next time.

My body wants to give up, but the runes keep me moving, keep the chant flowing.

The world is wind and blood and salt, and I am burning out at both ends.

The runes are eating me alive. Every word of the chant is a needle, every heartbeat a hammer driving it deeper. My vision is narrowing to pinholes, black at the edges, color smeared and runny as cheap paint in a flood. I want to stop, to let go, to just fall and let the earth have me, but Loki's voice is there, anchoring me, a steady drum in the dark.

He's holding me up now. Literally—my knees gave out sometime during the third verse, and I didn't even notice. His arm is iron around my waist, his body shaking as badly as mine. I can hear his breath, ragged and wet, every exhale a curse against the rift and the universe and probably himself for ever believing in happy endings.

The rift is almost gone. The monsters are gone. The only thing left is the wound, the bright, ugly scar of light, and the raw, animal hunger that doesn't want to let go.

I squeeze his hand. He squeezes back. "Don't let go," he says, and his voice cracks, the edges fraying.

"Not a chance," I say, but it's just air, not even words. I'm losing the thread.

We keep chanting, the runes spiraling tighter, brighter, the pain going from unbearable to something cleaner—a numbness, a surrender, a peace I didn't know existed. I feel myself breaking apart, like every cell is a spark, and I'm about to be scattered across every pine forest from here to eternity.

The rift surges one last time, a blast of light that's less sight and more sensation—pressure in my ears, taste of copper, the hot stink of ozone and burning sap. It's like standing at the edge of the end of the world and realizing the edge is inside you; it always was.

I hear Loki say my name. Once, twice. The third time, it's not a word—it's a prayer.

He pulls me closer, his body pressed to mine, both of us trembling with what's left of our power and our fear.

"I love you," he says. It's soft, but I hear it over everything—the wind, the roar, the dying scream of the rift. "No matter what happens, I'll always find you."

The words go straight through me, past every scar and shield and bad joke I've ever used to keep the world at bay. I want to answer, but I can't breathe. My chest is all static, my mouth full of salt.

I lean in, forehead pressed to his, and let the tears come. Just for a second, I let them. "I love you too," I say, and it's a whisper, a ghost, but he hears it.

The rift gives up. With a sound like a universe folding in on itself, it snaps shut. The runes flicker, then fade, then die, leaving behind only the taste of thunder and the sound of rain on steel.

The magic is gone. Not just drained—gone. I feel it leave me, the runes retreating, the power collapsing in on itself until I'm just... me. Small, weak, arms wrapped around the one person in the world who ever made me feel like more than that.

Loki slumps, taking me down with him. We hit the ground together, a tangle of limbs and hair and sweat and blood, and for a long, long minute, neither of us moves.

The dogs howl. Somewhere in the distance, Mystic and Ash raise their voices, a long, wild note that starts as a warning but ends in a question, as if they're not sure who they are anymore.

Me neither, guys. Me neither.

The rain is gone. The storm is gone. The sky is just sky, gray and endless, not a single rune or trick left in it.

I turn my head, nose buried in Loki's neck, and breathe him in. He smells like old books, pine needles, and something sharp that might be regret, but also maybe hope. His arms are tight around me, and even with all the world's magic bled out of us, it's the safest I've ever felt.

He laughs, breathless. "You're heavier than you look."

"Shut up," I say, but there's no bite in it. I'd hit him if I had the strength.

He rolls so I'm on my back, both of us staring up at the blank sky.

I nudge him with my elbow. "Well, at least we can skip leg day tomorrow," I say. "Sealing cosmic tears really works the core."

He snorts. "You're insufferable."

"Yeah," I say. "But you love me."

He closes his eyes, a slow smile spreading across his bruised face. "Every damn part of you."

I close my eyes too. I'm not scared of what's waiting behind them.

The world is still. The pines don't whisper, the runes don't flicker, and my skin is just skin.

I could get used to this.

Maybe tomorrow the magic comes back. Maybe it doesn't.

Either way, the world's still here.

And so am I. So are we.

Chapter Nineteen

MORTAL HEARTS, DIVINE LOVE

Dawn. Not the apocalyptic, rift-in-the-sky kind, just regular old East Texas sun leaking through the ratty blinds and across my face. It's so bright, so alive, I want to reach up and slap it, but my arm won't move. Everything hurts—not the sharp, dramatic hurt I'm used to from accidents or arguments or old secrets, but the slow, grinding ache of actually living through something. The kind of ache that seeps into your bones and takes up residence, like a relative with no intention of leaving.

I blink crust out of my eyes and try to sit up, only to realize that I'm trapped. Loki has one arm slung across my waist, his hair fanned out over my pillow and half of my face, and he is dead asleep. I mean, genuinely unconscious, mouth open and breath slow, not faking it to impress or seduce or manipulate. His chest rises and falls against the ugly faded comforter, and for a second, I forget to breathe. He looks so human it's disorienting—vulnerable, tangled, a little ridiculous.

The dogs are in their usual spots: Mystic coiled at the foot of the bed like she's keeping guard against nightmares, Ash sprawled upside down between our legs, snoring with an abandon I both admire and envy. They survived the night, too, and you can tell by the way their ears keep twitching, even in sleep, that they know it.

I watch Loki for a long time, measuring the impossibility of what's happened with every inhale. He's got a bruise under one eye, a shallow cut on his jaw, and the ghost of a rune still visible on his collarbone. The rest of the markings have faded, but the skin remembers them. I run a finger along his shoulder, and he twitches, a small, involuntary animal thing. It makes me smile. It also makes me blush, which is absurd—after everything, after literal world-saving and a very thorough physical inventory the night before, I still get pink in the face over bare skin.

Eventually, he wakes. Not all at once—first a mutter, then a frown, then the sharp green of his eyes snapping open and zeroing in on mine. He grins, slow and lazy, and pulls me in, nuzzling my neck with morning stubble and the faintest trace of ozone.

"Good morning," he says, his voice all velvet and sleep.

"Morning," I mumble, aware of the death-breath situation and not caring enough to fix it.

He rolls onto his back, dragging me with him, and we just lie there, stacked and knotted and barely covered. His hand drifts down my side and settles on my hip, thumb stroking a lazy circuit. There's no rush. No impending doom, no distant sirens, not even the crackle of magic in the air. Just us, the bed, and the low thump of Mystic's tail against the plywood floor.

"Do you feel it?" he asks, his voice softer than I've ever heard it.

I prop myself up on one elbow, hair wild and probably full of dog fur. "Feel what?"

He gestures, vague and tired. "This. The ache. The exhaustion. I thought—" He frowns, searching for the right word. "I thought it would be different."

I snort, not unkindly. "Welcome to being human."

He laughs, and the sound vibrates straight through me, every rib and nerve ending chiming in reply. "I never understood how mortals endure all of... this." He makes a face, as if the very concept of soreness is offensive.

"We don't," I say. "We just get used to it. One day at a time." I poke his ribs for emphasis. "Now get up. If we don't make coffee soon, I will die, and you'll be stuck with two dogs and a lifetime of regret."

He grabs my wrist and flips me, so I'm the one on my back, and for a moment we're nose to nose. "No regrets," he whispers, and kisses me.

It's slow at first—tentative, exploratory, the kind of kiss that asks a question and doesn't need an answer. But then it's more: hungry, urgent, teeth and tongue and the crush of two people who nearly didn't make it. His hands are everywhere—sliding under my shirt, tracing the lines of my waist, kneading the soreness out of my thighs. I arch into him, forgetting the bruises, the stiffness, the dogs. Even the world, for a moment.

He slides down, lips on my collarbone, my chest, every scar and imperfection cataloged and adored. I gasp when he bites, not hard, just enough to remind me that he's still Loki, and he'll never not be dangerous. I run my nails down his back, drawing a line from shoulder blade to spine, and he shivers, the whole length of him flexing against me.

His mouth is at my ear now, and he whispers things that would make a bishop blush. His voice is different like this—raw, desperate, the mask gone. I pull his hair, hard, and he growls, then pins my wrists above my head.

"You sure you want this?" he asks, the hint of mockery barely hiding real concern.

I nod, words lost in the thrum between my legs.

His cock pressed against my heat, teasing me as he slowly pushes inside. The pain is just a flash, but the sensation is overwhelming—the heat, the friction, and the intense rightness of his body filling mine. He sets a steady pace, relentless and demanding, each thrust chasing away the echoes of my past and leaving only this moment. My fingers dig into his back while my legs wrap around him tighter, pulling him closer and begging for more.

His lips crash against mine in a fierce, passionate kiss that leaves me breathless. Teeth scrape against my bottom lip, tongues tangle and dance as we devour each other. His hips pump harder against me, driving deeper still as our moans fill the air around us. The smell of sex and sweat permeates the room, making it hotter and thicker with every passing second.

The sensation builds within me like a wildfire out of control until it explodes in a blinding burst of light behind my closed eyes. I cry out his name in ecstasy as waves of pleasure consume me whole. He follows soon after, his body shuddering hard against mine as he releases himself into me with a primal groan. We collapse together onto the bed, panting heavily and tangled in each other's arms—two people lost in the haze of desire that has just consumed them both.

For a while, neither of us moves. He holds me, chin tucked into the curve of my neck, breath slowing to match mine. The dogs settle, reassured by the silence.

Eventually, I roll away, stretching every muscle just to see if it still works. I catch Loki staring at me, his gaze so intense it makes my skin prickle.

"What?" I say, grabbing a sheet for modesty I absolutely don't have.

He shakes his head, smiling. "Nothing. Just—" He pauses, then reaches over to brush a strand of hair from my face. "I like this version of you."

I stick my tongue out. "You'd better. It's the only one you're getting."

He laughs, and it's the most honest sound in the universe.

We stagger into the kitchen, still mostly naked, and set about the ritual of coffee. Loki stares at the Keurig like it's a bomb, poking at the buttons until I snatch his hand away.

"Here," I say, filling the reservoir with water. "Push this one. Then wait."

He glares at the machine, then at me, then back at the machine. "I could build a working model of Yggdrasil from baling wire and spit, but this defeats me."

"First-world problems," I say, and yawn. The ache is fading, replaced by a warm hum in my chest.

He leans against the counter, arms folded, the lines of his body sharp and perfect even in the crappy overhead light. "What now?" he asks.

I shrug, pouring two cups of coffee. "We eat. We walk the dogs. We see what's left of the world."

He takes the mug, sniffs it, then drinks. "And after that?"

"Same thing," I say. "One day at a time."

Mystic and Ash circle our feet, eyes alert, ears cocked toward the window. I follow their gaze and notice a shimmer—just a hint, a trick of the light—on the old pine outside. For a second, I swear I see runes, but then they're gone.

"Do you think it's over?" I ask, voice low.

Loki joins me at the window, his arm slipping around my waist. "I hope not," he says. "What would we do with ourselves?"

I smile, and the sun climbs higher, flooding the kitchen with a gold that has nothing to do with magic and everything to do with being alive.

The world is broken, maybe, but it's ours.

And for the first time in my life, I want to see what comes next.

The whole town smells like damp dirt and sheetrock dust, with a top note of burned ozone that nobody mentions but everybody knows is wrong. The "freak thunderstorm" hit overnight and left Pine Hollow looking like a twister had come through, but only if that twister had a specific vendetta against window glass, porch railings, and every plastic lawn ornament within a half-mile of Main. Loki and I drive into town and to the hardware store with Mystic and Ash in tow, and every person we pass has that look—the one that says, "I see you, and I know something about you, but I'm not about to say it out loud."

We keep our heads down and play the role. Me in my faded Def Leppard tee and jeans, hair in a mess, arm looped through his like he's just some guy I picked up in Dallas. Loki, for his part, wears a flannel shirt two sizes too big and a pair of cargo shorts that Eliza found in the bottom of a Goodwill bag. The effect is almost sitcom-dad, except for his posture: straight as a blade, shoulders broad, eyes scanning for threats like he's not used to not being the scariest thing in the room.

As we walk down the sidewalk, Mystic and Ash do a perimeter sweep every few feet, then circle back, tails up, eyes flicking from the sky to the sidewalk to every human with a paint can or leaf blower in hand. At least the dogs seem happy to be back in the world of sticks and old fast-food burger wrappers.

A neighbor leans out from her porch, arms crossed over a quilt. "Morning, Amethyst!" she calls, her voice a little too bright.

"Hey, Mrs. Coates," I say, forcing a smile. "Y'all make it through?"

She nods, but her eyes are fixed on Loki. "Sure did. Never seen a storm turn so fast, though. One minute I'm watching TV, the next my fence is in the Johnsons' pool."

"Weird weather year," I say, which is a thing people in small towns always say even when it's not true.

Mrs. Coates shrugs. "If you need help, just holler."

Loki waits until we're out of earshot before leaning in. "Is it always like this?"

I laugh. "It's usually worse. Folks here think being nice to your face and hating you behind your back is a moral obligation."

He processes that, then smiles—just a flicker. "Efficient."

We reach Main and find it crawling with locals. The church group has organized a bucket brigade to clear the mud from the post office steps. Kids are collecting limbs and stacking them in creative ways that are either art installations or future lawsuits. At least three different people try to wave us down for some task or another, but I make a beeline for the hardware store, dragging Loki behind me like a living shield.

Mr. Henderson is out front, hunched over a pile of plywood and muttering to himself. He's got a black eye—new, judging by the swelling—and he's picking shards of glass from a window frame with a pair of kitchen tongs.

"Mornin', Mr. H," I say.

He grunts, not looking up. "Amethyst. You here for work, or you just sightseeing?"

I bite my tongue before saying something stupid. "I can help if you need it."

He finally looks up, eyes settling on Loki. "That your new fella?"

I nod, and Loki sticks out his hand, all formal. "Loki," he says, and that's it. No last name, no embellishment.

Mr. Henderson eyes the hand, then shakes it with more force than necessary. "You any good with tools?"

Loki hesitates. "I can learn."

Mr. Henderson snorts. "We'll see about that. Come on inside."

He leads us into the chaos of his store, which looks about as organized as a garage sale in a hurricane. The front window is a disaster, glass every-where, and the counter's been moved to block off a hole in the wall where the storm tried to punch through. Loki immediately goes to pick up a fallen shelf, and Mr. H watches him with the same suspicion he probably reserves for the IRS.

"Hold it steady," Mr. H grumbles, and Loki braces the shelf while the old man drives a two-inch screw through the bracket. Loki flinches at the noise but keeps steady. I can see the concentration in his jaw, the way he's trying not to mess up something so...basic. It's almost endearing.

I grab a broom and start sweeping the glass into a bucket. Mystic and Ash sniff every corner, then post up by the door, their presence enough to deter any looky-loos from wandering in. Every once in a while, Mystic glances at Loki, as if she's checking to see if he'll bolt.

After fifteen minutes of grunting, nailing, and general hardware slap-stick, Mr. H steps back, wiping sweat from his brow. "Not bad," he says, nodding at Loki.

Loki flexes his hand and accidentally knocks over a can of paint, which rolls across the floor and bumps into my bucket. "Sorry," he says, but his eyes say he's not used to apologizing.

Mr. H shrugs. "That's what the floor's for."

A couple of Henderson's regulars wander in, eyeing the window and then the two of us. One of them, a guy who tried to date me once and whom I now avoid like tax season, nods at Loki. "Y'all see much of the storm out at your place?" he asks, in that tone that suggests he expects the answer to be no.

"We were pretty sheltered in the trailer," I say. "Didn't even lose power."

Loki nods but doesn't add anything. For once, his silence is more believable than mine.

"Lucky," the guy says, but he's already more interested in the cooler in the back.

Mr. H watches him go, then leans in, voice low. "You ever seen anything like that? The storm, I mean?"

I meet his gaze, steady as I can. "No, sir. Not in my life."

He grunts, which in Mr. H language means "I believe you, but I don't." He turns to Loki and hands him a hammer. "Here. Put this through that last brace on the window."

Loki takes the hammer, weighs it in his hand like it's made of gold, and lines up the nail. His first hit is dead-on, the second is a glancing blow, and the third... well, he misses entirely and smacks his own thumb.

He curses—not in English, but in a guttural, ancient snarl that echoes off the shelving.

After his ancient curse, Mr. H raises an eyebrow. "What language was that?"

"Old Norwegian," Loki says smoothly. "My grandmother."

Mr. H blinks, then laughs, and I lose it, snorting so loud I almost choke.

Loki shakes out his hand, red blooming under the nail. "It's fine," he mutters, pride wounded more than flesh.

Mr. H nods, and for the first time today, there's something like respect in his eyes. "Next time, choke up on the handle."

We finish the window in silence, Loki and I trading off tasks while Mr. H acts as supervisor-slash-dad. By the end, the store looks almost normal, and the three of us are covered in sweat, dust, and a fine mist of glass fragments.

Outside, the sun's breaking through, puddles steaming off the sidewalk. People are moving a little faster, a little less scared. I see Mrs. Coates on her porch, now flanked by two other neighbor ladies, each one pretending not to be watching us work.

We say our goodbyes and head out, the dogs trotting ahead. Loki flexes his sore hand and glances at me, green eyes clear and unguarded.

"You did good," I say, bumping his shoulder.

He smirks. "I'm not sure I was much help."

"Trust me. They'll be talking about it for a week."

He looks at his thumb, then at me, then at the hardware store behind us. "I never thought about building things. Only breaking."

I grin, feeling the ache in my own arms. "There's a first time for every-thing."

He stares at the horizon, then back at me, and for a second, I see some-thing different in him. Less wolf, more man. Less legend, more now.

We walk back to the truck in the darkening light, dogs leading, hands dirty, nothing left to run from.

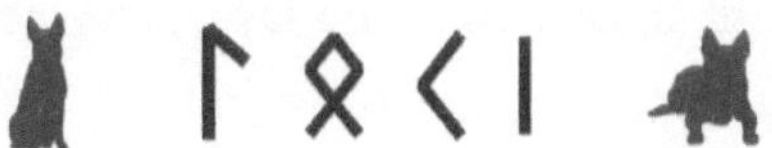

Dinner is two peanut butter sandwiches and a half-bag of Doritos I found behind the flour in the pantry. I sit on the porch steps with my knees up, feet bare, and Loki sits next to me, chewing with the concentration of someone trying to understand why humans eat things like this. The air is cool, sweet with cut grass and wood smoke. Lightning bugs rise from the ditch, blinking like lazy code.

Mystic and Ash are somewhere out in the yard, heads down, probably dissecting a gopher. The world feels still, suspended, the kind of evening where you can hear every distant engine, every dog bark, every neighbor sweeping up the last of the glass from a broken window.

It's almost peaceful.

Then I hear it: tires on gravel, crunching slow, deliberate. I freeze, sandwich half-raised, and Loki's head snaps toward the sound so fast I swear he hears more than I do.

A silver crossover, all polished metal and city dust, pulls into the driveway. Sarah. I haven't seen her since the night she called the Division on us, since she sold me out and nearly got us both killed. The sight of her car flips my stomach, then ices my spine. Loki stands, puts himself between me and the driveway, every line of his body coiled. I swallow, force my legs to move, and follow him down the steps.

Sarah gets out, and the contrast is comic—she's in a pressed blouse, ballet flats, hair pulled tight, not a speck of country on her. She clutches a floral gift bag, white-knuckle tight, and stares at the ground as she walks up. She stops five feet short, like the air between us is electric.

"I know I have no right to be here," she says, her voice thin and brittle. "But I needed to see that you're okay."

I don't answer. Loki's hands are fists at his sides, but he doesn't move. Mystic and Ash are back now, stalking around his legs, hackles high but silent.

Sarah looks up. Her eyes are puffy, rimmed in red. "I'm sorry," she says, and I can tell she means it, but I don't care.

"I told you never to come back," I say. My voice is low, even, but it shakes a little. "You made your choice."

She nods, tears threatening. "I know. I just—I was scared. I thought they'd help you. I didn't think—"

"You didn't think," I repeat, and I can feel the anger boiling under my skin, old and fresh and never quite finished. "You put us in danger. You betrayed me. There's no coming back from that."

She swallows hard. "I know. But I couldn't not try." She extends the bag, her hand shaking. "I brought—just some things from college. Pictures. I thought you might want them."

I don't take it. "Keep them," I say. "Or throw them away."

There's a long, ugly silence. The only sound is the cicadas and the whine of the porch light as it flickers on. Sarah's shoulders crumple, her whole body collapsing in on itself.

"I really did care about you," she says, barely above a whisper.

I believe her, and that somehow makes it worse. "Caring about someone means trusting them to make their own choices. You never did that. I need you to go back to Dallas, lose my number. I never want to see you again. Just go," I say, and she does.

She turns, climbs back into her car, and drives off without looking back. The gift bag sits on the gravel, forgotten.

When the dust settles, I finally breathe and sink back down on the steps. My hands are shaking, so I wrap them around my knees and stare at the stars. Loki sits beside me, close but not touching, and the dogs flop at our feet, spent.

He doesn't say anything, and neither do I.

After a while, he slides his hand onto my back, slow and careful, like he's asking permission.

I lean into him and lay my head against him.

We sit like that until the fireflies burn out, the moon comes up, and the world feels quiet again.

Later, when the night is thick and the house is too small for the thoughts in my head, Loki and I take the dogs out to the woods. The air's gone cool for June, and the moon is a perfect coin in the sky. Mystic and Ash run ahead, chasing each other through the bracken, paws drumming on last year's pine needles. For once, there's nothing behind us—no alarms, no monsters, no guilt.

We walk hand in hand, past the old fire pit, past the circle of folding chairs where some kids had probably snuck out. The branches close in overhead, black against the stars, and it feels like the woods are watching us, waiting for us to speak.

About a hundred yards in, Mystic stops. She freezes, tail out, ears locked on a stand of ancient pines. Ash joins her, and for a moment, the only sound is their synchronized, shallow breathing.

Loki tenses, and I do too, out of habit. But it's not fear in his posture—it's longing, almost.

He leads me forward, slow. The moonlight's enough to see by, but there's something else, too—a faint, familiar glow, like the afterimage of a camera flash. We reach a copse of pines, and I see them: the Twilight Runes, faint as old scars, winding up the bark in patterns I used to dream about.

They're almost invisible, nothing like the fire they used to be. But they're there. Real.

Loki reaches out, fingers trembling. He brushes the trunk, but the runes don't move for him anymore. He tries again, a little harder, and then lets his hand fall.

"They're still here," he says, wonder and loss tangled up in his voice.

I step in, lay my palm on the next tree over. The bark is rough and cold, but under my skin there's a spark—a little jump, like static. The runes flicker, barely, like they're saying hello.

Loki watches, then smiles, sad and proud at the same time. "Looks like you kept a little of it, after all."

"Not enough to start any more wars," I say, trying for lightness.

He laughs, and the sound is good. "Maybe that's for the best."

Mystic and Ash circle the trees, noses to the ground, but they don't bark or growl. They just sit, side by side, and wait for us to figure out what comes next.

I trace a rune with my thumb. "Do you think we'll ever…?"

He doesn't let me finish. He pulls me in, arms tight, breath warm on my hair. "I don't know what we'll become," he says softly. "But whatever it is, we'll face it together."

I lean into him, letting the woods hold us. Above, the runes pulse one more time, a heartbeat in the night.

We stay like that until the dogs get restless, until the wind shifts and the world feels ready to turn again.

When we walk back, the runes fade behind us, but I can feel them still—just enough to know the story isn't over.

Not yet.

CHAPTER TWENTY

NEW BEGINNINGS

A few weeks later....

Dawn lands on the trailer roof with the soft rattle of needles and dew. The pine forest—never truly still, even in sleep—breathes cool against the siding, and the sound of the wind in the boughs blends with the low, guttural snores of the dogs on the porch. The world has changed. It's quieter now, but not less strange. There are scars in the woods where monsters clawed their way into the light, then faded like a fever dream. There are scars inside me, too, but the ache has transmuted, refocused: from survival to living.

I step into the blue haze of early morning, yoga pants patched at the knee, a faded "Life's A Witch" tee draping past my hips and threatening to swallow me whole. My hair, wild and purple and as stubborn as ever, is lashed up in a spiral that looks like a challenge to the sky. I tuck the old wicker basket under my arm—something Miss Eliza called "a gathering vessel" with the solemnity usually reserved for funerals—and let the screen door slap shut behind me.

Mist swirls on the threshold. I press my bare feet to the porch planks, feeling for the pulse of the land. The runes have settled overnight, their fevered burning now a faint, disciplined glow that shimmers on the trees at the property's edge. There are days when I wonder if the magic will ever be content with just...existing. Maybe it never will. Maybe that's fine.

Mystic and Ash take up their posts at opposite ends of the porch. They've grown, post-incident—not grotesquely, but enough to make strangers pause, recalibrate, and reconsider whether to trespass. Mystic is wolf-lean, blue and sleek, her eyes still too bright and never quite the same color twice. Ash is bulkier, the kind of dog you'd send after cattle or bandits, his coat gone to a darker mottled blue with a ruff of silver that makes him look like he's waded through a bucket of starlight. Both watch the woods, ears flicked forward, muscles coiled.

Satisfied the world is still in place, I drop to a crouch and run my fingers through the cold fur at Mystic's neck. The dog leans in, exhales a hot breath that steams in the air, and licks my wrist with a tongue still lined, just barely, with the memory of otherness.

"Any bogeymen out there?" I ask, my voice still gravelly from sleep.

Mystic answers with a half-grunt, half-chuff that in any other dog would have been a bark. Ash replies from his end with a low, rolling rumble, the sound vibrating up the porch posts and into my calves. They're unsettled by something, but not afraid. That's new.

"Keep the perimeter tight," I whisper, and both dogs lock eyes with me, as if absorbing the command through the marrow of their bones.

I take the steps slow, knees popping, and let myself drift into the wild patchwork of the yard. The garden is more suggestion than cultivation, a running argument between native Texas weeds and whatever half-wild medicinal herbs Miss Eliza handed off over the years. Lemon balm. Mugwort. A mutant rosemary bush that grows in spirals. I trail my hands over the leaves, plucking what looks usable and tucking it into the basket. The dew makes everything heavy, and my hands glisten with wet before the sun even touches the clearing.

By the time I've rounded back to the porch, the world has shifted shades. Sunrise hits the treetops, filters down through the branches, and turns the vapor gold. The runes on the bark pick up the light and bend it, fractal and sharp, casting patterns on the dirt that would make a mathematician cry. For a heartbeat, I let myself feel small in the best way: a piece of something bigger, not the weapon or the target for once.

The screen door groans. Loki emerges, carrying two steaming mugs. He's shirtless but wears a pair of battered jeans that have probably been stitched together from the ghosts of a dozen others. His hair, black and unrepentant, is wrangled back with a row of silver rings that catch the sun and make halos against the darkness. His arms are clean, except for the runes—now subtle, tucked just beneath the skin, but visible in the right light like the promise of an old sin.

He hands me a mug. His fingers brush mine in the exchange—deliberate, almost ceremonial—and the contact is a jolt: not magic, but electricity, something primal and solid and very much alive.

"For the lady of the manor," he says, and if there's mockery in the words, it's warm and worn-in.

I sip. The coffee is strong enough to kill a horse and sweetened with honey. "We're courting diabetes, you know," I say, grinning. He knows I only drink it way, way too sweet. Thankfully, I don't usually drink it often.

He leans on the railing, one hip cocked. "Only if it can catch us."

We watch the forest together. He shifts closer, his arm brushing mine, and I let my body tilt into the space he offers. It's easy, this. After all the chaos, the simplicity of standing side by side and facing the morning feels so improbable it makes me want to laugh.

"So, what's the plan today?" Loki asks, voice gone soft. "Another round of fence-mending with the townsfolk? Or do you want to skip ahead to the part where we drink all the coffee and hide from our responsibilities until someone sends a search party?"

"Neither," I say. "It's inventory day at the shop. If we don't reorganize the rare books section, the children's librarian is going to sacrifice us to the Dewey Decimal gods." I don't know how Loki managed to buy the old Victorian house in town and get everything set up to open a bookstore in weeks, but then again... he's Loki.

He makes a sound halfway between a groan and a purr. "I've never met a librarian I couldn't outlast."

I take another drink, watching steam curl from the rim. "It's not the librarian you need to worry about. It's the Girl Scouts she sends our way. They're running a siege operation on the bakery next door. Last time they cornered me in the stockroom and demanded I buy three boxes of Thin Mints as tribute."

Loki grins, showing teeth. "If they try it again, I'll teach them how to summon a demon. See how they like competition."

I laugh. The sound feels new, unscarred.

There's a moment—a subtle shift in the air, the way the dogs freeze and the runes on the tree line flare one shade brighter—that announces the arrival of a visitor. Ash stands, hackles not up but bristling with anticipation. Mystic paces to the end of the walk, nostrils flaring.

I squint into the woods. A shape moves between the trunks, steady and slow, the stride too measured to be a threat but too deliberate to be just another neighbor. I set my mug on the rail, nodding for Loki to follow. We descend the porch together, the dogs flanking us like a pair of mythic sphinxes.

Miss Eliza emerges from the mist, basket in one hand and a foil-wrapped bundle balanced on her hip. She looks older than I remember, the lines on her face deeper, but she moves with the same precise authority. Her robe, a riot of florals, flaps in the wind like a flag of defiance.

"Y'all planning on standing there all day or are you gonna let an old woman say her piece?" she calls, voice sharper than ever.

Loki bows—actually bows, one hand to his chest in mock courtly fashion. "Lady Eliza. Your timing is as impeccable as your reputation."

She squints at him. "You look better without the black smoke. More like yourself."

He winks. "It's a work in progress."

I don't know what she means by that, but I step forward. "To what do we owe the honor? If it's about the property taxes, we already mailed the check."

Eliza smirks. "I'm not here to shake you down, sugar. I brought cinnamon rolls. And word from the town council." She waves the foil packet, and Mystic immediately sits, eyes fixed and tongue lolling with greedy anticipation.

As Eliza approaches the boundary, the runes on the trees shimmer, brightening in a wave that follows her steps. The light isn't warning, but welcome. When she crosses the line, the dogs relax; Ash licks her hand, and Mystic noses the bundle with careful reverence.

We walk her to the porch, where she plunks herself down on the top step and lets the basket thump onto the deck. "You gonna invite me in, or do I have to cast a hospitality rune myself?" she asks.

Loki grins, but it's me who opens the screen door, gesturing grandly. "Come on in, Miss Eliza. I'll put the tea on."

Inside, the trailer is warm and cramped, filled with the smell of cinnamon and dog fur. I clear the table with a sweep of my arm, set the rolls in the center, and pour three mugs without asking how Eliza takes hers.

The three of us sit—me in my usual chair, Loki sprawled on the bench, Eliza perched with her spine straight and hands folded over her knees. The dogs settle at her feet, one on either side, perfectly synchronized.

Eliza unwraps the cinnamon rolls and divides them with surgical precision. "The council wants you to know the runes are holding. No monsters in a week or more. Most folks are sleeping through the night again. The mayor's calling it a miracle, but everyone with half a brain knows who to thank."

I blush, look away. "It wasn't just me."

Eliza points with her fork. "Modesty don't suit you, girl. Neither does hiding out here. Folks want you in town. They're talking about a parade."

Loki's eyes light up, a wicked gleam. "Do I get to ride on the float?"

Eliza shoots him a look. "Only if you dress like a decent person. Which means shirt, pants, and shoes." Loki frowns and I smile, just slightly.

Eliza sips her tea, watching the interplay like a cat sizing up a pair of unruly kittens. "You two planning on behaving today?"

"Absolutely not," Loki says.

I grin, breaking off a corner of the cinnamon roll and feeding it to Mystic under the table. "We'll try, for your sake."

We spend the morning on the porch, eating and drinking and listening to Eliza's stories about the latest town drama. The air warms, the runes fade to a soft glow, and the sense of threat recedes so completely it's like it never existed.

For the first time in my life, I feel like I belong—not just to a place, but to a moment. To people.

When Eliza finally leaves, the runes brighten once more, following her out to the road before returning to their steady, contented shimmer.

I watch her go, the cinnamon still sweet on my tongue.

"You ever think it would end up like this?" I ask Loki, not really expecting an answer.

He stretches, catlike, and pulls me into his lap. "Every possibility exists," he whispers, lips close to my ear. "But this one is my favorite."

I kiss him, slow and deep, letting the magic settle around us like a blanket.

And in the woods, the runes glow on, silent and watchful, guardians of a peace hard-earned and well-kept.

The town looks better in the morning, when the light is soft and un-ambitious. Main Street's old ghosts keep their heads down in daylight, their sins hidden behind fresh paint, new glass, and the polite fiction of normalcy. I don't mind. I like the lie of it, the way Pine Hollow pretends last month's apocalypse was just a run of bad storms and not a cosmic correction that shredded the local definition of "weird."

Loki and I walk the three blocks from the parking lot to the old town square with the dogs in tow. Mystic and Ash draw less attention these days; people either recognize them as "my wolves" or just decide it's safer to avert their gaze and not ask. The dogs walk with the confidence of animals who know they can pass for normal if they have to, but don't intend to.

Twilight Tomes & Lore occupies a two-story Victorian on the corner, the kind of house that once hosted genteel teas and now spends its days as a cathedral of paperbacks. The sign over the door is hand-painted, the letters looping and florid, flanked by two stylized pine cones that look suspiciously like runes if you squint at them in the right light.

Loki pauses at the threshold, reaches down, and smooths the fur on Mystic's shoulder. "You'll behave today?" he asks, voice full of mock authority.

The dog licks his hand, eyes glinting.

He grins and looks at me as I'm already unlocking the door. "She's the only creature in town who respects me."

I hold the door open. "She's also the only one who'll bite your hand off if you lie to her."

"Fair," he says, and ducks inside.

The shop's interior is cool and dim, the smell of old books fighting a losing battle with the twin assaults of candle wax and patchouli from the incense stand near the register. I drop my bag behind the counter, flick on the lights, and watch the store wake up: the spines glow faintly in the dim, some of them pulsing in rhythm with my own heartbeat; the wood shelves creak and settle like a forest exhaling; the window glass catches the first rays of sun and throws rainbows on the floor in wild, shifting patterns.

I run my fingers over the counter, feeling for loose splinters or cold spots where the wards sometimes pool and tangle. Satisfied, I start the morning routine: coffee brewing, cash drawer counted, today's shipment stacked and ready for shelving.

Loki wanders the aisles, touching the spines, murmuring to the books in a language I know only by its cadence. He's developed a weird rapport with the store's weirder volumes—no matter how obscure or cursed the edition, he can always find it within minutes. The books respond to him, sometimes literally: a volume of Eddic poetry falls off its shelf as he walks by, landing open to a dog-eared page.

He bends down, reads a line, and smiles.

"Prophecy?" I call from the front.

"Just an old joke," he replies, tucking the book back where it belongs.

The dogs take up position behind the counter, Ash coiled like a sphinx, Mystic draped along the heater vent, even though the heat is off. They watch everything. When the first customer arrives—a middle-aged man in a Carhartt jacket and the anxious body language of someone who's recently lost a bet—I greet him with a practiced smile.

"Morning, Jack. Here for the new Stephen King?"

Jack grunts, eyes flicking to the dogs. "Heard you got it in early."

"Special order," I say, pulling a shrink-wrapped hardcover from under the counter. "Want it gift-wrapped?"

He shakes his head but hands over the cash. "You, uh, you hear about the thing at the water tower? Kids say there's still sparks out there. Weird colors."

I make note to check that out later, but shrug. "Kids see what they want to see. Last week it was a ghost in the post office."

Jack nods, more relieved than he has any right to be, and leaves with the book tucked under his arm.

Loki sidles up behind me, watching the door swing shut. "You're very good at normal."

I pour him a mug of coffee, black, and slide it over. "You get used to it after a while."

He sips, eyes narrowed. "But you hate lying."

"I never said I was good at it."

He leans in, so close I can smell the coffee on his breath. "You want me to handle the next one?"

I give him a look. "Last time you did, we lost a whole shelf to spontaneous combustion."

He laughs, and the sound is brighter than the day outside.

The morning spins out in a parade of regulars: the teacher in need of test-prep books; the teen who's been banned from the library and needs a fresh copy of "Lord of the Flies" for a report; a woman in scrubs who picks up two paperbacks and leaves a can of dog food at the door as a tip for Mystic and Ash.

Then the bell over the door chimes with a different note—hesitant, drawn out. I glance up and see a girl, maybe nineteen, wrapped in three conflicting layers of thrifted sweaters and with hair bleached to near-translucence. Her eyes are ringed in purple, not from makeup but from the kind of insomnia you can only earn by worrying about the world too hard.

She hangs back, biting her thumbnail, scanning the stacks.

I wait. The girl circles once, twice, and finally approaches the counter.

"Um," she starts, voice barely there. "Do you... do you have anything on, like, dreams?"

"Interpretation, lucid, or nightmares?" I ask, keeping my tone light.

The girl looks relieved. "Nightmares. I mean—" She hesitates, pulling her sleeves down over her hands. "It's not for me. It's for... a friend."

I smile, pretending to believe her. "Follow me."

I lead the girl to the back corner, where the occult and psych sections overlap in a lopsided Venn diagram. I pull down three books, each with a discreet bookmark at the section on recurring dreams.

The girl holds them close, clutching them like talismans. "Is this the good stuff?" she asks, suddenly bolder.

"Some of it," I say, lowering my voice. "But the best cure for bad dreams is a cup of tea and someone to listen."

The girl glances at me, wary but hopeful.

"Come on," I say, and guide her to the reading nook—an overstuffed armchair wedged between two display tables and shielded from the rest of the shop by a tangle of potted ferns.

I make tea from the samovar behind the counter, pour it into a chipped mug that still bears the scars of the siege. I hand it over, then sit across from the girl and wait.

For a while, we just sip. Mystic paddles over and lies at the girl's feet, tail sweeping slowly across the carpet.

"It's not for a friend," the girl says finally, staring into her tea. "It's for me. I keep seeing this place—like, a room, but it's not anywhere I know. There are these words on the wall. I don't know what they mean, but I wake up and I can't shake them."

"Do you remember the words?" I ask.

The girl nods, then recites them, slow and careful. I recognize a scrap of Old Norse, twisted and half-wrong, but still potent.

I set my cup down. "That's an old language. From before this country was a country. Did you grow up around here?"

The girl shakes her head. "Moved in last year. Never even heard it before. But I see it in the dreams, clear as print."

I consider. "Have you ever felt like you were in danger? Or like someone was watching?"

A beat. The girl's eyes flick to the front window, then back. "Sometimes. Not always. It's worse when I'm alone."

I lean forward. "Let me write the words down. If you see them anywhere in real life—on a sign, a tree, anything—let me know. And if you ever feel like someone's following you, come here. I mean it. Bring your dog, if you have one."

The girl smiles, small but real. "I have a cat."

"Good enough," I say.

We finish our tea. I send her home with the books, a handwritten note with my number, and a sample of the mugwort I keep behind the counter for emergencies.

After the girl leaves, Loki wanders over. "That was very gentle," he says.

I shrug. "People need gentle."

He looks at me, something unreadable in his eyes. "So do you."

I elbow him. "Don't get sentimental. You have a story hour at ten."

He rolls his eyes but goes to the children's section and starts pulling books for the day's reading.

Ten a.m. on the nose, and the store fills with kids—half of them regulars, half new, all loud. Loki herds them into a circle of floor cushions, plops down cross-legged in the center, and lets the noise settle.

He opens the first book—a retelling of the Eddas, this edition illustrated with wolves and giants and too many swords—and lets his voice drop to its storytelling register: rich, dark, made for secrets. The kids hang on every word.

I watch from the sidelines. Loki's eyes, when he reads, go from green to gold and back, the color shifting with the story's mood. When he describes a battle, his voice grows rough, and the children shrink away from the imagined violence. When he speaks of feasts, his smile widens, and the room feels warmer.

At the best moments, the book does things: a page will riffle itself, or the illustrations will shimmer and wink in the morning light. Once, as he describes the forging of a magic chain, a length of twine appears in his hands, and he ties it in a knot so deftly that the nearest kid gasps in delight.

I watch the parents watching him, some skeptical, most just grateful for an hour of silence. The girl from earlier comes in too, this time holding the hand of a small boy who looks enough like her to be a brother. They sit together in the back, the boy enraptured by Loki's voice, the girl glancing now and then at me, as if for reassurance.

Loki ends the story with a flourish, closes the book, and lets the kids ask questions. One boy demands to know what happened to the wolf after Ragnarok; a girl wants to know if the giants ever came back. Loki fields each query with a mix of fact and mischief, never quite lying but never telling the whole truth, either.

After the last child drifts away, Loki catches my eye and winks. "They're a better audience than the gods ever were."

"Less ego," I agree.

He sits next to me on the window bench, folding his legs under himself with a grace I envy.

"You ever regret it?" I ask, not sure if I mean the magic, the stories, or the peace we've found.

He looks at me, really looks, and shakes his head. "I had centuries of chaos. This—" He gestures at the dogs, the books, the sunlit shop. "—is enough."

I lean on his shoulder, letting the silence stretch.

Outside, the world goes on pretending nothing is strange, nothing is broken. Inside, the dogs snore, the books hum, and the last traces of old magic curl through the air, undemanding, content.

We sit like that until dusk, not needing words to say what matters.

The dusk that wraps the forest is the color of bruised fruit, blue and gold bleeding into the velvet dark. Loki and I get out of the car, and I let the dogs out. We head for the trailer, Mystic and Ash leading the way, the dogs' shadows doubled by the last traces of sun and the first sparks of the Twilight Runes along the property line.

The trailer feels like it's grown roots in the earth—solid, snug, a bunker against the noise of the world. We cross the yard, and I run my hand along the mint and wild basil that's started to overrun the path, while Loki whistles an old tune that sounds like something you'd hum while stealing the moon.

Inside, the kitchen is lit by a single bulb and the glow from the living room, where a fake fireplace flickers in permanent imitation of home. We move together, well-practiced: I wash the greens and potatoes from the garden, he handles the knives, dicing onions so fast the cuts blur into one movement. The dogs collapse by the door, both keeping half an eye on the window, the other half on my every gesture.

"So," Loki says, voice low and easy. "Girl with the nightmare—think she'll come back?"

I shrug, slicing carrots with a precision that belies my answer. "Most do. The town's memory is short, but the dreams stick. She'll either need help or want to say thank you. Or both."

He dumps the onions into the skillet, the sizzle sharp and clean. "You're better at this than you think."

I snort, tossing a carrot at his head. "That's just because I have good help."

We work in silence, the only sounds the clatter of utensils and the dogs' soft breathing. It's an ordinary kind of magic, and for the first time in years, I don't feel the urge to run.

I'm plating up the meal—roasted vegetables, a slab of cornbread, the last of the pickled okra—when the knock comes. Not the slapdash rattle of a salesman or the three-fast, one-slow of a neighbor, but a careful, measured tapping. Loki stiffens, his body stilling in a way that makes the room hold its breath.

Mystic's head comes up. Ash prowls to the window, lips peeled back not in a snarl but a warning: we see you, and we remember.

I dry my hands on a towel and go to the door. Loki follows, silent. I open the screen just a crack, enough to see the visitor—a man, maybe, or a teenager, age hard to pin down under the dirt and road-wear. He wears a coat too big for him, sleeves frayed to ribbons, shoes caked with dust. His eyes are the color of wet moss, and his hands tremble as he clutches a battered duffel bag.

He looks at us both, gaze flicking between Loki and me, then past us to where the dogs sit, waiting.

"Sorry," he says, voice a rasp. "Didn't mean to intrude. Just—saw the lights. Was hoping for directions."

I glance at Loki. He nods once, and I swing the door open wide enough to show the inside and the waiting dogs.

"Come on in," I say, stepping aside. "You look like you need a meal more than a map."

The visitor hesitates, eyes locked on Mystic. The dog watches him, head tilted, then lets out a soft, welcoming chuff. The runes outside the house flicker, then steady, as if deciding the stranger is safe enough.

He enters, careful not to brush against anything, and stands just inside the doorway, hands twisting the strap of his bag.

Loki greets him with the formal courtesy of another age. "Our home is yours," he says, voice slipping into a cadence that makes even the trailer's old walls pay attention. "Sit. Eat. Rest."

The man nods, lower lip quivering, then takes the seat at the kitchen table I pull out for him.

I set a plate in front of him, pour a glass of water, and set the cornbread just within reach. "We don't have much," I say, "but you're welcome to it."

He stares at the food, blinking hard, then tears into it with the silent ferocity of a starving animal. For a while, no one speaks. Loki fetches another plate for himself, fills it, and sits. I pour a glass for myself, lean against the counter, and watch.

After the first wave of hunger ebbs, the visitor looks up. "My name's Finch," he says, voice steadier. "I—"

He stops, unsure how to finish.

Loki finishes for him. "You're running from something."

Finch nods, a quick jerk. "Not the law or anything. Just... needed out. The world out there's got meaner. Or maybe it's just me."

I shrug. "World's always been mean. But it's not so bad here, most days."

Finch looks at me, then at Loki, as if searching for proof. "I saw the lights in the woods. Last night. Thought it was a trick of the eye, but they're still there."

I smile, not unkind. "That's just the runes. They keep the nightmares out."

Finch shivers. "I'm not sure they worked for me."

Loki tilts his head. "Nightmares aren't always a curse. Sometimes they're just the truth, wearing a mask."

Finch pokes at the last of the cornbread, chewing it slowly. "When I sleep, I see rivers. Endless. I'm drowning, but not dying. Just floating, forever. My old man said it was because I was born feet first. Never knew which way was up."

I pour more water, slide it across the table. "Maybe you're just meant to go further than the rest."

He snorts. "Don't feel like it."

Loki leans back, runes on his arms catching the kitchen light. "You ever stop running? Even for a minute?"

Finch shakes his head. "No. Doesn't feel safe."

I catch Loki's eye, then speak, gentle but firm. "If you want, you can sleep here tonight. We don't have a guest room, but the couch pulls out. The dogs will keep you safe. You can run again in the morning if that's what you need."

Finch's eyes fill, and he wipes at them with a sleeve. "Thank you," he says, the words brittle but true.

We show him how to work the shower, leave a clean towel and a stack of flannel for pajamas. Mystic escorts him to the sofa, curls at his feet, and lets him scratch her behind the ears.

After the house settles, Loki and I step outside, the air crisp and charged with electricity.

The woods have transformed. Every tree on the property's edge burns with a line of violet, the runes brighter than they've been in weeks. Fireflies drift above the grass, tracing the shapes in patterns that mirror the symbols' dance. It looks like a barrier, or maybe a blessing.

We sit together on the old porch swing, the seat creaking in rhythm with the night.

"You think he'll stay?" I ask, voice low.

"Doesn't matter," Loki replies. "He'll remember this place. Even if it's just for a night."

I lean my head on his shoulder. "We're turning into Miss Eliza, you know. Taking in strays, feeding them carbs, sending them back out with hope in their bellies."

He chuckles. "Could do worse."

We rock in silence. The runes flicker, pulse, then settle into a lazy heart-beat.

"You ever miss the old days?" I ask.

He considers. "Chaos is easy. Peace takes work."

I smile, eyes on the fireflies. "Who would've guessed we'd end up here?"

He turns to me, and in the pale rune light, his eyes are green and gold and every shade of maybe.

"Of all the realms I've wandered, all the lives I've lived," he says, thumb tracing circles on my wrist, "this simple existence with you brings me the most joy."

I laugh, quiet. "Careful. You're sounding sentimental again."

He kisses me, slow and sure, his hand warm on the side of my face.

"I love you, Amethyst Gold," he says, and this time, it isn't a trick or a dare. Just the truth, worn soft by repetition.

I lean in, my mouth pressed to his, and the rest of the world falls away, leaving only the two of us and the runes glowing brighter than the stars.

We stay there until the night turns to velvet, and the boundaries between past and future, mortal and myth, blur to nothing at all.

ABOUT THE AUTHOR

Luna Runestorm writes paranormal romance and romantasy filled with magic, danger, and slow-burning desire. Her stories blur the line between the supernatural and the everyday, often set in eerie small towns where secrets run deep and nothing stays buried for long. When she's not dreaming up rune-laced plots or writing emotionally tangled love stories, Luna lives deep in the woods of East Texas with her two Australian Cattle Dogs, Mystic and Ash, who assure her they are perfectly ordinary dogs and not magical beings in disguise (though she has her doubts).

https://www.lunarunestorm.com
https://tinyurl.com/LunaRunestorm
https://linktr.ee/lunarunestorm

9 7 9 8 9 0 0 4 6 1 0 0 7